the elm stone saga

chosen

shayla morgansen

The Elm Stone Saga: Chosen

A copy of this publication can be found in the National Library of Australia.

ISBN: 978-1-742844-65-7 (pbk.)

Published by Book Pal
www.bookpal.com.au

Contents

prologue

The late autumn night was crisp and cool. A brisk wind sliced through the dying trees in the garden, relieving them of their burden of dead brown leaves. The darkness in the marbled courtyard was broken only by the soft, haunting candlelight glowing in the large ring of lanterns. Thirteen white-robed adult figures stood in a circle within this enchanted ring.

Tonight, in this Connecticut home's courtyard, the government of the magical world, the White Elm council, had been called to an emergency meeting by their leader, an old, white-haired man whom they, along with the rest of their world, called Lord Gawain. He stood as part of the circle, and wore a royal purple sash over his white robes, as did the middle-aged black woman to his right, and beyond her was a tall, attractive man wearing an emerald green sash.

'Blessed be,' Lord Gawain began in his commanding voice. The twelve sorcerers responded, and a murmur of *Blessed be* resonated around the courtyard and into the surrounding gardens. 'Firstly, our thanks to Susannah, who has provided us tonight with her beautiful yard as a venue for this last-minute conference.'

'Never a problem, Lord Gawain,' a 40-something American sorceress replied with a smile. Her wavy brown hair was clipped back from her fresh, pleasant face and her manicured hands, although obviously freezing, were ungloved and open, relaxed at her sides.

'As a sign of honesty and purity, all members of White Elm traditionally keep their faces and hands uncovered,' Lord Gawain said, beginning the meeting. Two of the twelve pairs of candle-bright eyes dropped from Lord Gawain's face and two pairs of hands quickly appeared from underneath robes, and he knew, but he continued as if he hadn't noticed. 'This is one of many traditions we as a government have upheld for hundreds of years to ensure peace within the White Elm body.'

The council was silent. Lord Gawain continued.

'I apologise for the surprise meeting, but, as always in history, the White Elm has dutifully responded to their leader's call, knowing that I would only break the cycle for a great emergency. I am grateful for your faith. Your loyalty to your leaders, your adherence to the council's ancient code and your purity of spirit prove to the world your worthiness of ruling the magical people. Few other councils would gather so quickly at their leader's bidding.'

A couple of sorcerers smiled at their leader's

sentiment.

'So, when you felt my call, where were you, Lady Miranda?' Lord Gawain asked his co-leader, the 55-year-old black sorceress to his right.

'Finishing my shift at the hospital,' she answered smoothly, her British accent sharp.

'Lisandro?'

The attractive man on Lady Miranda's right blinked through his long, loose black hair at his Lord's word.

'With a woman,' he answered simply, in his New York accent. No one asked for details.

'Qasim?' Lord Gawain asked of the next man in the circle, the imposing Saudi.

'Reading to my children,' Qasim answered.

The White Elm immediately continued answering in the order Lord Gawain had been questioning – highest ranked to lowest – and most answered with honesty. However, the massive African American Jackson cast his vision down for a tiny instant and blinked a few times too many.

'Asleep,' he said. Lord Gawain felt the flicker of nervousness in the air, which accompanies a lie, and knew otherwise, but kept quiet. He needed to be sure of the others.

The stick-thin Russian woman next in the circle glanced oddly at Jackson, having felt the same flicker, before speaking.

'Meditating,' she murmured honestly.

'Asleep.' Tian still looked tired.

'Reading the paper,' Peter said, too quickly.

He is the second puppet, Lord Gawain thought.

Who is their master?

Emmanuelle, a beautiful French sorceress, admitted to being on a date. She blushed a little, but she wasn't lying. The youngest, the handsome and mysterious Renatus, spoke last.

'I was scrying,' he said. His violet eyes flickered to Lord Gawain.

A few other members of White Elm shared subtle ominous looks. They didn't trust Renatus. But Lord Gawain understood the very young man's meaning. After all, it was on Renatus's advice that he had called this council.

Peter and Jackson are traitors, Master, Renatus had said hours earlier, confirming Lord Gawain's already strong suspicions. Lady Miranda agreed. Now they only had to find the third traitor, the leader. But whoever it was had covered his or her lies so well that even Lord Gawain, Lady Miranda and Renatus couldn't work out who it was.

Lord Gawain had known for some time that a rival force was forming elsewhere. Rumours of black magic beyond that which the White Elm could imagine; whispers of a powerful leader no one could actually name. Similar little tales popped up every now and then, and usually died down, but these murmurings were persistent and becoming louder. Most disturbing was the realisation that this apparent rival group (if it existed) was said to be led by a member of White Elm.

'Three of you are lying,' Lord Gawain said after a minute of absolute silence. Two sparks of nervousness flickered briefly in the circle. *Who is the third*? 'There can be no lies in this council. Peter, Jackson, why are you lying?'

'I'm not,' they both lied at once.

'Where were you both before this council was called?' Lady Miranda barked, startling them both.

'Sleeping,' Jackson answered, keeping his eyes firmly focussed on Lady Miranda's face. *Clever.* He didn't want to give in to instinct and glance at his leader.

'Sleeping,' Peter agreed. The circle was silent.

'You said before you were reading a newspaper,' Emmanuelle said softly, staring at Peter. The young Scotsman met her eyes fearfully. They were friends – they had bonded when they had been admitted into the council at the same time. Now it seemed that bond – and Emmanuelle's trust – was crumbling.

'I'm sorry, Em,' Peter whispered.

'Why would you lie?' she asked. The others watched. 'You know our oaths – we may never lie here. You wouldn't break those oaths, Peter. You wouldn't.'

'But he has,' Lord Gawain reminded Emmanuelle. He turned back to Peter. 'That's not the only oath he's broken, either, is it?'

Peter stared back at him for a long moment, like a deer caught in headlights.

'Peter?' Emmanuelle prompted. Her voice broke his frightened paralysis.

'No,' he said shakily.

'What have you done?'

'I-'

'Peter.' Jackson's warning tone had more than a hint of menace, and even though Lord Gawain was quite sure that Jackson wasn't capable of instigating this situation, it was clear to him how the hierarchy worked. Peter was at the bottom, just along for the ride – and he knew why.

'Peter, you know I have to ask for it back,' Lord Gawain said to the youngest traitor. Peter's mouth tightened and his hand clenched. 'It needs to change hands.'

'Peter, don't be weak,' Jackson spoke up. 'You knew this day was coming. You told us so.'

Us. Proof that there *was* at least one more, although Lord Gawain had been near-certain already.

'Seeing a future event and living it are quite different,' Peter threw back. He chanced a look sideways at Emmanuelle. 'Living it, it doesn't feel like I thought it would.'

'You mean getting us both caught out isn't the thrill you thought it would be?' Jackson asked snidely. 'Maybe if you weren't such a crappy liar. There are no points for honesty now, matey. Ship's sailed.'

'Jackson, I think it's time you stopped talking,' Susannah snapped. 'What have you both done?'

'They have broken sacred oaths to this council by lying, and further by devoting themselves to a second power – a rival,' Lord Gawain said, not allowing his sadness into his voice. 'Is this true?'

'I...It's...' Peter stammered, looking desperately to Jackson, but the older American didn't seem to care.

'Yeah, alright, it's true,' he said, laughing suddenly as though surprising himself. He'd always been odd, the sort of character who laughs at all the wrong moments, and some kind of head injury seven or eight years ago had exacerbated his unbecoming traits. Luckily for him, this had roughly coincided with the council's discovery of Renatus, and in their collective efforts to dislike him even more, the councillors had seemed to readily accept the damaged Jackson. Their narrow-sighted mistake, obviously. Now they shook their heads and stared in disbelief, disgust and shock as Jackson laughed again, louder, and continued.

'It's true! We've lied, cheated, sold secrets, all the things we promised not to do. And? So what? We're finished with you. We're leaving this sorry council. We've found a higher calling; our values and ideals just don't fit in here. The White Elm is outdated and ridiculous. Your time is up.'

Jackson, still laughing, pulled his wand from his robes. Immediately, eleven wands were pointed at him.

'Drop it,' Anouk warned as she backed away from him.

'Drop it,' Jackson mocked. He took a step towards her, in the process of casting a strong stunning spell at the Russian, but Fate intervened: his toe caught on an uneven tile in Susannah's paved courtyard and he stumbled, looking down for just an instant. Anouk took that instant to deflect his spell straight back at him, knocking him to the ground without a fight.

'I thought you were trained better than that, Jackson,' she growled, advancing, but Lady Miranda moved forward and caught her arm.

'Leave him, he's harmless,' she said. She looked around at the now-disorganised circle. 'Who has done this to him? Whose lust for power? Speak, whoever you are. Your cowardice is pathetic.'

'There were only two liars, that I detected,' Lisandro said to Lord Gawain, leaning behind the high priestess and observing the council quietly. 'The leader has covered his tracks. Boy!' He motioned to Peter, who miserably came forth. Lisandro was known for his natural charisma and interrogation skills. The fact that he was the only witch in the world legally allowed to study and practise dark magic probably wasn't helping Peter's level of confidence. 'Who is your leader, Peter?'

'Lord Gawain,' Peter said dutifully, but his eyes revealed his difficulty. He felt bad. He felt guilty. The guilty were the easiest to break.

'Your other leader – the one you've betrayed Lord Gawain for.'

'I...I can't say. I'm sorry.'

'You must know what I'm going to do if you don't choose now to speak up,' Lisandro said, and Peter nodded.

'I understand. I'll submit to your questioning, but you won't get anything from me.' He shot a final look at his French friend, whose bright blue eyes were filled with tears. 'I *am* sorry.'

'Take the ring off and put it on the ground in

front of you.'

Peter knelt and did as he was told, removing the White Elm's weapon from his hand and placing it gently before him. Lisandro touched his wand to Peter's temple. For a moment nothing happened. Then the younger man screamed in unexpected pain and clenched his fists against his knees as Lisandro's presence entered his brain, forcing dark magic against his resolve.

'Stop it! You're 'urting him! Stop!' Emmanuelle begged, but she did not attempt to interfere, possibly understanding that this was Lisandro's job; this was what he had been trained for.

'Why does he hide from us? Why does he not come forth?' Lisandro drilled. Lord Gawain and Lady Miranda stepped forth to stand at the shoulders of their colleague, subtly transferring their own power slowly into Lisandro. Peter looked more fearful. The others stood back in silence, except for the few who bound Jackson.

'He is not afraid,' Peter muttered monotonously. 'He says… He mocks you even now with your deep trust in him. He says it's pathetic. His victory grows greater with each moment that passes with your faith. I'm sorry, I'm sorry…'

So the hidden traitor was a man. This was not particularly useful information, as only four of the council's thirteen members were *not* men. At least, however, it excluded Susannah, Anouk and Emmanuelle – Lord Gawain knew already that it could not have been Lady Miranda, the person he trusted most in the world.

Well, he trusted everybody present, but two had been proven unworthy of that trust, and one other remained to be discovered.

'And who is he?' Lisandro asked of Peter, his voice and his applied magic twisting together into a threat only Peter could feel.

'I will never tell,' Peter said loudly, closing his eyes resolutely. Many of the others were now slowly pouring their own energy into Lisandro's interrogation and Peter was becoming overwhelmed. Lord Gawain let his magical senses probe the garden. Why was Renatus not helping? *It couldn't be him...he's too young...*

'You will tell me,' Lisandro murmured, his bronze-coloured eyes getting brighter with power.

'I won't, I won't!' Peter cried tearfully, clearly in pain. He was completely unable to physically resist the increasing power of the strongest witches in the world being forced into his mind.

'Fine. Then where were you before this council was called?' Lisandro demanded, mentally and magically pushing against Peter's resolve, now trying another angle, seeking the weakest point.

'With him. Jackson and I were with him, planning...'

'And who is he?'

'No...' Peter choked on a breath and began coughing pitifully.

'You will tell me. Do you remember who I am?'

'Yes,' Peter mumbled, sobbing. 'L-Lisandro, Dark Keeper of the White Elm.'

'That's right. And you will tell me the name of

your leader.'

Lord Gawain felt his power draining but kept it up. This was vital information. When Peter finally gave in and told, Lord Gawain would be too weakened to pose as an immediate threat to anyone with full power. But even if it proved to be Renatus, at least Lisandro would be able to overpower him. Maybe. Lord Gawain could not imagine who on his beloved council would betray him, and though he trusted the young man with the dark family tree, he could not believe it of any of the others, either. Unfortunately, despite his deep trust, it seemed one more of them *had* betrayed the White Elm, and that person could arguably be anyone other than Lady Miranda and Lisandro.

Though it killed him to admit it, that person could very easily be Renatus.

'You will tell me *now*,' Lisandro said forcefully, punctuating his final word with a strong mental push against Peter's determination that even Lord Gawain felt.

'NO!' Peter screamed, his features twitching with his mental strain. 'I can't! I won't. He'll kill me if I do!'

Lisandro removed his wand from Peter's forehead and all energy transfers ended. Peter collapsed. Emmanuelle sank to her knees at Renatus's feet and hid her face in her hands, sobbing. A few weakened White Elm stumbled or sat down. None had expected Lisandro to use so much of their energy.

'You are incredibly loyal,' Lisandro said,

brushing some of his long black hair from his face and looking down at the twitching Peter with something close to admiration. He turned to Lord Gawain. 'Any more would have killed him.'

'Any more would have killed everyone else here, too,' Renatus said. Everyone ignored him. He was the prime suspect.

'I'm sorry...You'll kill me...I won't...' Peter mumbled, twitching violently.

'And you got nothing from him?' Lord Gawain asked Lisandro, trying not to sound too disappointed. 'You couldn't dig deeper?'

'I could get nothing. I probably could have dug deeper – but not legally or safely. There'd be nothing left of his mind.' The attractive American frowned and lowered his voice, adding, 'As it is, I may have overdone it.'

'I won't...I won't...Never tell...You'll kill me...' Peter whispered, his voice dropping away as his consciousness slipped.

Lisandro glanced back to Peter and shook his head, looking amused. 'Like I said, he's incredibly loyal.'

'To you,' Renatus said sharply. Lisandro turned to the much younger man. Lord Gawain glanced between them, their physical similarities appearing to him, not for the first time. The black hair worn long, the pale complexions, the tall and slim build, the strong air of unbelievable power and potential... But now he saw something else – the conviction in Renatus's eyes.

And Lisandro looked...surprised. Not offended,

but just surprised.

No...That isn't possible...

'That's right, to me,' Lisandro agreed. Long moments of silence followed. Everyone stared in absolute shock. Lisandro eyed Renatus over. 'I never really liked you, Renatus. You always know more than you should.'

Lisandro? No...No, he couldn't. Not the White Elm Dark Keeper. Not Lisandro...

'Why?' Lady Miranda said finally.

'Because he's the same as the rest of his family,' Lisandro said, still eyeing Renatus with mild distaste. Lady Miranda frowned.

'Why would you turn Jackson and Peter against us? Against their oaths?'

Lisandro sighed.

'This council has become outdated, and it's occurred to me on numerous occasions over the last few years that it might be time for us to upgrade,' he said, as if discussing his requirement for a new phone. 'Just think about it a minute – the magical community is fast losing faith in the White Elm. We haven't had the popularity we once did in a very long time. This council was never voted in; the power it holds is false. It is time for a newer model I'm afraid. It doesn't have to be a bad thing. Give the people the choice between what they've known and what could be. The White Elm has become obsolete, and Magnus Moira is the future. Peter and Jackson see what I see and want to create the same future for our world.'

'Magnus Moira?' Qasim repeated sceptically.

Others in the group looked as though Lisandro's words were swaying their judgement, but Qasim was difficult to manipulate.

'It's just a name,' Lisandro answered casually. 'A sort of club. Everything sounds more legitimate when you give it a name. Our people deserve an alternative option to the White Elm, and I'm ready to provide that. Jackson and Peter are VIP members, but you're all invited to join, too. This council is a sinking ship. I'm offering you all a life raft. There would be some serious reshuffling of ranks and responsibilities,' he conceded, glancing at Lord Gawain, 'but I'm certain I could find spots for everyone. Even you,' he added to Renatus.

'I'll pass,' Renatus replied coldly.

'If this isn't a bad thing, why didn't you share earlier?' Elijah asked of Lisandro. 'Why the secrecy and sneaking about?'

'Most of you weren't ready – still aren't.' Lisandro elegantly brushed some of his long hair away from his face. 'This has come out a lot earlier than I'd hoped. Peter wasn't ready, obviously – look what's happened to him. I didn't want that happening to the rest of you. I felt you needed more time to be able to understand.'

'Understand what, exactly?' Lady Miranda demanded, her voice harsh. She was clearly upset.

'That the time has come to let the White Elm dwindle to its natural end, and to start afresh.'

'We don't know anything about your "fresh" council. Why would we want to give up on what works to follow you into the unknown?' Glen asked reasonably.

'Well, you could trust me, but it sounds like you need something more convincing than that,' Lisandro said. 'First of all, I'm not really seeing Magnus Moira as a council. A council of thirteen takes too long to get anything done. I'm seeing a totally different structuring.'

'You see *you* in charge,' Lady Miranda guessed.

'Well, obviously. It wouldn't be much fun otherwise.'

The council members glanced amongst each other quietly, uncertain.

'What happens if we aren't interested in your proposal?' Susannah asked finally.

'The council will fall, whether you're in it or out,' Lisandro said. 'I'm not really fussed. I won't take it personally; neither should you.'

'You want to end the White Elm?' Qasim asked, still the sceptic.

'Yes. And I will. Slowly and decisively, I will bring this council to the ground, where it belongs, under the foundations of the new government – Magnus Moira. Or more precisely, me.'

Lisandro is an enemy. He led Jackson and Peter to betray us...

'Is this a power grab, Lisandro?' Lord Gawain asked, letting his devastation show. How could the leader be Lisandro? Lord Gawain himself had elected Lisandro to the chair of Dark Keeper – the White Elm's secret weapon against uprisings of sorcerers illegally using dark magic. They had worked side-by-side for eleven years now. How could Lisandro have kept his intentions so well hidden?

'Partly, yes.'

'You are the third-highest ranking member of the magical world's government. You hold the most honoured and trusted position in the world.'

'I hold a position that is secret outside of this council,' Lisandro responded coldly. 'No one else even knows that the Dark Keeper exists. To any sorcerer on the street I'm just another White Elm idiot.'

'Why do you need recognition, Lisandro? Isn't it enough that *we* trust you so highly?' Lord Gawain asked. *Lisandro...why you?*

'Your trust amuses me,' Lisandro answered. He looked around. 'You've revealed me as a traitor and a rival – as the manipulator of Jackson and Peter – and yet none of you have your wands out. No one is prepared to attack me. Your trust is so innate and leaves you exposed and vulnerable.'

A few White Elm raised their wands. Lisandro laughed.

'I speak and you all move – so predictable.'

'You tortured him...' Tian said, staring at Peter, who had now fallen unconscious, fingers curling around the power ring he'd been trusted to protect for them. They'd have to grab that back before Lisandro tried to get it. 'Though he was your friend and supporter, you tortured him. How can we expect any different if we follow you?'

'I needed to test his loyalty. I had no idea he was so dependable,' Lisandro commented. He clapped his hands once. 'So, who's coming with me?'

The council members glanced at one another again, and Lord Gawain felt his heart thudding in his chest. How many of his councillors were *his* and how many could be swayed by Lisandro's easy charm?

'None of us,' Qasim said finally, apparently speaking for the group. 'We are White Elm. We swore oaths to this council, and unlike some, we have the honour to hold to those oaths.'

Lisandro lifted his chin slightly as the other councillors nodded firmly, encouraged by Qasim's strong words. Lord Gawain felt himself relax. Lisandro was *not* the most powerful force here, after all.

'Well, you had your chance,' Lisandro said with a shrug. 'I'm sorry it has to end like this. You should know by now that *nothing* stands between me and what I want, so please make the effort to *not* be obstacles. I'd hate to have to kill any of you.'

'Don't be melodramatic,' Lady Miranda scoffed.

Emmanuelle started pulling herself together.

'Lisandro destroyed Peter,' she accused, struggling to stand. Her foot caught the hem of her robe and she stumbled. Renatus grabbed her by the elbow and pulled her to her feet, but he continued watching Lisandro. 'It wouldn't bother 'im to 'urt any of us.'

'*You* nearly destroyed him,' Lisandro replied carelessly. 'His friendship for you was weakening his resolve. If he'd given in I would have killed him.'

'Lisandro...What went wrong with you?' Lord Gawain asked. He was really struggling to understand why this was happening.

'Honestly? You, Gawain. *You* are what went wrong with me. Watch out, kid,' he added to Renatus, before turning back to Lord Gawain. 'You, my friend, my mentor, my leader, are responsible for anything I do henceforth, because *you* failed me in the exact moments I needed you not to. Think back: you remember the moments, the times I needed something and you ignored me.'

'Your needs were selfish,' Lord Gawain rebuked, thinking of one such time quite easily but having difficulty recalling any more.

'Maybe so, but I've noticed that the world is ready for a change, and realised that *I* could be it. It's a very empowering feeling.'

'What will you do now?'

'Destroy you. Bit by bit.'

At the opposite side of the dismantled circle, the energy levels spiked as someone relinquished their self-control and anger burst forth.

'You deceitful monster!' Emmanuelle screamed, her usually smooth blonde hair ruffled. 'How dare you? How dare you ruin this council, after all it 'as gained you? How dare you destroy Peter?' She continued ranting in furious French and started forward as though to attack her friend's manipulator, but Renatus caught her and held her back. Glen hurried to Renatus to help restrain her.

'I think that's my cue to leave,' Lisandro said cheerfully. He tapped Peter's motionless form with his wand and the young Scot disappeared, displaced.

Lord Gawain froze mid-step – *the Elm Stone!* Why hadn't he bothered to look into the future to see this coming? He'd been so focussed on the events unfolding in the *now* and now the ring, the White Elm's greatest source of emergency power was *gone*!

'No! Bring 'im back!' Emmanuelle cried, fighting against those who restrained her. Renatus held her tightly, his face expressionless, while Glen transferred soothing energy to her. It wasn't working.

'Someone needs to shut that little girl up,' Lisandro commented, waving his wand in her direction; she dropped as though dead, but Renatus was quick to catch her before she hit the ground. An automatic check of her aura confirmed that she was alive and unharmed, just stunned. Lisandro smirked at Renatus. 'Pretty girl, that one. Not as pretty as your sister was, though.'

In an instant Renatus had released Emmanuelle and shouted an ancient-sounding word. A bolt of too-fast misty blue energy ripped through the air, aimed at Lisandro's green-sashed chest. Lisandro saw it coming. He dropped his wand.

The result of his unexpected spell was instant. With a deafening, unexplainable noise, the entire garden was shrouded in poisonous black smoke. The candle flames that had lit the space were immediately snuffed. The White Elm began coughing painfully as soon as they inhaled the smoke. It was toxic, constricting the throat and lungs in a way that normal smoke did not. Lord Gawain dropped to the ground, his lungs already desperate for air. He had no idea how to reverse this dark magic. That was Lisandro's job as Dark Keeper, but no doubt

Lisandro had displaced himself by now.

Because, impossibly, the council's secret weapon had backfired and Lisandro had betrayed them.

'What is this?' Susannah asked, her voice forced.

'I don't know!' Lady Miranda said, coughing and sounding lost.

'It's exhaust,' Renatus said. His voice was calm and easy, his sudden anger of moments earlier lost. Lord Gawain looked around for him but the smoke stung his eyes. However, the smoke was thinning. Within a few seconds it was gone. Renatus was the only one standing, his wand out.

'Exhaust?' Lord Gawain asked, slowly standing and looking around. Sure enough, Lisandro, Peter and Jackson were gone. The other White Elm were getting to their feet.

'It's an old, old piece of dark magic,' Renatus said smoothly. 'It's the negative energy left over after dark magical spells, turned physical. It's called exhaust. Most of the time this energy dissipates but Lisandro obviously knows how to manipulate it into exhaust.'

'How do you know this?' Lady Miranda demanded, standing and pointing her wand at him threateningly. Renatus handed over his wand obligingly but didn't answer. 'Is it from your spell?'

'Partly. Mostly your own energy you imparted to him-'

'He's done nothing wrong, Miranda,' Lord Gawain said immediately. He knew Renatus's family's reputation, like everyone present, but now wasn't the time to pretend it mattered. 'We need to focus on Lisandro.'

Lisandro's gone.

The Elm Stone's gone.

Both weapons, and two other talented councillors, gone – lost in a matter of minutes. In this moment, there was no obvious course of action.

chapter one

Heavy rain slashed at the windows, so hard they could have broken and no one would have been surprised. A flash of lightning briefly relieved the stormy darkness, but was followed by an eerie flickering of the living room lights and television. The thunder clap was immediate, and the image on the television blinked out. A cold and shaking hand grabbed mine – my equally terrified sister trying to comfort me, trying to remind me that inside, we were safe, surely. The wind howled, and whole branches were ripped from the massive tree in the yard. The two men I loved most in the world ducked as the wind intensified and flung a neighbour's post box over their heads. There was a huge, sickening crack from outside, totally unlike the thunder and many times worse, and the tree began to fall…

A harsh rumble like thunder jolted me awake, and I sat up suddenly.

'This is your stop, isn't it?' my bus driver asked kindly, smiling at me in her rear-view mirror. I nodded, blushing as I got to my feet and hurried to the front door.

'Thanks,' I mumbled, grateful that my bus driver, at least, knew what I was doing. I apparently didn't. Falling asleep on the bus? That was something new, and stupid. The next stop wasn't until the Catholic neighbourhood, and, well, I wouldn't exactly be welcomed there. As far as they were concerned, I was a Protestant through and through, and this *is* Northern Ireland, after all. You're one or the other, even if you're neither, which is my category. I suppose someone in my family, way back, might have been a real one, but I didn't think so.

You don't get many Protestant or Catholic witches.

'No worries,' the driver said, waving once as she closed the doors behind me.

The bus rumbled again, its ancient engine sputtering loudly as it continued on its journey. That's what had woken me. No big deal. Nothing to be paranoid about. I looked up at the sky. I needed to get a grip. The clouds were grey and low, but harmless. The weather lady on the news had predicted rain this afternoon, but no storms. I could relax.

Naturally, I'd forgotten my umbrella, despite the weather lady's warning, so if I was to avoid being rained on I should probably hurry and get home. I zipped up my jacket and hurried along the quiet street.

I'd lived in this neighbourhood for three years, but it still didn't feel like home. I didn't know any of my neighbours, not even the people in the houses right next to mine, whereas in my childhood home I'd known the whole street and heaps of kids living nearby. Other witch kids, mostly, because our old neighbourhood had been home to several witch families. Maybe that was the problem with this neighbourhood. No magic. Sorcerers just didn't tend to live in secluded, dull North Irish suburbia, or at least not within like twenty kilometres of our place. You'd hardly think *anyone* lived around here, I reflected as I crossed the silent road. People just stayed inside their houses unless they were getting into their car to go somewhere more interesting.

I turned a corner and kicked a stone. It clattered across the road and rolled into a puddle from yesterday's rain. I felt that disappointment you get when your game ends prematurely. Oh, well. There would be other rocks, no doubt.

As I passed the puddle, something compelled me to look down. My stone lay prone in the murky water amongst other stones. Was it a trick of the light, or was something glinting? I tilted my head, and saw again the glint of something shiny. A coin? The first drops of rain struck the surface of the water, marring my view, so I leaned down and scooped it out. At first, I felt nothing in my hand, and reached again, but noticed that my fingers had indeed closed around something.

My prize was more of a river pebble, I saw now, smooth, round and flat. Bizarrely, weightless, like it was hollow. Unassuming, and unshiny, until I turned it in my hand and saw a silvery engraving on its other side. The design was of a roughly symmetrical tree, like a Celtic tree of life. I knew I'd seen it before, probably many times, but for a long moment couldn't place where.

It came to me suddenly.

'White Elm,' I murmured, recognising the tree as the symbol of the magical world's governing council. Thirteen of the world's most gifted sorcerers worked together to regulate the use of magic, maintain secrecy of our kind from the non-magical community and monitor the goings-on of sorcerers everywhere. They were like our politicians, our judges, our police and our social workers all rolled into one entity. I'd never met any of them, but three years ago, immediately after the tragedy that had killed my parents and older brother, I'd received a letter from them, offering condolences and providing my sister with best contact details for emergencies now that she would be a teenager raising a minor on her own. Days later, we'd received another letter, congratulating my sister on coming of age on her twentieth birthday – the first day of adulthood in magical culture.

We'd kept the second letter, but tossed out the first one in a clean-up five months ago when we'd realised that the directions we had for an emergency were to contact one Lisandro, a man who no longer even worked for the White Elm. Worse, he'd deserted it in a controversial political bust-up and not been seen or heard from in almost half a year. It had all been very exciting at the time, with the White Elm publishing weekly public safely messages, acting like their former councillor was an escaped convict on the loose, but nothing had come of it, and things had been quiet on that front for quite some time now.

I turned the pebble over in my hand again, wondering what it was doing lying around two streets from my house. Maybe a sorcerer had been this way, and dropped it? Random. Maybe a councillor from the White Elm had left it here for me, a message? Doubtful.

Giving up on my dumb theories, I slipped the pebble into my pocket and turned to continue on my way home. I stopped immediately.

A man was standing there. He certainly hadn't been there seconds ago, and he wasn't puffed like someone who might have just bolted out from one of the houses behind me. Where had he come from?

'Hello, Aristea,' he said. For a long second, I just stared. Where had he come from, and how did he know my name?

'Hi,' I responded, warily. His appearance didn't tell me much – mid-fifties, Arabic in descent, skin the colour of dark coffee, deep soulful eyes, curling dark hair, short beard, powerful build, tall, dressed in a suit – so I tuned into my other senses, my witch senses. They were like long, invisible fingers I could brush over things nearby to feel for energies. I could sense straightaway that he was a sorcerer, and one of the strongest sorcerers I'd ever encountered. His energy field was fuller and stronger than that of anyone else I'd previously met. What he was doing here, I couldn't guess, so I probed deeper, looking for feelings and intentions. I felt curiosity, mild interest, but nothing frightening or threatening about his emotional state.

How someone feels isn't always a perfect indicator of how they intend to act, so when he moved towards me I jumped back and opened one hand instinctively. Unseen, an energetic shield, a ward, blossomed from my hand, blocking him. The man paused, sensing what many others wouldn't. He wouldn't be able to walk through it. He shifted his weight to a standing position again and extended his hand, probably what he'd been doing in the first place, I reflected now.

'My name is Qasim,' he told me. 'I belong with the White Elm council.'

My ward lost its fizz and dissolved as relief washed over me. No weirdo. No escaped convict. This was one of the good guys.

'Aristea Byrne,' I said, stepping forward to accept his hand. His handshake was warm and firm. 'You gave me a fright.'

'My apologies, but I couldn't arrive here before being sure you would pass the test,' he said, sounding far from sorry. He had a businesslike tone that I wasn't sure I liked, but I overlooked this for the moment in light of what he was saying.

'What test?'

'Just a test of faith,' Qasim said, nodding once at my left hip. I reached into my jeans pocket and withdrew the weightless pebble. Before my eyes it vanished. 'You passed, or I wouldn't have come.'

I'd passed because I'd kept the stone?

'Where did it go?'

'It was only an illusion. Its purpose is met; it no longer needs to exist.'

'But how did you even know I'd kept it?' I countered, confused. Could he go invisible? Had he been here all along?

'I saw you.'

'Where were you?'

'Dublin.'

I stared at him, realising what he was saying. He could *scry*. He had the power and the skill to observe events remotely with his *mind*. It was something I'd always, always wanted to be able to do, and something I'd never, ever been able to perform.

'Are you a scrier?' I asked, suddenly tentative.

'I am *the* Scrier for the White Elm,' Qasim answered. 'I have been monitoring you, among others, for a number of weeks.'

I bit back on my mildly hurt feelings about my broken privacy. He'd been *watching me*. From other places. I'd been spied on, for weeks, and not even known it. Was he even allowed to do that?

'Among others?' I asked politely, and he nodded briskly.

'I'd rather discuss this with your guardian present, if that suits you fine,' he said. 'The White Elm wishes to present you with a special opportunity, but because of your age your guardian will need to be fully informed and give her consent if you are interested.'

Interested? I was beyond interested, especially now.

'Okay, I live just this way,' I said, pointing up the street and leading the way. Qasim followed silently. 'So what is this about?'

'An opportunity,' he said again, and I got the distinct impression that it was all he was going to say until we reached my house, so I gave up. He would tell my sister, I was sure. He would love my sister. Everyone did.

The rain mostly held off except for occasional little drops until I unlocked my front door and held it open for Qasim. He walked inside, and I followed, shutting and locking the door behind us.

The small house was quiet, but I'd seen my sister's car in the driveway, so I knew she had to be here somewhere.

'Ange?' I called, leading Qasim into the sitting room. I hurriedly dusted off a seat for him – the couch in front of the TV and DVD player was still littered with crumbs from my chips and other assorted snacks during my movie last night. My highly domestic sister couldn't have been home long, or this room would have been spotless. 'Angela?'

I heard a door opening, probably the bathroom, and heard the drone of the hairdryer. It quietened down, momentarily clicked down to a lower setting.

'Aristea?'

'Yeah, I'm home,' I called, nervously rearranging the coffee table, still covered in DVD cases. Last night I'd enjoyed a marathon of all three *Pirates of the Caribbean* movies (I don't count the fourth because it doesn't have Orlando Bloom in it), which had obviously been excellent at the time, but they're long films so I'd gone to bed without bothering to clean up, and then this morning woken late and had to hurry to catch the bus for my casual shift at the crystal shop in town...'We've got a guest.'

'Alright, I'll be one second,' Angela promised, and I heard the bathroom door shut.

'She'll just be a second,' I repeated to Qasim, although he'd probably heard it from the source, just as I had. I stood awkwardly beside the DVD cabinet, stuffing the cases into any old slot. Angela would no doubt reorganise these later. It felt weird, almost embarrassing, to be seen handling objects as mundane as DVDs around someone like Qasim. I wasn't sure whether he was one of them, but I knew that many of the councillors on the White Elm lived lives in varying degrees of tradition, some shirking modern, technological life altogether.

Angela and I were very modern witches. We lived very normal lives, paying rent, going to work at normal jobs, watching DVDs at night, going shopping on Saturdays, getting places by car or bus. We just happened to be sorceresses, with the ability to perform a couple of magical acts. No flying brooms, no black cats...Our rental agreement wouldn't allow the cat anyway.

The bathroom door opened and I heard footsteps as my sister approached. I looked over my shoulder as Angela entered the living room. She smiled politely at Qasim, but the look she shot me spelt out exactly what she was thinking. Who needed telepathy? We'd never mastered it, but I could tell that she was wondering why I'd brought home a well-dressed, middle-aged Arabic man and seated him on our lounge suite.

'Hi, I'm Angela,' she said, speaking with both friendliness and easy authority.

Angela Byrne was my very favourite person in the entire world. She was six years older than me at twenty-three, six times cooler and six times more beautiful, although everyone claimed that I was her spitting image, just "coloured in differently", as my uncle joked. She was slim and fair, with bright blue-green eyes and straight blonde-brown hair, and bordering on tall for a girl, though at almost the same height, I never noticed this unless we were out with other girls or with our much shorter cousin. Angela and I lived alone in this small two-bedroom flat in the suburbs of Coleraine, which was not our first preference of living arrangements but still worked quite well. We got along fabulously, by which I mean I idolised her and she doted on me.

Qasim stood and offered his hand.

'Qasim, with the White Elm,' he explained, shaking her hand. Her polite expression immediately smoothed to one of genuine welcome.

'Oh,' she said, glancing at me again. 'What can we do for you?'

'As you may have noticed, the White Elm has been somewhat publicly *quiet* in recent months,' Qasim began, sitting down again when Angela did. I plopped down beside her, wishing immediately that I'd sat down more elegantly. Qasim didn't seem to notice; he wasn't even addressing me anymore. 'One reason for this has been an attempt to starve

Lisandro of information. The less access he has to our plans and movements, the closer he has to come in order to get it.'

That made sense, I supposed, although that plan hinged on the notion that Lisandro *wanted* to know what his old council was doing. I'd assumed he was just in hiding, but this sounded like the White Elm thought otherwise.

'The other reason is that we have been in the process of establishing an institution, a sort of academy, for instructing young sorcerers in the finer magical arts. We are finding, more and more in this integrated, fast-paced world we live in, that the younger generation is missing out on the instruction their parents or grandparents might have had in such areas as healing, Seeing, displacement, scrying or spell-writing, among other things. This academy is due to commence taking students in just a few weeks, and would serve the dual purpose of getting skilled sorcerers out into communities where they are lacking, and also improving the skills within the pool of young people from which the White Elm selects its members. Several councillors within the council are at a stage in their lives where taking an apprentice would seem prudent, and this academy would provide opportunities for appropriate matches to be found.'

He'd had me riveted from "scrying", but I still wasn't sure what he was saying. Was he talking about a magic school? Only I was pretty sure that the White Elm themselves had been fighting against that one for decades or centuries, insisting on social and educational integration with mainstream and trying to remain as inconspicuous as possible. My sister seemed to be thinking along the same lines.

'That sounds like a good idea,' Angela agreed, 'but how does that sit with the White Elm's social integration policy?'

'The White Elm council still maintains that the only way forwards is side-by-side with our mortal counterparts,' Qasim answered smoothly. 'We are not seeking to replace mortal schooling with our system. Conversely, our new academy would be open to highly gifted sorcerers who have completed compulsory mortal schooling and may be interested in developing their special skills to carve a place for themselves in *this* world, for example as healers or even by, eventually, joining the White Elm council.' He finally shifted his gaze back to me. 'We would like to offer Aristea a place at this academy.'

I blinked, startled, and looked at my sister for confirmation. I had *not* expected this, although of course I should have – why else would he have bothered testing me and then telling me about the school?

'But...you said it was for gifted people,' I stammered, sounding stupid. 'I'm not gifted.'

'Your name came up,' Qasim said simply. 'We are looking for sorcerers between sixteen and twenty with a high capacity for power and a pre-existing relationship with, or at least a positive attitude towards, the White Elm. You fit our criteria.'

'How, though?' I persisted. 'How did you pick me out? Is there a list or something?'

It had to be a dodgy list.

'No, I possess the ability to mass-scry,' Qasim said, like he was talking about a good catching arm or something equally commonplace. 'I was looking for the world's fifty strongest sixteen-to-nineteen-year-old sorcerers, and I have been monitoring them since.'

I should probably just shut up. Qasim could not only remotely view scenes, people and events, he could view *fifty of them at once*. Anything I said now was going to sound really dumb and pointless.

'I didn't realise there was so much magic in the family,' Angela commented, looking me over curiously. I wished she wouldn't. I didn't like the idea that something made me different from her.

'You're the same,' Qasim said, kindly. I felt immediate relief. 'You're both very powerful. It probably comes from a long way back. These things usually do.'

'So where is the school?' Angela asked, crossing her legs. I almost mirrored her but stopped myself. No copied movement was going to make me anywhere near as ladylike as her. I would only succeed in looking awkward, like usual.

'Not far from here, actually.' Qasim looked out the nearest window and nodded to the west. 'I can't give you the exact location at this time but I can say that it is nearby, at the home of a White Elm councillor. Students would be completely protected and perfectly safe boarding there, while also enjoying open channels of communication with families.'

'Will they have access to phones and internet?'

Angela asked, and Qasim shook his head.

'Unfortunately, that is impossible. Electronic devices fail to function within the walls of this particular property because of the protective magic encasing it. Phones would short out.'

'Is there electricity?' I asked, a horrible image of a candlelit existence occurring to me. 'And running water…?'

'Of sorts, yes,' Qasim said cryptically. 'Lights, taps and toilets function exactly as you would expect them to. I assure you, this property is not lacking in any modern luxury, except perhaps power points.'

'What would be the main mode of instruction?' asked Angela, ever focussed.

'The councillors of the White Elm will be scheduling time each week to teach their area of expertise to classes of students.'

'Lady Miranda will be teaching healing, then?' Angela checked, shooting me an excited smile. The White Elm's High Priestess was the world's most talented healer, and extremely well-known in our world for the countless miracles she'd performed while working as a surgeon in a hospital in London.

'And you'll be teaching me scrying?' I asked Qasim, because though healing was great and all, nothing appealed to me like the ancient art of scrying. He nodded once.

'Yes, I will be taking the lessons on scrying,' he answered. He turned back to Angela. 'You don't need to decide today. I'm just here to let you know about the opportunity. If you are interested, we will send further information and the enrolment forms in about a week.'

I looked hopefully at Angela.

'And if we're not interested?' she asked, politely, and I forced a smile to match, but inside I was screaming at her. I wanted this.

'I won't bother you again,' Qasim promised.

'I hope a refusal wouldn't be taken as a show of disloyalty, because that would not be the case.'

Angela was so diplomatic, I reminded myself. She was just exploring our options. She was just checking all avenues for holes. That's all. She wasn't trying to turn Qasim down without even asking me. She wasn't like that.

'The White Elm is satisfied with your family's commitment to our principles and would understand that a refusal in this case is well within your rights,' Qasim assured her. Angela looked at me again.

'There's a possibility that Aristea might be chosen as an apprentice due to her involvement at this school?' she said, looking at me critically like she always did when forced to think like a parent instead of a sister.

'There is every possibility,' Qasim agreed. 'Such a selection would create a guaranteed position for her on the White Elm some day. Not everyone will get this opportunity, of course, but even those who do not will have access to learning and skills they would otherwise not have developed. We anticipate that this school will have at least as many benefits for the community as it does for the council itself, if not more.'

'And how long will she be staying at the

school?' Angela was still watching me, still trying to decide how best to act as my guardian.

'At this time, we are planning for a one-year-long training program,' Qasim said. 'That may be extended for some or all students, although that need will become apparent throughout the year.' He paused, waiting for Angela. She said nothing, so he asked, 'Should I put your family down as interested, or should we leave this here?'

I looked back at my sister intently, silently begging. I wanted to go. I was going to learn how to scry, and maybe join the White Elm one day and matter and make big decisions, but right now, my sister stood between me and that future.

'It's not a family decision,' Angela said finally. She shrugged. 'I'm not Aristea's mother; I don't make decisions for her. If she wants to go, that's up to her. Are you interested?'

I stared at her. I shouldn't have been surprised. Angela was always like this – totally perfect.

'Yes,' I managed. I swallowed. 'Yes, I'd love to attend the White Elm's academy.'

'Excellent,' Qasim said, standing. Angela and I did the same. He shook our hands. 'I hope you'll understand when I request that this conversation does not leave this room. At this time we are trying to keep this very quiet, so I would prefer that you do not disclose anything pertaining to my visit to anyone until Aristea actually enrols.'

'We understand,' Angela agreed immediately. Qasim nodded once, grateful, and withdrew a card from his pocket. My sister accepted it.

'You can write to the White Elm at this post office box. I'll be in touch with further information. Thank you for your time.'

'Yes, the same to you,' Angela said, walking with him to the front door. I stayed where I was. Had all that really just happened? I heard them exchange goodbyes and I heard the front door click shut. Had Angela really just said goodbye to Qasim, *the* Scrier for the White Elm? It sounded insane; I had to have imagined it. I hurried into the front room and wrenched open the door Angela had just closed.

Outside, there was nobody to be seen. Our quiet street was as devoid of activity as the rest of the suburb, and the rain had settled into a sort of drizzle.

'I did imagine it,' I murmured, shutting the door again. Angela laughed and locked it.

'No, he was here. But he'd be long gone by now. He's probably in Cambodia by now.'

'Cambodia?'

'Well, probably not, but he wouldn't have hung around waiting for a bus, would he?'

I realised that the White Elm contained some of the most powerful sorcerers in the world, to whom displacement was probably easier than running. Why had I entertained the thought that our visitor might be walking to fifty houses around the world? He'd popped up out of nowhere when I'd pocketed that stone. Qasim was clearly an accomplished Displacer.

'So, what have you gotten yourself into?' Angela asked, smiling as she went back into the sitting room and began to tidy. I followed, continuing my earlier work of dusting crumbs off the chairs.

17

'I'm not really sure,' I admitted, honestly. I crouched beside one seat and picked a couple of bits of potato chip from the upholstery. 'Do you think it's a good idea that I go?'

Now that Qasim was gone I didn't feel so certain about the whole plan. Angela started rearranging the DVDs, putting them back in the order only she understood. She looked thoughtful.

'I think anything's a good idea if it's what you want,' she said eventually.

'Way to be cryptic,' I said, taking my crumbs to the kitchen bin. Angela followed, leaning on the breakfast bar as I washed my hands.

'This is pretty amazing,' she said, handing me a hand towel. 'You're going to learn to heal and displace and scry and all that. You are being handed a massive opportunity. I don't think Mum and Dad ever learnt those finer arts.'

'Mum could heal little things,' I said quietly, and we both fell silent, as we often did when one of us accidentally mentioned our deceased parents or brother. It had been three years since the tragic day a storm had rolled in from the sea, destroyed our seaside family home and killed our mum and dad and big brother Aidan. It still hurt every day, and every night, when I relieved it all in my dreams.

'Yeah, she could,' Angela agreed softly. She reached over the breakfast bar to take my hand. 'You could be healing all sorts of things in a few weeks from now. You could be displacing all over the countryside. You might be writing your own spells.'

'I'll be scrying,' I added, perking up again. 'I

18

might even be able to start scrying you.'

Despite my love of the art, I'd never been able to perform it. I'd heard that it was easiest to begin with things or people you know really well, but I'd never even been able to scry my own sister.

'You might be the next White Elm Scrier,' Angela suggested, squeezing my hand. We both laughed, because that was a little optimistic.

'How good do you think the chances are of people getting picked as apprentices?' I asked, and Angela shrugged lightly.

'I suppose there would be a few councillors old enough to be looking, but I think a lot of them would be too young,' she said thoughtfully. 'I think you have to be about forty or something to have an apprentice.'

'If I learn enough, I might even have my *own* apprentice one day,' I said, allowing my imagination to run free. Angela released my hand and went to get the vacuum cleaner from its cupboard.

'Maybe you'll teach your apprentice to clean up after herself,' she teased. I rolled my eyes and went to take it from her. I could take a hint.

'When I have my own apprentice, I'll be too busy saving the world to have to clean up my own messes,' I told her as she plugged it in. 'You'll see.'

It wasn't until much later that I learned this, but even as I joked around with my sister, my experience was being repeated, four dozen times over, with young sorcerers all around the world. An eighteen-year-old surfer paddled back onto Australia's sunset-soaked beach and noticed a silvery gleam in the shallows. He scooped the pebble out of the sand, and, surfboard under one arm, walked to shore where he met a smiling, unfamiliar wisp of a man. In South Africa, a dark-haired girl was hanging out her laundry. A wet towel brushed against her glasses, marring her vision, and as she took them off to clean them against her dress, a blurry glimmer of silver caught her attention. She returned her glasses to her eyes to bring into focus the engraved pebble sitting amongst her laundry. She admired it for a long moment before closing her fingers around it experimentally; a fresh-skinned, round-faced woman with soft brown hair approached out of nowhere. In Japan, a brother and sister pair danced energetically at a nightclub, surrounded closely by friends and acquaintances. The younger of them, the sister, had had too much to drink, and stumbled. Her brother laughingly pulled her up, but both paused when they saw the little stone on the floor beside the girl's spike heel. Both snatched for it at once and fought for it even once they were upright. A man just a little too old to be there tapped their shoulders and beckoned them to follow him away from the pumping music. There was a pretty sixteen-year-old sorceress in north-east England curling her hair; a German teenager coaching junior soccer; a pair of identical twins outside Vancouver on a horse-riding camp...There was even a homeless boy in Manchester reaching into a drain, hoping desperately to find money, even just a few pence. He spotted something shiny and his cold and dirty fingers closed on the pebble.

In short, my life was not the only one changed that day, nor was it the most significantly changed, and it would take me many months to really realise it, but my life was about to drastically transform and this was the day it started.

chapter two

My life had been changed drastically before.

    None of us had foreseen this storm. It had rolled in out of nowhere. I was upstairs in my room when it hit, reading. I'd hardly noticed it coming, except to realise that the sunlight had suddenly dulled, forcing me to switch my light on. The rain was heavy and fast, pounding on my window, strong winds lashing tree branches against the house walls. It wasn't until a branch was ripped from a neighbour's tree and flung at my window, cracking the glass, that I got scared, grabbed Cedric (the stuffed rabbit my grandmother Merit had handmade for me for my first Christmas, completely out of scraps of material) and hurried downstairs to find my family. My mother, Elysia, I met on the stairs, coming up to find me. She led me to the sunken dining room, where my older siblings, Aidan, twenty-one, and Angela, not quite twenty, were waiting, looking panicked. I asked them where our father Darren was, and they told me he was outside. Mum left Angela with strict orders to stay inside with me, while she allowed Aidan to go outside and help Dad tie down the outdoor furniture. She herself went upstairs to collect all the most important family treasures and bring them to the much safer sunken dining room.

Outside, I heard a sickening, crunching snap as a massive old tree was uprooted from the dirt. Angela and I ran to the nearest window to helplessly watch as Dad and Aidan desperately struggled to get back to the house despite the high winds, before the huge tree toppled towards the big house, its thick trunk mostly obscuring both men from my view, almost as though to protect Angela and I from watching their deaths. Angela gave a strangled cry of horror, but an instant before either of us could move or call out to Mum, there was a deafening crash, and the entire house shook as the tree landed on it, smashing through the roof.

My sister and I screamed, clutching each other in terror and collapsing to the floor as the ceiling above us caved in, furniture from Angela's bedroom pouring on top of us along with leaves, twigs, small branches and a lot of sharp rain. Without thinking, I cast my first ward around myself, Angela and Cedric with only my hand, protecting us from harm and preventing any physical object from passing through the invisible bubble…

I opened my eyes, and the entire scene melted away immediately, immaterial like the dream it was. The more real knot of fear and grief in my stomach lingered. I stared at my ceiling as my heartbeat slowly returned to its normal pace. I was accustomed to this daily ritual. It was the same every night, and every morning.

Mum and Aidan were killed immediately. Dad officially died upon arrival at hospital, but his heart had stopped in the ambulance and the paramedics weren't able to restart it. The coroner later said that with head injuries like his, regaining a pulse wouldn't have been enough to give us our dad back. He was gone, really, at the same time as his wife and son. Angela and I lost them all at once.

Eventually I dragged myself out of bed and set about making myself presentable. It always took a long hot shower, several changes of clothes and about ten minutes of hair styling before I chose to simply leave my hair out, wear the clothes my sister had just washed and laid out on my bed the day before, and felt prepared to face the dull and uneventful life that was mine.

'Why, good afternoon,' somebody joked as I entered the dining room of the flat. I glanced at the clock above the kitchen sink – not yet eleven. It was a Sunday. Eleven a.m. on a Sunday was practically equivalent to seven a.m. on a weekday.

'Hi,' I replied to my aunt. She smiled indulgently and pulled out the chair beside her so I could join the family at the table for a late breakfast. I'd forgotten that they were coming over, although I shouldn't have, because Aunt Leanne, her husband Patrick, and their daughter Kelly often came over on Sundays.

'Did you have a good sleep?' my aunt asked,

affectionately brushing a stray lock of my hair out of my face.

'Yes,' I lied with a convincing smile. She suspected nothing, and was not sensitive enough to notice the teensy flick of energy that always accompanies untruth. It was a white lie, more of a half-truth really, because yes, I had slept all night and was well-rested. She didn't need to know that I'd had a bad dream, and she especially didn't need to know that it was the same bad dream I'd had every night for over three years.

'Orange juice?' Uncle Patrick offered, reaching for my glass even before I nodded.

'How many pancakes, sweetheart?' Aunt Leanne asked while her husband filled my glass. She patted my hand kindly as though I were a little girl. At seventeen, not far off eighteen, I was definitely not a little girl anymore, but in this family I would always be the baby. My sister Angela and our cousin Kelly were twenty-three, and I'd once also had an older brother, who would now be twenty-five if he were alive. It was very hard to convince my aunt and uncle that I was grown up now, especially considering that they hardly considered Ange or Kell to be adults.

'Um, just two,' I said, looking around behind me so I could see into the kitchen where my sister and cousin were standing over the stove frying pancakes. They were the same age, and shared blood, but from behind, Angela and Kelly couldn't have looked more different. Kelly looked much like her father, with her freckled white skin, her thick red curls and curvier, shorter shape. Angela, on the other hand, was taller and slimmer, very fair skinned, and her hair was straight, some strange colour caught between blonde and very light brown. She looked like *our* father, I supposed, as did Aunt Leanne, his surviving sister.

Following the tragedy I relived in nightmares every night, Angela and I were taken in by Aunt Leanne for a few months. It was lovely to be loved and supported, but the tension ignited between my aunt and sister as they'd both petitioned the courts for custody of me had made the experience uncomfortable. When Angela was made my guardian, we'd moved out of my aunt's place, and their relationship had improved dramatically.

'You really should sign up for the newsletter,' Aunt Leanne was telling Angela as a plate of pancakes appeared in front of me. 'It's not like those mortal newsletter people, where they pass on your details to marketing companies. The White Elm's not like that. Your details are safe; it just opens up a direct channel of contact between you and the council. It means they can send you updates and information at any time. And if you signed up, I wouldn't have to bring over mine every month.'

She said that, but she would, anyway I knew, just like she brought over bread rolls, milk, junk mail and random coupons. Aunt Leanne wouldn't want us to go without a thing – especially not potentially important news direct from the magical government.

My entire family were witches (people with old magical blood, the opposite of mortals) and sorcerers (people who could produce spells). Some witches were not powerful enough to do sorcery, and hence were only witches, and some who practiced sorcery were not witches. Blood didn't necessarily determine power or ability to use magic (after all, there were cases of powerful sorcerers born into families in which there was absolutely no witch blood) but it was generally a pretty good indicator. Magic went back a really long way through Dad and Aunt Leanne's family, the Byrnes, beyond the scope of the family tree, but none of us had ever been able to produce particularly impressive magic when we tried. Except me – just that once.

We didn't know anything about Mum's side, except that *her* mum was Greek and her dad (a writer, apparently) had disappeared just after she was born.

'I will, I just keep forgetting,' Angela said, glancing at me significantly and returning to the kitchen to retrieve her own plate. Aunt Leanne had been on her case to sign up for the monthly White Elm newsletter ever since the Lisandro incident half a year ago. What she didn't know was that the White Elm had managed to find us without us ever signing up to the newsletter, and that next time we received anything from the council, it was likely to be much more informative than a public newsletter.

'The White Elm needs as much support as it can get these days,' Aunt Leanne said, cutting her pancakes into little pieces. 'It's important to show where your loyalties lie.'

When one of the council's most prominent members had very suddenly and publicly mutinied, our society had been rocked in a very real way. The White Elm council had always been trusted and followed, if sometimes grudgingly, so what reason could their most popular councillor have for wanting to leave? It had to be a good reason, many people determined, and they'd cancelled their subscription to the White Elm's newsletter, trying to cut off the council's ability to contact them further. The White Elm had been fiercely discouraging this, especially as whispers of Lisandro's travels became louder and more persistent. Rumours said that he'd been seen in Hungary recruiting followers, and that Jackson, who had left the council with him, had been spotted repeatedly in parts of Western Europe and along the east coast of the USA. According to Aunt Leanne, however, by the time these rumours reached the White Elm, there was no trace of any of their former councillors. Some people thought that this was a good thing – that Lisandro was clearly much cleverer and more gifted than the council, and a powerful contender for their loyalty should he ask for it.

Aunt Leanne was not like those people. A staunch believer in the council, she read the newsletter every month and occasionally wrote in to share her support. She frequently quoted the newsletters like they were scientific journals, and religiously drilled into her daughter and nieces the importance of supporting your chosen side.

'They're being very careful with their words these days,' Aunt Leanne commented as she skimmed over her newsletter for the thousandth time. 'They've put into action a long-term plan to protect communities and the council's future from threat, but they haven't written what they're actually going to do.'

I silently ate my breakfast, avoiding everybody's eyes. All things going smoothly, I was part of that plan. If I were on a council and I had spent half a year looking for a former colleague who had managed to totally evade all attempts to locate him, and I had absolutely no clue where he was or who among my society were even still on my side, I probably wouldn't be publishing my grand plans in a monthly newsletter, either.

'And they aren't putting photos in anymore,' Kelly complained. 'They haven't published a single picture of any of the new three councillors. Usually when they bring somebody new on, they do a huge feature so you can sort of get to know them. Then they hired these new people and just did a small article, with no pictures or last names or anything! No one seems to have seen them or to know who they are. You don't even know if they're real people. What're their names again, Mummy?' Kelly paused and looked to her mother, but Aunt Leanne's mouth was full, so Kelly took a guess. 'Jadon, Therese...Audrey?'

'Aubrey,' my aunt corrected once she'd swallowed, 'Teresa and Jadon, from France, Romania and America, respectively. That's all we know.' She took a sip of her cooling coffee. 'I suppose they've got their reasons for withholding their youngest councillors' identities. It's not that important that we know what they look like, after all. It was good to see that they brought on another sorceress this time around – brave girl.'

'More juice, Aristea?' Uncle Patrick asked me. I looked up at him. Uncle Patrick shared no blood with me, but a lot of the time I liked him more than either his wife or daughter. He was easy-going and slow to anger, a perfect combination in a mentor, which he'd become for me when I hit adolescence. A former teacher, he'd home-schooled me through my secondary school years and also worked with my mother to correct my various emotional issues.

At that moment there was a sharp knock at the door. Angela looked straight up at me.

'Uh, yes, please,' I said, looking over my shoulder towards the front room as my sister got up to answer the door.

'Are you expecting someone?' Aunt Leanne asked, always nosy. I shrugged while Uncle Patrick poured me another juice. It had been almost a week since Qasim had appeared and told me about the White Elm's academy, and so far we'd heard nothing else.

Angela returned a few minutes later with a thick stack of envelopes.

'Post on a Sunday?' Uncle Patrick asked. Angela shook her head.

'Who was it?' I asked, wishing we'd mastered telepathy long ago so she could tell me everything without ever opening her mouth.

'It was Qasim,' she said, handing me most of the letters. I shoved my plate away and ripped the first envelope open. My aunt frowned.

'Qasim? There's a Qasim on the White Elm.' She opened her newsletter and began skimming through it.

'Yes, he was just here,' Angela said, sitting down again. 'He was here last week, too.'

Aunt Leanne said nothing for a few seconds, and though I knew she was dying to ask a thousand questions, she was also feeling slightly insulted that we hadn't thought to tell her this already. She was extremely interested in everything anyone in her family got up to, from what I was doing on the weekend to what Angela got up to at her dull but well-paying receptionist job at an optometry clinic in town. I understood the possessiveness – her baby brother had died suddenly and tragically, and she'd taken it upon herself to take his place in loving and protecting us, his daughters – but that didn't make it any less annoying at times.

'We were asked not to tell anyone he was here,' I told Aunt Leanne, guessing from Angela's openness that that rule had been lifted. My aunt visibly relaxed, and I felt it, too, as she decided that this made it okay.

'Of course, they're being very careful these days,' she agreed, buttering another pancake. 'Didn't you want to invite him in to join us for breakfast?'

'He had lots of other people to visit,' Angela answered, her blue-green eyes skimming the letter she'd opened. I finished reading my first letter and waved it at her excitedly.

'They want me at their school!' I said, because this handwritten letter made it feel more official. 'I can start on the first of March!' I looked around for the calendar and spotted it on the wall. I silently counted the days. 'That's less than two weeks away!'

'You'll be boarding there – you'll have to quit your job,' Angela commented. I felt a twinge of regret for that, because I liked my little job at the crystal and occult store. I liked being surrounded by the pretty things, the books and the positive energy of my eccentric customers. It would be a worthwhile trade-off, I reminded myself, when I learnt to scry.

'I'll tell them tomorrow,' I said, because I always worked Mondays.

'I'm very confused,' my aunt said pointedly. 'Which school is this that you're talking about?'

'The White Elm has started a school for gifted sorcerers, and they've offered Aristea a place,' Angela said before I could answer. 'It could lead to a position on the council one day.'

'Oh,' Aunt Leanne said, clearly too surprised to think of anything else to say. In the silence that followed, I reread my letter.

Dear Aristea Byrne,

Congratulations on your acceptance into the White Elm's Academy of Sorcery. We hope that you will enjoy the classes being prepared for you and your classmates. Along with this letter, you will also have received a letter addressed to your sister and guardian, a list of items you are required to bring, a list of classes you will be studying, a key to your dormitory at the Academy, and a contract you and your guardian will be expected to sign before your enrolment in the Academy is finalised.

Upon arriving at the Academy on March first, the date of term commencement, you will find your shared dormitory, which is home to three other students besides yourself. Each student will be supplied with a bed, a closet for clothing and a second cupboard for excess belongings.

Please advise the White Elm of your travel needs as soon as possible. We are happy to provide displacement services to families requiring this.

Please be advised that pets are not permitted at the Academy. We apologise for any inconvenience but this is for the comfort of all students.

Please do not bring electronic equipment, such as mobile phones, CD players, MP3 players, laptop computers, hair dryers or electric toothbrushes onto the Academy grounds. These will not function due to interference from the many layers of magic encasing the estate.

Please be advised that consumption of alcohol and the use of illicit drugs are strictly prohibited at the Academy. Smoking will be allowed in a designated outdoor area only. It is suggested that students begin planning for these lifestyle restrictions now.

Students will not need money during their stay at the Academy. All food and other necessities will be provided to students at no cost. Due to restrictions on movement in and out of the school grounds, it is unlikely that opportunities to spend money will arise.

Meals will be provided and prepared by Academy staff. Students with special dietary requirements should detail these in immediate return correspondence. Students from all cultural backgrounds are encouraged to supply

*the Academy with recipes for favoured dishes and will
have opportunities to share culinary knowledge and skills
with house staff through the preparation of meals.*

*Please keep your key with you at all times throughout
the school year. It is only with this key that you will enter
your room, your closet, your cupboard, many of your
classrooms, and other various places around the school.*

*Thank you for taking the time to read this letter, for
accepting this opportunity to take up your offered place at
the White Elm's Academy of Sorcery and for your support
in our creation of this facility. Without enough numbers,
the school would not have gone ahead.*

We anticipate your reply.

Sincerely yours,
Glen
Blessed be.

I was in! I was in a magic school!

'It's right here in Northern Ireland,' Angela said,
finishing her letter. 'It's inland a bit, but it's really
close to Coleraine City.'

'The school?'

'Yes. It's only about an hour's drive south from
here.'

When our parents and Aidan were alive, we
lived north of the city of Coleraine, near the ocean.
After the storm, Angela and I moved south to the
city, where freak storms rolling in from the sea
couldn't hurt us.

'Well…Well done, sweetie,' my uncle said
finally, forcing a smile at me. 'It's very impressive.

I'll be very proud one day to say I have a niece on the White Elm.'

I smiled back. Uncle Patrick was so nice.

'Do you think I'll get a place in the school?' Kelly asked her parents. I loved my cousin, my only cousin, but she totally lacked the maturity of Angela.

'We're too old,' Angela said, letting Aunt Leanne take the letter from her hands and begin to read. 'It's for younger people; they're looking for apprentices.'

I opened the other envelopes and tipped their contents onto the tabletop. My booklist was for a few exercise books, some pens, a set of runes and a wand if I had one. I did. I'd inherited my Greek grandmother Anthea's old one on my thirteenth birthday. I was also advised to bring as many clothes as I wanted/could fit into one small wardrobe and four drawers, and that there was a laundry service organised by the house staff.

A small silver key tinkled as it fell to the tabletop amongst the paperwork. This was the key to my future, I knew it. It was so pretty and delicate, very complex-looking.

'This will be interesting – you'll be sharing rooms,' Angela said, amused.

'What's wrong with that?'

'It'll be just your luck to be put in a room with the nastiest girl in the school. I know I always was on school camps.'

Unlike Angela and Aidan, I'd never been enrolled in high school, so I'd not really had the same experiences, like camps and schoolyard bitchiness.

I'd been home schooled until I'd completed all the requirements of compulsory schooling. This White Elm school was going to be so new for me.

'I'm sure there'll be cool people there,' I said simply. I read over my list of subjects. My eyes skimmed right through to scrying. I'd learn how to scry! Only a very small fraction of the magical community knew how to scry. In fact, apparently some of the White Elm couldn't even do it outside of the actual council! That made sense, I supposed, because not all sorcerers were specifically scriers. Once they entered the council, however, they were granted group powers, such as the ability to scry each other.

'We have to sign a contract,' Angela mentioned, and I handed the final sheet to her, still reading my subject list. She read through the contract carefully. 'It looks pretty straightforward. It basically says that we can't tell anyone else where this school is, because it's a secret.' She looked up at the rest of our family. 'That includes you guys. It also says that you have to adhere to the code of conduct on the back of your letter.'

I checked it. It wasn't a very strict one – I'd have no trouble behaving myself.

'I have to keep my key to myself, act lawfully, respect my teachers and fellow students, stick to the curfew and stay within the school grounds,' I said. 'How hard can that be?'

Angela took the code of conduct and gave it a once-over.

'I notice it doesn't have a no-boys-in-girls'-

rooms rule,' she said, surprised. 'Then again, you'll all be more or less adults…And rules wouldn't really prevent anything.'

'I'm not going to do anything,' I told her, teasing. I read through the contract. 'So, can I go?'

'Aristea, honey, you don't really want to do this,' Aunt Leanne said, finally speaking up after sitting in silence for several minutes. 'It's going to be very hard work and you might be away for a long time. It's not really your thing.'

I sat back in my chair, momentarily deflated. I wasn't much accustomed to hard work. I'd not been away from my sister since we'd lost everyone else. Did I really want to do this?

Yes.

A part of me wouldn't hear logical arguments against my newest life plan. A part of me was absolutely certain that this was *right*, beyond any reason.

'I want to go.'

'Sweetie, the White Elm are politicians but they're also peacekeepers. They began as a band of warriors. Sometimes their work is dangerous. It's not work for little girls.'

'She's not a little girl,' Angela defended me. Her tone gave strength to my determined side.

'I really want to go,' I told my aunt. I took the contract from Angela and grabbed a pen from the jar in the centre of the table. 'Something tells me that this will be really good for me.'

Maybe it was intuition, but I couldn't shake that feeling that March first would be the first day of my new life. Something important was happening, some huge, special change in my life. I signed the contract and pushed it away, waiting for the response my rashness would bring from my older family members.

'Darling, I really don't think this is right for you,' Aunt Leanne said again, glancing at her husband for support. He stayed silent, unwilling to get involved.

'You're always saying how important it is to show the world what side you're on,' I reminded my aunt. 'Consider this my ultimate demonstration of loyalty to the White Elm.'

'When I say that, I mean when you're grown up,' Aunt Leanne insisted. 'I mean you should sign up to receive the newsletter, not enrol in their training program. I don't think it's a place for girls.'

'You said that new councillor, the woman, she's brave,' I said, starting to feel annoyed. 'You said it's good for girls to be brought onto the council. Maybe one day I will.'

My aunt sighed.

'Honey, I'm sorry, but I'm not signing that,' she said finally. For a second, I felt my hopes sinking, but then my sister reached over and took the contract back.

'I am,' she said, keeping her hand extended, waiting for me to hand her the pen. I felt a huge smile grow across my face. Angela was my legal guardian. Aunt Leanne may be the head of the family, but legally, only Angela could make decisions like this for me. I pretty much had the best sister in the whole world.

'Angela, you can't be serious,' our aunt demanded, apparently shocked that her niece would overstep her authority like this. 'It could be dangerous-'

'Aristea knows that,' Angela said easily, signing her name. 'She's a big girl; she can take care of herself. I've got the address and I can go and get her whenever I want, and she can take herself off the enrolment register whenever she wants to. This is a huge opportunity for her, and since nobody present is her mother, nobody present gets to tell her what she can and can't do. If she wants to go,' she dropped the pen, 'she can go.'

In a flash of pale purple, the contract disappeared from the tabletop. We all jumped a little, startled by the unexpected disappearance.

'Well,' my aunt said, visibly deflated, and then said nothing more on the matter. The remainder of breakfast was quite awkward, my aunt acting as if none of the preceding conversation had occurred, and I was quite glad when they left.

'Whoa,' Angela muttered as she locked the door behind Kelly. 'I hate it when she does that.'

'Tries to control us?' I guessed, clearing the table.

'Acts like parenting you is a competition,' Angela corrected, coming back to help me. 'I'm sure she thinks I'm an epic failure.'

'Well, I think you're pretty awesome,' I said, carrying the plates to the sink. 'Maybe the very best sister anybody ever had, ever.'

Angela smiled and wrapped an arm around my shoulders in an affectionate sort of snuggle. She kissed my cheek.

'Don't you forget that when you're the rich, famous star of the White Elm.'

chapter three

On Sunday March first, at noon, the first students arrived. From the fourth-storey window of Renatus's huge study, Lord Gawain watched the gate with mild interest. Three White Elm members, Glen, Susannah and Emmanuelle, were standing guard, interviewing each person that came to the gate, checking their keys to ensure they still had them, probing their minds for signs of treachery, and separating them from their guardians. Lord Gawain watched as the gates were closed, locking out a pair of parents and locking in their teenage son now that they'd said their goodbyes. Emmanuelle led the boy to the manor, where, Lord Gawain knew, he would be left in the library with Aubrey and Anouk to await the coming of the other thirty-seven students who had signed the contract.

'Was the map clear enough?' Lady Miranda asked concernedly. She'd been pacing around the study for the past hour, unable to sit still. Most of the students had elected to be picked up by a White Elm councillor and displaced here, but some had decided to make their own way.

'I'm sure it will be fine,' Lord Gawain answered calmly. 'If anyone is still missing by this evening, we can have Qasim find out where they are, and send Elijah or Renatus to collect them and bring them here.'

Leaning relaxedly against his beautiful, antique, oak desk, Renatus nodded. Elijah was the White Elm's most reliable and most established Displacer – he could teleport an object, himself or anyone else with very little effort, and had been doing it since he was eleven. Renatus was also very good at displacing, although not as reliable and spot-on as Elijah because displacement was not his first skill. Of course, Renatus was very multitalented. The secretive position in the White Elm he'd inherited from Lisandro required him to be.

Another family had arrived on their own. This one had a pair of identical twin girls – Lord Gawain knew that these girls must be Kendra and Sophia Prescott. They had strong names (both meant wisdom) but were half mortal, on their father's side.

Magic was a complex and sometimes uncertain science. Hereditary power was more of a likely theory than a fact, because though the children of witches almost invariably showed the same promise as their parents, anomalies would appear and throw things into the air. Half-mortals, for example, tended to have powers at one extreme or the other – most were almost devoid of magical energy, while others, like these twins, were so powerful that they well and truly outshone even their witch parent.

Lady Miranda sighed as she stopped beside Lord Gawain and stared out the window with him.

'Twins,' she commented, as Glen touched one girl's temple to telepathically search her mind while Susannah questioned her sister. 'Qasim thought he'd made a mistake when he scried them – thought he was seeing a double image.'

Lord Gawain smiled at the thought, but Renatus remained expressionless, his violet eyes surveying the grounds of his inherited estate. Morrissey House was named for the family whose surname he had abandoned, and had been in the family for centuries, passed from eldest to eldest along with the family fortune, and, apparently, Renatus's hereditary power. As far as Lord Gawain was aware – and he'd met a lot of people in his sixty-seven years – no person alive had power like he did.

Four storeys below, Emmanuelle and Tian walked together from the manor towards the gates. The twin girls said their lengthy goodbyes to their mother and father, and then followed the French witch back to the building. Tian stayed with Glen and Susannah, awaiting the next group.

'Have the classes been decided yet?' Lady Miranda asked suddenly. Lord Gawain turned to Renatus for his response. Lord Gawain and Lady Miranda had many responsibilities, as well as mortal jobs and, in Lord Gawain's case, a family, so neither of them could be at the school on a permanent basis. Since it was his house, he was the highest authority in the council after the Lord and Lady, he didn't have a public face and was incredibly powerful, the White Elm had reluctantly but unanimously voted Renatus as the school's headmaster.

'Glen and Susannah will be organising the classes tonight,' Renatus answered, nodding past them at the distant gates. 'While they're poking about in the students' heads, they're also examining their strengths and weaknesses so that we can categorise them easier.'

Lord Gawain nodded and turned back to the window, watching as two families arrived at the same time.

'Would either of you like something to drink?' Renatus asked, surprising both of his guests. He wasn't usually the type to play host.

'Seeing as we have time,' Lord Gawain agreed, looking to Lady Miranda. She hesitated, and then nodded quickly.

'Tea?'

The two White Elm leaders nodded. Perhaps Lady Miranda expected Renatus to leave to make the drinks, but instead he blinked and turned back to the window. An Asian father and daughter had just displaced together outside the gate.

'This one will be Elijah's favourite student,' Lord Gawain commented.

'Her father probably displaced her,' Lady Miranda answered, but Renatus seemed interested.

'Do you suppose that any of the students would be able to displace or scry yet?' he asked.

'It's possible,' Lord Gawain offered. He smiled. 'I know Qasim was hoping to find an apprentice from this cohort, but only one is a natural-born scrier.'

Renatus half-smiled back, but it was a polite smile, without warmth or genuineness, used to cover his keen interest.

'I doubt Qasim was pleased,' he said. 'What's the student's name?'

'Aristea,' Lord Gawain answered, pretending not to notice Renatus's unusual curiosity. How ironic that he should ask about *her*, of all the fifty youths they'd investigated. 'Most of her family was killed in a storm, much like the one that struck here seven years ago. Apparently it was very sudden.'

Renatus's smile vanished.

'How did the girl survive?'

'You'll have to ask her when she arrives.'

'Don't, Renatus,' Lady Miranda said. 'Don't bring that up for her.'

The young sorcerer didn't answer. His fine features smoothed into an expressionless, impassive visage. It was clear that he wouldn't say anything else on the topic. It was rare for him to speak as much as he had today. He lazily flicked his fingers through the air.

The door opened, and Lord Gawain and Lady Miranda turned. Renatus didn't move. Still staring at the distant gate, he muttered, 'Your tea.'

A woman of about fifty awkwardly bustled into the study, carrying an elegant silver tray, upon which was a complete silver tea set.

'Good afternoon,' Lord Gawain said to her. Renatus's manor was also home to a staff of servants, and this one, he recognised as Fionnuala. The housekeeper smiled quickly, laid the tray on the oak desk, and hurried out. The woman had once disliked Lord Gawain, maintaining a grudge for decisions he'd made to protect Renatus, but in recent years she'd come to forgive him, he suspected, for his part in securing a place on the White Elm for her beloved master. Lady Miranda stared after her, mildly surprised.

'Fionnuala's family has worked for mine for eight generations,' Renatus explained before she could comment. 'I have a staff of fifteen.'

Lady Miranda nodded and fell silent while Lord Gawain poured the tea. Like many other councillors on the White Elm, she carried a barely-disguised fear and mistrust of Renatus. It was not baseless, but it was not substantiated by any real proof, either. The Morrissey family, from which Renatus came, had been known to the White Elm for generations as trouble. Though no charges had ever been made, rumours had always suggested that the family possessed all manner of dark objects, practised ancient branches of forbidden magic and were connected to various shady people and dealings. Dozens of inquiries and searches had turned up zero evidence, so the family's reputation was built entirely on hearsay and intuition, but that didn't stop people from believing.

Renatus, for his part, had never seemed bothered by the negative attention. Doubtless he was well-accustomed to it, although the reactions of others always disappointed Lord Gawain. Where was the necessity for quick, rash judgements? Even the council's newest recruits, who were very close in age to Renatus, avoided him.

Aubrey, Teresa and Jadon had been brought on in the unstable weeks following Lisandro's disappearance with Jackson and Peter. It had been a difficult process. Possibly because of the situation surrounding Lisandro, most of the young people approached by the White Elm had refused to apply for the positions, leaving only a very small pool of applicants. Teresa, a talented healer and illusionist, and Jadon, a quick-thinking twenty-year-old with an unexpectedly wide knowledge of spell casting, had been obvious choices. The good name of Aubrey's family line and his gifts of Crafting (bending magic – a skill the White Elm had lost with Crafters Lisandro and Jackson) had secured his position. They were all brilliant, in their own ways, but all young, all idealistic. Jadon was overeager and reckless, but willing to act when it was necessary. Teresa was patient and sweet, but lacked the initiative to fight, as the council all knew they might soon be forced to do. Aubrey was compassionate and good but remained unable to comprehend the difference between what was good for the people and what was good for the person.

In short, none of them quite lived up to the man whose betrayal had led to their employment.

Still leaning against his desk, Renatus straightened abruptly, his gaze focussed on the gate.

'What is it?' Lady Miranda asked, accepting her tea from Lord Gawain. Renatus was silent and still for a long moment, and Lord Gawain followed his gaze. A car had pulled up outside the gates and a dark-haired girl climbed out, closing her door.

'Nothing,' was all Renatus said, and he sat down at his desk and pulled a stack of paperwork towards himself. Clearly the conversation was over.

chapter four

I got out of Angela's car, apprehensive. She unloaded my bags from the back seat as I walked towards the Academy. Beyond the intricate, wrought iron gates stood a massive, stone structure, less a house than a mansion. It had at least four storeys, and looked to be the sort of place that had 'wings', like a hospital. A cobblestone path led from the distant, grand front doors directly to the gates, built slightly winding to complement the gently sloping, emerald-green hill the building was set upon.

Directly behind the gate stood two men, one Asian and one Caucasian, and a woman dressed in royal purple robes. I didn't recognise any of them, although if I'd read the newsletter back when they included photos, I might have. I forced a smile. They all smiled back genuinely. More confident, I walked to the gate.

'Hi,' I said uselessly.

'Hello, Aristea,' the Caucasian man said. I didn't

ask how he knew my name. His accent was Welsh, and his hair was blonde. 'I'm Glen. This is Susannah and Tian.'

'Your key will open the gate,' Susannah said. For a moment I stood silently, and then remembered my key, hanging on a silver chain around my neck. I unclasped the chain at the back and looked for the lock. My little key fitted perfectly. The lock clinked when I turned the key, and Glen pushed open the gates.

'Good afternoon, Aristea. Before you go up to the school, we need to do a few tests, if you don't mind,' Susannah said. She was in her forties, with wavy brown hair and a kind, round face. I could tell from the way she talked that she was from somewhere in America. She sounded like someone out of a movie.

Securing the chain around my neck again, I glanced back at Angela. She smiled at me, showing no signs of unease, so I nodded at the White Elm representatives.

Glen, smiling, touched my temple and said, 'Just relax, don't worry about me. Susannah will ask you a few questions.'

'Okay,' I said nervously, turning to the American.

'So, Aristea; you have been aware of magic your whole life. Have you ever displaced before?' Susannah asked pleasantly. I began to answer when I felt Glen's satiny presence slip into my mind. He was probing my thoughts. I ignored him.

'No,' I told Susannah.

'Can you scry?'

'No.'

'Have you ever healed another person's injury?'

'No.' I was starting to feel a bit useless.

'That's okay. You'll learn it all here. Now, I want you to think back through your childhood. People you've known, people you've loved, people you met in passing…Your parents, your siblings, your friends, your parents' friends…'

Faces from my memory popped to the forefront of my mind, and Glen scrolled through them. I did my best not to fight him. I knew which face he was looking for, and I'd never seen it, so I needed to give him a chance to realise that. I focused on Susannah's words.

'Neighbours, cousins, maybe someone you met on holidays?'

More faces, none of consequence, I was sure. I'd led a remarkably dull life for an orphaned witch.

'Your siblings' school friends…'

Aidan and Angela, only a year apart, had shared many friends, while I, the much younger baby sister, had followed them around like a little puppy. They and their friends had always put up with me and let me play, and Aidan had always stuck up for me when a friend had complained about my poor catching, my misunderstanding of the rules or my inability to keep up with the big kids. Those were much better times.

'Can you perform rudimentary level spells?' Susannah asked. I frowned. Couldn't Glen see all this information anyway, or was he just looking for links with White Elm enemies?

'Yes.'

'What is the most advanced level of spell casting you have reached?' Glen pressed. I turned to him as I thought this over. Glen was about medium height, with broad shoulders and light blonde hair. He was wearing robes of royal purple, like Susannah and the Chinese witch.

'Um, I can do wards,' I offered, unsure how else to answer. I didn't know what level that was!

'Reliably or only in controlled conditions?'

'She saved my life with her first ward,' Angela answered for me, shutting the car door now that my stuff was unloaded. 'Her wards are really strong.'

'I was in a panic – I didn't think about it,' I disagreed. 'I've never done anything like that again.'

Susannah smiled, and Glen withdrew from me. I felt his presence slide away. I fought the impulse to catch him.

'Thank you for your patience, Aristea,' he said. He indicated the Chinese man. 'This is Tian. He will show you up to the Academy once you have said your goodbyes to your sister.'

I turned to Angela, and her sad smile made me want to cry. She was my only immediate family and I was leaving her alone in our flat.

'Will you be lonely?' I asked, hoping I didn't break down.

'Kelly wants to come and stay,' Angela answered. 'Not sure how long I'll be able to handle that, but we'll see.'

Feeling tears stinging my eyes, I hugged her

tightly.

'Okay. She can have my room. And Angela – I'll miss you.'

'I'll miss you too. But make sure you write as often as you can. Okay?'

I nodded quickly. Keeping one arm around me, she reached through the car window and withdrew a folded woollen blanket.

'I think you'll need this more than I will,' she said, pressing it into my hands. I accepted it, confused, but as soon as I had I could feel that it was too solid and heavy to be just a blanket. I unwrapped a few layers and discovered the tattered old cover of our grandfather's book.

My mouth fell open. As a child I'd tried several times to sneak this beautiful old thing out of the bookcase to look at, and each time my mother had taken it from me and said it was too important to play with. It was her daddy's, she'd explained, and it was the only thing he'd left for her. The blanket obscured most of the cover but I knew the title: *Magic and Destiny*, by Cassán Ó Grádaigh.

'Ange-' I began to argue; this was a family heirloom, one of so few things we had of our ancestors, but she pressed it more firmly into my hands and spoke over me.

'Aristea, it's yours. I have everything else at home. Besides, I've read it. It's about time you did.'

I hugged her again and wished this moment would last forever. Angela smiled as she pulled away from me. She turned and got back into the car. Glen shut the gates behind her. The clang of iron on iron struck me as very final and my chest tightened.

'Angela!' I said suddenly, speaking through the iron bars of the gate. I felt very alone and stupid now – why had I been so eager to come here and be separated from the only person I had left in the world? She smiled at me through the open window of her car.

'I love you too, Aristea,' she said, saving me the trouble. Looking sad, she turned the car on and drove away quickly.

'Come on, sweetie,' Susannah said kindly. I turned to them numbly, feeling small and ridiculous. What was I doing here? Glen extracted a polished platinum wand from his robe pocket and tapped the pile of my belongings. They disappeared. Displaced, undoubtedly.

'Would you like those sent to your room, too?' he asked, nodding at the book and blanket in my arms. I held them out wordlessly and then they were gone. Like Angela.

Tian led me along the cobblestone path towards the magnificent building that was the school. His elegant royal purple robes brushed the stone beneath his feet. I looked down at my own outfit. Jeans that had been washed yesterday instead of worn and a fleecy olive green sweater. I looked *presentable*, which differed from usual by a great deal.

'My sister told me you have to be twenty before you can join White Elm, so how come you want teenagers?' I asked Tian. The Chinese man smiled.

'Some of the senior members of the council are considering the option of taking on an apprentice from this cohort, if a suitable person should be present,' he said, taking care with his English. 'If they do, it is expected that they will adhere to the age-old traditions of the White Elm council, which dictate the ages of the master and apprentice, the genders and the levels of skill. Those people who are already twenty years of age are ineligible for an apprenticeship according to the old guidelines.'

'If we become somebody's apprentice, are we White Elm? Technically?'

'Not exactly,' Tian answered. 'A sorcerer's apprentice is bonded to him, or her, and so in the case of the White Elm, an apprentice is usually treated as an extension of the council – not as a councillor, but as an honorary member, with a distant telepathic link to the council's whole and the right to observe council meets.' He smiled and tried not to laugh. 'In the past, White Elm apprentices have been referred to as *White Leaves*.'

He seemed to think the nickname was quite funny, so I chose not to voice my own opinion – I thought it was a good name. Better than *White Twig* or *White Branch*, anyway.

We had walked the entire length of the winding stone path and now stood before the manor. It was even more beautiful up close. The windows were full-length and the glass was panelled, with clear glass in the middle and intricate patterns of stained glass framing it. I looked up at the monstrous structure and saw a huge arched window in the centre of the fourth storey. I wondered what was in that room.

'That's the main study,' Tian said as though I'd asked a question. 'It will now be the office for the Academy's headmaster.'

'Whose house is this?' I asked as he stepped across the threshold and into a high-ceilinged entrance hall. I followed, gazing up at the massive open doors. They opened outward, letting sunlight spill onto beautiful medieval-style papered walls. Opposite me was the beginning of a wide sweeping staircase, which I assumed took you all the way up through the houses' levels. Tapestries and huge paintings hung everywhere, darkening the room. Thin, tall doors took the rare, small spaces between wall hangings. One was open. Tian stopped in front of it.

'It belongs to a high-up member of White Elm,' he offered, although seemed unwilling to share much information on the person. 'It's been in his family for untold generations. It's covered in wards and other protective spells. It's a very safe place to be.'

'But who is he?' I pressed keenly. 'Is it Lord Gawain?' I'd heard that he lived here in Ireland.

'No. This house belongs to a White Elm named Renatus.'

I frowned, stopping beside Tian. I hadn't heard much of Renatus. He'd only entered the council within the past two years. Not many people talked about him. Not many people *wanted* to talk about him, perhaps. The only way I knew about his existence was that Aunt Leanne had mentioned one morning that the White Elm had enlisted a young sorcerer named Renatus – and she thought it was a strange choice. I hadn't cared enough then to ask further questions. Tian didn't seem willing to answer them anyway.

'This is the library. This is a resource that will be open to you throughout the term, but you must treat it with respect. It is also the official meeting place in times of emergency. Today it will be where you will wait until all students have arrived. Enjoy your term.'

With a final smile, Tian turned and walked back out of the house. Feeling apprehensive, I entered the library through its odd, thin door.

As I walked down the few steps into the sunken library, I knew I would be spending a lot of time here if I could. The library was high-ceilinged, old-fashioned and housed dozens of ridiculously tall, thin bookcases, all packed with books of all kinds, sizes, colours and ages. It was twenty times better than the little occult bookstore I'd been working at. I couldn't wait to get a good look at the titles on the spines of those thousands of books.

But as I reached the floor and was itching to run to the bookshelves, I realised that I was not alone. The library was quiet, but it was then that I noticed at least twenty other presences. The library was practically crackling with magical energy. These were some of the most potentially powerful teenage witches in the world. Some were browsing shelves. A few were standing around talking quietly. Most were sitting, either in the comfy-looking chairs against the walls, or in one of the wooden chairs that faced a podium. The wooden chairs didn't look like permanent fixtures to the library – they were probably there just for today's orientation.

Most of the kids were dressed like mortals – jeans, skirts, t-shirts, etc – but two people, definitely not teenagers, were not. Like the other White Elm members I'd encountered today already, the young chestnut-haired man and the rake-thin woman sitting side-by-side in chairs on the podium were dressed in long robes of royal purple. They smiled at me when they noticed me. All the White Elm people, besides Qasim, seemed nice, open and warm people. I wondered how far up in rank these two were. They were obviously keeping an eye on the students waiting here in the library.

Would I be able to befriend any of these other teenagers? Carefully, so as not to touch their presences with mine, I brushed my senses across the entire room. I didn't feel any hostile presences, but then again, I wasn't getting close enough to notice anything but general stuff. They were all strong sorcerers who were generally nice people and were quite nervous.

With a small sigh, I began browsing the nearest bookshelf. I was in the herbs and plants section. Herbs and plants were fine, but I wasn't too interested in that category. I couldn't wait to learn more spells like my wards. I wanted to learn scrying.

Scrying. Where would books on scrying be? I wandered around, not forgetting about the other nervous students. Were they eager to learn to scry, too? Or were they all experts at it already?

It was about ten quiet minutes later that I found

the scrying section. Granted, I hadn't been looking too hard, slowly meandering through the shelves, stopping to examine every book with an interesting title or attractive cover, but I was glad to have found it. This Renatus guy had a good collection of scrying reference books.

I started pulling books out, examining them and judging them all by their covers, before I realised that I wasn't the only person in this row. I was in the advanced magic section, and an Asian girl of my own age was slowly making her way towards me, gazing at the spines of the books. She hadn't noticed me yet. Her shiny jet-black hair was cut on a funky diagonal, from her chin on one side to her opposite shoulder, and it looked like she was trying to grow her fringe out. Her skin was porcelain white. She was very thin, very pretty in a doll-like, dainty way, a bit shorter than me, and was all but flat-chested.

She noticed my attention and looked up. Somehow, I knew that she was Japanese, which was odd because my knowledge of Asia was limited to what I'd seen on TV and I had never spoken to a Japanese person in my entire life. I forced a smile. Did she speak English?

'Hi,' I said awkwardly, pushing a scrying book back into its slot on the shelf.

'Hi,' she responded.

'I'm Aristea,' I said because I had nothing better to say, and also because I had to say something now that I'd initiated a conversation. 'Aristea Byrne.'

'My name is Hiroko Sasaki,' the Japanese teenager answered, smiling. It didn't sound like

English was her first language. She shifted her books into her other arm and offered me her hand. Smiling back and relaxing, I shook her hand. 'How long have you been here?'

'Fifteen minutes,' I said. 'How about you?'

'One hour, I think. No one else here seems willing to talk to me, so I want to read about displacing. Do you like displacement?'

'Aye, it would be pretty cool,' I agreed automatically, earning myself an awkward pause.

'My father and I searched for Irish colloquialisms online so I could learn,' she said finally. 'Aye means yes.'

I caught the twinkle in her dark eyes. She was amused. I cracked a wider smile, too. I immediately liked this girl.

'Do you want some help finding the displacing books?' I asked, pushing my handful of scrying books back onto the shelf. Displacing was interesting, too.

Hiroko looked pleased.

'Yes, please,' she said. 'If you don't mind.'

I shook my head and walked down the row with her, looking for books with 'Displacing' printed on the spine.

'My main objective of coming here this year is to learn to scry,' I told Hiroko. 'I always wanted to learn how to do it. What about you?'

'I'd like to learn,' Hiroko agreed, 'but first I want to perfect my displacing. My father has been teaching me for some past years.'

'You can displace already?' I asked, impressed.

She nodded, her pale cheeks turning to a delicate shade of pink.

'Not reliable. I cannot displace myself very far. My father helped me to get here. But I can displace objects almost perfectly now, and I am studying very hard to displace myself properly. I want to study the theory more and get better with this.'

For half an hour, we chatted, getting to know each other as we searched the shelves for displacement reference books. Hiroko's English was very good, although it was quite obvious that it was a language that she had learnt through study rather than through necessity. Finally we found the books we'd been searching for. The selection was quite small it turned out, and was on the very bottom shelf, practically on the floor. We sat opposite each other on the carpet, sorting through the twelve displacing books and talking.

Hiroko *was* from Japan – she was from Sapporo, Hokkaido Island. She was also seventeen, but had no siblings. She lived with her father in a flat in the city. Surprised by our similarities despite our cultures, I told her that I also lived in a flat in the city with one guardian.

I must have been there for going on three hours (Hiroko must have been there for almost four) when I heard someone close the tall, thin door through which everyone had entered. Hiroko heard it too, and we both peered apprehensively through the shelves towards the door, which was now on the far side of the library. We'd managed to find two comfortable chairs right at the back of the room.

Eight purple-robed figures had just entered. The other kids in the library were putting their books away and respectfully hurrying over to the chairs set out before the podium. With a quick glance at one another, Hiroko and I got up and walked as fast as we could towards the crowd, ensuring that we didn't run. You can't run in a library.

Of the thirteen chairs set up on the little platform, ten of them were now occupied. I personally recognised some of the occupants – Tian, Susannah, Glen, and Qasim (the Scrier!) – but the other six sitting down were unfamiliar, nameless. The eleventh man was old, bearded and radiant with compassion and warmth. He was standing at the front of the podium, waiting. I'd never seen him before but I knew immediately who he was: Lord Gawain, widely regarded as the greatest sorcerer of the time, head of White Elm and the leader of the magical world. He was nearing seventy, I saw, and was tall and broad. His purple robes sported a white sash. His face was lined but friendly and he had a certain air, an aura of greatness that could not fail to impress his audience.

Hiroko and I found seats next to each other. She was in an aisle seat, with no one to her right. To my left was a boy who looked to be fifteen or less, except of course he must be at least sixteen to even be here.

Once everyone was silently seated, Lord Gawain began to speak.

'Good afternoon, my friends,' he said. His voice was quite soft, and, like Glen, he had a Welsh accent, but it carried. I was surprised – I had never known that Lord Gawain was Welsh. Everyone said that he lived here in Northern Ireland, so I'd assumed he was a local. 'Welcome to the White Elm Academy. I would firstly like to thank you all for your generosity in giving your time to come here this year. I assure you all it will not be a waste of time – all of the White Elm have skills we are willing to share with you and pass on to you. For those of you who are not aware, my name is Lord Gawain, head of White Elm.'

Like anybody here was dumb enough not to know that, though, I thought a second too early, because the boy beside me flinched in utter shock. I resisted the urge to roll my eyes. Who else would the man be?

'Seated behind me are ten of my White Elm colleagues,' Lord Gawain continued. He did not look back at them but listed their names from left to right as though he were looking at them. Could he sense them so distinctly that he knew exactly where they all were? 'Qasim, Glen, Susannah, Elijah, Anouk, Tian, Emmanuelle, Aubrey, Teresa and Jadon. Some have been working here at the Academy all day to ensure that your first day runs as smoothly as possible; others have been transporting many of you from your home countries so that you may be with us today.'

I scanned the row left to right, trying to memorise the names of the White Elm. The first three I recognised; Elijah was next, a fragile-looking man with unruly brown hair. He looked like he might be blown away in a strong wind, never to be seen again. The fifth was the rake-thin woman who had been in the library when I arrived, and the sixth was Tian.

The next woman was exceedingly beautiful and I guessed (as I had with Hiroko) that she was European. Her hair was long, wavy and blonde – Emmanuelle. Next was Aubrey, who had been here with Anouk when I'd arrived. Teresa was petite and of evident eastern European descent, and Jadon was slightly gangly with close-cropped hair.

They were sitting, I noticed, in such an order that the older councillors were seated at one end and younger ones at the other. I didn't know any of their exact ages, but I assumed that they must have seated themselves according to rank, which must have been organised by age.

Still, the first three seats were vacant. One must be Lord Gawain's. Who else was missing?

'Tomorrow morning, after breakfast, a list will be posted here in the library to inform you all of which White Elm members will be teaching which subjects. Your classes are being decided tonight, and the class lists will be posted at the same time. Each class is being arranged with age and abilities in mind.'

I wondered if Hiroko would be in my classes. She was my age, but she seemed quite more advanced than me.

'You will have eleven subjects in all, but no real timetables have been created – our schedules are much too busy and prone to change for us to even attempt to organise a workable, structured timetable for you all to follow. Your week's subjects will be posted by Monday morning each week in this library. Because of this flexible timetabling, you may find sometimes that two classes are scheduled for the same time. In this instance, we remind you that you are all young adults: you can elect which class to attend, according to your own preferences or areas of need.'

I guessed that Lord Gawain was one of the White Elm councillors not teaching. After all, he was much too busy for something as unimportant as teaching schoolchildren. He ran a nation, more or less.

'Your meals will be served in the dining hall, which is through the door opposite the library,' Lord Gawain was saying now. 'Your dormitories are on the second level of the school. Some house three students, others four. Your key will fit only one. Each key is unique and different. They all fitted the simple gate lock, and will all unlock the front doors of this school, but only students living inside a dormitory will be able to gain access with his or her own key. Your closets are accessible only with your own key. Your roommates' keys will not fit the locks on your cupboards and closets.'

I, like most of the other students around me, got my key out and gazed at it.

'Now I would like to introduce you all to a pair of extraordinary people,' Lord Gawain said suddenly, causing us all to pocket or hide away our keys quickly. The impressive, white-haired man waved his hand towards the library door. Every student turned to stare at it. It was closed.

But then it opened, and, as promised, two people stepped inside the library. The first was a shortish woman of almost sixty. Her black hair was streaked with silver and the very dark skin on her kindly face was starting to wrinkle. Her royal purple robes also bore a white sash, like Lord Gawain. I'd seen photos of this woman before, in mortal newspapers – she was Lady Miranda, second-longest serving current White Elm and co-leader to Lord Gawain. She was a most gifted Healer – once she had succeeded in bringing someone back to life almost a minute after his heart had stopped, using her talent. She worked in London as a surgeon. The mortals there thought she was just good at her job. They had no idea who she really was, how great she was to us.

The man following her was a stranger to me, but he drew my attention (and, I realised, the attention of every other person in the library) immediately. His robes were emerald green, a huge contrast to the purple of the White Elm. His complexion was pale and smooth, but not unhealthily white. His hair was silky and jet-black, longish but not untidy. He wasn't old – in his early twenties, I guessed, about the same age as Angela. He was tall and lean, but not lanky. In fact, he looked very comfortable in his body. He was graceful and had a demandingly strong air.

The energy surrounding him was incredible. He was the most powerful sorcerer in the room, easily, and more powerful than anyone I'd ever before encountered or probably ever would again.

This *had* to be Renatus, the owner of the house. The tall, thin door through which he passed seemed built for his frame. After closing the door, the young man turned back to the silent crowd, ignoring us all, and I heard a few girls gasp as he neared the podium.

He was *beautiful*. Staggeringly beautiful. His features were perfect and carefully formed, like artwork. His dark eyebrows were not too heavy – they were of a perfect thickness, and made him more striking, and hung perfectly over a pair of mesmerising violet eyes...

I blinked as Hiroko nudged me. Trying to hide her smile behind one hand, she pointed discreetly towards a girl a few rows in front of us. She had a high, strawberry blonde ponytail, cute features including an upturned nose, and a couple of freckles. Her bright eyes were fixed upon the man in emerald green and her pretty face sported an awestruck, predatory look. I'd never seen anyone look so intense. I smiled at Hiroko, hoping we didn't giggle. I was glad she'd nudged me – I might have looked just as creepy as that strawberry blonde girl.

'Lady Miranda, my co-leader,' Lord Gawain continued, although it seemed that many minutes had passed, 'and Renatus, your headmaster.'

While no one in the audience spoke as Lady Miranda and Renatus took their seats, I felt the surprise and the restlessness of the students. They all desperately wanted to murmur amongst themselves, but knew it would be disrespectful to Lord Gawain. I understood their surprise. Headmaster! Renatus was one of the youngest White Elm councillors present. He was about the same age as my sister, and I knew Angela would not be able to handle the responsibility of that post.

Well, she probably could, if it were her only responsibility. I doubted whether she would have time to run a school *and* clean up after me.

I realised that Lord Gawain was talking again, but I, like everyone else, wasn't really listening. Something or another about respecting each other and property. We were all busy staring at Renatus, who completely ignored us. He was *impossible* to ignore. He listened to Lord Gawain with mild interest, although wore no expression.

Then it was his turn to speak, and we held our breaths. Lord Gawain sat down beside Lady Miranda amongst polite applause, and Renatus stood. The clapping stopped abruptly. He seemed not to notice, and walked to the front of the platform.

'This school is my house,' he said simply, his voice low, silky and somehow intriguing. He actually sounded almost bored. The strawberry blonde girl looked ready to faint. 'I trust you will treat it with respect during your time here. Smoking will not be tolerated inside. You will not litter. You will find that electronic equipment will not function in or around this house. Your evening meal is being served now in the dining hall. Afterwards you will be informed of your dormitories. A White Elm member will be assigned as your dormitory supervisor. This is the person to whom you will forward all of your requirements, complaints and questions. He or she will give you a tour of the Academy building, ending at your room. Your keys will open your door. Your belongings are already inside your rooms. Please enjoy your studies throughout the term.'

It was such a short speech that when he stepped off the stage and walked out of the room, we students simply remained where we were, silent and unsure. The White Elm stood and filed off the podium, so, with a nervous glance at Hiroko, she and I stood. The others quickly followed our example, and we all left the library.

This was going to be an interesting year.

chapter five

Our buffet meal was delicious – roast chickens with a hundred golden potatoes to go around, and plenty of steamed vegetables for those who didn't eat meat. I wasn't one of those people. I loved meat, but I dumped a pile of steamed beans onto my plate as I passed the buffet table, thinking of Angela's health-thing.

The hall itself was long, with the same height ceiling as the entrance hall, high enough to give a feeling of spaciousness without the room having to be particularly sizeable. There was one huge oak table that looked made for the place, and I wondered as I walked in the main doors how anyone had managed to get it in here. It was wider than the door frame, and seemingly all one piece. Was it built inside this room? Straight-backed timber chairs were tucked neatly along both sides. Another, smaller table, much newer and a different colour of wood, obviously added later, was situated to the side with thirteen chairs. It seemed clear that this was where the White Elm would sit, while the big old table was for us.

Hiroko and I sat together at the long, elegant, oak table, chatting over our meals. Opposite us was a pair of identical twin girls. They had chest-length brown hair, sweet faces and crystal green eyes. They looked about my age. I wondered if they'd be in any of my classes.

One of them caught my eye and smiled.

'I'm Kendra Prescott,' she said. Her sister had a mouthful of roast potato, so she added, 'This is Sophia.'

'Aristea,' I answered, glad to meet more people.

'I'm Hiroko,' my friend added. 'Where are you from?'

'Canada,' Kendra replied. 'Vancouver. That's where our dad lived when Mom met him. She's a witch from the States – he's a mortal.'

'Where do you live?' Sophia asked. She and her sister sounded almost identical, but I noticed very slight differences in their voices. Cautiously, I allowed my sixth sense to sweep against their presences. As could be expected, there were more differences in their personalities than in their shared appearance.

'Sapporo, in Japan,' Hiroko said. 'With my father.'

The twins turned to me expectantly.

'I live about an hour north from here with my older sister,' I said. 'We used to live by the sea but now we live in the city.'

The four of us talked for the entirety of the meal. I finished my dinner, arranged my cutlery in the centre of my scraped-clean plate and leaned back. Just as I started to agree with Hiroko's last statement, someone appeared at my elbow to take my dishes. I glanced at the maid in surprise. Where had she come from? She hurried away before I could say anything.

When everyone was done, Lady Miranda stepped forward, and the cheery chatter died away. She had a list in her hand.

'Your dormitories have been organised according to age,' Lady Miranda explained. 'When your name is called, will you please come and stand at the front beside me, where your group will be assigned a supervisor, who will then begin your tour of the school.'

Hiroko and I glanced at each other, and then met eyes with the twins across from us. Where would we all be put?

'Dormitory one: Noah, Michael, Miguel and Brennan,' the famous Healer read from her list. Slowly, four boys stood and made their way towards her. One of them I recognised as the boy who had been sitting beside me in the library. He looked too young to be here. The other three, I noticed, weren't much older. They must be the four youngest boys in the school. 'Your White Elm supervisor is Jadon. Please follow him now for your tour. Enjoy your term.'

The last White Elm member, the young man with short brown hair, smiled at the boys and led them from the room.

'Dormitory two: Leilani, Jacinta, Willow and Iseult. Your supervisor is Teresa. Enjoy your term, girls.'

The four girls who followed the young sorceress Teresa didn't look as terribly young as the boys before them had, somehow. Perhaps they were more confident, not having to go first.

'Dormitory three: Selby, Daniel, Heath and Sylvester. Your supervisor is Tian. Enjoy the term.'

I watched the boys file out of the room and then directed my gaze along the table. Twelve of the thirty-seven students were gone now. Was I next?

'Dormitory four,' Lady Miranda said, stealing back our attention, 'Xanthe, Sterling, Aristea and Hiroko.'

I stood slowly, stunned by my good fortune. How lucky to meet someone lovely and then be placed in a dormitory with her! I was disappointed not to be with the Canadian twins. It would have been cool to be put with them, but surely our other roommates would be just as great. I smiled goodbye to Kendra and Sophia and walked with Hiroko to the front of the room. As we passed, most of the White Elm smiled encouragingly at us – they were such nice people. Standing beside Lord Gawain was Renatus. He wasn't smiling, but he was watching me. *Me.* He finally wore the slightest trace of an expression – he looked thoughtful, intrigued. His irresistible violet eyes followed me. I dragged my gaze away.

'Your supervisor is Emmanuelle,' Lady Miranda said when Hiroko and I reached her. The beautiful blonde French sorceress stepped out of the line and smilingly led us from the room. Hiroko and I followed her along with the other two girls. One of them tugged on my arm excitedly, and I recognised her as the strawberry blonde girl who had been practically drooling over Renatus in the library.

'I am *so* jealous!' she whispered as we left the dining hall. 'He was watching you – he is *so, so* gorgeous...'

In the entrance hall, Emmanuelle stopped us.

'From the entrance 'all, you can access almost every other part of the school,' she explained, her French accent melodious and lilting. Her "th" became a z sound; she missed out the h in hall.

'The library, the dining 'all and the ballroom, where you as students will be able to relax between classes.' She indicated the doors to which she referred, then pointed to another one and said, 'Through this door is the old servants' wing, but we don't call them that now. The 'ouse staff still occupy this section. Students are not permitted. The staff run a laundry service – 'ave your clothes in the 'amper by nine in the morning to 'ave it washed that day – and they're very lovely, so if you need anything else, tell them.' She gestured to the huge staircase at the end of entrance hall. 'This leads to the second floor, which is devoted to bedrooms. Through this door,' she nodded at the lonely door against the back wall, directly opposite the front doors, 'is the kitchen, which is off-limits to students except in special circumstances, such as bringing a message or serving detention.'

'Hi, I'm Sterling,' the strawberry blonde girl said to me as we followed Emmanuelle's shimmery, wavy blonde hair up the stairs.

'I'm Aristea,' I said, cheering up. I was still disappointed that I wasn't with Kendra and Sophia.

'I can't believe how hot our principal is!' Sterling said. She was American. Hiroko, the other girl and I laughed. Even Emmanuelle glanced back in amusement. 'Well, he is!' Sterling added defensively. 'I expected our principal to be old and ridiculous – not a model!'

'Renatus is not a model,' Emmanuelle said, smiling. 'I think 'e would be appalled at the notion of posing for profit.'

'Doesn't he realise how much money he could make through modelling, though?' Sterling asked, shocked. 'Doesn't he know how gorgeous he is?'

Emmanuelle thought for a moment as she waited at the top of the steps.

'I think that if a person is truly beautiful, they must not know it,' she said slowly. 'An attractive man who believes 'e is attractive is less charming than a man who is attractive but doesn't know it. Don't you think?'

All that did was confuse me – it didn't really answer Sterling's question at all, but the American girl seemed incredibly moved by this advice. She nodded eagerly.

'Did you see the colour of his eyes?' Sterling sighed. She turned to the fourth girl. 'Xanthe, is there something wrong with me?'

Xanthe, I realised then, was Greek. Her

colouring was considerably darker than mine, and she was taller than the rest of us. I started to feel at home here at the White Elm Academy – I had at least two nice roommates, two nice acquaintances outside of our dorm, and my final roommate was Greek – we were sure to have heaps in common.

I had always been fascinated by my Greek heritage. My grandfather Cassán had met his wife Anthea when he had travelled to Greece as a young man. He had married her and brought her back to Ireland, where unfortunately she had lived a sheltered and antisocial life, considered by many in their town as an outsider. Luckily, their daughter (Elysia, my mother) had been considerably fairer than her foreign parent and had been better accepted. Perhaps Xanthe could tell me more about where my grandmother had been born.

Emmanuelle didn't treat us like kids. She spoke to us as equals, which was cool of her. She showed us the third floor, full of large rooms that would be our classrooms, and the fourth floor, which was where the White Elm stayed overnight.

'In an absolute emergency that I am somehow not already aware of and if I am on the premises, you can find me in this room,' she said. She showed us the door to her room. She made us memorise how many doors down it was from the staircase. She carried on and we followed in silence, fully aware that this was not a part of the house we were welcome to hang out in normally. 'This,' Emmanuelle said finally, stopping in front of a heavy, thin oak door with no handle or lock visible, 'is the 'ead's office.'

'Renatus's office?' Sterling asked keenly, her already bright eyes sparkling with interest. 'How does he get in? There's no doorknob.'

Emmanuelle laughed, sounding a tiny bit resentful.

'No one can enter this room from the outside – except Renatus. It's enchanted. The spells on this estate are incredibly powerful. Renatus's spell-casting abilities quite outshine those of the rest of us, I'm afraid.'

'Even Lord Gawain couldn't enter this room?' I asked, shocked. No *way* could Renatus be that strong. Emmanuelle smiled.

'The spell guarding this door only allows Renatus to open it. Once open, anyone may enter, with 'is permission.'

'But Lord Gawain can't open it?' Xanthe pressed. Emmanuelle hesitated.

'I'm not sure 'e's bothered trying,' she said finally, as another group, led by the unbelievably skinny Anouk, approached. 'I don't believe 'e 'as. It isn't considered polite to enter a man's office without 'im, especially if 'e 'as put up spells such as Renatus's.'

I smiled at two of the three girls in Anouk's group – they were the twins. Emmanuelle directed us away before we had a chance to talk, so I waved, hoping to see them again the following day.

'Is Renatus stronger than Lord Gawain?' Sterling asked as we headed for the second floor.

'I can't answer that,' Emmanuelle said instantly,

as though the answer was rehearsed. 'The question lacks a context.'

Sterling badgered the White Elm sorceress all the way to our new dormitory. Emmanuelle was clipped but patient. I would have snapped at the American witch by now – Emmanuelle obviously had a very small knowledge of Renatus, and had apparently shared everything she knew.

'Your keys, girls,' she said as we all reached a tall, thin door that matched nearly every other door in the mansion. In the hallway, a few other people were entering their rooms one at a time. I unclasped the chain around my neck; Hiroko and Xanthe pulled their keys from their pockets. Sterling, interestingly enough, had hidden hers down the front of her top.

'You never know,' she said when we stared at her. 'You can't trust most people.'

'Alright, you should enter one-at-a-time,' Emmanuelle explained to us when we had our keys in our hands. 'Only six keys fit the lock – each of yours, mine, and the master key in Renatus's office.'

'Renatus can enter?' Sterling asked excitedly, her bright eyes shining.

'I'm sure the keys 'ave already been tested but it would not 'urt to check,' Emmanuelle continued as if Sterling had not spoken, 'so once you're inside, pull the door shut behind you. It will lock automatically. Then the next person can check that their key works, too. Hiroko?' I could hear the French sorceress make a concerted effort to pronounce the h at the beginning of Hiroko's name. 'Would you like to go first? You're the eldest.'

'I am?' my friend asked, surprised.

'Yes,' Emmanuelle said, equally surprised that Hiroko hadn't worked it out herself. 'The girls in Dormitory Two are predominantly sixteen-year-olds – the four youngest female students. You are the next four, and so forth.'

I realised that the Prescott twins must be older than Hiroko and me. I doubted it was by much.

Hiroko did as she was told. She unlocked the door and pushed it open. I could see a good-sized room beyond it, with plush beds, and a pile of suitcases and bags on the floor in the middle. She walked through and shut herself in.

The Greek girl silently slid her key into the lock, turned it, and walked in. Sterling went next. Her key was perfectly fine. I desperately hoped that mine was, too. When the oak door shut behind her, I drew in a breath and slid my key into the lock. It fitted. Good. I slowly turned it but there was resistance on my arm. I felt myself stiffen, panicking. Was I going to be rejected from my own room? But then I realised that the resistance was Emmanuelle's hand on my elbow. I sighed, relieved.

'You needn't worry about things like your key not working; you *are* meant to be 'ere,' Emmanuelle said. She smiled and let me go. 'If you 'ave any questions, remember that you and the other three can always come to me. Alright?'

I nodded and smiled back, then entered the dormitory. Was everyone on the White Elm a telepath, or just scarily intuitive? I saw Emmanuelle turn away just as I took my key back. The chain, still hanging from the silver key, swung around my fingers as I turned and pulled the door closed. Hiroko, Sterling and Xanthe were disentangling their possessions from the pile in front of the door. My blanket and book were right on the top.

The first thing I noticed was that my new room had no windows, giving it a timeless feeling. How would I know day from night here? The room had four beds, all with the headboard against the same wall as the door and with a round little reading table to the left of the pillow. Four beds, four tables, four desks at the foot of each bed, four chairs, and four closets. There were two other oak doors, one on each side of the room.

Sterling and Xanthe had chosen the beds of the right side of the room (the beds that had been on my left when I first entered the dorm) and Hiroko had the far left one, so I took the bed between her and the door.

'Just check that your key fits that closet,' Sterling suggested, pointing to the wardrobe opposite my bed. 'Ours all fit these ones. When's your birthday? Xanthe thinks they're in age order too and I just thought it would be a good idea for us to have the bed that corresponds with the closet we've been given.'

'July,' I said as Sterling tipped a suitcase out onto her chosen bed.

'Then that one should definitely be yours, because you're between my birthday and Hiroko's,' she confirmed. 'Just check though.'

I did as she suggested, and found that my key

fitted this lock perfectly, too. So this was my wardrobe. That was my new bed. This was my desk.

This was my new home.

For about twenty minutes we unpacked our clothing into the closets opposite our beds, discussing our lives. Xanthe didn't talk much, but she told us she lived in Greece in a big house with her eight brothers and sisters, and had a red Mexican walking fish called Elmo. Sterling had a younger half-brother and three older stepbrothers – her witch parents were divorced, and she lived between their houses.

'My dad remarried, and they've had a son – that's my brother Jamie – but my stepmother is an idiot,' she explained as she hung an expensive-looking jacket up in her closet. 'She's got so much mortal blood and so little magical talent you'd laugh if I tried to tell you she was a witch. She's got another two sons from her previous relationships. They're the laziest jerks you can imagine.'

'What about your real mother? Is she remarried, too?' I asked, glad I could ask questions with these girls and not expect them to get upset.

'Yes. My stepdad's not so bad. He's got another son, too, but he's cool. He drives me places.'

'I wish I had brothers and sisters,' Hiroko mentioned.

'Why don't you take a few of mine?' Xanthe asked, and we laughed. 'I've got enough to spare a couple.'

Once done unpacking our clothes, we put our herbs and tools and stuff into our lockers. Each of us found the locker whose lock matched our keys. Last of all we arranged our personal items on our desks and bedside tables. I was glad to see that I wasn't the only one propping up photo frames next to my bed – Hiroko had a picture of a man and woman who had to be her parents; Sterling had two frames, one with a little boy of about nine and one of a Border Collie; and Xanthe hung a big photo of her large family of eleven above her bed.

I looked back at my own. One frame contained a photo of Angela and me together, taken by our cousin Kelly at a family gathering about seven months ago. The other was old, taken by me nearly six years ago in front of our family home by the sea. Mum, Dad, Aidan and Angela smiled at me through the dusty glass and through the many turbulent years that had passed since my camera had snapped that shot. It wasn't even that good of a photo – Angela's blue-green eyes were closed against the glare and Dad's face was blurry with accidental movement. But it was the only one I had. We'd never been the photographic sort of family, and other than a few bath time and playtime pictures of us kids, this was the closest thing I had to a family portrait. I loved it as much as I loved Cedric, who I now removed from my bag thoughtlessly.

'Oh, how cute!' Sterling exclaimed to me. For a moment I stared at her, and then realised she was talking about my toy rabbit. I blushed.

'My grandmother made it for me,' I muttered, laying him on the bed. How embarrassing. But Sterling reached into her bag and extracted a squishy purple lump that looked vaguely like a stegosaurus.

'This is Stuart,' she admitted, her freckled cheeks colouring. 'I was so scared I'd be the only girl who brought a toy. But I couldn't leave him behind.'

I smiled, rearranging Cedric into a position I suspected would be much more comfortable for him if he were able to distinguish the difference between comfortable and not.

'His name is Cedric. I've had him forever. I can't sleep without him.' *Not that he really improves my quality of sleep, admittedly...*

Sterling laughed. She sat down on her bed and started brushing her shiny, strawberry blonde hair.

'I was totally nervous about bringing Stuart – I was scared people would tease me. But I guess it doesn't feel right when I'm not holding something, you know? In any case, I'm glad I'm not the only one.'

Before bed we checked out the other two doors, which turned out to be our bathrooms. We were spoilt, with two ensuites. Both were tiled entirely in different shades of blue and the far wall was lined with cubicles. Two were toilets and two were showers. The wall to our right had two pedestal basins, two mirror-door, medicine cabinets, a little rubbish bin and a tall glass cabinet full of fresh towels. The left wall was just a mirror – full-length and full-width, the entire wall.

I found my toiletries and began organising it all into the first medicine cabinet while Hiroko claimed the other one. We brushed our teeth and got changed.

The beds were clean, snug and plush – just perfect. I wondered if I'd have nightmares here, too.

The four of us stayed up for at least another hour after that, talking. I learned that I had absolutely nothing in common with Xanthe. Sterling talked almost endlessly about Renatus, although eventually she *did* stop talking about the headmaster and started describing her past boyfriends and why they no longer were her boyfriends. Hiroko was the first to drop off to sleep, and after that I lost interest in the conversation. It wasn't long later that I dozed off, too, into a remarkably dreamless slumber, wrapped warmly in my sister's woollen blanket.

chapter six

The black waves of the unpredictable, wild night sea crashed repeatedly into the smooth paleness of the shore. Lisandro found the rhythmic pounding to be soothing and beautiful in its consistency. The men and women around him, he knew, thought it a little foreboding, only now recognising and fearing its awesome destructive power. It was a necessary sacrifice, Lisandro thought to himself. None of them would really understand, but Peter did. He and Peter had talked about this all week.

Peter had always been a risk to have onboard – his conscience and his affection for that blasted French witch had unsettled the loyalty he had for Lisandro. It had been a concern of Lisandro's from the outset that Peter might one day lose his senses and go running back to Emmanuelle and White Elm with their location and anything else he might have overheard.

For several weeks after that fateful night in

Susannah's garden, Lisandro had wondered whether letting both Jackson and Peter in on his plans, and bringing them both along with him, was as good an idea as he'd first thought. Jackson was a little unstable, but greedy and determined and more than willing to be led into victory. He'd proven his loyalty years before, failing in his task but proving his willingness to do anything Lisandro asked.

It was because of Jackson's failure seven years ago and Lord Gawain's selfish refusal to grant Lisandro the power to fix things that he'd needed to convert Peter. Peter...Peter was weak. The idea of rivalling the White Elm had excited him at first, a couple of months before their desertion, but the reality of abandoning his code and betraying the trust of the woman for whom he harboured a secret love had been more than Peter could handle. He had shown loyalty and great strength of character when Lisandro had interrogated him, but Lisandro had watched over the past few months as Peter's resolve had slowly crumbled away.

The murder of Peter had become an unfortunate necessity, although it would serve multiple purposes. Dead, Peter no longer had the option of abandoning Lisandro, nor of rejoining White Elm. Dead, Lisandro theorised, Peter's Fated custody of the White Elm's greatest treasure should end and the power to rekindle a spirit or crush an enemy would be his.

Well, technically speaking, he already had it – he'd taken the thing a month ago during a heated argument with the younger former councillor. But he hadn't realised that the lore surrounding it was all true. The treasure remained loyal to its last guardian, and would not yield its gifts to Lisandro unless Peter freely gave it...which he wasn't going to do. Surely, if Peter died, the power would lose its loyalty to him and would become available to Lisandro.

Scattered across the beach, looking nervous but invigorated, were fifteen men and women he'd found in bars, nightclubs and at poker tables in the past year. They were all lost, they were all empty, and they had all fallen hard for the ideas he'd fed to them like honey. They were devoted now, devoted to Lisandro and his false beliefs and many of them were probably more committed to the cause than he was.

A frigid wind cut through their hooded cloaks, and many of them shivered. Lisandro did not. He saw movement further up the beach, and one silent minute later, Jackson and Peter stepped through the wall of wards and enchantments that kept this section of rough Irish beach secret and kept the tidy cabin Lisandro was staying in totally invisible to observers. Jackson wore the same crimson robe as the others. Peter wore torn jeans and a grim expression. He was a Seer, and a good one. He had to know what this was, and what the outcome would be.

'Peter,' Lisandro greeted him cheerily, 'so glad you could make it.'

'Found him in France,' Jackson said darkly, casting a resentful look at his one-time friend that told Lisandro that Peter hadn't made this easy for Jackson.

'Just making some arrangements,' Peter said coolly. The nervousness and under confidence that had always characterised him were gone without a trace. He knew, and he was ready. Lisandro couldn't help but feel impressed.

'My friend, I've been trying for months to come to an arrangement with you, but you've been making it very difficult, running away and hiding and whatnot.'

'Your terms were unacceptable,' Peter said simply. 'Had I known a year ago what you *really* wanted...we wouldn't be here now, let's just say that.'

'You wouldn't have come,' Lisandro knew, and Peter laughed, surprising him.

'You wouldn't be alive to come with,' he corrected. 'I would have told him and he'd have ripped you to shreds.' He stopped laughing and gave Lisandro a level look. 'I think one day he will.'

Lisandro understood the implication.

'At least when that does happen, you'll be long dead,' he said with a smile. 'Unless, of course, you do the smart thing now and just give it to me.'

Peter laughed again and tucked his gloved hands into his pockets, glancing around at the waiting hooded figures with amusement and disdain.

'Just this once, I'm going to try the honourable thing instead of the smart thing...and say no. I think she would be proud of that.'

Jackson lost it, shoving the smaller man with unreasonable force. Peter fell onto the sand, a bubble of energy springing up around him to protect him from further attack.

'She'll never be proud of you again,' Jackson snarled, yanking his wand from his pocket and pointing it threateningly at Peter. 'You're nothing.'

'Perhaps,' Peter said, slowly getting to his feet and dusting the sand from his clothes, 'but I'd rather be the nothing she cared about than the somebody she rejected.'

Jackson lunged again but bodily rebounded from Peter's wards. The younger Scottish sorcerer quietly took his wand from the back of his jeans, and Jackson paused, unsure.

'Let's get this over with,' Peter said to Lisandro, snapping his own wand across his knee and dropping the pieces to the gritty sand. His ward dissolved, and this time, Jackson stayed back.

'Aw, Peter, why do you have to become all noble and strong tonight, of all nights?' Lisandro asked as he rested a hand on Peter's shoulder. 'It makes me wish I didn't have to kill you.'

'I suppose I'm just pumped from stealing the Elm Stone back,' Peter answered. Even those who couldn't hear him froze suddenly when they saw Lisandro's expression of shock and disbelief.

'Where is it?' Lisandro whispered, telepathically barking at Jackson to check on the treasure's hiding place. He displaced immediately. Lisandro tightened his grip on Peter's shoulder, feeling cold fury building, and used his other hand to pull the gloves from Peter's offered hands. No rings.

'It's no longer mine to give,' Peter said. He was not worried. He had *known*, and he had prepared. Blasted Seers. 'Killing me won't help, but by all means, go ahead. I'm not scared of you.'

Lisandro grasped Peter's collar and strode into the cold North Sea, dragging his captive with him. Peter did not fight him, which only annoyed Lisandro more.

'You know that all the enchantments in the world – and I know you've got nearly all of them on this place – won't keep a murder from Qasim and Renatus,' Peter commented as Lisandro forced him to his knees in the turbulent surf. 'Congratulations on starting the chain reaction to your own undoing.'

It was true that the White Elm's scriers were the best in the world right now, and they would undoubtedly scry this Fate-altering act in days to come as the acid nature of murder burnt away all magical concealments, but Lisandro wasn't worried about that. They would never find his hideout. He forced a cold smile, feeling the earlier anger abate to be replaced with quiet calm.

'I know,' he agreed. 'Let them. Let them see what I am capable of.'

Jackson reappeared behind Peter.

'It's gone. Where did you take it?' he demanded, smacking the back of Peter's head roughly. 'You can't ruin everything like this!'

Says the one who ruined everything in the first place. Jackson was deeply, personally invested in putting things right for Lisandro after what he'd done.

'It's hardly ruined, Jackson,' Lisandro said calmly. 'This is just a setback.'

'A pretty big setback. Let me kill him.'

'No,' Lisandro snapped. He rolled his sleeves

up. 'I said I would kill him; so I will.'

Frustrated, Jackson turned his wand on an oncoming wave and blasted it apart, showering them all in cold droplets of salty seawater. Still angry, he bore down on Peter, only refraining from attacking him because Lisandro still had a controlling hand on the Scottish sorcerer's shoulder.

'I'm going to kill *her* for this, you understand?' he snarled. 'I don't care if takes years. I'll find her and I'll kill her. Maybe I'll have some fun with her first – who knows what she'll be willing to do to save her own fantastic ass?'

Peter looked up over his shoulder.

'I've already seen you try,' he said, 'and I've already seen you fail. I've seen how you'll die; it's a pity I won't live to see it in action. Your death would be good to see play out, too,' he added to Lisandro. 'So just, so perfect, so…poetic.'

With a firm downward thrust, Lisandro forced Peter's head underwater.

'I've already heard this story from a greater Seer than you, so don't bother elaborating,' he said, though Peter couldn't hear. At first there was no movement, but as his lungs began to burn for oxygen, Peter's shoulders tensed and he started to push upwards. Lisandro remained strong, keeping him there to the count of twenty-five, Peter's age in years. Then he pulled his head free of the sea to watch him sputter and gasp desperately. Jackson chuckled, sick as he was, and Lisandro asked, 'Any regrets yet?'

'One,' Peter managed to say after a moment of

deep breaths. 'I never told her I love her.'

Lisandro thrust him back into the sea and used both hands to keep him there.

'Wrong answer,' he muttered, and held Peter under the waves until his struggles stopped.

On the beach, Lisandro's followers were high on terror and amazement. They discreetly backed away as he passed through the middle of the little crowd. They were afraid, but drunk with possibilities. Suddenly, killing people who pissed you off was an option. Lines had been redrawn. Witnessing murder changed a person's soul and opened the soul's eye to the darkest of magic, and these people were forever changed.

'See how the White Elm brainwashes the weak-minded,' he commented, gesturing at the body floating out to sea on the retracting tide. 'They poisoned his heart with illusions of love, leaving him erratic and without sense. He had no idea what he was doing. He couldn't even reason or make his own decisions. They just used him to sabotage our cause.'

'We're stronger than they know,' one man, Saul, spoke up. 'We'll pull them down, whatever it takes.'

'They won't poison us, or anyone else if we can help it,' a woman named Catherine agreed. The murmurs of concurrence spread through the little crowd, quickly gaining volume and passion.

'Tear the White Elm apart!' Saul shouted.

There was a resounding cheer, and Lisandro smiled.

'Yes, we will,' he agreed, pleased with their self-motivated hatred of the White Elm. 'From the inside out.' He turned to Jackson, at his side, and said quietly, 'Get a message to our friend within the council. Make it known that the ring is missing and I want it back.'

Jackson nodded once and displaced.

Lisandro wondered presently how long it would take for the White Elm to learn of Peter's death. He wished he could be a fly on the wall when they did – it would be so delightful to see their expressions. He envisioned his well-placed spy faking horror. He imagined with relish the look on Lord Gawain's face when he realised that the man he had worked with and trusted for eleven years had not only betrayed him, but had committed the murder of a colleague and a loyal follower.

Let them see what I am capable of.

chapter seven

Blackness…Back-of-your-eyelids black…Utter silence, not a sound…And peace…

The next morning I was woken by a bell at 7am, and had to blink a few times blearily, taking in my surroundings, before I realised where I was.

The White Elm's Academy.

I got dressed. Angela had packed my bags. The clothes she had picked out for me to wear during my term here were presentable, neat and simple with clean lines. It was mostly stuff she'd bought for me over the last few years. She had mentioned that schooling here was almost like attending a year-long job interview, and that I should look the part, and I had reluctantly agreed. My net skirts, high-waisted belts, tights, purple tartan and platform Mary Janes had remained at home.

The morning meal was set out like dinner, but there was a lot less energy from my classmates. Most looked exhausted despite a night of sleep. I realised that the majority of students were currently adjusting to a new time zone and would probably take a few days to get used to the times.

'How are your roommates?' one of the twins asked Hiroko and I as we finished breakfast.

'Sterling and Xanthe. They're both very nice,' Hiroko answered diplomatically. 'How are yours?'

'We only have one,' the same twin said. 'Marcy. She's nice.'

'Kendra,' the other said, yawning, and lightly nudged her sister and nodded discreetly towards the buffet table as we passed on our way out. Kendra snuck a glance. I did the same, out of curiosity. A tall guy with spiked-up jet-black hair and the sort of warm, even tan you get from living a lifetime in the sun was filling his plate with bacon rashers, all the while admiring the twins.

'Yeah, I guess he's alright,' Kendra murmured, linking arms with her sister and steering her away.

'He's really cute,' Sophia murmured enviously as we stepped into the reception hall. 'It'll be you he's checking out, of course, now that I've said that.'

Our week's lessons had been posted in the library this morning, and it'd taken me so long to decipher the strange time-tabling system that I'd only bothered to write down today's classes. Each lesson, it seemed, went for two hours, and was scheduled for whatever time of day that particular councillor preferred.

This term was going to be the best few months of my life, I realised as Hiroko and I met Sterling at our dormitory to collect our classroom equipment.

We had the coolest subjects and the world's most talented teachers…and I'd already made a heap of new friends.

We reached our classroom on the next floor right on eight am. The classroom was airy, spacious and well lit with full-length windows all along the back wall, displaying a gorgeous view of the estate's well-kept grounds. A teacher's table was there with a couple of sheets of paper, a jug of water and a stack of plastic cups on it. The desks were perfectly spaced in four straight lines on the right side of the classroom, facing a free-standing chalkboard. The rest of the room was carpeted and spare; perhaps a practical area. I hoped so.

The three of us sat down in a line and arranged our belongings on our sturdy wooden desks just as Jadon began the lesson.

'Welcome to your first class of the term,' he said. His voice was a cheerful and upbeat one. I could tell he was American, although I had no idea which state or part he came from. 'For those of you who do not know, my name is Jadon. I have been with the White Elm for about half a year. During your lessons you are encouraged to address me and the other White Elm by our names rather than by titles such as "Sir" or "Miss". This room will be our classroom for every lesson. Even if I tell you ahead of time that our lesson will be outdoors, we will meet in here first.'

He looked up as a girl blushingly walked in late. 'Spell-casting is one of the fundamental practices of basic sorcery. We will cover energy transference, spelling techniques, energy spiking, wand-making, correct wand use, and the benefits of hand and voice-initiated magic. We will also learn assorted useful spells, such as forces and animation, and you will learn how to research and select suitable spells for your use. Once we reach that point, I intend to let you experiment with some of the spells you discover, and that can often be a lot of fun.'

I understandably became more interested at this point. Hiroko and I smiled at each other. How much cooler could life get?

'Unfortunately, the curriculum plan I worked on with Lord Gawain requires me to begin with the dull stuff, so for at least the first couple of weeks I'll be working with you on the transference of energies,' Jadon continued, now sorting through a few papers on the front desk. 'It's a useful talent. However, many of those who study this subject have found it to be tedious, repetitive and difficult to appreciate at first. Learning the nature of energy is not particularly fun in its early stages, particularly the theory, but it is the basis of many more advanced subjects, and so I hope you'll listen and learn regardless.'

I'd not really done any conscious energy transferring. I'd done a lot of silly, little, made-up spells and I frequently played around with scrying exercises (and frequently failed), but I'd never sat down and tried to transfer energy between stuff.

Jadon was handing out smooth clear quartz pieces. I accepted mine with a murmured thank you and looked over it briefly. It was very standard, roughly polished and shapeless. I placed it on my desk in front of me.

'The stone you have received today will be yours for the remainder of the year,' Jadon said as he distributed the crystals. 'They should be stored with your other tools when not in use. I expect that you all have crystals of your own but these will be the ones we will use to learn energy transference, as they are almost identical to one another. We will begin practical transference shortly, but first, please open your notebooks and copy this down.'

For the next hour and twelve minutes my interest in this subject rapidly dropped as we dutifully copied sentence after uninteresting sentence off the board. Theory and legislation were indeed incredibly boring. Thankfully, it was eventually over, and I was glad to put down my pen and pick up my quartz once again. Soon everyone was finished and gazing silently and attentively at our teacher. Jadon waved his hand vaguely and the writing on the chalkboard disappeared.

'Thank you all for writing down those notes, and I am sorry for boring you so badly on your first day,' he said as the chalk dust floated weightlessly to the floor around him. 'Now: generally, what colours, according to the chart you just copied down, are positive energy?'

I glanced down at my page, but Hiroko already had her hand up. Jadon selected her.

'Positive energy is often green, Sir, but also is white in its purest form,' she said, reading directly from her page. Nodding approvingly, Jadon smiled and reminded her to call him by his name.

'That's correct. Pure energy is the whitest white,

but I don't expect anyone here to be capable of producing pure and untainted energy from within yourselves. Inexperience inhibits your abilities, but with practice and clarity of mind, you will improve.'

That sounded like meditation. Damn, I sucked at any kind of meditation. I hoped my other subjects didn't require much of this.

'You just wrote down the theory behind the "orthodox" method – the method I'm meant to teach you, because this is how you cast spells. You've all done magic before, and the first time you cast a spell it was probably more a reflex than any conscious effort. Essentially, this is what happens each time you cast a spell: you draw magic inside you; you decide what you want done with it; you channel it and it comes out, hopefully as the spell you'd intended. Put like that, it sounds very simple. Give it a go. Try to transfer energy into those crystals.'

Looking at him dubiously, most of us had a go, to no success, of course.

'You need to mean it,' our teacher reminded us.

Jadon closed his hand and reopened it, a few glowing balls of light suddenly in his palm. He tossed them into the air, and, while we all looked on enthralled, began to juggle them. Very quickly, though, all three little lights faded to nothing, and Jadon dropped his hands.

'No energy or emotion can remain forever unless made to. Like everything, it moves on. The stronger the intent and power of the transference, the better the effect. For example, in order to transport energy from a healthy person to a sick person, as is often required in healing, you need to really mean it. Without a strong intention, the energy dissipates too quickly. The same applies for any spell or transference.'

I examined the crystal in my hand for a moment. My failed attempt to push energy inside it had stirred a question in my head. How much energy could a little thing like this hold? How much energy could my body hold? As I thought this over, Jadon said my name. I blinked and looked up.

'Aristea, you read my mind – or, more correctly, I read yours, and you were thinking just what I wanted to talk about next,' Jadon said with a smile. I tried to smile back, but felt slightly shaken.

'Oh,' was all I said at first, then, stupidly, 'how did you read my mind?'

'I'm a Telepath by trade,' he said jokingly. He sat down on the edge of his desk. He was so, so young, I noticed then. He must have been only days past twenty when the White Elm had brought him on. I tried to stop thinking about it; clearly he could read my thoughts and I didn't want him overhearing that, but he seemed not to notice, or at least said nothing about it.

'Essentially, Aristea was wondering about capacity. How much power can an item hold? How much can *you* hold?'

Jadon reached for the jug of water on his desk and placed an empty plastic cup on the desk of a girl in the front row.

'Imagine this cup is you. You are a vessel, capable of channelling "x" amount of energy at once.

You draw power to you,' he poured water in until it was about a third full, 'and expel energy in your desired form, perhaps a spell or an effort to heal a cut,' he picked up the cup and poured it back into the jug, 'hence returning the power to the universe. You borrow and direct magic; *you* are not a creator of magic. Magic is only energy; it cannot be made nor destroyed, only manipulated. The idea behind spell-casting is that you manipulate the power you draw in to suit your purpose.'

He had poured water back into the cup; now he haphazardly tipped the cup over the jug, swirling the cup as the water trickled out. The thin stream glowed and sparkled and ignored gravity, falling slowly and pausing in the delicate spiral in which it had been poured. We all stared, mesmerised by the glass-like mobile he'd created. Then the spell broke, the water fell back into the jug and a murmur of appreciation ran through the class.

'Now, I mentioned capacity,' Jadon went on, arranging a line of ten plastic cups on his desk, in order of smallest to biggest. 'Every vessel has its limitations. A rowboat can only carry so many people, and *you* can only channel so much magic.' With the cups arranged, he began pouring water into each one, filling them to their brims. 'Capacity for energy is often historically referred to as a sorcerer's "strength". In the 1700s a magical theorist called Emile Trefzer devised a widely popular scale which identified a sorcerer's capacity for energy, from one being barely psychic to ten being unstoppable. The factors and algorithms behind the Trefzer Scale are incredibly complex, so I won't try to explain exactly how it's worked out, but really, once you start getting a true sense of others' abilities and of your own, you don't really need a big, confusing scale to work out whether or not someone is stronger than you. These days the Trefzer Scale is considered quite politically incorrect in academic circles anyway, because it labels people, but I still think it's worth learning.'

Nine cups were now full, and the jug almost empty.

'Every person in this room weighs in as level six or above on the Trefzer Scale, making you all reasonably powerful sorcerers,' Jadon said, pouring water into the last, and biggest, glass. 'While it's great to know your own awesomeness, it's also wise to know your limitations. Your body, though strong and amazing, *can only hold so much power*. Attempting to channel more than one's capacity…' He kept pouring, and the water level reached the brim. The water's tension held it together for an instant as it raised above the edge, and then it spilled over the edge and onto the desk.

'How anticlimactic,' Jadon commented, still holding the now empty jug above the overflowing cup. 'That doesn't illustrate my point properly at all.'

He flicked a finger, and the spilling water paused, then, impossibly, began moving backwards like it was on rewind. Trickles slid back up the sides of the cup, and a stream flowed up from the cup back to the jug until the cup was only just full. Another wave of his hand, and a thin, glassy film spread across the top of the cup like a lid.

'This should be a more impressive and accurate representation,' he said, pouring once again. The water fell through the film of energy (maybe a ward of some sort) but did not spill back out. It continued to fill, and overfill, and the cup shook with strain, but there was no outlet…

There was a collective cry of shock from the class as the cup exploded, shards of sharp plastic and huge blobs of water bursting outwards across the room. I ducked, closing my eyes to protect them, but nothing touched me.

'As I was saying, you can only hold so much power,' Jadon said, and I looked up to see the explosion frozen in the air like a special effect from a film, water droplets floating alongside suspended chunks of plastic. 'You are not a cup, with a hole in your head where dangerous excess power can slip out. If you draw it in, you need to expel it. If you take in more than you're capable of expelling…' He gestured to his impressive floating demonstration. 'Well, I've never heard of anyone actually *exploding*, but people have died from trying to overextend themselves and "burning out".'

There was a quiet moment of sombre reflection as everyone let this sink in.

'When you say "burning out"…?' one boy asked in a tone of morbid curiosity. A few girls shot him disgusted looks.

'I mean, not much left, Miguel,' Jadon confirmed. 'Charred remains.'

'So it's true you can catch on fire?' another boy

asked excitedly, receiving his own dark looks.

'There're no recent reports of that, but some historical eye-witnesses claim it, yes. And it makes sense. The excess energy would burn its way out of the overfilled vessel.'

This lesson seemed geared towards telling us not to attempt big magic on our own. I was convinced. I glanced silently at Hiroko, sufficiently horrified for one day.

'People aren't the only things that can hold energy,' Jadon said, turning his finger lazily in a "rewind" gesture. The still-suspended explosion began to reverse itself, droplets joining together to create larger droplets and plastic shards fitting themselves together. 'With control and intention, energy can be channelled into objects, such as crystals or jewellery, for storage and later use. Normally this would just transform and fade over time as it leaks out through natural outlets, but with appropriate spells, objects can be made to hold power for years, decades...maybe centuries.'

I turned the quartz over in my hands. How much could this little crystal hold? Could I learn to transfer my energy into it, and ask it to hold onto it for me, to use it later to stay up late cramming for an exam or watching a movie marathon?

'Aristea, I'm certain you can demonstrate active transference to the rest of the class,' Jadon said with a smile.

'I've never done it,' I admitted, hoping everyone wasn't staring at me. Jadon's smile widened.

'Give it a try,' he suggested. 'Here, stand up.' I

did. 'Think about this, Aristea,' Jadon continued, looking at me directly. 'Emotion is made up of energy, like all things – it is like a mask, something that can be peeled away to reveal something pure. All I'm asking of you today is a transference of your feelings. Easy as.'

I nodded, turning the quartz slowly in my hand.

'Concentrate on a happy feeling, Aristea,' Jadon said. 'Just do whatever you need to do.'

Jadon let me think in silence for a few moments. I searched my memory for a time when I was truly happy. I came to the conclusion that I hadn't been truly happy since my parents were alive, and after extensive digging through my cluttered memory, I selected a fleeting memory of Christmas when I was nine. Aidan and Angela were both in high school and I was dying to go. They always seemed to get everything better than me. But this Christmas, I got the most beautiful present in the world – a tiny silver locket with a diamond set into the front. At the time I was incredibly overjoyed to receive that locket. It was so delicate and beautiful – I'd never felt so entrusted. I was so happy to see that my parents loved me and trusted me with something so lovely.

'You've got it,' Jadon said quietly. 'Now...'

I closed my eyes tightly and remembered that Christmas, the pride I felt about getting the beautiful necklace, the colourful presents, the warmth and love from my family – and mentally shoved it all out of my mind and into the quartz. I opened my eyes and smiled when I saw it was glowing green.

'That was quick. How long will that stay green?'

a boy asked. I sat down.

'It depends on the intensity of Aristea's emotions and her intent,' Jadon explained. 'Intent is a powerful force.'

I studied my glowing green stone. Mum, Dad, my whole family, the necklace, that Christmas...It might be in the past but it was still very real, right here in my hand.

'True, untainted energy is white, as Hiroko told us, so when an emotion masks energy, it takes on a colour to signify the intent,' Jadon was saying. 'Positive and benevolent emotion is green. Negative and often harmful emotion is red.'

A girl near the front tentatively raised her hand. She had shiny, straight black hair and very fair skin.

'Yes, Willow?' Jadon asked, turning to her.

'If someone did a spell, with a wand...and there was, like, a beam of light,' she added quickly, sounding nervous. She was British. 'Does that mean that the light would be either green or red?'

'That's an interesting question, Willow.' Jadon entwined his fingers and cracked his knuckles. I was one of the people who shuddered. 'As with most everything in the world, magic has evolved over the centuries. Old magic could take on many colours, but with recent regulations and changes in methods, modern magic is more or less restricted to three possibilities – good, neutral, or negative intent. Most of the older forms of magic have been lost throughout the years.'

'Does that mean we'll never see a stone glowing purple?' Miguel asked.

'You misunderstand. Your emotions are not the same as magical energy. Emotions have not changed over time, and emotions are also not restricted by laws or modern society to a range of good, bad and neutral. At first, during your studies, you will not be able to differentiate emotion from energy, and most of your spells will be tainted with feeling. But soon you will learn.'

I silently took all this in, wondering whether that last statement was true. There seemed so, so much to learn that I couldn't imagine ever getting through it all.

Considering the sheer dullness of the first half of Jadon's lesson, it was a total and complete success, inspiring a lot of excited dialogue between classmates on the way out. I'd loved it, mostly for Jadon's fun little tricks. What level of control did one need to be able to manipulate magic like that? They were just party tricks, really, nothing of real use, but so showy and well-done that I couldn't wait to progress through his subject and juggle my own specks of light.

My excitement didn't fade – I knew that I had a telepathy lesson next with Glen as my instructor. I'd noticed that Hiroko and the twins were in my class with me, so thankfully, I wouldn't be alone.

'Have you ever read anyone's mind with telepathy?' Hiroko asked us, sitting cross-legged on the floor beside her bed and picking through her things. I glanced at Sterling, hoping that I wasn't going to be the only one who couldn't even mind-read my own sister. Thankfully, she shook her head.

'Once I thought I mind-read my stepmom's thoughts, but then I realised she was just talking to herself about what she needed to get in the groceries,' she answered ruefully. I smiled.

'I can't do it either,' I agreed. To my surprise, Sterling giggled.

'*Can't*,' she repeated, trying to imitate my speech. '*Either*. You talk so cute, Aristea. You sound so Irish.'

For a moment I stared at her blankly, before bursting into uncontrollable laughter at her stupid comment.

'That's because I *am* Irish,' I said, laughing. Hiroko shook her head, trying to hide her smile. After our laughter subsided, and we'd pulled ourselves together, I added, 'There are people here from all over the world. Haven't you met Irish people before?'

Sterling spoke, but her response was broken by occasional leftover giggles.

'Not really,' she said. 'I saw Irish people on MTV once, though. An interview.'

Eventually the time came to go to our next class, by which time Sterling had managed to turn the conversation about Irish musicians into one about Renatus.

'He's Irish, too, you know,' she said vaguely, collecting her things. Again, I stared at her incredulously.

'I noticed,' I said, trying not to laugh at her, 'seeing as I am Irish, too, and seeing as we are in Ireland.'

Sterling giggled.

'I just wonder how a man that looks like him, with a home like this, manages to *not* be married!' she commented as we left the dorm.

'You don't know he's not,' I said cheekily, and she stuck her tongue out at me.

'I looked last night and he wasn't wearing a ring, but I'm sure that if he had a wife, she would have made herself known by now to prevent students like me from gazing after her gorgeous husband,' Sterling responded. We filed down the winding stairway. 'I certainly wouldn't want any young girls mistaking my hubby for a potential boyfriend.'

'Even without a wife, he is not a potential boyfriend,' Hiroko reminded Sterling. 'He is headmaster of this school, and you are a student.'

Sterling waved one hand dismissively, as if everything Hiroko had just said was as completely irrelevant and off-topic as a comment about starfish.

'Besides, we would know if he was married,' Sterling continued. 'Emmanuelle would have said something yesterday.' She stopped and looked back up the stairs. 'Where am I going? I'm meant to be upstairs learning about history.'

She said goodbye and hurried back upstairs. Hiroko and I looked at each other, and then continued outside.

It was a beautiful day, with a somewhat clear blue sky and a warm yellow sun shining down on Renatus's rolling green grounds. Though it did seem odd to be having lessons outside, I couldn't see any reason why not. Winter had been kind this year.

'This place is so beautiful,' Hiroko said, admiring the unspoilt land. 'If it were mine, I would not make it a school.'

'Me either,' I agreed, waving as we rounded the side of the massive building and the twins came into view.

'Kendra and I visited a farm like this when we were young,' Sophia said when we repeated our sentiments to her. She turned to her sister, adding, 'You remember, Uncle Joseph's farm. We played with the baby chickens.'

'I only remember the lambs,' Kendra answered, looking distractedly through the small group of other students gathered around Glen. Her cute admirer wasn't present. The White Elm sorcerer was kneeling on the soft green grass, stroking a small dove that he held in his cupped hand. He seemed not to notice the gaggle of young adult students at first; his attention was entirely devoted to the gentle creature in his hands. He was humming a soft, indistinct tune that I could barely make out, but the dove seemed to like the sound, blinking serenely and making no attempt to fly away. We all stood around in what might have been uncomfortable silence, except that we were all staring at the lovely scene of gentle Glen and his dove, and were all bathed in the aura of his kindliness.

It occurred to me what good people the White Elm really were. These were people who *cared*. Good, honest, kind-hearted, *real* people. There had been complaints from the public in recent years about the

White Elm and its "old-fashioned policies" and its "slipping grasp of political power", but I had never heard anything actually *bad* about the council. A few of its members had *turned* bad, and left the council, but there had never been reports of the White Elm causing anybody harm. It made me wonder, quite suddenly, what the other side was like.

'Thank you all for being on-time,' Glen said pleasantly, patting the grass invitingly. 'Take a seat, please, and make yourselves comfortable.'

We did so; I settled myself on the squishy green grass between Hiroko and Kendra.

'Telepathy has many uses, and there are many branches of it,' Glen began. 'Some will find it an easier subject than others, depending on your natural perceptivity and concentration skills...'

Already, my heart was sinking. Natural perceptivity? And as for concentration, well...I'd already stopped listening. I made an effort to tune back in.

'...the simplest of which is detecting deceit or untrustworthiness,' Glen was saying now, 'a skill we will work on here, and the most extreme of which is magical interrogation – which you realise, of course, is not only illegal but deeply wrong,' he added flatly. 'There are three main goals we will work towards in this class. First: to learn how to enter another's mind *legally and safely* without putting that person's dignity or safety at risk. Second: how to recognise and resist an unwanted presence in your mind. Third: to learn how to communicate with others using the powers of the mind and the aura. There are many ethics and laws associated with our first and third goals, which we will cover in theory; not so many laws for our second. I suggest you worry less about protecting an intruder than protecting your own precious minds in the event of a mental attack.' His soft features went serious. 'These are not stable times. There are people outside these walls, everywhere, with the ability to break into the minds of others, to harm and control through means of telepathy. You are talented, good sorcerers – it is important you remain safe from his dangers.'

The dove fluttered nervously in Glen's hand, and immediately he dropped the ominous tone and reverted back to his air of steady calm. We, the students, glanced at one another with slightly unsettled expressions. By *his*, we had to assume that Glen was referring to Lisandro, the former White Elm councillor who was now apparently attempting to undermine them.

'Yesterday, when you arrived here for the first time, you gave myself and Susannah permission to search your minds,' Glen said, pleasant and informative again. 'All of you. By gaining your permission and following certain ethical restrictions on what we could and could not view, Susannah and I acted within the law. We accessed enough memory, personality and emotion within your minds to be sure of your identities, your trustworthiness and your skill levels, but left everything in its original "place", so to speak, without disrupting the natural order of the mind. This is a part of telepathic safety procedures, which you will all learn before you do any deep-mind diving. I learned enough about each of you to be able to recognise your minds at first touch. Mind-touch is something I expect you all to be familiar with.'

The lesson began swiftly – we were paired up and instructed to search for the other's aura. I'd never seen an aura, although I had a pretty good idea what I was meant to be looking for. Theoretically, there should be a glowing frame of colour around my partner, representative of the energy that radiated from every living thing. I'd always been able to feel them, sense them, but never actually *see* them.

Sophia, with whom I was partnered, squinted at me for a while before insisting that I had no aura.

'Of course I do,' I said, although I had never before seen it, nor anyone else's.

'I can sometimes see them,' Sophia admitted, 'but either you don't have one or I'm not looking hard enough.'

'I would say that you weren't looking hard enough,' Glen said, looking over me as he passed, 'but Aristea possesses a very unique aura. It has...holes.'

'Holes?' I asked, worried. That sounded bad, like I was faulty or something. Glen laughed.

'I've not seen that particular characteristic in many individuals, but it's nothing to worry yourself about. It's like a birthmark, I'd guess. Irrelevant.' He turned to address the class. 'In order to properly view auras, one needs to slip into a different frame of mind. Staring at the physical world isn't going to

113

give you access to what lies just outside your visible spectrum.'

Annoyed, I realised that this was more meditation.

'I *hate* meditation,' I told Sophia bitterly. Glen glanced over at me, and I realised I'd spoken a little too loudly.

'It's not really meditation,' he said, putting a hand over my eyes, obscuring the grassy green grounds and Sophia's face from my view. 'It's more like…focussing your eyes. Try again.'

I felt his presence brush past mine, felt him alter something in my mind. When he took his hand away, it was like he took away something else, too, like a veil or something equally immaterial. I blinked, and my mouth fell open.

Sophia, who hadn't moved, stood before me, a misty turquoise green glow around her body. She seemed unaware of the change, and was watching me curiously. I looked around at the others, who were facing their partners, squinting and screwing up their faces in concentration. Kendra's aura was similar to her twin's, although probably bluer. Hiroko glowed with slowly swirling shades of red and pink. I turned back to Glen, and was impressed by his very solid aura of shimmery ivory and its shining outline of the brightest white – the White Elm influence on his life, I supposed.

'How did you do that?' I asked him, but already the glowing auras were slipping away. I had lost my focus.

'I'm not doing anything,' Glen answered. 'This

is *your* ability, Aristea. All I did was remove its biggest obstruction – doubt.'

chapter eight

That evening at dinner, I sat with my new friends and we shared stories of our first classes. Hiroko had her telepathy notebook open in front of her and was reviewing the laws and ethics we had written down. Sterling was telling the twins and me about her earlier class – spell-writing.

'I always thought writing your own spells was, like, illegal or something now, 'cause there was this thing my mom used to rant about, years back, something about people getting in trouble for trying to write their own spells,' she was saying. 'So I asked Aubrey about it, and he told me that all new spells that are written need to be approved by White Elm before they can be performed and put into practice, and what they teach us here about writing spells is a council-approved method, and that everything we write will be reviewed by one of them before we can use it.' She picked at her nail-polish. 'Aubrey's kinda hot, too, actually, but he's got nothing on Renatus.'

'I had sword-fighting practice this morning,' Kendra said cheerfully. 'Tian studies martial arts and sword combat. He was saying that swords and knives are typical weapons and tools for witches and that it can be useful to know how to use them for more than magical purposes.' She grinned. 'It's so much more fun here than I expected.'

'Yeah, I thought there'd be a lot of hardcore study and examinations and whatnot,' Sophia agreed, swirling her peas around her plate, wistfully gazing in another direction with her crystalline eyes out of focus. 'I expected some kind of urgency, I suppose. This is a much more comfortable pace.'

'This place is absolutely awesome,' Kendra added, stealing a lamb chop from her twin's plate.

'It is a beautiful location,' Hiroko agreed, looking up from her notes. 'I have never been so far away from home as here before. It was far to displace. Ireland is very different to Japan.'

'Is it more difficult to displace over large distances than within a smaller vicinity?' I asked her. She nodded.

'Yes, it becomes harder to, uhh…pin…' She hesitated, searching for a word. 'Harder to get it right.'

'Pinpoint?' I suggested, and Hiroko nodded.

'Yes, exactly,' she said, blushing slightly. 'It becomes harder to *pinpoint* an exact location when the distance is greater. When my father and I arrived yesterday, we were very lucky to arrive so close to our intended destination. We knew the general location and knew we could expect to find ourselves anywhere within a one kilometre radius of this property.'

'I can't wait to start learning stuff like that,' Sterling said enviously. 'Displacement and healing and all that.'

'I had a healing lesson this morning, with Lady Miranda,' Sophia said. 'She's so amazing. There was a newborn foal from a farm not far from here that had deformed ankles – it wasn't going to be able to walk properly, left alone. And she fixed it. We didn't do much more than transfer positive energy from ourselves to one another and take notes about ethics and laws and stuff like that. I can't wait to have a go at it myself.'

'Soph has always been really good at that sort of thing,' Kendra said, now stealing potatoes from her sister's plate, having finished the lamb chop. Sophia was still staring absently in another direction, but lowered her fork over the third potato when Kendra attempted to relieve her of it.

'Really?' I asked, amused by their behaviour.

'*Natural ability*, our mom keeps saying,' Kendra continued, digging into the potatoes she had already taken. Once she had swallowed, she continued, 'We used to have a mouse, when we were about ten, and it managed to get its foot trapped in its little running wheel thing. Its foot and toes were all demented and stuff.' She twisted the fingers of one hand around in a way that was obviously meant to convey a mouse's broken and mangled foot. 'Soph picked it up and held it, and did...well, something, and she healed it.'

Sophia didn't appear to be listening, and it was

to my surprise that she nodded in response. Some more people entered the dining hall right then; some students, some White Elm. Sterling's attention was riveted when Renatus entered, followed closely by a small fan group of female students. These three girls were some of the oldest here, and they were practically falling over themselves to keep up with Renatus's quick strides as they flashed bright, flirtatious smiles and all tried to talk to him at once.

I watched, along with most of the students in the dining room, as Renatus strode up to the White Elm table, followed by his admirers. He stopped, and turned to face them – blatant annoyance was, I thought, an easy expression to read, even on an unfamiliar face. The girls either could not recognise it, or chose not to, because they kept smiling, though they stopped talking now.

'That's all *very* nice.' Renatus's low voice carried to where I sat with my friends. 'Perhaps now you'd like to find a seat and have your evening meal?'

The girls, beaming, turned and hurried towards the buffet table, giggling and whispering frantically to one another. Sterling looked outraged.

'They shouldn't be bothering someone like him!' she hissed across the table to me. 'He's the headmaster! He's obviously been working hard all day, and he wasn't at lunch – it might've been all day since he's had a break to eat anything. And all they're doing by following him and badgering him with questions is prolonging his wait for his dinner.'

The twins and I laughed, and Xanthe, who had not said much since we'd started dinner, now spoke up.

'You're very defensive of our headmaster, considering he's a person you've never actually spoken to,' she commented slyly.

'He might be an ass, once you get to know him,' Kendra agreed.

'He may not be very nice,' Hiroko said, having apparently not understood Kendra. The Canadian kindly explained to her, in an aside, what an ass was.

'He might be gay,' Sophia added quickly.

'He could be a total creep,' I suggested, but Sophia's comment was the best, being the only possibility that would mean Sterling could *never* have him.

'He can't be gay, there's no way,' Sterling disagreed confidently. 'I have a very good gaydar. He's definitely batting for the side I need him to be.'

We all laughed as she continued, 'And there's no way he's a creep or an ass or whatever, I can just *tell*. Look at him. He's *beautiful*.'

I did as she said, and knew that she was right – Renatus was a prime example of physical human beauty – but I knew as well as the next person that external beauty had very little to do with internal beauty.

'Maybe he knows it, too,' I said, turning back to Sterling. 'Remember what Emmanuelle said yesterday? Maybe she was alluding to something. You reckon he's not into lads, but he could still be in love with himself.'

'Mightn't be any room in his life for you,' Kendra teased, but Sterling was too busy laughing at my comment to hear her.

'*Lads*,' she giggled, trying not to choke on her mouthful. She managed to swallow. 'Aristea, you say so many things that are just *so cute*. I *adore* your accent.'

This time I didn't laugh, though I did smile pleasantly. The girl was in Ireland...what did she expect the locals to sound like?

'That cutie's looking at you again, Ken,' Sophia said softly, staring into the distance once more. Her sister casually turned a little to itch a spot on her back, and stole a glance over her shoulder. I resisted the urge to look as well, not wanting to give the act away.

'Are you sure?' Kendra asked, her voice doubtful as she turned back to her dinner. 'He glanced up when I looked, but he wasn't staring or anything.'

'He has been,' Sophia responded, finally turning her attention to her dinner plate, which, after Kendra's raids, was somewhat empty.

'Does anyone know yet what classes we have in the morning?' Hiroko asked, looking mainly at me. I shook my head.

'We should check after tea,' I suggested. 'And we should probably write down the entire week while we're there.'

Just as I had suggested, the six of us finished our meals and visited the library. Very few people were here (most were still finishing up dinner) so we had an easy time reaching the noticeboard and finding our names amongst the lists of subjects, days and times.

'I have scrying on Thursday morning!' I exclaimed, leaning close to the noticeboard to read the details. 'Level 3 Scrying, with Qasim. Hey, Xanthe, you're in my class!'

She looked up from her handwritten timetable to give me a vague smile, although it was not a particularly warm or excited smile. I turned back to the noticeboard. Well, *I* was excited about the prospect of learning to scry.

'The rest of us have scrying tomorrow afternoon,' Kendra commented. 'Level 2. You two must be more advanced than us.'

I wondered whether there had been a mistake – I certainly had no prior knowledge of scrying, nor any experience. Maybe enthusiasm made up for lack of talent.

Later that night I wrote to Angela, telling her about all the subjects I had and everything I was learning. I told her about my new friends, and how different they were from me and from each other. I withheld a smirk as I wrote about Sterling and the fascination with Renatus that she shared with half the female students in this school. I left the letter on my nightstand, uncertain as to how to go about sending it, and went to sleep.

When I awoke the next morning from another refreshing, dreamless sleep, I was surprised to discover that I hadn't slept in. The other three girls were just starting to wake up, too. Apparently the breakfast bell had just sounded.

There was something very magical about this

place, and it could have been due to any number of things. I was sleeping better than I had been in years. My dream had left me alone for two whole nights.

Throughout the day, I tried my best to concentrate as Anouk spoke about the history of the White Elm and its purpose in her warm, purring Russian accent, as Aubrey explained the ins and outs of spell-writing, and as Elijah dictated the laws surrounding displacement. I knew it was important, all of it, and I made sure I took notes in case I needed to reflect on these lessons, but my mind was very firmly stuck on Thursday morning's scrying lesson. It didn't help at all that while I was carefully writing out law after displacement law, Hiroko, Sterling and the twins were all in their own scrying lesson, learning the beginnings of everything I had ever wanted to know.

One might even go so far as to refer to this phenomenon as "unfair".

At dinner I drilled the other girls on their scrying lesson, desperate to know everything they had learnt.

'It wasn't that exciting, to be honest,' Sterling said in a bored voice, as she scooped a meatball out of her spaghetti with her fork. 'We wrote a whole lot more laws and ethics and stuff, and then did some visualisation exercises. It wasn't much different from our other classes. And Qasim's too old to check out.'

'That's all you did?' I asked Hiroko as she sat beside me, trying to quell my disappointment.

'Yes, it was very basic, but as with everything I am sure we will begin more difficult tasks later on once we have a grasp of the regulations,' she said encouragingly. 'Your class may be more involved than ours was.'

'I'm excited to start divination with Susannah,' Kendra said. 'Soph makes it sound boring but I'm pretty sure my class will be much more exciting. I'm in Level 3.'

'I've been reading the timetables that are up in the library, and I can't see Renatus's name beside any subject,' Sterling commented in a slightly concerned voice. 'I don't think he's teaching a subject.'

'Like you said yesterday,' Kendra pointed out, 'he's the headmaster, and probably extremely busy already without the added stress of organising his own class.'

'What do you suppose he's got to do?' Sterling asked after a moment of thinking. 'I'm sure he is very busy, but it's not as though he's writing school newsletters or signing class reports, is it?'

'Usual White Elm business, I'd assume,' Sophia suggested without a lot of interest. She turned to me and firmly changed the subject. 'That cutie that keeps checking Kenny out was in our class today, in scrying. He came over and talked to us.'

'His name's Addison and he's Australian,' Kendra continued with sparkling eyes. 'His accent is gorgeous.'

Hiroko and I willingly joined in this conversation, lest Sterling captured our attentions and started on Renatus again.

By seventeen, most girls have been in some kind of relationship, serious or otherwise. I was probably sitting very firmly in the late bloomer category. I'd never been involved with anyone; never had a real boyfriend. I attended primary school with the mortal children but never attended mortal high school so I missed out on all that. When I was young I liked a boy in my neighbourhood called Shane, who was a year older than me. His family were sorcerers as well, and his parents were friends with mine. When I was eight I told my parents I was going to marry Shane when we grew up, because he kissed me at the park. We stayed friends until he started high school and I didn't. He made new friends and we started to drift apart. I hadn't seen him since my parents' and Aidan's funerals.

I'd never really had any particular interest in any particular individual (other than Orlando Bloom, but he doesn't count because you can't count celebrity crushes) and it had never really concerned me, either.

Kendra, it seemed, was much more boy-savvy than myself, or least that was the impression I got as she talked. It was probably right to expect that every girl here was more experienced with the male species than I was.

Oh, well. There were worse things in life than not needing a boyfriend to function.

It seemed to take forever, but eventually, Thursday morning arrived. I was awake and dressed before the other girls had even woken up. To use up my extra time before breakfast, I spent as long as I could manage inside the bathroom, trying out different hairstyles with the assorted ties and clips

Angela had packed for me. Finally, I settled on a look, and checked my watch.

I'd only wasted fifteen of my extra forty minutes! Annoyed, I strode from the bathroom and headed for the door. My letter for Angela still sat patiently beside my bed, waiting for me to work out how to send it. I grabbed it. With the other three girls still sleeping quietly, I opted to go to breakfast early rather than risk waking them by pacing agitatedly. I slipped on my shoes and left for the dining hall.

As I walked, I tried to admire the tapestries on the walls and to read the dates on the older-looking portraits – anything to take up more time. I noted with vague surprise that even those paintings that appeared positively ancient were dated as no older than from the late nineties. The oldest painting I found, a Renaissance-style epic of fat baby angels and a cowering man, had *1997* scrawled beneath the artist's unintelligible signature.

Unfortunately, the more time I tried to waste, the less time seemed to actually pass. All too soon, I was walking into the dining hall.

I had intended to sit around for a quarter of an hour in the silent and empty room and try my best to not go insane, but when I arrived, I saw that the hall was not empty. A maid was attending to the long buffet table, adding a plate of fried eggs to the array of dishes. Nearer to the door, an older maid was speaking to a tall figure I recognised as Renatus.

'It can't have been a nice thing to see,' the woman was saying as I entered the room. Her tone implied a level of intimacy not usually present between an employer and his staff. 'You could have told me. It's not like a simple bad dream, now, is it?'

'No, it's not, Fionnuala, but I'm fine,' Renatus said in his soft voice, laying a hand briefly on her shoulder. He glanced over at me, having obviously felt my presence as I walked in on their conversation. I quickly looked about for somewhere to sit as he second-glanced me. 'This is my job. I'm good at it. I can handle it, I promise.'

'Since you promised,' Fionnuala said, and turned away with a smile and a respectful bob of her head. Renatus turned back to me as I began charging towards the table.

'Aren't you going to get something to eat before you sit down?' he asked, sounding very slightly amused.

'Yes,' I said, turning and hurrying back towards the buffet table and feeling like an idiot. I grabbed a plate, then stopped, and turned back to face Renatus. He was still standing in the same place, watching me. 'I'm sorry if it seemed that I barged in on your conversation. I didn't mean to. I didn't think anyone would be here.'

He didn't answer, so I went back to choosing my breakfast. There were still a few spaces on the buffet table, spaces for the dishes not yet brought out from the kitchen, but the pancakes looked great and so did the sliced strawberries, so I loaded my plate up with these and went to sit down. Renatus hadn't moved, but now followed me and, to my surprise, sat opposite me as I started on my breakfast.

'What's your name?' he asked, just as I took an

uncomfortable bite of pancake. I chewed quickly and swallowed.

'Aristea,' I said nervously. 'I haven't done anything else wrong, have I?'

'No. Can you see auras?'

'No. Can you?'

Renatus almost smiled.

'It's not difficult once you have unblocked your senses,' he said. 'Your aura looks familiar to me, although I can't think why.'

I didn't really know how to answer this, so I pulled Angela's letter free of my pocket.

'How do I send letters here?' I asked. 'I already put a stamp on it.'

'Usually, just give it to one of my staff,' he said, taking it from me, 'but I'll send this one for you.'

'Thanks,' I said. A few White Elm councillors entered the room, and Renatus stood as Emmanuelle approached him. She looked as though she hadn't yet slept.

'Good morning, Renatus. This would 'ave to be your first interaction with a student, wouldn't it?' Her tone was slightly cool, and I got the impression that these two were not on the best of terms.

'Aristea and I were just having a little chat,' Renatus said. He stared at her meaningfully but said nothing else. I wondered if they were communicating telepathically. Emmanuelle's bright blue eyes narrowed in his direction, but when she turned back to me, she smiled.

'I 'ope you 'ave an enjoyable day,' she said. She strode from the room, followed closely by Renatus.

At the door they stood together for about half a minute, speaking quietly, until Emmanuelle shook her head, smiled thinly and left.

I finished off my pancakes and strawberries as maids brought out the rest of the food and the White Elm councillors helped themselves to an early breakfast. The seven o'clock bell's ring brought a steady stream of students into the hall.

chapter nine

As the students ate breakfast and prepared for the first class of the day, Lord Gawain strode towards Renatus's office, where, he could see, Qasim and Lady Miranda were already waiting outside. The Healer looked worried; the Scrier looked annoyed.

'Who are we waiting for?' Lord Gawain asked as he approached. Qasim scowled.

'You, apparently. He must know that we are here but he hasn't let us in. I need to get to my first class.'

'We're not waiting on anyone,' Lady Miranda said, with a reproving look at Qasim. 'We thought it would be best to keep this amongst ourselves until we'd spoken to Renatus and compared his vision to Qasim's. I assumed you would like to be present for that.'

'Yes, thank you for calling me here,' Lord Gawain said. He had been at home, enjoying a pleasant breakfast with his wife Davina and their youngest daughter, twenty-seven-year-old Radella, but the news Lady Miranda had contacted him with was very concerning and required his immediate attention.

Without hesitation he knocked twice on Renatus's office door. Almost instantly, the magical lock released and Lord Gawain was able to push the door open and enter the office. Behind the massive desk sat Renatus himself, poring over yet another pile of paperwork. Due to the others in the White Elm taking on the responsibility of teaching classes, Renatus had offered to take on more of their usual tasks in order to reduce their overall workload. Now he spent most of each day carefully analysing every home-written spell sent to them for approval; he read and answered dozens of letters; he organised upcoming trials and researched reports of dangerous or illegal magical activity. This morning, already, somewhere amongst all of his other jobs, Renatus had managed to find time to receive psychic visions. He did this as a normal state of being, much as Qasim did, but Lord Gawain had wondered whether the excess workload would dampen Renatus's natural gift of perception. Apparently, it had not.

'There's been a report of a mortal teenager most unusually injured in a fistfight with a sorcerer of the same age,' Renatus said without greeting, looking up at Lady Miranda. 'The hospital cannot explain why his cuts won't heal despite weeks passing since the incident. No weapon was found and the victim's testimony has brought up no mention of a knife, but the injuries are described as '"deep lacerations inconsistent with the victim's memory of open-hand strikes".'

'I'll have to investigate further,' Lady Miranda said with a slight frown. 'I might be able to do something for the young man. Hopefully it's not what I'm thinking of. Where is this report from?'

'One of ours; a nurse in Budapest,' Renatus said, handing her the relevant paper. 'The attacker is being charged with assault by the mortal authorities, but if he's used dark magic aside from assaulting the mortal, we'll have to take it even further.'

'I'm told that you experienced a vision today, Renatus,' Lord Gawain said as his co-leader scanned the report. The young man looked to him and nodded.

'Will you share with us what you saw, or should we go and stand outside for a while until you're ready?' Qasim asked scornfully.

'Next time you'd like to see me, Qasim, perhaps you'll try knocking,' Renatus responded coldly, before turning back to Lord Gawain. 'Peter is certainly dead. Lisandro must have shrouded the incident at the time, because I have only just received the images.'

'You are certain that Lisandro murdered him?' Lady Miranda asked, pocketing the report from the Hungarian nurse and looking concernedly between Qasim and Renatus. Qasim nodded.

'Absolutely. My vision was very clear; Lisandro drowned Peter,' he confirmed.

When both Qasim and Renatus, two of the world's most gifted scriers, experienced the same vision, Lord Gawain could always be certain that their visions were correct. This time, though, he found himself hoping that somehow, they might both be wrong.

'We'll need to compare the two, and ensure they're not false visions sent from Lisandro,' he said, scratching his stubbly chin and considering what repercussions could come of these tidings. Peter's family would need to know about this. Emmanuelle…what would he tell Emmanuelle?

Qasim and Renatus looked at one another coldly, but did what they had to – unblinkingly holding the other's gaze, their minds met and shared images of their ghastly vision. Within a few seconds they had broken eye contact and turned back to the White Elm leaders.

'His is the same as mine,' Qasim reported solemnly. 'Lisandro drowned Peter in waist-deep seawater by holding him under the waves. There were a dozen or so others standing around, wearing dark red cloaks.'

Lord Gawain felt his morale sinking. Peter was now lost forever. He had retained slim hopes of Peter's feelings for Emmanuelle dragging him back into the light eventually, but now that hope was dashed. Lisandro was a murderer – Lord Gawain had known that his former friend was indeed ruthless, but to have his true capabilities revealed was quite crushing.

It had been devastating to discover that Lisandro was a traitor. It was even worse to learn that he was able to kill a loyal friend, but somehow

Lord Gawain found it much easier to take in. He had been slightly more prepared for this blow. Lady Miranda sat down on one of the cushy chairs and rubbed her temples.

'Do you know *why*?' she asked finally.

'We aren't empathic,' Renatus said. 'Qasim and I can only scry and receive images and sounds – the solid and the physical. Feelings and thoughts are beyond our grasp.'

'But we can guess,' Qasim added, confirming Lord Gawain's terrible fear. The Elm Stone. Peter had been its keeper when he'd disappeared, and they'd all immediately assumed the worst. The Stone was an ancient store of intense energy, and if tapped, could grant its keeper unknown power. No White Elm council in living memory had ever needed to use it, but they still kept it, still fuelled it, forever strengthening it. The Elm Stone was a weapon. Insofar as the public knew, it was their *only* weapon. They weren't to know about the Dark Keeper; they weren't to know that when Lord Gawain had lost Lisandro and Peter, he'd lost *two* weapons.

But when Lisandro hadn't suddenly risen up and blown them all apart in the days, weeks, and then months following their disappearance, Lord Gawain had begun to wonder and hope. Maybe Peter hadn't given the Elm Stone to his new master – because the Elm Stone could only be given, never taken. Maybe Peter was holding out until the right moment to return. Maybe Peter, a talented Seer, knew something they did not.

But no.

'Does Lisandro have the Elm Stone?' Lady Miranda asked worriedly. Renatus shook his head and Qasim said, 'He searched Peter for it but he didn't have it on him. He said it was no longer his, so who knows where it is now.'

Lord Gawain sighed and wandered over to the large arched window. Renatus's beautiful estate of hilly, green pastures dotted with large trees stretched into the distance until it met the orchard. The branches of the ancient trees, stripped by the season, swayed in the early morning breeze. It was a stunning property. By looking at it, one could never guess the tragedies that had occurred here – the bad memories, the pain, the loss, and the stain of hundreds of years of dark practices were invisible to the naked eye. But Lord Gawain had a better idea than most as to the truths behind the beautiful scenery.

'We should keep this amongst ourselves for now, at least from Emmanuelle, until the council next officially meets,' Qasim mentioned. 'By then we'll have given this situation further investigation. Emmanuelle doesn't need to know yet. I see no reason to accost her at breakfast and tell her in front of the whole council and the students that her old friend has been murdered.'

'She knows something is wrong,' Renatus said immediately. 'I just saw her. She said she dreamed of Peter's death last night and asked whether it was a vision.'

'And you said?' Qasim prompted.

'I said it's unusual for a talent like scrying to

develop so late so it was probably just a dream. I didn't know how to tell her.'

Lord Gawain released the breath he hadn't known he was holding. Renatus was not the most tactful councillor – it would be preferable for Emmanuelle to hear this news from someone else, and later on.

'Alright, that's good, Renatus,' he said. 'That gives us time. I think we can agree to keep this from her?'

Lady Miranda and Qasim nodded and Renatus frowned.

'What if she asks again? We can't lie to her,' he said, but his words were unheeded. No, they would not lie to her, but they didn't have to give her any information regarding this conversation, either.

'Well, my day has certainly gone downhill,' Lady Miranda said with a mirthless smile. 'Did either of you happen to see where this happened? We'll need to find the…the body…and perhaps search the surrounding area for clues as to where Lisandro went next.'

What she meant was, they needed to find Peter quickly so they could track down what he'd done with that ring he'd taken with him months ago. This was the closest they'd come to it all year.

'The crowd seemed very cold – my best guess is to start with the northern hemisphere, not that that helps much – but it was at night, so there wasn't much to see of the shoreline except that it was mostly sand with a rocky outcrop beside a small structure on stilts,' Qasim said. 'They were quite far away from the structure, but the water wasn't very deep, so I assume the tide was going out. Unless Peter's body washed up on that beach, and assuming they left it alone, there's no telling where it might be now.'

Lord Gawain felt a wave of sadness to hear Peter spoken of in such an objective sense.

'Was there anything said that gave any clues as to the location?' he asked his colleagues. 'Was anything said at all?'

Qasim and Renatus shared a look.

'I agree with Qasim that we should investigate this further,' Renatus said, choosing to ignore the question completely. He stood for the first time since the others had entered the office. 'I don't think we should keep this from the other councillors, but it must be kept quiet from the students until we are certain of what has gone down. They needn't be panicked. If I come by any further information, Master, I will certainly forward it to you.'

Strictly speaking, Gawain's title was Lord, but Renatus had always referred to him as Master, like an apprentice might. Lord Gawain had never taken the boy on as a formal apprentice so there was no necessity for it; it was just Renatus's personal choice.

'Thank you, Renatus, but you didn't answer my question,' Lord Gawain said, meeting the younger man's violet eyes. 'What did you hear, when you had the vision of Peter's death?'

For a moment, he wondered whether Renatus would answer. The White Elm's leader had never experienced any direct disobedience from his protégé but sometimes wondered whether this respect would last forever. As always, though, Renatus acquiesced.

'Lisandro pulled Peter out of the water for a few seconds to watch him splutter and beg, but Peter didn't beg,' he described dutifully. 'Peter caught his breath and spoke.'

'What did he say?' Lady Miranda asked when Renatus didn't continue. Qasim finished for him.

'He said, "I never told her I love her"'.' Nobody in the room had any doubt as to who "she" was.

chapter ten

Despite leaving breakfast early, Xanthe and I were not the first people to arrive at the doors of our scrying classroom. A couple of dark-haired guys stood around, waiting patiently, and a pretty girl of about my age was sitting cross-legged on the floor. She was extraordinarily pale, especially compared with those of us around her, with very thin, almost white blonde hair, and very fragile features. Approaching where she sat, I could tell that she was not only extremely powerful, but also very capable – she knew more magic than most of us here. My senses discreetly brushed past hers as I lined up with Xanthe, and my immediate impression was of a wall of ice. I opted to stay out of this one's way.

A couple more people arrived as the minutes ticked by, and when Qasim turned up to let us inside, I counted only eight people in my class.

The room Qasim had chosen as his classroom was darker than most of the other rooms in the massive house. It looked like an old parlour of some description, and hadn't been much changed for lessons. A number of cushy couches were arranged so that people sitting in them could easily converse with people sitting around them without having to turn a lot. The middle of the room was devoted to an ornate rug and a spindly coffee table. Candlesticks lay in the centre of the table.

I was not the only student who hesitated in the tall, thin doorway, somewhat put-off by something I couldn't explain. It wasn't anything visual, or a funny smell or anything else so obvious. It was something else. Something...blank.

'How did you get the room like this?' the little blonde asked, her accent similar to mine. 'Did it take long to wipe down?'

The rest of us looked to Qasim, confused for a second before we clicked, one by one. The room had no feelings. No atmosphere. Usually, when you walk into a room, it *feels* like the energy that has been left behind in it. If people argue, the tension is tangible in that space for some time following. A warm, loving home will feel warm and loving. The rest of this house felt like various things, although you didn't think so until it was mentioned. The entrance hall felt busy, the library felt sombre, the hallways felt a little creepy and abandoned. Every room has its own feeling, whether you notice it or not. This room felt blank, which was slightly disconcerting for reasons I couldn't understand yet.

'It was already like this,' Qasim answered. 'It's why I chose it. No distractions. Take a seat and try to clear your minds,' he directed as we stood around awkwardly. 'This class varies more than either of my others in skill, but your abilities in my subject are all roughly equal. I think. I want to get a clearer idea of where to start with this group.'

Well, that answered my question as to why I was in this class if I'd never scried before. I had *natural ability*. With a thrill of excitement, I grinned at Xanthe. She forced a smile and sat down. She was nowhere near as excited about this as I was, obviously.

When everyone was seated, Qasim moved to the centre of the room.

'To begin today's lesson I would like for everyone to close their eyes and allow for me to analyse your current level of skill in my subject,' he said. 'If anyone has any objections, please voice them now.' When nobody spoke, he continued. 'Good. After I have gauged your skills, we will begin some simple exercises. Everyone in this class has been put here because of advanced abilities, so I'd like to move you all along at as quick a pace as you can manage. The ability to scry is one that the White Elm highly prizes, and one that you will find most beneficial in life.'

He turned to one of the older males in the group.

'I will start with you, and make my way around the room. Everyone, please close your eyes and try to quiet your minds.'

I did as I was told, and closed my eyes. Calming my thoughts was much more difficult. My excitement over what I could be about to learn, and my concern over whether I would be as good as everyone else, bubbled away in my head, setting off dozens of other thoughts before I had the chance to catch them all and stow them away.

By the time I felt Qasim's mind reaching into mine, I had barely started with quietening my thoughts. I felt his annoyance, but he probed through them anyway, ignoring them and searching for a part of my mind I'd never used. I focussed hard on letting him in, and did my best to avoid clamping down on the silky tendrils of probing presence the way you clamp down on thoughts you don't want to have. Qasim seemed to find what he was looking for and seized it. I heard his voice inside my head.

This is very deeply concealed, Aristea. You have great ability but even with regular exercises it will take some time before you can progress to the level I need you at. This far back in your mind, you might never reach your potential. I can draw it forward, but it may be painful.

I didn't know how to speak with my mind, so I tried to send him enquiring thoughts. I wanted to know a little more. He seemed to understand.

Your abilities are blocked, probably by doubt and grief. Both can be powerful in prohibiting progression. You're being held back by your own mind. Naturally it would take many years, much reflection and a lot of painful personal growth to move past the issues in question. In this class we don't have time for that. I can pull your talent through all of that if you like. It will probably still take a few sessions and will probably hurt but will be much quicker than the years of couch therapy you'd need otherwise.

I tried not to be offended by his offhanded and less-than-sensitive comments about my need for therapy and tried to just consider what he was offering for a moment. I'd gone to counselling after my parents and brother died but had never spoken a word to the funny little man except to say hello at the start of every hour-long appointment and goodbye at the end. He was nice and had never pushed me to talk, but perhaps I should have. I decided that a little pain would be worth it if it meant I'd be able to scry. It made sense that my deepest abilities would be blocked by my grief over the loss of my family – I hadn't done much magic since their deaths and it had affected me very deeply. I wanted to learn to scry, more than anything, so I did my best to think affirming thoughts. *Yes, yes, I want to learn to scry.*

Without answering, Qasim's mind took a stronger hold of my scrying abilities. Again, I felt excited. I felt a slight pull and a small twinge as Qasim tugged at my abilities. It hardly hurt at all. I was just starting to wonder what else I'd start to be good at when Qasim yanked, hard, on that part of my mind. I cried out loud. The sensation of a sudden, splintering headache was enough to leave me dizzy. It felt as though a delicate little part of me had just been dragged through a solid brick wall and out the other side.

It *hurt*. My head was aching immediately. What he had found was talent, something insubstantial, but the pain was as real as anything physical. When Qasim pulled a third time, I covered my mouth with my hands to avoid shouting again. The poor little segment of me that had just slammed through a wall was now being dragged through a thicket of thorns. Qasim withdrew, and I opened my eyes, which were slightly watery. My head was throbbing; memories of the storm that had destroyed my family swirled about the forefront of my mind, almost as painful as the day it had happened.

The others in the class were watching me closely, startled. No doubt I'd disturbed them with my shouts of pain. Qasim stood in front of me.

'I apologise for the pain caused,' he said, though he didn't sound particularly sorry. 'The wall you felt is your self-doubt and the second pull took your attention through your most painful and grief-stricken memories. It may take a few more lessons to pull your abilities clear of its blockages and to ensure you don't regress. We'll leave it there today. I still need you able to concentrate for the remainder of the lesson.'

The rest of the lesson? It felt like someone was pounding the inside of my head with a brick. The abilities that had remained dormant and unnoticed for so long were extremely obvious to me now – it was hard to ignore what felt like a very sore physical body part.

Apparently I'd been the last person to be analysed, because Qasim went straight into the next part of the lesson. I tried to tune in.

'…art of scrying has very distinct levels of skill,' he was saying. 'The first level is the type of scrying performed by most sorcerers around the world, and that is tool scrying – the use of a tool such as a crystal, flame, bowl of water or a mirror in order to view images sent to the quiet and concentrated mind. Most who practise sorcery do not have the discipline or talent to scry without a tool. In this class, we will touch only very briefly on this type of scrying, because each of you have the ability to perform much greater feats.'

Qasim collected the candles on the table and began to hand them out.

'In the next lesson, which I have scheduled for Monday, we will move onto the second level of scrying, which is the level I expect each of you to be able to master by the end of this semester,' he continued as he handed me my candlestick. 'That is scrying without a tool and using your own mind to consciously receive and view images. I have complete faith in each of you,' he added when one of the boys looked doubtful. 'Scrying without a tool is a much more precise and focussed art form. You will receive much clearer impressions and will yield better results overall.'

The throbbing in my head had begun to lessen, and my thoughts, which had been so jostled and upset when Qasim had been messing around with my head, had begun to reorganise themselves.

'Passive scrying, the ability to scry without conscious thought, is a level we will work towards but not one I expect anyone to achieve for probably a number of years. A great deal of discipline and focus is required for this skill to develop. Very few of you here possess the quietness of mind necessary.' Qasim glanced momentarily at me before continuing. 'It is this skill that allows the White Elm to effectively police the magical world. While teaching this class, a part of my mind is focussed elsewhere, indiscriminately accepting visions of events around the world. Right now, a sorceress in Arizona is helping her young son to take his first steps. Such events are irrelevant to the White Elm, however, and so I can change my focus and accept visions only of sorcery being performed. This is how we can immediately know when someone is misusing their powers.'

I had often wondered this, and again, my question was answered.

'There are variations of each of these forms,' Qasim continued. 'Tool scrying can lead to future-seeing, if the scrier has that ability. Conscious scrying can be developed to a point that the scrier can mass-scry, as I did to find you all. There are other forms of scrying, but these involve the detachment of the consciousness from the body and are illegal. The use of these methods carries very harsh penalties, including imprisonment.'

My seven classmates and I sat in tense silence as Qasim dusted his hands on his robe.

'Stand, all of you, and bring your candles to me so that I can light them,' he said. We all stood and waited in a short line, each grasping our candlesticks in one hand. The powerful blonde girl stood at the front. Now that she was standing, I realised that she was actually very short – probably only up to my shoulder – and proportionately tiny. The white fingers wrapped around the candlestick she held were small and skinny, with neat fingernails.

Qasim made a fist momentarily, and when he opened his fingers, a flame ignited in his open palm. A few of us leaned around those in front to see better. Qasim offered his hand to the little blonde student, who held her candle's tip into the flame. One by one we did the same, lighting our candles before sitting back down in our places. Qasim closed his hand, and the flame disappeared.

'Perhaps Jadon will be able to teach you that one,' he said, when someone asked how he'd created the flame. 'This now is a simple exercise to open your minds to the art of scrying. You'll need a partner, which shouldn't be hard, as there's an even number of you. One partner, stand behind the other.'

I glanced at Xanthe. She shrugged and stood, rounded the couch and stood behind me.

'Good,' Qasim said, pacing slowly around the group. 'Since there is truth to the saying that nobody knows you quite like yourself, you will find that it is quite simple to scry yourself. Those of you sitting, you need to close your eyes and envision yourselves exactly as you are. Those of you standing, choose a number between one and ten and hold up that number of fingers behind the head of your partner.'

I closed my eyes tightly against the dull pain in my head and focussed on myself. I was sitting on the left seat of the plush two-seater couch. I was wearing skinny jeans and a neat little jacket that would have looked more appropriate on Angela. I had black shoes. The top half of my dark hair was tied back; the rest hung loose over my shoulders. My eyes were closed. The studs in my ears were peridot. The candlestick in my hands was thin and tapered, and the flame was very still.

'Hold that image in your mind, very tightly,' Qasim said into the silence, 'and open your eyes. Focus on that image as you stare into the flame.'

I did as I was told. The flame flickered only a little with each exhalation I made. I concentrated on the image I had of myself and tried to see it within the flame. A few times I thought I'd done it, but then I'd lose focus in my excitement. After several minutes, Qasim called for us to stop.

'When you scry yourself, you also see your surroundings, which would enable you to see and count the number of fingers your partner is holding up,' he explained now. 'Did anybody succeed?'

The tiny blonde raised her hand.

'What number did you count?' Qasim asked.

'Eight,' she answered. Qasim glanced at the dark-haired boy behind her, who nodded, faintly surprised.

'Excellent. Now swap places with your partners and see if the rest of you can do it.'

I swapped places with Xanthe and picked the number three. She sat very still for several minutes, staring intently into the flame. Opposite us, an Asian teenager exclaimed, 'Two!' The other three attempting to scry themselves were distracted long enough to give him nasty looks before they went back to what they were doing.

Holding three fingers up behind Xanthe's head

felt extremely unproductive. My head was still aching a little, although nowhere near as badly as it had at first. The candle in my hand was dripping hot wax onto my fingers, burning momentarily before quickly cooling and solidifying. I was quite relieved when Qasim called for an end to Xanthe and the others' turn at scrying.

'Did anyone other than Isao manage to count their partner's fingers?' Qasim asked. The Asian teen looked abashed. Another lad raised his hand tentatively, and Qasim nodded appreciatively.

'Good. We will continue this exercise until the end of the lesson, by which time everyone here should have made some progress. Tiredness is not,' he added, and though he didn't look at me, I felt the pointedness of his words, 'a reason to slack off. It is in exhaustion that we can reach the furthest, so I should see you working *harder* as the lesson goes on.'

For the next hour, Xanthe and I continually swapped places, taking turns at staring pointlessly into the flame. As the class's end approached, Xanthe managed to scry herself, and by extension, her surroundings, including the four fingers I held up behind her. Qasim was impressed; by this point nearly everyone had begun to yield results. I determinedly took her place on the couch. There was no way I was going to be the only failure in the class. Absolutely no way.

I closed my eyes, shoving away thoughts of my aunt telling me this school was not for little girls like me. She loved me but she didn't know what I was really capable of. She didn't understand. With that thought I breathed deeply and opened my eyes to behold the little flame for what had to be the tenth time. The candle had lost a lot of length as it burnt away the time, but the fire still burned brightly.

Though it still twinged, I tried to stretch the part of my mind that Qasim had uncovered. *In exhaustion we reach our furthest.* Sounds like the crap Angela's gym instructor had spouted that time I'd gone with her – you know, that crap that makes you want to kick them. The latent gift was sluggish and largely unresponsive, but the more I tried to use it, the more obvious it became. Very slowly, something *clicked*. As I strained, something moved; something happened.

In the flame, I could see me.

It was like trying for the first time to lift a limb that has been bandaged to your side your entire life. It was difficult and felt alien, but it responded if you tried hard enough.

The tiny, fuzzy-outlined Aristea sitting on the little couch in the fire was staring intently at the dripping candle in her hands. I realised I was *scrying*, and in the excitement that suddenly rose from me I nearly lost my focus. The image I had finally managed to procure faded and became obscured, and I had to fight down my feelings in order to regain concentration.

Slowly, the image refocussed. I could see a tiny Xanthe standing behind me. I was unmoving; she was fidgeting and looking about in utter boredom. One hand held her candle. The other was by her side. She wasn't bothering to hold up any number of fingers for me to count.

My annoyance snapped my concentration, and my first scried image dissolved. I became aware of the rest of the room once again. Qasim was just passing by me; I felt a slight movement behind me.

'Did you succeed this time?' the councillor asked me. I nodded, but my talent had started to hurt again, making my head swim with dizziness. I put it down to exertion. 'What did you count?'

'She wasn't holding up any fingers,' I said, putting my free hand to my head as the pain continued to increase. Both Qasim and I turned to Xanthe, who, to my surprise and then anger, was displaying one index finger – one index finger that I *knew* had not been there before.

'Your mind is very disorganised, Aristea,' Qasim said. He waved a hand over my candle and snuffed the flame with a flick of his energy. 'You should not be too discouraged – you have great talent, so with some practice you should be able to grasp the concepts eventually. I'd hoped you would be able to keep up with the progress of the rest of the class regardless of your mental blockages, however. Before our next class, you should do this exercise each morning before breakfast, when your mind is quietest. Take that candle with you. That way, when we return on Monday, you will hopefully not be too far behind the others. It will also help to prevent your talents from regressing.'

Before I had the chance to argue, Qasim turned away and addressed the class, snuffing each candle that was not blown out by the students.

'Overall I consider today's lesson a success,' he

said. 'Neither of my other two classes is at the stage that you have reached today. Well done to those of you who succeeded at this first task. We will begin each lesson for the next few weeks with similar exercises, as they are good for preparing the mind for scrying. I will see you all again on Monday.'

With that dismissal, I stood and left immediately, seething.

chapter eleven

'That is very unfair,' Hiroko agreed quietly, with a sympathetic expression. We were sitting cross-legged on the floor of the library in the displacement section, and I had just finished recounting the story of my first scrying lesson. Aside from learning that I had a fantastic innate gift for scrying, and aside from scrying for the first time, the class had been a complete disaster. Qasim had been very unsupportive, Xanthe had been nasty, and on top of it all, my head had hurt then and ever since, although it had decreased once again to a dull throb.

'She wasn't holding up any fingers – I *saw* her with her hand by her side, she just couldn't be bothered,' I went on passionately, though I kept my voice down, 'and when Qasim came past I felt her move a little, and then suddenly she's got her hand behind my head!' Scowling, I held up my index finger to demonstrate. 'He thought I just wasn't disciplined enough. He gave me extra work to do between lessons, to *make up for it*.'

'I am surprised by Xanthe's behaviour,' Hiroko said with a slight frown, going back to her book and running her finger down the contents page. 'She has been quite distant to me and does not often to speak to me. However, I did hope that she is nice.'

'So did I,' I muttered, glaring at the bookshelf beside me. Perhaps I was overreacting, but as far as I was concerned, there had been no need today for Xanthe to make me look like I'd failed. I dismissed the possibility that I'd misinterpreted the image I'd perceived. I *knew* I'd scried, just as I knew my name and knew I liked the colour purple. I *knew*.

I'd not spoken to Xanthe since our scrying class, and had made a point of sitting far away from her at both lunch and dinner. She'd made no attempts to talk to me, either. I wondered, not for the first time, what her problem was.

'At least Sterling is still pleasant to us,' Hiroko said, flicking to the page she wanted. 'Sterling is very talkative and speaks to everybody.'

'As long as you want to talk about Renatus,' I added, and we both smirked. Despite my strong Irish accent, and Hiroko's inconsistent ability to fully express herself in English, we understood one another perfectly and shared the same sense of humour. By this point we'd known each other only a few days but had already really connected.

I ran my fingers along the smooth spines of the books on the nearest shelf. *The Physics of Teleportation* and its neighbour, *Advanced Displacement*, were both very old books with peeling gold lettering. The author's name, Griffon, was flaking steadily away. I was too scared of having the ancient texts fall to pieces in my clumsy hands to dare remove the older books from the shelf, but the romantic in me still drew my fingertips magnetically to them, even if just to admire them.

'What is this word?' Hiroko asked me, passing the book over and keeping her finger pressed to the page, indicating the offending word. 'Foo-row?'

I took a quick glance at the sentence: ...*causing a slight furrow in the Fabric of space but NOT of time...*

'Furrow,' I corrected, handing her back her book. 'Like a crinkle.'

'Like a fold?' she asked, and I nodded. 'Thank you. Have you yet had a lesson in displacement?'

'Yes, but we only talked about laws and ethics and examples of things that can go wrong,' I told her. I subconsciously began flicking through one of the less deteriorated books that Hiroko had not yet started on. 'There was no practical aspect. But that's fine, because I already know that I'll be no use at it.'

'You should not be so quick to doubt yourself if you have not yet tried,' Hiroko warned me. 'Qasim has told you, doubt holds you back. You may be blocking much other strength.'

Eventually, as it started to get late, Hiroko and I headed back upstairs to our room. She was telling me about her first attempts at displacement. I was listening, but part of my mind was focussed elsewhere, dreading facing Xanthe. What if the reason she'd been so difficult was because I'd done something wrong? What if she'd told Sterling to act the same?

Upon entering the room behind Hiroko, though, I discovered that I had nothing to worry about. Xanthe was sitting silently on her bed, writing in a diary, and Sterling was, as usual, practically bouncing off the walls, animatedly describing her day to her friend. Xanthe, it seemed, was temporarily deaf and was not taking in a word of it; Sterling either didn't notice or didn't care. She turned on Hiroko and me when we entered and jumped onto her bed, beaming.

'He spoke to me,' she said as I dislodged Hiroko's key from the door and handed it back to its owner. I glanced at Sterling. She was wearing her pyjamas and her strawberry blonde hair was secured in two braids.

'Who?' Hiroko asked, innocently, though I was pretty sure I already knew the answer. Sterling's smile widened, and her bright eyes brightened further.

'Renatus. He spoke to me,' she explained in near ecstasy. 'He *spoke* to me.'

'Yeah, what did he say?' I asked, deciding against telling her that Renatus had also spoken to me, and had probably spoken to hundreds, if not thousands, of other people in his life.

'Well,' Sterling said, arranging herself so that she was kneeling on her bed, 'I was having dinner, well, dessert by that point, I guess, and nearly everyone else was already gone. Then I finished my ice cream and left the dining hall, and was coming up here, and was halfway up the stairs when *he* came down and nearly walked into me!' She grinned and pressed her hands against the sides of her face in excitement, as if nobody in the world could ever have asked for such a blessing as being walked into by a headmaster. 'And he sort of righted himself and said, 'Excuse me', really softly...Really vaguely. He's got the most beautiful voice; really, it's so soft and silky; really low, too. Then he, like, averted his eyes, totally cute, and hurried past me. He looked really intense, like he was thinking a hundred other things...Aristea, Hiroko, don't laugh at me – he's just *so sexy*.'

Dramatically, Sterling threw herself back onto her bed, grinning at the roof. Hiroko and I shared an amused glance. Pathetic.

Xanthe said nothing for the entire night. Sterling made up for it by talking almost non-stop until she fell asleep.

In the morning, I again woke up earlier than the others. My sleep had once again been refreshing and dreamless, and my mind felt clear and alert – perfect to practise tool scrying. I quietly found my candle and a box of matches and let myself into the bathroom. I settled myself cross-legged against the mirror and lit the wick. I had nobody to hold numbers behind my head but that hardly mattered – my objective was to get a clearly scried image of myself and to hold it.

Taking several deep, relaxing breaths, I imagined myself, sitting cross-legged in the bathroom in my pyjamas, my hair unbrushed, my feet bare and a little cold, my hands clasped together over a lit candlestick. Slowly, I opened my eyes and stared deeply into the steady little flame.

My mind was a bad one for wandering, and it did this more times than I bothered to count, but I persevered and held my self-image securely in the forefront of my thoughts. I found my scrying talent after some searching, because for some reason it was not in the same place as it was yesterday. Though it was an effort, I forced the talent to show itself. Again, like yesterday, it responded lethargically, like an underused limb suddenly being asked to lift a heavy piece of luggage.

With a push, I managed to get a little bit of it to work. Something slid into place, and then an image appeared inside the flame – a tiny little Aristea, sitting on the bathroom floor in her pyjamas with bare feet and messy hair.

I felt a rush of excitement, and immediately the image blinked out. My talent stopped exerting itself.

I tried twice more and got the same results – a brief image of myself before my feelings overpowered and drove the image away. It was enough, though; enough for me to know that I could scry.

On Friday afternoon I had my first lesson with Susannah. She was a talented Seer, or so Kendra had gushed admiringly.

The round-faced American sorceress was waiting for us in the grounds on the crest of a grassy hill, asking students to sit down on the large picnic blanket she had laid out for us. Wrapped in jackets and scarves, we did so.

'Our work here will be to develop your ability to See, with a capital S,' she told us. 'Often confused with the related art of scrying, my preferred art is to do with the divining of the futures. Scrying, as most of you should know, is to do with observing events as they *are* – usually actual events from the past, or current events as they unfold. Seeing relates more to what *could be*. It is less precise but, to me at least, much more fulfilling.'

I'd never foreseen anything, not really. Like most witches (like most humans, actually) I had experienced intuition, but a gut feeling and a rush of metaphorical images are very different.

Susannah went around the group, asking everyone to voice their experiences with Seeing. Everyone here had known already that Seeing was not synonymous with scrying, but most had not done much more than dabble in some card reading or rune casting. Just like me. I felt relief.

'All of you are sitting at about the same level of skill in this area,' Susannah said when the last person had finished speaking. 'You're all aware of Seeing and how it can be used, but none of you here is a natural Seer – that is to say, nobody here identifies with this art in the way that the Level 3 class does. You,' Susannah smiled directly at Hiroko, 'are a Displacer. It's your talent; your interest. Just as yours,' she looked at one of the boys we'd followed over from the house, 'is telepathy.'

I opened my mouth to speak, to ask her what I was – most sorcerers knew instinctively what their gift was, but all I seemed to be good at was wards and making messes.

'Do you know a lot about gifts?' one of the few other girls in our class asked suddenly, British accent sharp, half-raising her hand as she spoke. I recognised her after a moment as being a student in my energy-transferring class with Jadon. Willa? Willow. Her very shiny, straight black hair was twisted into a bun this afternoon.

'I can sense a burning question,' Susannah said with a small smile. 'You're a Healer, as I'm sure you already know.'

'Yes…and I know this has very little to do with the actual topic…but, I'm a Healer, and all of my family are Seers,' Willow explained hesitantly. 'All of my dad's family is. None of them are Healers. And it hasn't come from my mum's side, because she's, well, not a witch.' Willow lifted her chin suddenly, as though daring anyone to laugh. Nobody did.

It was not my own opinion, but there were some pure-line witches who considered anyone of mortal birth to be second-class. Willow had obviously come across this animosity before; she was not ashamed, but knew there were people out there who thought she should be. I could sense that she would defend her mother's dignity, and her family's right to call themselves sorcerers, if she had to.

I thought of Kendra and Sophia and how easily they'd let me know that their father was mortal. Was the pure-line supremacist problem different on different continents? I supposed that witchcraft had deeper roots here than it did in those nations settled by Europeans, and probably deeper prejudices, too.

'So your mother is mortal?' Susannah asked, making it clear that this was just another casual subject to her, and not something she would judge her student by. Willow relaxed visibly.

'No, she's a sorceress,' she said, 'but her parents weren't. She's a Seer, too, just like Dad.'

'Well, Willow, while there's an abundance of research done of this topic, I cannot tell you conclusively why you are a Healer,' Susannah said, settling into a more comfortable position. 'Research shows us that magical power in pure lines is inherited, so if your ancestors were powerful in magic, you will be, too, but there's no evidence to suggest that talent is exclusively linked to that. In some cases we see families in which every child has a different talent. For example, take my own family. My husband is a Displacer, and our son Dean is a Crafter – that is, he can write and create magic in his mind. A very unusual gift, and not one he got from anyone in our immediate living family.' She smiled helplessly and shrugged, hands spread wide as she did so. 'I can only assume that a gift is just that – a gift – and has nothing to do with genetics. We don't know why it happens. Just as sometimes we come across sorcerers with no witch blood, like your mother, Willow. Magic, I'm afraid, is a complicated science.'

The lesson, following that insightful dialogue, went on to be extremely boring. We copied down laws *again* and made some half-hearted attempts at Seeing. I'd never been much interested in future sight, and I wondered whether my disinterest would hinder me.

Hiroko and I went for a walk when the lesson ended while the other people went back inside with Susannah.

'Have you done a lot of future-seeing work?' I asked as we headed further away from the grand house. I realised that I had asked Hiroko this before or after nearly every class. I knew why, too; I wanted assurance that I wasn't going to be the dummy in the class during this term.

'Yes, sometimes, but I am not very good at it,' Hiroko responded, taking a long stride to avoid a small rabbit hole. She paused, and turned back to it. I stopped as well, waiting for her. 'Is this for rabbits?'

'Aye, that is,' I agreed. 'We get a lot of hares, too, but they don't dig burrows.'

'Are they very cute, like rabbits?' Hiroko asked, now walking again, although slower, looking around. I fell into step beside her.

'They're pests,' I said. 'Though sometimes, I suppose, they're cute. Don't you have rabbits and hares in Japan?'

'We do,' said Hiroko, 'but not in the city. There are no rabbit burrows in Sapporo.' She smiled at me. 'It is very different in Sapporo from here. One day, you must visit me at my house.'

'Definitely,' I agreed. 'And you should visit me, too, and meet my sister – you'd really like her, everyone likes her, and you have a lot in common…'

And I realised suddenly that this was true. Hiroko was responsible, level-headed, caring and sweet. Just like Angela. No wonder I'd latched onto her.

'When you come to Sapporo, you will meet my father,' Hiroko continued enthusiastically, 'and you can see the shops where I go and you can meet my English teacher. She is very nice with me.'

We didn't really have a destination, but after half an hour or so of aimless wandering and chattering, we found ourselves at the west edge of the hilly lawn. Here, the lush grass blended seamlessly with a sparser type of grass, and tall, gnarled apple trees grew, shading the grass with stark, spindly shadows and, oddly for so early in the season and considering the trees were only just budding with new leaves, dropping little apples everywhere. The spaces between the trees were roughly equal, which told me that this was an orchard, not just a place where a bunch of fruit trees had happened to grow. The ground was littered with the ripe, very early fruit and the rotten shapes of those apples that had fallen in the preceding weeks.

The orchard had the definite feel of something long abandoned, and I somehow knew that no one had been amongst those trees for many years.

'Why does nobody farm these trees?' Hiroko wondered aloud, voicing my own thoughts. This was a huge orchard; surely the apples could be used in the meals that were prepared in the mansion? Apple pies, or even just as snacks. I didn't think I'd seen apples yet on the buffet table.

I suddenly felt that these trees needed *somebody* to accept the delicious-looking fruit they produced season after season, and reached up and plucked a large red-green apple from a low-hanging branch. While Hiroko silently watched, I took a hesitant bite.

It was probably the sweetest, most flavoursome apple I'd ever tasted, and I told Hiroko as much.

'We won't be in trouble, will we?' she asked, eyeing the fruit. I shook my head confidently.

'There's no way anyone will notice a few missing apples in an orchard this size,' I assured her.

That said, I picked a second apple for her, and then we continued walking along the orchard's border, munching away.

We eventually passed a big gap in the apple trees, which on second glance proved to be a wide dirt path leading into the orchard. Even the grass didn't grow there. I slowed and allowed my gaze to wander down the long, straight pathway. Thirty or so metres into the trees, where the land rolled away out of sight, the path ended at a low, cast-iron gate. Because of the trees either side of the path and the gate, it was difficult to see what lay beyond; however, both Hiroko and I sensed the significance of it. This was a powerful place. The trees lining the path seemed stiller than the others, which all rustled softly in the breeze. No apples had fallen onto the dirt path, but dozens lay rotting either side.

We stood for some time, staring as though entranced by the gate. My head began to ache very slightly. There was something special – and, somehow, frighteningly familiar – about this path that I couldn't quite identify. Just being this close, I felt invigorated like I'd just had a hit of caffeine, yet also a bit unwell, like I was lactose intolerant and had forgotten to ask for soy. For a wild moment, I felt an urge to follow the path and satisfy my burning curiosity. What lay just beyond that gate? What was so special about this place that made my senses tingle nervously?

I must have made a movement along the path, because Hiroko closed her hand over my wrist.

'We shouldn't,' she whispered, as though afraid of being overheard. 'It is...not nice. I am thinking of dead things and dark.'

Her words shocked me out of my little trance. She was right. Now that she had verbalised the problem, I could feel exactly what she meant. I felt slightly ill. Where had I felt something like this before?

Together, we turned away. Every step I took in the opposite direction made me feel better. The ill feeling went away. My head cleared. I took another bite of my apple and felt my senses relax. It was not hard to forget the experience as we walked across the sunny, hilly lawn and started talking again.

We eventually settled ourselves atop a small hill and finished our apples. Other classes must have finished at similar times, because we were soon joined by Sophia and Kendra, and their friend Marcy. Marcy was quiet but seemed nice. She was shorter than me, with long dark hair and glasses. She was South African, she liked healing, and that was pretty much all I learnt about her.

Between the two of them, the twins more than made up for their friend's shyness.

'We were with Sterling as well,' Kendra

explained presently, 'but she decided that she needed to study once we passed the library doors.'

'Study? For what?' I asked, perplexed. Sophia and Kendra shared identical smirks.

'Here's a clue: he's not a book.'

Hiroko and I groaned.

'The headmaster was inside the library?' Hiroko guessed. The twins nodded.

'He must have been walking behind us on the stairs,' Sophia said. She'd started making a daisy chain. 'As we passed the library, he slipped past us and went inside. Sterling – you should have seen her face – just stopped completely.'

'Then she followed him,' Kendra finished, now ripping daisies out of the lawn for her sister's chain. Again, too early in the year for daisies, yet here they were. 'She didn't even say a word.'

'It's a little creepy,' Marcy said quietly, gazing off into the distance.

'He *is* hot,' Kendra admitted on Sterling's behalf, sending the rest of us into a fit of giggles. 'He *is* prominent and influential and wealthy. But he *is* also a teacher. And a politician, so therefore *probably* a douche bag. And there's a difference between admiring somebody and stalking them. A big difference.'

We all agreed, and the topic changed as soon as we saw a dejected Sterling herself in the distance, meandering towards us from the mansion. By the time she reached us, we were discussing the jobs we hoped to hold one day, either as a part of, or independent to, the White Elm.

'I think I want to work as a Healer in a hospital, like Lady Miranda does, and do that sort of work, where it's needed,' Sophia said, weaving her daisies together placidly. 'I've never really thought of what else I could do. I guess, in the White Elm, I could travel and do similar work, but it's hard to know whether I'd get the chance to do as worthwhile work. Or as much work.'

'I think it would be wonderful to be the Healer in the White Elm,' Marcy commented. 'The travel opportunities would be fantastic. But there's only one Healer position, and Emmanuelle's still young. That spot won't come up again until we're old.'

'Doesn't mean the council can't have other Healers,' Sophia countered. 'Emmanuelle coming in didn't stop Lady Miranda from keeping her job at the hospital.'

'I do not know now what I will like to be,' Hiroko said with a slight frown. 'Before I get – *got* – the letter from White Elm, I have always thought I must have a mortal job like my father, because there is very little place in Japanese society for magical life. The only magical job that can be used in the mortal world is healing, and I am not a Healer.'

'Me neither,' Kendra said cheerily. 'I'm a Seer. Soph and I used to joke that she'd be a brain surgeon and I'd be a cheesy telephone psychic.'

'You have different gifts?' I asked, surprised. Susannah had said that different gifts often occurred within families and that genetics didn't seem to be the only factor. But Kendra and Sophia were identical twins – same genes, same childhood, same experiences, probably the same diet for most of their childhood, too. What other factors could there be?

'I've never been able to see anything in my head other than my own thoughts,' Sophia said, 'but Kendra sees things before they happen. And Kendra can't heal yet.'

'Once you get to know us, you'll be less surprised,' Kendra added, smiling. 'We're not really very alike. For instance, Sophia is the boring one.'

'And Kendra thinks she's the funny one,' Sophia said dryly. She glanced up at Sterling, who had just reached us, and shielded her eyes from the sun with one hand. 'You caught up, then?'

'He just disappeared!' Sterling said, dropping herself right in the middle of the daisies that the twins were picking. 'I just went inside to read up on Seeing-'

'Sure,' Kendra interjected, and though Sterling tried to ignore her, when she continued, she was smiling slightly.

'He was just pulling books off shelves, skirting through them, then putting them back, like he was looking for something,' Sterling explained, picking at a knot in her shoelaces. 'He went into a different aisle and then he just vanished.'

'Do you think it's possible that Renatus might have been avoiding you?' I asked, knowing that Sterling would take the jibe for what it was – harmless teasing. She smiled.

'I just want to get to know him,' she insisted, although everyone present, who knew better, burst into fresh giggles.

chapter twelve

From his office window, Renatus watched as the last of the students finally trooped back inside. The sun was setting, and dinner had been called. Despite feeling rather hungry, he had no intention of attending the evening meal. It was an awkward experience he could do without, sitting at a long table of colleagues who wished he'd just disappear, avoiding the gazes of the dozen or more admiring young female students, his troubled mind elsewhere. No; he could have Fionnuala bring him something later. Perhaps he'd just join the staff for their evening meal once the students had gone to bed.

Earlier, while reading a letter from an elderly Welsh sorceress demanding that the White Elm assimilate with Lisandro for the good of the magical world, Renatus had felt a sickening jolt in his heart that had nothing to do with the stupid letter. He had known immediately what it had to mean.

Pain. Loss. Revenge. Guilt.

The orchard.

He had moved to the large arched window of his study, and stared out across his estate. Straight away, he had seen them – two students, girls, standing at the edge of the long-abandoned apple orchard, staring down the path. Could they feel it, too? Could they sense the significance of that place? He imagined so.

Renatus had waited, watching the girls as they deliberated with themselves. Unconsciously, his senses brushed their intentions. The Asian girl was understandably repelled by the darkness of the path, but the other...the other, though frightened, found the darkness familiar.

Renatus recognised her, then, by her energy. Aristea, a young Irish student with an affinity for scrying, according to Qasim. The only natural scrier at the Academy, Renatus found her fascinating – so fascinating, in fact, that he'd broken his own rule of not speaking to the students. Ever since Lord Gawain had mentioned the death of her family, Renatus had taken an objective interest in the girl, as though she were an extremely unusual museum exhibit.

He'd taken the time to talk to her, and he almost wished he hadn't. Aristea was just like *her*. Her energy was so similar, and her demeanour (timid, yet also defiant) took him back a decade to better times.

After a few seconds, the friend had pulled Aristea away, and with every step they took, Renatus felt himself relax along with them.

He should have known that with thirty-whatever students running around the estate, somebody would eventually stumble upon that place. Just because he had avoided it for seven years did not make it invisible to everyone else.

Unsettled, Renatus had been unable to return to his paperwork. The disgruntled Welsh crone could wait until later. His every thought had been of the pathway into the orchard, and what he could do to stop students from following it and learning his secret.

One of his secrets, anyway.

He had suddenly remembered a book in his library, written by his own great-grandfather, which outlined methods of hiding dark presences and the traces left behind where dark magic is used. Surely he had poured over it a dozen times, but maybe he had missed something? And there were other books, too. Books he knew he had read before. But he didn't want to think about the orchard anymore. He didn't want to worry about anyone wandering down the path and seeing what was there and feeling what awful things had been done there. *Everything* could be lost if anyone learnt that one truth.

He had gone straight to the library, ignoring his surroundings, the giddy whispers of young girls, with his mind everywhere else as it usually was.

He had only stepped through the library doors when yet another student noticed him and decided to follow. Renatus felt a flash of annoyance, although only a very strong Empath would have been able to feel that – his aura and his emotions were always well-guarded. He couldn't even walk around his own house without picking up a trail of obsessive fans. In many ways, he couldn't wait until the students' educations were finished, or until the White Elm decided to give the young people a holiday. They had been in his house for a week and already, Renatus was getting sick of it.

At the same time, having the students here was a good thing. They were the most powerful young sorcerers in the entire world, and they were here, able to be watched, observed. They were powerful blobs of potential, like clay, waiting for someone like Renatus to take one of them into his hands and mould that student the way he needed them to be.

He could wait. He would wait patiently for that *one* to present him or herself.

Aware of the strawberry-blonde student's keen gaze, Renatus had moved into another aisle and stepped directly into what seemed like a normal book case. The next step he took was through the wall of his study, back where he'd started.

There were a number of these secret little wormholes all around the house, designed by a distant but brilliant ancestor to assist him and his family to escape if ever the estate was attacked. The openings of the wormholes were sensitive to Renatus's bloodline, along with most things in this house, and so no one but a blood relation of the family could use the wormholes or even sense them – which, of course, suited Renatus just fine.

But there was nothing to do in his office but to work and glance out the window at the orchard, and he hadn't even managed to retrieve the book before he'd lost patience with being stalked and returned. So he spent the remainder of the day pacing the study, staring out the window, and occasionally managing to get some work done. He knew that tomorrow he would regret wasting this afternoon, but he knew that he was much too unsettled to get anything important done. His thoughts were locked onto the orchard.

Now, Renatus watched the sun disappear behind the apple trees. Perhaps tonight was the night to be brave. He turned away and waved a hand; the study door opened, and he left. Instead of following the hall, however, he walked directly into the wall opposite his door, activating yet another wormhole, and stepped out of the pantry door of the large underground kitchen.

Fionnuala looked up at him and smiled, as though it were perfectly common for the man of the house to stride out of her pantry.

'Master Renatus, you should be at dinner,' she scolded lightly. 'You haven't eaten all day. I had the girls make your favourite; roast duck, with vegetables and potatoes and gravy.'

Renatus paused beside the large, steaming dish. It *was* his favourite.

'Save me a plate,' he said. 'A big plate, if it isn't too much trouble.'

'Don't be silly,' Fionnuala beamed, already preparing a heaped plate to go back beside the oven to stay warm. 'It's never too much trouble for you, Master Renatus.'

She reached up and briefly touched his cheek adoringly, like an aunt might, and Renatus felt the usual wash of warmth. It was wonderful to feel loved; to know that for at least one person, the world would not be better off without you.

Grateful for her unconditional love, Renatus leant down and kissed Fionnuala on the forehead. She'd mothered him and fussed over him since before he could remember. She'd always treated him as though he were a little prince, instead of the son of a reclusive and selfish sorcerer. She'd read to him as a toddler, given him treats from the kitchen in the middle of the night as a growing child, and supported any decision he had ever made as a young adult. Fionnuala adored Renatus, and wouldn't hear a bad word against him – and it would destroy her, he knew, to discover some of the things he had done.

Another reason why something had to be done about the orchard.

'I'm going for a walk,' Renatus told her, squeezing Fionnuala's bony shoulder affectionately. She beamed at him.

'Come in before it gets too dark and cold,' she ordered lovingly, as though catching a cold were a real concern of his, as though he had never faced worse things than a darkening sky as part of his life and work, as though anything dangerous could possibly occur to him, the White Elm's Dark Keeper, on his own estate.

'I will,' he promised anyway, before leaving the kitchen.

As could be expected, nearly everyone was inside the dining hall, and the entry hall was completely abandoned. Renatus strode past the open door, preparing himself for the onslaught of teenage attention, but no one noticed him, either because the diners were too absorbed by their conversations or because the entry hall was not well-lit enough for Renatus to be easily seen.

Either way, he didn't care.

Darkness was creeping over the grounds now. Renatus, in his black cloak, blended straight in, heading purposefully across the grass towards the orchard at the edge of his property. Knowing where he was going, thinking about his impending destination, he began to feel slightly ill, as he always did whenever he tried to visit his past.

The past should be left be, Lord Gawain had said. He was a wise man, with Renatus's best interests at heart, like Fionnuala. But could he really understand? He had not lost that day. He'd witnessed Renatus's loss. Renatus had lost everything, and gained nothing but anger and a thirst for revenge. And he had thought he'd had his revenge, but now there was only a need to get it right this time, to do better.

Lord Gawain could not understand. And he would not. Not ever. Renatus would ensure it.

Some things were best left in the past, and the past should be left be.

Renatus had reached the edge of the orchard and stopped at the beginning of the pathway. The darkness was strongest right here, on this pathway, the site of his first act of darkest magic. The beginning of a lifetime spiralling downward. The stain of such an act was not something that simply washed away in the rain.

He had not been back here in the seven years that had passed since that day.

However, in the past week, he had begun to wonder whether his one act of evil had been enough. New information has a way of shedding new, and sometimes concerning, light on old situations.

Somebody would pay for this. Somebody already had, but it wasn't enough. It didn't bring back what Renatus had lost.

A soft and familiar presence was approaching. Renatus stared down the pathway to the cast iron gate, wondering whether he would ever be strong enough to follow this path to its end, open that gate and visit what lay beyond. Lord Gawain made his way over, closer and closer, until he was standing right beside Renatus, silent as well.

After several minutes, the older man spoke.

'My friend, they will not begrudge you for staying away so long,' he said gently. 'Is it finally time?'

Renatus stared through the trees at the tall grey headstones that stood, ghostly and elegant, beyond the gate in the family graveyard. Many he had visited as a child, ancestors he had never known. Three, he knew, had been there for seven years and had never been visited by a soul since the day they were buried.

'Not today,' Renatus answered finally, hating himself for his cowardice. But the fact was that he could not bear the thought of standing beside their final resting places, reaching out with his hands and feeling nothing but dirt; reaching out for them with his energy and feeling nothing at all. Knowing, all the while, that in some sick way even he could not comprehend, their deaths were his own fault. How could they not be, when their bodies and souls had been destroyed and he had been left virtually unscathed?

His soul had been destroyed, too, but that had been his own fault. He had chosen his actions.

He turned away.

'Then when?' Lord Gawain asked, turning in unison with his protégé and beginning the slow walk back to the house.

'Maybe tomorrow,' Renatus said doubtfully. *Maybe never*.

'Things will not always be as they are now, Renatus,' Lord Gawain commented. 'You of all people know how quickly life can change. Tomorrow is a new day, and it may be the exact day you are waiting for.'

'You always have the right advice to give me, Master,' Renatus said, feeling his stomach unknot as they moved further and further from that place. He finally met the leader's eyes. The cool blue was always lit with respect and fatherly love when he looked upon Renatus. 'You have given me so much.'

He thought of the first time they had met. Lord Gawain and Lisandro, close friends and colleagues then, had arrived at the estate's gates and had been let inside by one of Fionnuala's daughters. The two White Elm had come straight to the orchard, where already the servants were combing the fallen trees for the family of the house. Lord Gawain had been the one to find Renatus, only fifteen years of age then, in shock, standing over the unrecognisable body of his twenty-year-old sister, his black hair plastered to his face from the rain and his shirt spattered with blood. And, instead of assuming the worst of the boy, Lord Gawain had rushed past the dead body and gathered Renatus into a tight embrace.

'Thank heavens you're alright. Come away from here, my boy,' he'd said. His blue eyes then had been filled with an unbearable concern.

Concern that Renatus knew he didn't deserve.

Would Lord Gawain have been so loving and protective of Renatus had he known what the boy had done in the minutes before their arrival? Had he known where the blood on his clothes had come from, would he still have gathered the boy into his arms and half-carried him away from that place?

If he knew what Renatus was capable of, and what went through the younger man's head, would he have ever allowed him to rise to the position of Dark Keeper?

Certainly not was the answer to all questions.

chapter thirteen

That evening, I wrote to my aunt and uncle while Hiroko wrote to her father, Xanthe wrote to her family, and Sterling chattered about nothing.

'Damn,' Xanthe murmured, as her pencil's lead snapped. She glanced over her desk, and then turned to the rest of us. 'Does anyone have a pencil sharpener?' She held up her pencil to show us what had happened. Sterling shook her head and continued going through her clothes, all the while chatting about what she was going to wear the following day. She was easy to block out. I glanced at my pencil sharpener, glinting of dull silver as it sat, unused, in my disorganised pile of stationery.

'I don't,' Hiroko apologised. Xanthe frowned, and turned her attention to me. Her gaze met mine.

'Aristea?' she asked. I paused for probably a second too long, but I nodded, forced a smile and stood, pencil sharpener in hand.

'Aye, it's fine,' I said, walking over and passing

it to her. Perhaps I'd been too hard on her, I thought, as she thanked me, smiled quickly, and sharpened her broken pencil. She handed it back, and I went back to my desk, hoping that meant that our unofficial argument was over.

The weekend was uneventful but enjoyable. I spent a great deal of time doing very little, playing cards with Hiroko, leafing through Sterling's magazines, going for walks around the grounds with the girls (which was much more comfortable now that Xanthe wasn't ignoring me) and doing the little amount of homework I'd been set.

At breakfast on Monday, one of the servants, the portly little lady dressed in green I'd seen talking with Renatus (Fionnuala?), handed me an envelope with my name printed on it in Angela's handwriting. I didn't ask how she knew who I was.

To: *Aristea Byrne*
        House of Morrissey

From: *A. Byrne*
        9 Cairn Gardens
        Coleraine

I tore it open and began to read, eagerly.

Aristea,

I received your letter this morning (it's Thursday) and had to write back to you straight away. It sounds like you're having the most amazing time there. I laughed when I read what you said about your friend Sterling and her obsession with your headmaster – I had a girl in my class at primary school who always said that she was in love with our teacher.

In your next letter you must tell me everything there is to know about Lord Gawain and Lady Miranda! Are they as amazing and incredible as the rumours say? I don't want to just take Aunt Leanne's word for it...

What is Renatus like in true life? Kell and I were just saying last night that he's the one White Elm that you never hear anything about. All I know is what you'd hear from gossip, so I was surprised when you said he is your headmaster. I thought that surely Lord Gawain or somebody high up would be in charge.

Your new friends sound lovely and your classes sound fantastic – I'm almost drowning in envy.

Sorry that this letter has been so short. Nearly nothing has been happening in my life. Work is dull, household chores are dull (although the sheer amount of chores to be done has noticeably decreased since you left) and being by myself in the house is dull. Kelly has been coming over in the evenings to keep me company, though, so don't you worry about me. Just focus on your studies!

Make sure you write again soon.

Love you so much xox

~ Angela

I smiled and reread the letter. Angela's handwriting was so neat, precise and familiar; reading words written by her hand was almost as good as hearing her voice. She was a receptionist, with access to a computer all day every weekday, but I was grateful that she hadn't thought to fill in her spare time at work by writing to me. Typed letters, though often longer, simply did not compare to handwritten notes.

Hiroko, too, had received a letter, I noticed eventually. I glanced over the page, unintentionally peeking, but it didn't matter anyway. The entire letter was hand-printed in elegant Japanese script. To me, it was such a pretty and exotic-looking written language. I wondered whether it would be difficult to learn.

Breakfast finished, and since we had no classes first up, Hiroko and I went for a wander through the grounds. It was another beautiful day, and when Hiroko commented on this, I told her not to get too used to it. It wasn't going to last, it never did. We saw a young hare bounding across the grass, and I pointed out to Hiroko the differences between the hare and a rabbit.

'My father has been very busy with work,' Hiroko informed me as we peered into a rabbit hole, waiting to see if anything came out. 'He works for the biggest bank in Sapporo. It is not a very magical job but he likes it very much and he must work so I can learn English and go to good schools.'

'My father built furniture,' I told her, remembering how Darren Byrne had always been good with his hands. 'One year, when I was only very young and hardly old enough to even play in it, my father built a tree house in our yard. It was mainly for my brother and sister, because they were older and they could climb to it. But when they outgrew it, it was all mine.'

'And now, you live only with your sister?' Hiroko added hesitantly. She glanced at me sideways, obviously hoping not to upset me, but curious all the same. For a long time I didn't know what to say. I hadn't talked to anyone about this, except relatives, at any point since it happened. I hadn't even spoken to the grief counsellor. Was I up to it? How to even start? Hiroko was still waiting, but she wouldn't be affronted if I declined to discuss the matter. She would understand. With that in mind, I sat down on the grass and I just said it.

'My parents and brother died when I was fourteen.'

'How awful,' Hiroko stated, sitting down beside me. 'What happened?'

'There was a big storm, and a tree fell in the wind and killed them,' I said, expecting tears and tightness in my throat. Surprisingly, it didn't hurt as much as I expected it to. It felt kind of relieving to share my experience with someone who cared and honestly wanted to know. 'My sister and I had to find somewhere else to live, and we've had our aunt and her family for support.'

'My mother is dead, too,' Hiroko told me, without hesitation. 'She died in an accident, in a car, when I was a five-year-old. She was pregnant. So, I have no brothers or sisters.'

I tried to imagine losing my mother at age five. Who would have kissed better my bruises? Who would have sung me to sleep? Who would have read

183

to me? That was when I'd needed her the most. I'd lost my mother after fourteen years of love; Hiroko had lost hers after only five.

I tried to imagine life without my siblings, as an only child. I tried to imagine my father's hands building a tree house intended for me alone. I tried to imagine wanting anything for my own reasons, instead of just because my brother and sister had one. I couldn't. Hiroko would have been a big sister, I realised, had this accident not taken away her mother. And I knew she would have been a fantastic one, just like Angela.

'I'm sorry,' I said, and it was true. I'd never felt sorrier for somebody else in my life. It was a strange feeling, to pity her instead of myself. Hiroko smiled.

'There is nothing to be sorry for,' she said, getting up and beginning to walk again. I did the same and fell into step. 'Life can still be happy without a person I love. I can still have my father; you can still have your sister.'

I thought over the wisdom of her words. She was basically telling me to be grateful for what I still had. In truth, I realised that Angela and I would not be as close as sisters had we not lost everything else. I imagined that Hiroko and her father, too, would have come together following the death of the late Mrs Sasaki.

Even though I already liked Hiroko, and already felt a connection with her, I felt another level of closeness form. We had so much more in common than I could have imagined a week ago.

Before my scrying lesson, I spent half an hour

practising with my candle. I'd spent every moment of my weekend alone-time staring into that stupid candle, staring and concentrating and straining until my head ached and my normal vision was swimming.

Qasim was staying at Morrissey House for much of this week, so we were to have a scrying lesson almost every day, except Wednesday, when apparently too many other classes were running for him to be able to have an uninterrupted lesson. I couldn't wait to get into this week, to get better and to show Qasim how good I could be at his subject.

Trying to ignore the dull ache in the back of my head, I sat down in the scrying classroom with Xanthe. Hopefully we'd leave this lesson on better terms than we had the last.

Did you do the exercises? I heard Qasim's voice clearly in my head. I looked at him, but he carried on with preparing his lesson. I tried to think affirmative thoughts. I felt his mental fingers probing my recent memories and witnessing my candle burning out, minutes before, from overuse. I felt his surprise.

I'm glad you didn't shirk this, he said. *I worried that without this work, you might have regressed. Another few good tugs and it should be free of its blocks.*

'To begin, we will continue with last week's exercise,' Qasim said to the group. He began to hand out candles, lighting them as he went. 'One partner stands behind the seat of another, holding up a number of fingers. The seated partner scries themselves and their own surroundings, and counts their partner's fingers. Please begin.'

I stood as soon as I had my lit candle, allowing Xanthe the first turn at scrying. I positioned myself behind her where she couldn't see my hand behind her head and held my open hand up – five.

When it was my turn to scry, I got it within seconds – three fingers. Xanthe smiled, a small smile but a smile nonetheless, and we swapped places. After five minutes, Qasim stopped us. My head was swimming again.

'As promised, today we will begin working towards scrying without tools,' the Scrier said, taking a seat in an armchair. 'Put out the candles.' We did. 'This next step requires a great deal of mental strain and effort. The jump from tool to unaided scrying is a difficult one, but I am confident that you will all show progress very quickly, and with the potential contained within the people in this room, I don't want to waste time teaching you different ways to tool-scry when you have the ability to take the next step. Knowing how to tool-scry is useless when you can't light a flame or have no access to crystals or mirrors or water.'

He paused, and we were silent, considering this truth. Qasim looked around at us.

'Please close your eyes and regulate your breathing,' he said. I did as I was told, although I felt disappointment – I *hated* meditation. 'You must turn your attention inward. You must locate your talent and try to exercise it in the same way as when you have a candle. It is difficult to receive the images without a tool at first, but the methodology is the same.'

He continued to speak and give instructions, but I couldn't listen to him *and* follow his instructions at the same time. I couldn't concentrate like that. Instead, I blocked out his voice and began searching the back of my mind for my scrying talent. I knew exactly where to find it, hidden at the back, throbbing dully with overuse. I tried to think of exactly how I had used it only minutes before with the candle flame, but it wasn't something I could really explain to myself, let alone anyone else. It was like making a fist. You don't know exactly how you do it – there's some unconscious nerve and muscle involvement, certainly – you just *do*. When I had been practising scrying, I'd just *done* it. I tried to break it down, but all I could really identify was a stretching and straining sensation that didn't really answer my question. That was how it *felt*, not how it was *done*.

Overwhelmed by the impossibility, I opened my eyes. All seven of my peers were sitting silently, concentrating madly. Qasim met my eyes.

If you think it's impossible, then it is, he said. *Just give up.*

It sounded like a taunt or a challenge, and I resisted the urge to glare at him. I worked to keep my expression neutral. I would *not* give up. This subject was my dream. I was going to try, and I was going to *succeed*, regardless of what the Scrier believed or said.

It took all week for me to show any signs of progress. Why did my dream subject have to be so difficult? I practised every morning and night and any moment I had to myself, but nothing changed. One by one, throughout the week, my classmates announced that they had started to see things, and with each person's success I felt more deeply panicked. What was wrong with me? My friends reported almost daily of their adventures in their preferred areas of magic – Hiroko was teleporting herself all over the place, apparently, and Sterling had foreseen something I hadn't cared to listen to – so why wasn't I getting any better at mine?

'You will,' Hiroko assured me optimistically at dinner on Friday when I quietly voiced my concerns. 'It will only take time.'

In my memory, the days of that week all blurred together, one big blob of time filled with fuzzy everyday motions, lots of attempts at scrying and an ever-worsening headache. Each successive lesson was every bit just a repeat of the previous day's feelings of frustration and failure. Qasim's scrying lessons were getting steadily more intensive and I didn't seem to be improving at the same rate as everyone else. After a full seven days of nothing – bringing me into my third week at the Academy – the White Elm councillor asked me to stay back after the other seven students had left. I sat back down in my seat, ignoring Xanthe's curious backward glance.

'Aristea, you have a lot of potential in this discipline,' he began, sitting down in his armchair. 'I understand that you have an interest in the art of scrying. Are you motivated to learn what I can teach you?'

'Yes,' I said honestly, wondering why he couldn't tell how tired I was, how achy I felt.

'Are you practising?'

'Aye, all the time.' I tried to sit a little straighter, wanting to be taken more seriously. But no matter how I sat, it wouldn't change the fact that I sucked at the one thing I wanted to be good at. I slumped down again. 'I don't know what I'm doing wrong.'

'Here,' Qasim said suddenly, handing me a fresh candle and lighting it with his hand. 'Look into it and scry. Expect an image. Think of nothing. Do not scry yourself.'

I did as he said, staring into the flame and willing an image to magically present itself. Was it so easy?

'Yes, it is that easy,' Qasim said, reading my thoughts. 'With an aid, you should find this simple and natural. It is the jump between aided and unaided scrying that is difficult.'

Some time passed, maybe as much as ten minutes. Qasim said nothing. Very slowly, a bubble appeared to me in the middle of the flame, and expanded into a moving image. A vision.

'I can see a beach, a stony beach,' I told him, trying not to allow my excitement to destroy the image. 'There are a lot of birds flying around. There's something in the water, in the shallows, that they're after.'

I paused, paying closer attention. The birds were hungry, I knew that much. The bulky thing in the low surf looked like a rock, black and wet, but was shifting a little with the tide.

'It's not a rock,' I said, still trying to decipher this vision. 'It's something dead. Maybe a seal or something? Although…'

Qasim had gone very still. His eyes were burning with intense interest.

'Don't look at the seal, Aristea,' he instructed firmly. 'Look around the beach. Where is it? Can you see any signs or buildings?'

I drew my attention away from the dead thing drifting in the water and tried to sort of zoom out. It turned out that I could. I looked around and saw a small, hand-painted wooden sign.

'"Smithy's beach",' I read. '"Private property. Keep out". It's a cold beach, and there're no people. There's a small house a few hundred metres up the beach, but there's no one living there. Maybe it's a holiday home? It has a garden and all the flowers are full-bloom.'

'Have you seen this beach before?' Qasim asked quietly, and I, stupidly, shook my head, breaking my eye contact with my scried image. 'Is there anything else? The birds?'

'The birds were black-headed gulls,' I told him, though I was uncertain as to what else he wanted to know. 'We used to see them a lot when we lived near the beach near Coleraine. I think they're all over the UK and Europe, though.'

Qasim abruptly put out my candle with a click of his fingers and took the candlestick.

'I am glad to see improvement, Aristea, but scrying with a flame is something all of your class can already do,' he said bluntly. I deflated rather quickly. 'You have potential to be great. Is that what you want?'

'Yes. Every day.'

'Good,' he said, itching a spot on his chin. His fingernail running across the bristles of his beard made a scratchy sound. 'I'll see some improvement by Thursday morning, then?'

I nodded and left, worried. What if the work I'd been putting in wasn't enough? What would happen if, come Thursday, I still hadn't shown any improvement? Would I be given more homework? Moved into a different class? Asked to leave the school for not being good enough?

I didn't even attend dinner that night, so busy was I with my scrying practice. I lay on my bed in the silence, my eyes closed, trying *so, so* hard to envision myself in third-person and then to actually scry myself. Just to scry *anything*, like that beach, would be fine. But nothing was happening. I wasn't even getting a flicker or a momentary change of focus, like I had with the candle when I'd first started. *Nothing* was happening, except that my headache was steadily worsening with each passing half hour that I wasted achieving nothing.

Was this what life was going to be like at the Academy from now on? A constant headache, literally?

The next day we played a hot potato-style game with a round, smooth quartz in Jadon's class. Each person in the circle would hold the quartz for five seconds, imbuing it with as much energy as the person could transfer in that amount of time, as pass it on. As the game progressed, the time in each hand was reduced to four seconds, then three and then two. The idea was for the crystal to never lose its glow, and to glow more brightly as it was passed between students – to hold the energy we gave it – and for us to learn how to transfer energy quicker as the game became faster. The lesson was fun (minus the write-up) and took my mind off my scrying concerns for a while. When it ended, though, I had the rest of the day free from classes to spend stressing. At dinner, Sophia commented on how pale I looked.

'No subject is worth this,' she chastised when I explained. 'You shouldn't be hurting yourself.'

'I'm not,' I insisted quickly. 'I'm just working really hard.'

'There might be a really good reason why you can't scry yet,' Sophia warned. 'I've read about cases where sorcerers have discovered gifts they never knew about because they were buried by the mind, like trauma and suppressed memories. The mind is a pretty amazing thing. You shouldn't mess with it too much.'

From what Qasim had said in my first class, I suspected that what Sophia had read applied to me, but I didn't say anything. She sighed and put down her fork.

'Can I try something?' she asked, offering a hand. 'I need your permission.'

'For what?' I slowly lowered my own hand towards hers, unsure what she wanted me to do.

'Sometimes, when our mom gets a headache, she has me try to soothe it.'

'She's really good at it,' Kendra added before I could refuse. 'She *is* a Healer.'

I shrugged and nodded, figuring that Sophia couldn't exactly make it any worse. I let my hand fall into hers and she closed her fingers.

'Just relax,' she suggested. I tried to do as she asked, closing my eyes and wondering how much good she could do with a pain that wasn't even physical. At first I detected no change, but I soon noticed her presence, silky and insubstantial, inside my aura. She brushed past my thoughts and I resisted the urge to shut down. She was going to help me.

When she found the source of the pain she worked quickly, and I felt the relief straightaway. I couldn't tell exactly what she was doing, because there was no injury per se and hence nothing to really *heal*. Regardless, my overwhelmed mind quickly quietened and calmed. The strained feeling faded. My worries fell away.

When Sophia removed herself, I opened my eyes and smiled at her. I felt blissfully calmer, and ten times more aware. My head was still throbbing lightly but it felt less intense.

'Better?' she asked. I grinned back.

'So much better,' I agreed. 'Thanks. You have the very best gift.'

I meant that. Even though scrying was my obsession, how cool was it to be able to undo migraines, stitch up cut skin, reverse broken bones and single-handedly fight off disease?

'Don't tell her that,' Kendra told me off light-heartedly. 'She pats herself on the back for it quite enough!'

We laughed and went back to our meals, but as we did, I glanced up and noticed several councillors of the White Elm watching us, concern on their faces. Their senses brushed over me one at a time, almost imperceptibly. I realised that they were making sure that Sophia had not tampered with my mind while she was inside. A sorcerer can do a lot of damage once inside another's mind.

I smiled briefly at Emmanuelle when she caught my eye, hoping that she would understand that Sophia was my friend and meant me no harm. She nodded once and tried to smile back, but the expression faltered on her face. I noticed, offhand, that she, too, looked rather pale. Her mouth was tight and her posture was tense. She'd been kind of airy and less-than-present during her lessons this week, too, I realised now, but I didn't know her well enough to know if this was unusual. I shifted my gaze to Elijah, beside her, and to Lord Gawain, beyond him. Both men were studiously eating their dinners, making no effort to make conversation with anyone else. I looked along the table at the only other councillor present – Glen – and noticed the same behaviour. Usually, their table was just as talkative as the student table.

'Where's Renatus?' Sterling asked, following my gaze to the councillors' table, at the same time that Hiroko asked Sophia, 'How long since you can first heal for headaches?'

'He's probably really busy, Sterling,' I said, as Sophia started relating her first memory of healing to Hiroko. 'He's hardly ever at dinner.'

'I guess,' Sterling agreed unhappily.

'And that was probably when I was about five. Or maybe six?' Sophia finished. Kendra swallowed her mouthful of soup and shook her head.

'No, we were five,' she insisted. She turned to Hiroko, sitting opposite me. 'When did you first learn to displace?'

I listened with interest as Hiroko said, 'I was ten years old when I first displaced by accident, and so my father began teaching me on the weekends when we go to the parks.'

'Kendra had a vision of our dad falling from a ladder when we were very little,' Sophia recounted suddenly, glancing at her sister. 'We didn't tell him because we thought it was a silly dream, but it happened that same day and he sprained his ankle. That's when our mother realised that Kendra was probably a Seer.'

Out of the corner of my eye, I saw Qasim enter the dining room and make his way over to his colleagues. I watched, paying only the vaguest attention, as he made eye contact with Lord Gawain, Glen and Elijah each in turn. All three men stood abruptly and left the dining hall with Qasim, leaving Emmanuelle alone at the table. She watched them leave, and I felt, distantly, a trickle of concern and sadness emanating from her. Were they keeping a secret from her?

'When I was seven, I had a vision of my mother in a hospital holding a new baby wrapped in blue,' Xanthe spoke up. 'Up until then they'd only had daughters, and my mother didn't even know then that she was pregnant again, so when I told them what I'd dreamt, they were pretty happy. I'd seen a few other things before that, but they just dismissed it as coincidence until my brother was born.'

'I've Seen a few things,' Sterling agreed, though she didn't go into detail. For once. 'It started for me when I was little. I don't remember when, exactly.'

The girls turned to me expectantly. My stomach flipped nervously. I didn't really know what my gift was, and I hadn't really ever done anything extraordinary to indicate what my gift might be.

'Have you scried anything before coming here?' Sophia asked when I didn't speak. I shrugged uncomfortably.

'I...No, I'm not quite as gifted as you all,' I said lamely, trying unsuccessfully to make it into a joke. 'Unfortunately, I've never Seen anything or healed anything.'

Sophia cocked her head to one side slightly, regarding me.

'No, because you're a scrier,' she said.

Sterling laughed and began talking about how sometimes she wasn't sure if maybe she was meant to be a Crafter, but I wasn't listening. I leaned closer to Sophia.

'You're sure?' I asked, keeping my voice soft and hoping she wouldn't laugh. 'Are you positive that I'm a scrier?'

'One hundred percent,' she promised in an equally low voice. 'I learnt to sense and feel energies very young, years before my sister. I was always able to classify the witches I met into six groups, though it wasn't until I was older that I realised that I was able to sense the energetic features that define the classes.' She shrugged, slightly embarrassed, and cleared her throat before continuing. 'Every class *feels* different – that is, Healers feel different from Seers or Displacers or scriers. Next time you're focussing on auras and energies, compare Kendra, Sterling and Xanthe. They're all very different but there's a part of them that's just the same.'

'I had no idea that anyone could read into energies that deeply, other than the White Elm,' I commented in an admiring tone. 'Is it something anyone could do if they tried, or is it just because you're a Healer that you can do it?'

'I've met others who can do it, not all of them Healers.'

'You're so lucky to be so talented,' I said, slightly envious. I looked around. 'Everyone here is really talented.'

'That's right,' she agreed, sipping her juice. 'That's why you're here, too.' She smiled as I blinked, then continued before I could argue. 'It turns out that anyone can learn to read energy. I was lucky, learning early. Kendra was just slower, but eventually she worked it out, too, to a point.'

'It probably helps that *she's* a Healer, being naturally attuned to others and energies,' Kendra interjected, overhearing. 'I might have learnt to read people sooner if my gift were one that actually involves other people.'

The twins bickered playfully for a few minutes, and my attention shifted inward. Sophia was *one hundred percent positive* that I was a true scrier. Qasim had indicated that I had a lot of potential as a scrier. Could it be?

That night, after dinner and after the usual chat with my roommates, I lay in bed smiling. Sophia's insistence that I was a scrier was a huge encouragement. Could she be right? How reliable was her opinion? She seemed like a knowledgeable and respectable sort of source.

Was it possible that I was already everything I'd ever wanted to be? Could it be that I just needed to work on fine-tuning my skills?

I wanted to believe it. Did believing make the difference?

I closed my eyes and concentrated, though not hard.

I'm already everything I've ever wanted to be. I am a natural scrier.

I pictured myself and the room, and instead of straining my mind for results, I allowed myself to wait. I kept thinking: *I'm a natural. I don't need to try. It will come to me.*

And it did.

Slowly, reluctantly at first, something shifted in my mind and a dim image of the room and its four unmoving occupants came into focus.

I was scrying. All by myself. *All by myself!* No candle, no crystal. Unassisted, unaided.

It was enough for me. I opened my eyes and allowed the image in the forefront of my mind to fade away. I wasn't going to be kicked out of my class for lack of improvement. Grinning uncontrollably, I rolled over and went to sleep.

I drifted off reasonably quickly, but soon found myself rising back to consciousness. I experienced an odd and unfamiliar sensation right before waking, though, of floating or flying. I flexed my shoulders by way of stretching, wondering what the time was, and opened my eyes.

I was standing in front of a window.

chapter fourteen

I gasped loudly and jumped backwards, shocked. *Where am I?* I had only just gone to bed, hadn't I? Was I dreaming? I seemed awfully conscious and aware for this to be a dream.

The window was arched and large, and overlooked a great deal of black. I could see nothing through it. I glanced around as my heart hammered against my ribs. *What's going on?* I turned slowly to my left, taking in the elegant bookcases, stiff armchairs and the spaciousness of the room I was in. Opposite the window was a tall, thin door, much like the others in the house.

At least I haven't left the house.

I turned further, noticed a large desk, and got another shock. A man sat at the desk, his narrow shoulders stooped over the letter he was writing, his dark hair obscuring his face. He hadn't noticed me yet. I wondered whether this was his office and whether I'd be in trouble for being here, this late at night. I realised suddenly that I was still wearing my pyjamas.

'Um, hi…I'm…' I began to apologise, but even as I spoke I realised that something wasn't right. The man didn't look up at me in response, or even startle at the sound of an unfamiliar voice in his private office. Perhaps he was deaf. I took a nervous step closer, and finally he moved. He craned his neck a little to stretch out a kink and used one pale, spidery hand to brush his longish black hair out of his face.

It was Renatus.

Sure that he'd be able to see me now that his hair was not covering his eyes, I began apologising once again.

'Uh, Sir, I'm really sorry about this,' I said, but nothing had changed. The headmaster continued etching word after word with his elegant fountain pen, the scratchy sound the only thing I could hear above my own thudding heartbeat. 'Sir?' I waved experimentally, but still, nothing. 'Sir? Renatus?'

He couldn't see me. He couldn't hear me. He was completely unaware of my presence. Was I dead? Surely not: I was young and healthy, how likely was it that I'd gone to bed and just died? This had to be a dream. And yet, it was so real. The desk was solid dark wood. It was piled high with tidily stacked papers and books. It was highly impersonal – no photo frames, no personal possessions…even the fountain pens were identical and lined up neatly in their own little space in the top left corner. Obviously, this was the workspace of a highly meticulous mind.

I thought to tell Sterling of this, then realised with another little jolt where I actually was. The headmaster's office – his private office that Emmanuelle had told us was so private, it had no doorhandle and was spelled to keep people out...

I hurried to the door, but already knew what I'd find. It had hinges, but where the doorknob should have been, there was nothing. I looked around for a way out. I didn't want to be caught here. What if one of his spells detected me and I got zapped or whatever? How much trouble would I be in when he finally worked out I was here?

I looked back at Renatus. Still, no response at all, no indication he had any idea he wasn't alone. I considered shouting his name, but I wasn't sure yet whether I was actually here or just dreaming, and it would be way too embarrassing to wake the other girls up shouting aloud the name of the headmaster. Xanthe and Hiroko wouldn't let me hear the end of it.

'What's going on?' I wondered aloud, moving away from the door and around the room. The bookcase was filled with some very old and mismatched books. Some looked like published texts; others might have been diaries. They spoke to me the same way the library ones did and I reached out to touch a particularly battered book's spine, but my fingertips had not quite extended far enough when there was a sharp knock at the door. Startled, I snatched my hand back and spun around.

Renatus had looked up and was gazing at the door with a thoughtful, calculating expression. I stepped closer to him, wondering how he'd heard that knock but still hadn't noticed me. He put his pen down and waved his left hand lightly through the air –*These are not the droids you're looking for*, I thought.

Instead, the door swung inward, and Emmanuelle strode in. Renatus sat straighter in his seat and his eyes grew concerned as she approached. I could see why. Her beautiful hair was ruffled; her cloak was sitting on her shoulders funny, as though she'd just thrown it on and not bothered to straighten it out. I couldn't see auras, but I could feel them as well as any other witch. Emmanuelle was flustered, upset and angry, and looked as though she were on the verge of tears.

'Emmanuelle…' Renatus said softly, sounding both resigned and concerned. She, too, ignored me, and marched up to his desk.

'When were you planning to tell me?' she demanded. Her voice was very high and she didn't sound far away from losing control. 'Is it true?'

Renatus regarded Emmanuelle for a moment, as though assessing what he should and shouldn't say. I stepped closer again, frightened by Emmanuelle's hysteria but curious all the same.

'Why don't you sit down?' Renatus suggested finally, but apparently it was the wrong thing to say.

'*Sit down?*' Emmanuelle repeated furiously. 'I don't *think* so. I'm just *fine*. Why don't *you* start by telling me what you know? If it's what I think it is, if it's about P-Peter, and you think I'm too delicate to 'ear it, then you're wrong.' Her voice broke at the name, contradicting her words. 'If you think I'm too weak-'

'I don't think you're weak,' Renatus interrupted her. He was still sitting at his desk, gazing up at her with intense violet eyes. 'We both know that you're a very powerful and gifted sorceress.'

'So,' she said, calming down a little, 'tell me what you know. Where 'ave Lord Gawain, Glen, Qasim and Elijah gone tonight?'

Renatus held her furious gaze for a few seconds, but eventually had to back down and look away.

'Emmanuelle, please take a seat,' he said softly. 'I'll have Fionnuala bring you a drink of something-'

'*No*,' Emmanuelle shouted. I jumped in shock and moved away, so I was standing near the darkened window. What had I dreamt myself into? Tears of frustration were glistening in the French sorceress's eyes now. 'I will *not* be treated as a child, and not by you. You *bastard*! You know! *Tell me*! 'ow dare you 'ide this from me? You told me scrying doesn't develop this late in life – you told me it was a dream. You let me think myself an idiot!'

Renatus finally stood up so that he was facing her, looking down at her slightly. She was a tall woman, but he was taller.

'I'm trying to *protect* you,' he argued.

'I don't need you to protect me,' Emmanuelle said furiously, but quickly softened, her sadness curtaining the anger. She struggled to control herself and, in a tight monotone, she said, '*S'il vous plait*; please...tell me – is it true, what I think? What I saw?'

Slowly, Renatus nodded. Emmanuelle seemed to crumple. The anger and tension left her, and suddenly she wasn't so tall. She took a step back.

'Tell me everything,' she murmured hollowly. Renatus rounded his desk and leant against its opposite side.

'Tell me how you found out,' he countered gently. Her return look was cold.

'You first,' she said firmly.

'It happened a little while ago,' he said delicately, watching her closely for signs of a breakdown or explosion. 'I'm not sure when, exactly. I've known for about a week. It was quick,' he added.

Tears had begun to stream down Emmanuelle's face.

'How?' she asked brokenly, pronouncing every phoneme in the word.

'Lisandro.'

I walked over and sat down on one of the stiff-looking armchairs in front of the desk. It was comfier than it looked. Still, neither councillor noticed me. What had Lisandro done? I didn't know what his capabilities were. This Peter person, whoever he was, seemed to have died, and according to Renatus, Lisandro was somehow involved.

'But *how*?' Emmanuelle insisted, although she was shaking by now.

'Quickly,' Renatus said again. When she looked up and opened her mouth to press him for details, he said, 'I'd rather not discuss the rest. What's important is that you remember him as he was to you.'

Emmanuelle was silent for several moments, trying to suppress sobs.

'It was a while ago,' she whispered after a wait. 'The night the students came 'ere. There was a note in my garden, I found it today. It was dated March the first. Peter's handwriting. It just said, "Forgive me, love". Why would 'e call me that? 'e never said it before. Did 'e...?'

'Did he mean it?' Renatus finished for her in a quiet voice. Emmanuelle nodded, crying openly now. 'We believe so. Don't you?'

Again, she nodded. She managed to choke out something unintelligible, and had to take several deep breaths before she could say it properly.

''e never told me,' she whispered. 'Why wouldn't 'e just tell me? Things might be different. *Peter*...'

'I'm sure he had his reasons. Maybe he thought he had more time.'

'I always thought 'e would come back. I *hoped*.' Emmanuelle stressed the word enough to make the h sound. She covered her face with her hands.

'We all did,' Renatus reminded her softly. She slowly dropped her hands and met his eyes.

Suddenly, Emmanuelle stepped forward and threw herself into Renatus's arms, wrapping her arms around his neck and back. She pressed her mouth against his and kissed him fiercely.

Shocked again, I jumped to my feet. *This* was unexpected. Emmanuelle, who had seemed to know so little about the headmaster when Sterling had badgered her, who had seemed even resentful of his power and magical abilities, who had spoken to him so coolly the other morning, was involved with

Renatus?

Emmanuelle's manicured fingers slid through her colleague's soft black hair as she kissed him deeply. Renatus leaned backwards, lightly knocking the closest pile of papers. A few sheets drifted to the floor. Emmanuelle pressed herself close and held him tight, as though concerned that he, too, might disappear from her life.

My cheeks burned with embarrassment. I wished *I* could disappear. I was trapped in an office, watching my two most beautiful teachers make out. I considered running to the door and slamming my fists against the heavy oak until it opened, but then thankfully, I was given a reprieve.

Renatus's hands tightened around Emmanuelle's upper arms and he pulled her away from him.

'Emmanuelle,' he said. 'Stop.'

It was a simple command, but without much force. Emmanuelle shook her head childishly and shook him off.

'No,' she said, pulling him close again for a second kiss. Again, it wasn't long before Renatus ended it, but while it lasted, it was intense. Emmanuelle kissed him with such force that I would not have been surprised if either of their lips were bruised. I'd never kissed anyone like that so I didn't know. She moved her hands to his cheeks and held his face tight.

'Emmanuelle,' Renatus said again, taking her shoulders firmly and holding her away. 'Stop. We both know it isn't me that you want.'

My supervisor stared at him with watery eyes, her skin flushed, her lips red. Then she dissolved into tears, dropping her hands to his shoulders and collapsing against him. Renatus ran a hand up and down her spine reassuringly for a few moments, then led her to one of the deceptively plush armchairs. He sat her down, and dragged the nearest one a little closer for himself. He conjured a tissue from thin air and handed it to her as though nothing had just happened between them.

'*Je suis désolée*, I'm so sorry,' Emmanuelle sobbed as Renatus sat down opposite her. '*Je ne l'ai pas fait exprès.* I didn't mean to…I don't know…I just…'

Renatus rested a hand on her knee. It was a supportive gesture, meant to convey understanding and sympathy. Soon, Emmanuelle calmed down. She hiccoughed and excused herself for it.

'Did you see it? The end, I mean,' Emmanuelle asked finally. Renatus nodded. 'I only saw 'im for an instant, underwater – 'e closed 'is eyes and then I woke up. Did 'e suffer?'

'His last words were, "I never told her I love her". Peter's main concern at his death was that he'd lost his chance with you. I think the root of his deepest suffering was that you might hate him for what he'd done.'

Fresh tears ran over the French sorceress's cheeks, but she smiled. Renatus hadn't answered her question about Peter's suffering in quite the way I'm sure she'd expected, but it seemed to be the right thing for her to hear.

'I don't *hate* 'im. I 'ope 'e knew 'ow much 'e

meant to me, too,' she murmured.

'You'll have your chance to tell him, probably tomorrow,' Renatus told her. 'Lord Gawain took the others tonight to retrieve the body. I imagine there will be a funeral service here tomorrow morning.'

'What will 'appen to 'im?' Emmanuelle asked, and Renatus hesitated. His intense eyes flickered towards the window, passing right over me without seeing.

'Does his family have a place of burial?'

'I don't think so. Nowhere in particular. The Chisholms are very scattered.' Emmanuelle sniffed delicately, and Renatus looked at his hands.

'If you would like,' he said slowly, 'Peter could be buried here. With my family. If you would like. It's entirely up to you – you knew him best.'

Even though I barely knew him, I could sense how reluctant Renatus was to give this – how much it cost him to even say it. His expression was conflicted. He wanted to give Emmanuelle this small consolation, yet something else was making him hesitate. Family pride? Emmanuelle smiled, and it seemed to light up the room, so genuine and hard-earned was the expression.

'*Merci beaucoup*, Renatus,' she said warmly. 'This offer means a lot to me. But if it is up to me, I think 'e should be cremated, and 'is ashes given to 'is grandmother. She was the only family 'e could count upon.'

Renatus visibly relaxed, and nodded smoothly.

'Other than you,' he said. 'I'm sure she appreciate the gesture.'

Emmanuelle nodded, and opened her mouth to say something, but hesitated. She stared at him in silence for a long, long moment.

'This is a stupid question,' she whispered, 'but I ask anyway…can I trust you?'

Renatus, too, hesitated.

'I hope you will learn to,' he answered eventually. Emmanuelle reached over and took his hand.

'And words spoken in this room…they are completely safe?'

'Absolutely. No one else can hear you.'

I shifted uncomfortably. Um, sorry, but I'm standing here denying your truth.

'Then…' Emmanuelle hesitated again, tightening her grip on his hand. 'There's something else. A list, with your name, in Lisandro's hand.'

'What?' Renatus tried to pull his hand away, but Emmanuelle held on.

'There are other names, too. Some dead, some alive. Some very unexpected. Don't stress, I don't 'ave it with me anyway,' she said. 'It doesn't matter, not in light of this.'

She looked significantly at their joined hands, and something changed. I peered closely. Her thumb seemed to be changing colour…No, a ring was appearing. A dull, wide, silver band with a big stone set in. A strong presence seemed to be growing in the room, too, and it was only after a bit of energetic searching that I realised with a shock that a strong welling of power was coming *from* the ring.

Renatus took a deep breath. Emmanuelle looked

up at him.

'It's mine now,' she said. 'Peter left it with the note.' She held his gaze. 'Do you want to take it from me? I won't stop you – we both know I would not win. You can 'ave it.'

Slowly, Renatus pulled his hand from hers.

'There's a very good reason why the weapons are kept separate,' he said, mystifying me. 'I won't take it from you. I won't accept it from you if you offer it. It's yours now.'

Emmanuelle stared at him for a long time, seemingly surprised but also apprehensive, as though waiting for him to change his mind. When he did not, she broke the silence with a choked, awkward laugh.

'I've never given you enough credit, 'ave I?'

A harsh, heavy knock sounded at the door, startling both Emmanuelle and myself. Renatus waved his hand briefly, and we all watched as the door opened again and Qasim entered. Renatus stood quickly, and Emmanuelle wiped her eyes. Qasim surveyed the scene before him, which apparently didn't include me, and glared at Renatus.

'What did you say to her?' he asked, his tone making his annoyance clear. 'I thought we agreed to wait.'

'He told me what I deserved to 'ear,' Emmanuelle said testily, standing also and glaring back at the Scrier. 'What gave *you* the right to decide what information is shared with other councillors?'

'I don't know what *he* told you, but the four of us agreed not to share this with you until we had all

211

of the information,' Qasim responded coldly. 'That is, Lord Gawain, Lady Miranda, Renatus and myself. I would have thought that the collective wisdom of the four of us would be sufficient.'

'Where's Peter?' Emmanuelle said sharply, changing subjects. 'Is 'e *here*?'

'Emmanuelle,' Qasim said, staring at her hand, 'is that-'

'Yes, it is,' she snapped. 'Peter passed it to me. Now, where is 'e?'

'Glen and Elijah are bringing him now,' Qasim said. 'This changes things. When did you receive that?'

'I took possession of it today, but Peter left it for me over two weeks ago.'

'Interesting,' Qasim murmured. He turned his attention to Renatus. 'Lord Gawain is waiting for you in the ballroom. He would like to discuss funeral plans with you.'

'Emmanuelle has already made a decision on that,' Renatus said.

'Where was 'e?' Emmanuelle pressed, and I saw the two men glance at one another.

'On a private beach,' Qasim said.

'And why tonight?' Emmanuelle added insistently. 'Why have you waited a week before retrieving him?'

Qasim's eyes narrowed at Renatus – apparently, the younger councillor had said way too much.

'Our visions were indistinct and dated,' the headmaster explained, ignoring the Scrier. 'We had no way of knowing where the event was taking place. One of Qasim's students had an accompanying vision yesterday that gave us some further information – a place name; the bird life; the season of the area.'

'One of the students? Who?' Emmanuelle asked, looking between them. They gave her nothing further, but I felt my jaw drop.

I had scried a private beach yesterday, with plants flowering in spring and birds circling something dead. I had thought it was a seal or something.

Could that dark shape have in fact been a person? It would explain why Qasim had directed me to pull my attention away from it, if he had suspected the seal to be this Peter.

'Emmanuelle and I will meet with Lord Gawain to finalise her plans for the funeral,' Renatus was saying. He looked back to Qasim. 'My housekeeper, Fionnuala, has prepared the basement room for the body. You may meet her in the reception hall, and Glen and Elijah may bring Peter there.'

Qasim nodded once, and Renatus gestured the other two towards the still-open door. Emmanuelle went to the doorway, followed by her male colleagues, before stopping and turning back to them.

'I…I want to see 'im,' she said in a small voice. I walked over, watching the expressions of the men she spoke to. Without even glancing at one another, both Renatus and Qasim said, in unison, 'No.'

Emmanuelle looked ready to argue, but then seemed to take in their stern, stubborn expressions.

She silently walked out the door. Qasim followed, then Renatus. I realised that I was about to be locked in here alone, and ran for the door as he walked through. It began to swing shut behind him, and I had almost reached it when it slammed in my face. I blinked.

Bang.

My eyes snapped open, but I couldn't see anything. My heart was thudding; my head was throbbing dully. I sat up. Hadn't I just been standing, running? I looked around. Incredibly, or perhaps not, I was back in bed, in my room, with Hiroko asleep in the bed to my right and Sterling and Xanthe on the other side of the room.

Did that mean it really had been just a dream?

I slowly lay back down. I felt massively disorientated, as though I really had just teleported straight from my bed, into the office and back again. The experience had been so real – I had been fully aware of my surroundings, and there had been none of the surrealism that typifies dreams. You know, changing landscapes, people morphing into other people, pink elephants, that sort of thing. None of it. I almost might have believed that I *had* teleported – displaced – to the head's office during my sleep, except that nobody else had been able to see me. If I had actually displaced, then I would have been physically present at the time and there should have been nothing stopping the other three from noticing.

This left me with my original suspicion. I had dreamt the entire thing. That meant that the conversation had not really happened, except in my head. Why would I dream something like that? Why would my mind make up an office for Renatus, complete with the arched window at the top of the house and the door with no doorknob, and play out such an odd scene?

I tried unsuccessfully to fall back to sleep. My mind kept going over the dream, as though it were a video on a loop. Maybe it was a prophetic dream, trying to warn me of...something? If that were the case, it might have been warning me about the death of Emmanuelle's friend Peter, or that the councillors of the White Elm were not as close friends as I had imagined. There had been a moment or two of obvious hostility between Renatus and Qasim.

But of course, it had only been a dream. I had to keep reminding myself that it wasn't real; that I'd invented the entire exchange, from the heated conversations to the tears to the kiss.

Of course, Qasim would be on my thoughts because of how hard I'd been working on scrying. Emmanuelle was the White Elm with which I identified the most, because, as my supervisor, she was more involved in my life than the others. It made as much sense that these two people might pop up in my dreams as if Hiroko or Kendra were to do.

Renatus? Well, I heard his name fifty million times a day from Sterling...obviously she'd talked enough rubbish that it had invaded my dreams.

By the time the other girls had awoken the following morning, I had almost managed to convince myself that my experience had been a perfectly rational dream. I forgot to wonder why, after three weeks of dreamless sleep, I would dream anything at all.

chapter fifteen

Unlike the previous few days, Thursday dawned overcast and gloomy. The sun made no attempt whatsoever to shine through, as though it knew already that it wasn't worth the effort. A few sunbeams weren't going to make Emmanuelle's upturned day any less horrible.

She'd been sitting in the ballroom of Morrissey House since just before midnight. It was hard to tell what time of day it was through the windows, because the sky was so grey, but she knew that many hours of numb nothingness had passed.

After Renatus had brought her here to speak with Lord Gawain about the funeral service, she had collapsed into a chair and he had left. She hadn't seen him since, and for that she was glad. She couldn't think of him without wanting to melt into a puddle of embarrassment. What had she been *thinking*? Obviously, nothing.

It was a weak moment, she kept telling herself. She

hadn't been thinking straight – she'd been distraught, thinking only of Peter and all the things she now wished she'd thought to say and do while he was alive. *Imbécile, Emmanuelle.*

Lord Gawain had sat with Emmanuelle for a while, wanting to know all about how the ring had come to her, as if that mattered. She'd offered it to him, and he'd shook his head.

'Fate has brought it to you. It's yours for now, and for a reason.'

He'd explained how the service would go. The students would be told at breakfast that they would be attending a funeral for a former White Elm councillor that morning. The service would be short, held in the ballroom, and would be used as an example of Lisandro's destructive power.

'I think Peter would approve of his death being used to incriminate his murderer and to educate young sorcerers against Lisandro,' Lord Gawain had said, not noticing Emmanuelle's miniscule flinch at the word *murderer*. Renatus hadn't said that Lisandro had *murdered* Peter – only implied it, and it hurt much more to hear the word. The word made it real and horrible. 'He was lied to and manipulated, and it's our responsibility to ensure that Lisandro doesn't get the chance to do the same to any of our students. Emmanuelle,' he had added when she just nodded. 'Peter was not White Elm when he died. We don't have to have any special ceremony if you would rather not…'

Emmanuelle thought for a few moments in silence. The idea of Peter's death being *used*, in any way, to promote an ideal or rule upset her. She would love for Lord Gawain to hand to her a decorative urn with Peter's name on it and to take it to Peter's grandmother, and to grieve in her own time and space. Alone.

If anyone asked, she would say that her friend had been killed by Lisandro. It wouldn't be shocking; it would be sad, and people would feel sorry for her. If the story circulated, it would change slightly with each retelling until Peter was no longer Peter and Lisandro was no longer a heartless killer. The story would not save anybody, nor would it do justice to Peter's life.

Emmanuelle thought of the students – particularly her four, the girls in her dorm group. Xanthe, Aristea, Hiroko and Sterling were just sweet children. They were powerful, with much potential, but, like all young people, they could very easily be led astray by someone like Lisandro. She shivered at the thought of strawberry-blonde Sterling being found dead in a field, or Hiroko's body in a third-world side alley, or Aristea in a creek or Xanthe in an abandoned apartment. Lisandro had given Peter enough empty promises to drag him away from his oaths and his love for Emmanuelle – what would he need to promise a teenager for their loyalty and involvement? A vague, fifth-hand story about a friend's cousin's friend's best friend being killed by Lisandro wouldn't save a student from Peter's fate.

Seeing a coffin, seeing it surrounded by white flowers, seeing Emmanuelle struggle with her grief openly, knowing that Lisandro had done this…That might.

'You must do what is best by the students,' she had said finally, and after a few more words of comfort, Lord Gawain had excused himself and left her alone, which was exactly what she'd thought she wanted, all along.

Now, she could hear the sounds of the early-rising students coming down the stairs and traipsing through the reception hall. She heard their chatter and their laughter. Their lives had not fallen apart at the seams – and hopefully, at Emmanuelle's expense, they never would.

Peter…

He had loved her, all along, and said nothing. They had met as hopeful twenty-year-olds, brilliant and powerful and eager to take the place of the two White Elm councillors who had recently passed on within weeks of each other. There had been other applicants, too, but they had been so ordinary, too intimidated by Emmanuelle's physical beauty to make real attempts at getting to know her. Peter had walked into the waiting room, seen the three spare seats, smiled and taken the one right beside Emmanuelle. She remembered thinking that nobody as nerdy-looking as Peter had ever dared to sit beside her.

She had initiated conversation, and quickly came to adore his off-kilter sense of humour, sweet disposition and odd, quirky personality. She'd found herself inspired by his insatiable idealism and passionate desire to be part of positive change. She had been delighted when they had both been initiated into the council. They had remained close friends, telling each other everything, almost. He had never indicated that he was working with Lisandro to overturn the White Elm; he had never shared his true feelings for Emmanuelle. What else had remained hidden within Peter's heart, and died along with him eighteen nights ago?

She heard hesitant steps, and looked to the door. Aubrey and Teresa had entered the ballroom, and both looked extremely uncomfortable.

'The service will start straight after breakfast,' Aubrey explained, while Teresa hovered near the door. 'It will be held in here. Lord Gawain suggested we be present in full uniform.'

Emmanuelle nodded. By uniform, of course he meant the white robe. She followed the two younger councillors from the ballroom.

Aubrey's chestnut hair was shiny, worn straight and cut like a nineties' boy-band star. His bangs hung into his eyes, just like the pop icons of the decade. He looked comfortable in his body; he was nothing like Peter. Did he know that he only had a job because Peter had left? Jadon and Teresa had been everybody's first choices after the initial interviews. Aubrey was more like a wild card – a distant cousin of Emmanuelle's, after all, had seemed a safe and reasonable choice.

Were Aubrey, Jadon and Teresa close like Peter and Emmanuelle had been? Were they friends? Did they hold secrets from each other? Did Aubrey love Teresa?

'Will you be alright?' Teresa asked, and

Emmanuelle realised that Aubrey was gone, and she was standing in front of the door to her own room in this house.

'I think so,' Emmanuelle said, fumbling for her key. Her hands were shaking. They hadn't stopped shaking since Lord Gawain had said that Lisandro was Peter's murderer.

Teresa gently took the key from her trembly hands and opened up the room.

Half an hour later, Emmanuelle was dressed appropriately and standing in the ballroom between Tian and Aubrey. This was her place in the White Elm, and it felt right to stand there. The students were seated in rows, all eyes glued to either the gleaming white coffin or to Lord Gawain, who spoke about Peter and how Lisandro had manipulated and destroyed him. Behind Lord Gawain, Lady Miranda and Renatus stood silently, like guardians.

Life is constantly changing, like the path cut by a river. Only a year before, Lisandro had been a colleague and an ally, and his place had been Renatus's. Emmanuelle's place had been between Peter and Renatus, and the year before that, her place had been right at the end, where Jadon was now. Though Renatus was several years younger than her, she had once again become the council's baby after his promotion – the last one in the line, until Aubrey, Teresa and Jadon had been initiated.

Emmanuelle gazed over the students, seeking those four that she felt most responsible for. She spotted them, sitting all together in a row with a pair of twins. She was glad to see their saddened and alert faces; this affected them, and so they would learn from it.

As her eyes moved along the row, Emmanuelle met Aristea's gaze. The girl was looking right at her. Aristea's eyes were wide, and she looked slightly frightened and ill.

What was important, though, was that Aristea would never fall under the illusion that Lisandro mightn't be so bad – today she had learned that he was a dangerous killer, capable of murdering even his allies and friends.

Today, the students had learnt the capabilities of their enemy. Tomorrow, or next week, or in thirty years, whenever the true war started, would they be as eager to destroy that enemy as Emmanuelle was right at that moment?

She lightly touched her fingertips to the dull, ward-protected ring around her thumb. The Elm Stone rarely chose female keepers, which might be the reason for its large size. On any of her other fingers, it would have slid straight off. As it was, it sat very loosely in its place, held mostly by her knuckle.

Was it possible that Peter had given her this ring to destroy Lisandro? He was a Seer, after all. He would have known the likely repercussions of leaving her this immense power. Was she meant to take it and destroy his killer, like she wanted to? Would she be able to stop herself if an opportunity arose?

Lord Gawain dismissed the students to their first class, which would be shortened due to this service. Emmanuelle had no class until that afternoon – she taught students how to create and structure protective wards. She had always been good with wards, but physical barriers were not enough to protect a heart from being broken.

Those White Elm with classes filed out after the students. Emmanuelle stayed with the others, as Lord Gawain and Renatus approached the coffin. Lady Miranda touched her shoulder supportively as she left, and Anouk and Susannah moved so that they stood either side of Emmanuelle. Pillars.

'Peter, your death is not unacknowledged,' Lord Gawain said, loud enough for the others to hear. 'What has happened to you will not be allowed to happen again…'

He spoke about Peter's good deeds and how much his former colleagues respected him still, despite his mistakes, but Emmanuelle wasn't listening. Her eyes were on the coffin and her mind was on the man inside. She'd gathered from light brushes against her colleagues' current thoughts more information about Peter's death – Lisandro had drowned him in front of an audience of dark sorcerers, and then left his lifeless body afloat in the surf. After two and half weeks at sea, the body Glen and Elijah had brought back had not been in any condition to be viewed by a friend of the deceased.

She was glad, now, that Renatus and Qasim had refused to let her see him. She didn't want the sight of his battered and rotting body to mar her memories. The gleaming white coffin she could endure.

Au revoir, Peter.

Lord Gawain nodded once to Renatus, and they stood facing each other at either end of the casket. Together they raised their hands to just above the coffin, and pale balls of flame burst to life in their palms. The little white-hot fires floated in space, even when the sorcerers took their hands away. Slowly, the balls expanded until the flames licked the white of the casket, and then the fires took hold, engulfing Peter's coffin entirely. There was no smoke.

Emmanuelle felt tears running down her cheeks, but she didn't care. They were freeing themselves.

Within a minute, there was nothing left but a disproportionate pile of ash. The enchanted fires burnt themselves out. No damage had been done to the beautiful ballroom floor.

Lord Gawain took out his wand. He conjured an elegant but plain vase from the air and swept his wand through the air over the ash. In a swirl of magic, the remains of Peter floated upward and fell obediently through the neck of the vase. Lord Gawain sealed the top with a neat little lid.

'Goodbye,' he murmured. His sentiment was repeated by many of the others. He stepped forward and handed the urn to Emmanuelle. She took it and marvelled at how steady her hands were now.

'Will you take this to Peter's grandmother?' he asked.

'I will,' she answered softly, and it felt like an oath. Peter's grandmother was an elderly Scottish witch living alone just out of Glasgow. She would be happy to see Emmanuelle, and she would appreciate the urn and the truth.

Lord Gawain left the ballroom. Anouk, Susannah and Renatus stayed back.

Without speaking, Susannah laid a hand across the side of the plain vase. When she removed her hand, Emmanuelle saw what she had added – a silver plaque with Peter's name engraved upon it. Anouk leaned forward and touched the vase in two places, either side of Susannah's plaque. In the spots where she touched the ceramic, two baby-blue crystals appeared; the colour of Peter's eyes.

The two older women left through the double doors behind them, and Emmanuelle looked over at Renatus. He was still standing where he had been when he helped to light up the coffin. He was gazing out of the huge windows.

Was he waiting back to talk to her? Her stomach clenched in embarrassment at the very thought of Renatus bringing up her indiscretion. She hadn't meant it, after all – she wasn't in love with him, and although *obviously* he was an attractive man, she felt no desire for him. Despite that he'd grown up, he was still *too young* in her mind. In many ways, she was still frightened of him. She had been since the day she had first met him.

She and Peter had just been initiated into the White Elm, and Renatus then had been an incredibly intense seventeen-year-old. Lord Gawain's informal apprentice in almost every way but by name, the boy had always been around a lot. His entire family was dead, she'd learned. They were dark sorcerers and their son had undoubtedly learnt a fair bit before they'd died and Lord Gawain had intervened. The boy was a mega-conduit, capable of magic others might never even consider. Even as a teenager, Renatus had scared the council.

The only obvious path for Lord Gawain, if he wanted to calm the council's fears and keep the orphan close enough to be watched, was to prepare Renatus for initiation onto the council. Everyone had been much happier with Renatus as an ally than with him running amuck, performing magic whenever and however he liked.

After today, though, Emmanuelle found that the young Dark Keeper did not scare her as much as he once had. He'd held her hand, with the Elm Stone…and he hadn't taken it. He'd given her the truth when those she trusted more would not. He'd offered her traitorous friend a place in his family's graveyard, though it had killed him to do it, simply to be kind. She'd not seen this side of him before – well, she hadn't really been looking. Eyes open, she could see now what Lord Gawain saw in him.

She walked over so that she stood beside him.

'Thank you for telling me the truth when nobody else would,' she said. 'I owe you a lot of respect and I think it is probably well overdue.'

For several seconds, Renatus said nothing. Then he, too, laid a palm on the vase. When he took it away, she turned the urn to look at the image.

He'd emblazoned a white tree, crossed through with a capital 'W', just above the plaque. It was the emblem of the White Elm, which Lord Gawain had originally omitted. Whenever a councillor died, the emblem was clearly marked in the urn or gravestone as a respectful tribute. Lord Gawain had chosen to leave it off Peter's urn – which was understandable, because Peter had chosen to throw in Lord Gawain's trust and his oaths to the council. But it would mean so much to one elderly witch to receive her grandson's remains in an urn marked with the official symbol. Emmanuelle began to cry again. It meant something to her, too, and she knew Peter was smiling somewhere, grateful for Renatus's gesture.

'Because we all make mistakes,' Renatus said, looking her in the eyes. His low voice was loaded with meanings. His fingertips lightly touched her wrist as he walked past her to leave.

Emmanuelle closed her eyes and allowed herself to imagine, for just a moment, that the fingers belonged to Peter, and that the departing footsteps might be his, too.

chapter sixteen

I had never collected my things for class so quickly. I was lined up outside Qasim's classroom before most people had even reached their dorms.

The short funeral service had been a shocking experience. Peter was *real*. He'd been murdered, by Lisandro. Emmanuelle had spent the majority of the service with her eyes glazed over, staring into space. She looked as though she'd not slept. Most of the council had looked in a similarly exhausted state.

Before breakfast, I had described my dream to Hiroko in detail. I told her everything I'd seen and heard. I trusted her, and she'd been a fantastic listener.

'I have never heard of such a thing,' she'd said when I finished. 'It could perhaps be a dream, as you say, but it seems unlikely. I have not yet had a dream here, nor has Sophia or Kendra.'

That had struck me as odd, too, because until last night, I'd not dreamt a thing here, either.

So now I stood at the scrying classroom's door, wondering whether Qasim was inside. The council had left the service after the students, but I had gone to my dorm since then, so there was a chance he'd managed to get here by now. I tentatively knocked. It wasn't very loud, so I knocked again, harder.

'Aristea,' Qasim called from behind me. I turned and watched him approach. 'You're here early.'

'I think I'm going crazy,' I blurted out. 'I knew this was going to happen – today, the funeral.'

Qasim unlocked the classroom door and let himself inside. I followed.

'You foresaw a funeral?' he asked, a little sceptically. I shook my head.

'No, I heard it was going to happen…' I trailed off, realising how stupid I sounded, and started again. 'I've never even heard of Peter, but last night I had a dream – or, I thought I was dreaming – and I saw Renatus, and Emmanuelle came in, really upset, and she was going on about somebody called Peter. She said she had a right to know, and eventually Renatus told her that Peter died a little while ago and he'd known for about a week. He said Lisandro did it.'

'Wait,' Qasim said, closing the door behind me and looking at me closely. 'Did you *scry* all of this?'

'I don't know,' I said, because the possibility hadn't occurred to me. It hadn't been much like ordinary scrying, which was like watching a movie. 'At first I thought I was just dreaming.'

'And this was all in the office?'

'Aye, all of it.'

'What else happened?' the Scrier asked, and it sounded like he was testing me, listening out for clues as to whether or not this had actually occurred.

'Well, they argued a little bit before Renatus told her,' I recounted. 'And Emmanuelle was really upset. She said that Peter left a note in her garden asking for forgiveness. "Forgive me, love", it said. I think Renatus said that he said, "I never told her I love her" when he died, so I guess that's why.'

Qasim's sceptical look vanished, and it was quickly replaced with one of curious wonder.

'What then?'

'They...' I froze, remembering what happened next. Emmanuelle had kissed Renatus. It had happened, and for all I knew, it might have been something that was okay to talk about. I had told Hiroko about it – she had suggested I not tell Sterling. But something stopped me from saying it to Qasim. I remembered how it had felt to be standing in the room with Emmanuelle, feeling her sadness and the pain she was in.

She hadn't been herself. No one was meant to have seen. It was none of my business, and not my place to share it with her colleague.

I felt my cheeks heating up as I remembered the scene, and felt Qasim's eyes on my face. I wondered whether my entire face was flaming pink.

'Um, they talked a while,' I muttered, looking away. 'Emmanuelle said she wanted Peter cremated, and Renatus said the funeral would be today. That's how I knew.'

'It's impossible,' Qasim said in wonderment,

apparently not noticing my blush. 'That office is scry-proof. It shouldn't be possible. Even *I* can't see into that study. Do you have any idea how many spells have been performed on that room over the ages?'

I shook my head again.

'Do you really think that I scried last night?' I asked. 'I've been practising heaps. Do you think while I was sleeping, it just…happened?'

'It seems to be the only explanation, if you really saw what happened in there last night,' Qasim mused, looking intensely at the door without seeing. 'Your emotional blocks must have finished clearing. Did anyone else join them?'

'You did,' I stated. He looked back at me with something like pride – I had finally proved it. I had scried, and he was pleased with me. My heart swelled with pride, too. I even smiled. I had scried, and impressed the world's most accomplished Scrier by scrying into a room that was spelled too tightly for even him to see into. 'You said that Elijah and Glen were bringing back the body from a private beach. Is that what I scried on Tuesday?'

'Yes, it was a vital clue,' he said, much more open with me and friendlier now that I'd gained his approval. 'It gave Renatus and myself a few pointers and helped us to narrow down our search. We've been trying to retrieve Peter's body for a week.'

I assumed that Qasim's search method of choice was scrying, which impressed me even more deeply.

'It must be really useful, being able to find lost things by scrying,' I said, sitting down on the arm of a two-seater. Something occurred to me. 'When you're scrying, if you're looking for something, are you able to pick things up and move them around?'

'What do you mean?' Qasim asked, his fascinated and proud expression growing slightly quizzical.

'Can you pick things up?' I was thinking of the books in the office. I hadn't quite touched them, so I hadn't even known if I'd be able to feel them or if my hand would just go straight through them. I hadn't fallen through the chair, door or floor so I was still subject to the basic rules of physical space, but did the same rules apply if I wanted to relocate something? If I'd been able to take a text from the bookshelf, and Renatus still hadn't been able to see me, would he have freaked out to see the book floating out of the bookcase unassisted?

'Aristea, scrying is entirely observatory,' Qasim reminded me. 'You just watched an event. Do you mean, if you scry yourself, can you still interact with objects around you? I'm sure I've told you about passive scrying. You learn to scry and carry on with daily activities simultaneously.'

'Yes,' I said patiently. 'I mean, while I was there, I was going to pick up some books. I didn't get the chance to, so-'

'When you were where?' Qasim asked, a little sharply. I frowned a little. *What have I been talking about for the past two minutes*?

'In the office,' I said.

'You weren't there. You *saw* it.'

'No, I was walking around,' I corrected. 'I even ran to the door when you all left to meet Lord

Gawain. Nobody could see me.'

Qasim's excited expression slowly slipped away. He said, 'You were there? Actually there?'

'Yes, I just turned up beside the window,' I said. Something about this wasn't right. 'Why?'

'Did you actively scry?' Qasim demanded, a new expression slowly spreading over his features. It was darker, and I already didn't like it.

'No, I was trying to sleep.'

'Did you or did you not travel into that office as a whole entity?' he said, his voice getting louder and angrier with each word. I shook my head slowly, uncertain of how to answer. *Whole entity*? I didn't travel anywhere. I'd been sleeping. 'Aristea! This is serious. Active scrying is an illegal activity. You could be excluded from the school or arrested.'

My heart skipped a beat, and I blinked in horror. *Then I didn't do it, whatever it is...*

'But I didn't mean to,' I said reasonably, 'so it wasn't active at all.'

'That's a technicality,' Qasim said tightly, glaring at me now. 'Active scrying is highly dangerous. It is what some people call astral travel and others call Haunting – your soul leaves your body unattended to walk around. Most practitioners report a floating feeling beforehand. Does this sound familiar to you, Aristea?'

It did.

'No,' I said. The air around me flickered with my lie. Qasim's glare narrowed and I wanted to run away. I hadn't meant to do anything wrong. They wouldn't really expel me, would they? I imagined going home to Angela and having to tell her I'd been expelled already.

'Luckily, there's a simple way to be sure,' Qasim said in a tightly controlled voice. He continued to glare at me, and I felt the silky tendrils of his mind begin to enter mine. He was going to take a look at the memory. Could he tell from that whether I'd really been there or just viewed the scene? Of course he could – from the part when I looked down at my pyjamas, or when my hand reached out for the old books.

In a flash, I thought of Emmanuelle, crying her eyes out, clinging to Renatus. I shouldn't have seen any of that – it wasn't mine to share. I hadn't said it, so I wasn't going to let Qasim see it, either.

'No,' I said forcefully, and as I said the word, I fought back with my mind, clamping down on Qasim's presence as I'd not known I could do. I threw him out and raised my hands, instantly building up a dozen wards all around my mind. I felt his anger – I felt him trying to get in. But my wards were strong.

'Aristea!' His voice was a furious one, and I felt terror coursing through my blood. How much trouble was I in now? 'Let me see the memory.'

'No.'

'Now, Aristea!' Qasim shouted. 'If you've committed a criminal act, it's in your best interest to cooperate. Now, show me the memory of what you've done.'

'No, it's mine,' I said, feeling childish. I snatched out my wand, intensely threatened. 'You can't just break in and look around.'

Qasim stared at me, and I wondered whether he was going to hit me. *Oh, god, oh, god...*

'I can't,' he repeated, nodding to himself. He grabbed my wrist roughly and pulled the door back open. He dragged me through it, into and along the hall, where my classmates were lining up. They watched on in curious silence. I met Xanthe's eyes. Would I see her again? Was I about to be literally chucked out?

'Where are you taking me?' I asked. My voice was small and high – I was terrified. Qasim would not look at me. I could feel the fury emanating from him in waves. I asked again, louder. 'Where are we going?'

'To speak with the headmaster,' he said harshly. 'I mightn't be able to break in...but *he* can.'

I tripped on an uneven floorboard. Renatus could break through my wards?

We stopped at the heavy oak door with no doorknob. Qasim knocked. It was a hard, urgent knock that the occupant couldn't ignore. After a moment, the door swung open. Giving my wrist an unnecessarily hard tug, Qasim pulled me inside after him.

I froze, staring around the room. It was *exactly* as I'd seen it in my dream. *Exactly* the same, except that now it was day time. The bookcase, the huge desk, the papers piled up neatly. I stumbled slightly as Qasim pulled me forward so that I was standing in front of the desk.

As he had been the night before, at the desk sat

Renatus, placidly writing something.

'I have honestly only just sat down, Qasim, so this had better be important,' he said without looking up. His voice was low and smooth, with only a hint of impatience.

'Aristea scried you last night,' Qasim said in the angry, harsh tone that scared me. Renatus looked up. 'She scried you *in here*.'

'She what?' the headmaster asked, looking from the Scrier's face to mine. His gaze was very intense, but I couldn't look away. He'd seemed kind of nice with Emmanuelle last night, but Qasim didn't bring me here for Renatus to be nice to me. Was he going to put a truth spell on me? Was he going to force his way into my mind and rip through my thoughts? Was he going to expel me? Arrest me?

Was Emmanuelle's dignity worth all that? I barely knew her.

I began to shake.

'She *Haunted you*, Renatus,' Qasim said angrily. 'She broke the law.'

Renatus regarded me a little longer before turning back to his colleague.

'How do you know?' he asked, his tone cool and expressionless.

'She described the events of last night, and everything that was said inside this room. There's only one way to scry into this office.'

Renatus's violet eyes flickered to me briefly.

'Have you examined her memory to be sure?' he asked. 'Active scrying is a serious charge, Qasim.'

'I was about to when she refused me entry and

drew her wand,' the Scrier spat, pointing at my right hand. My wand was still clasped tightly in my trembling fingers, hanging limply at my side. I wished now that I hadn't taken it out. I had already broken the law – I didn't have to make it worse by drawing a weapon on a White Elm councillor. 'She put up wards and I can't get through.'

Renatus nodded. I tensed nervously – was he about to smash down my hasty wards and break into my thoughts? But I felt nothing. He gazed at me for a while, and then turned back to Qasim.

'Those are good wards, too,' he commented. Qasim's eyes narrowed.

'We need to know the extent of her crime,' he said in that tight voice he had used earlier. It sounded as though he was struggling to control a lot of ugly emotions. 'Then we need to inform Lord Gawain. *You* can get through.'

'Yes, you're right,' Renatus said, placing his pen down on the table, in line with the other pens. I swallowed, but my throat was dry. 'I can, but surely it would be easier to examine the memory with Aristea's permission.'

'Aristea has already refused,' Qasim said, dropping my wrist and folding his arms.

'Then I refuse, too,' Renatus said smoothly. Qasim stared at him.

'You refuse?'

'Yes.'

'You refuse to follow up a charge as serious as this? Where is Lord Gawain?'

'Lord Gawain will not be back here until

Sunday,' Renatus answered, folding his hands together neatly. 'He left straight after the funeral. He has asked me to fill out summaries of important incidents for him to read upon his return. He is working today, tonight and all day tomorrow as a mortal in court, and this weekend is his wife's birthday. He does not wish to be disturbed except in urgent circumstances.'

'I think this counts, Renatus,' Qasim said coldly. 'A student has performed an act of illegal and highly dangerous magic-'

'Aristea,' Renatus interrupted, as smoothly as ever, 'did you intentionally and actively scry last night, transporting your consciousness into my office, with the intention of causing harm and knowing that it was unlawful?'

I quickly shook my head. My throat wouldn't have worked, anyway.

'Well,' Renatus said, turning back to Qasim. 'I don't think there was anything particularly important said last night, anyway.'

'Ignorance of the law is no excuse!' the older sorcerer snarled. 'Her intention is irrelevant. What she heard or saw is not important. The fact is that she was here! She witnessed private White Elm business. Lord Gawain must be contacted, and Aristea must be excluded from the school, as it is stated in the form she and her guardian signed.'

'Actually, I believe that the form states that *a student who acts in an unlawful manner may face exclusion from the school, at the discretion of the headmaster*,' Renatus recited, 'or something to that extent. As that's me, I don't think that we need to discuss this any further.'

'You're not expelling her?'

'No, I don't think so,' the headmaster said.

'I'm going to speak to Lord Gawain about this,' Qasim said after a long moment of stunned silence. 'He has a right to know.'

'Well, Qasim, he's asked not to be disturbed,' Renatus reminded the Scrier. 'There's nothing he can really do about it for you, either, because you all put *me* in charge of the school, which makes *my* word final on all matters relating to the students and their enrolment here.' He held up a blank sheet of paper. 'This is the report I'll give Lord Gawain on Sunday when he visits. Anything I deem important enough for him to worry about will be written down on here. You may be the next Lord, Qasim, but you're not there yet. I'm still one step ahead – and so it is me who will decide what Lord Gawain needs to know, and this is not one of those things.'

I didn't dare look at Qasim right then. I felt his anger and thought he might implode if he tried to hold it in any longer. He had brought me here, intending for Renatus to back him up and beat a confession out of me. Instead, Renatus had pulled the rug out from under his feet and taken *my* side, completely out of the blue.

chapter seventeen

The tension and silence that followed was horrific. Eventually Qasim turned away, muttering loudly in an unfamiliar language, and strode out of the office, fuming. His pride was damaged; I'd gotten the better of him, and I knew he'd hate me for it.

But at least now I'd be around to be hated.

Right then, my legs gave out beneath me, and I collapsed backwards into one of the stiff-but-comfy armchairs. Relief made my head feel light. I wasn't expelled.

Renatus, I noticed, was watching me. I swallowed twice, trying to make my throat work.

'I'm really sorry for all this,' I said uncertainly. 'I honestly didn't mean to do anything. I didn't know I could scry like that.'

'I'm not angry,' he said, and I relaxed a little more. 'I would, however, like to know what you saw last night.'

I swallowed again and said, 'Everything, from

when Emmanuelle came in. I was standing there.' I pointed to the space in front of the window.

'I take it then that you heard our conversation about Peter.' It was a statement, not a question, so I said nothing. He asked, 'What else?'

'You talked about Lisandro, or mentioned his name, and then talked about Peter and the funeral,' I answered, shrugging uncomfortably. I had recounted most of what had been said to Qasim because I had wanted to prove I was there; recounting the same information to Renatus was discomforting. For one thing, I now knew that I'd been performing illegal magic and didn't want to further incriminate myself to the one person who could cancel my enrolment. Secondly, Renatus had actually *been* there. It felt odd to be telling him stuff he already knew.

'What else did you see?' he asked.

'You were there, you should know,' I said before I could stop myself. I looked down at my lap. 'Sorry.'

'You're not in trouble,' he responded, 'and nothing you say will get you into any trouble, provided that you are honest with me.'

'I saw Emmanuelle kiss you,' I muttered, avoiding his intense gaze and wishing my cheeks wouldn't feel so warm.

'Did you tell Qasim *everything* that you saw last night?' he asked.

'No,' I said pointedly, looking away. I didn't like talking about this. I did *not* want to discuss my teachers' personal lives with them. I wished I'd never scried myself into this office.

'Why not?'

I stared at him, disbelieving.

'Because it was none of his business,' I said strongly, but then looked away, less confident. 'It was none of mine, either. I shouldn't have been here and I shouldn't have seen anything. Neither of you knew I was watching.'

Renatus reclined slightly in his chair, regarding me.

'Emmanuelle doesn't need the entire council and student body to know that she made a mistake – especially one that she couldn't control. It would embarrass her, and that's not something I want to do. Do you?'

'No.'

'I'm very grateful for your respect thus far, Aristea,' Renatus said sincerely. 'Emmanuelle has suffered a great loss – she has just lost a friend that might have been her soul mate. Your discretion is appreciated, as is your determination to keep this secret from Qasim. You are correct – it is none of his business, or anyone else's. To that end, I suppose we can agree that what you saw will not be shared with anyone else, by either of us, and perhaps that it never even happened?'

'Okay,' I said, and stood so I could shake his hand when he offered it. His skin was cool, as if his blood had more important things to do than warm and oxygenate his hands. I released his hand after shaking it once, but his long fingers held on.

'If nobody hears about *what* you scried, then technically, nobody else on the council needs to know that you scried at all,' he said, holding my gaze in his.

'Qasim knows, and he's going to tell Lord Gawain,' I reminded him, my stomach clenching. What would happen when Lord Gawain found out?

'Qasim won't tell anyone anything,' Renatus said dismissively. 'He's just blustering. He's angry and his ego is bruised. He won't want anyone to hear the full story, in which he didn't just catch a student out for misbehaviour, but also had his authority overstepped by me. He already dislikes us both. Today has made that worse. He will be very, very angry if you are not punished. He could make life very uncomfortable.'

I swallowed once again, nervousness flooding back.

'To avoid that,' Renatus said clearly, 'it needs to seem to him that you have been punished. I am issuing you three weeks of detention, to be served in the evenings of weekdays, in my office, for one hour a night. There will be no chores or lines or scrubbing of floors – only time spent here. Does that sound fair to you?'

I nodded, too relieved to say anything. I had expected some kind of suspension or removal of privileges. An hour a night lost for three weeks was a thousand times better than writing to Angela to say I'd be coming home early, or watching my friends attend classes while I sat in my room, banned.

'Perhaps you can spend the time practising scrying properly so that you can get back into Qasim's good books,' Renatus continued. His hand still grasped mine across the desk. 'If you are serious about becoming a Scrier for the White Elm, you'll want to be able to go to him for advice. So, you will serve three weeks of detention with me, and because the rest of the council and the students aren't to know that you ever illegally scried, you will tell anyone who asks that your punishment is for refusing to follow an instruction given by Qasim. You argued with him over whether or not his technique was correct. It was a silly argument and you don't even remember why you said it. The council knows his tendency to overreact and his love of discipline, so nobody will think twice.'

It took me a moment to realise that the headmaster was inventing a story for me to tell anyone who asked for it. Was he was asking me to *lie* to the White Elm?

'Don't think of it as lying,' he said, as though he'd read my thoughts. I was sure he hadn't, couldn't have, because my wards were up, shielding my mind and all of its facets. I glanced at our hands, clasped across his desk. Did skin contact make my wards useless? 'No, your wards are very good – impenetrable to most sorcerers.'

'Then how can you get through and read my thoughts?' I asked, wondering why I didn't feel more threatened. Renatus almost smiled – his mouth hardly moved, but his eyes softened and brightened a little.

'You may not yet have noticed, but I'm not like *most sorcerers*,' he answered. 'You'll have to work with Emmanuelle to perfect your wards. You're already very established at protecting yourself from telepathic attack, but there's room for improvement. Anyway,' Renatus said, getting back on track, 'the story about your argument with Qasim is the story that we will allow to circulate, because there is nothing in that story that implicates you in any crime.'

'Why are you helping me if I've done something so awful?' I asked carefully, not wanting to sound ungrateful. I wondered whether he had fought Qasim on the matter for my sake, or simply because he didn't want to agree with the Scrier.

'Because in this version of the truth, everybody wins,' he said simply. 'Emmanuelle's pride is kept intact. Qasim is secure and placated knowing that you are disciplined for your wrong doings. You are able to continue with your studies without fear of exclusion, which I feel is in the best interests of both yourself and the council. And *I* will be in much less trouble if Lord Gawain or Lady Miranda ever learns that I chose to ignore and conceal a serious breach of magical law. At least this way I can defend my actions by showing that you have been punished.' He paused, as though waiting for me to interject or ask a question. When I did nothing but stare at him silently, he said, 'So we are in agreement?'

'Yes, Sir,' I said, and he shook my hand again and finally released it.

'Good. Your detentions start this evening. Please avoid Qasim until your next lesson, or until you really must see him – I intend on doing the same. I expect he'll need some time to cool off.'

'Will he even let me back into his class?' I asked,

feeling doubtful.

'Absolutely. He wouldn't pass up the chance to teach you everything he knows – you're a once in a lifetime opportunity for him. He just needs some time to remember that.'

'I don't understand.'

'You don't need to,' Renatus answered. He stood and walked to a tall, thin cabinet behind his desk. The glass was smoky and too dark to see through. He opened the door of it and withdrew a small box. 'It seems that your accidental Haunting was caused by putting your mind under a great deal of stress and pressure to scry. I imagine that during your practices, you may have flipped the switch, so to speak – opening yourself up to your potential. With your mind still open, you went to sleep, a deep state of relaxation, which is when your soul left. Very few sorcerers have the power to Haunt. However, Qasim is right. It is an extremely dangerous activity. Your body was defenceless, and had you touched one of us, you would have possessed that person. Unskilled as you are, you may never have been able to disengage; it may have been permanent. It mustn't happen again, or I really will have to expel you.'

I blinked, shocked. No wonder Qasim had been so angry; no wonder it was illegal. I remembered almost touching the books in the shelf. What if I had tried to touch Renatus or Emmanuelle on the arm or shoulder to get their attention? I shivered.

Renatus held out the little box to me, and I hesitantly took it and looked inside. The box held a roughly cast pendant on a dark silver chain. The carved symbol on the pendant was entirely unfamiliar to me.

'What is it?' I asked.

'Very old,' Renatus responded. 'It will lock your magic inside your body and prevent you from scrying at all, so if you wear it at night until you learn to control your abilities, it will stop this from happening again. Don't wear it during the day – *always* take it off first thing in the morning. It prohibits a lot of magic.'

'Thank you,' I said, re-examining the pendant. Renatus nodded his acknowledgement and raised his hand, and in the corner of my eye, I saw the door open.

'Please don't return to class,' he said. 'Enjoy this spare lesson. I'm glad we had this talk. I will see you this evening straight after tea.'

I nodded, recognising the dismissal, and headed for the door. I didn't look back until I heard the heavy oak click shut behind me.

I went to my empty dorm room and sat down on my bed. My head was reeling. So much had happened in the past day.

I kept thinking about the things Renatus had said. He was correct in saying that he wasn't much like *most sorcerers*. What was it that made him different? How had he read my thoughts, without me even noticing? He hadn't broken my wards, so how? Hasty wards could often be smashed down with enough mental force (it had never happened to me, but it was common knowledge – like a wobbly, badly constructed fence, a strong shove could push it down). However, I imagined I'd feel the sort of strength that would be required.

He'd suggested I use the detentions as time for scrying practice so I could impress Qasim with my skill. He'd said I presented an opportunity that Qasim couldn't pass up. He'd implied that I had the potential to become a Scrier for the White Elm...

I looked at the pendant again. It looked very old and handmade. When I lifted it from its box by the chain, I found that it was heavier than I'd expected. It seemed heavier *out* of the box than when it was in it. I stared at the pendant and tried to focus on its energy, but I felt nothing at all. Was it even real? I touched it with my fingers. It was cool and rough. Experimentally, I looped the chain over my neck and settled the pendant against my chest.

It was the magical equivalent of turning off a light. My magical senses immediately shut down and beyond my skin, I could feel nothing. Even the feelings of others, which usually passed over me constantly, were unreachable. I took my wand in my hand but it was like holding a stick. I felt dim and powerless, and I didn't like it. This was what it was like to be mortal. No idea what was around me, except for what I could see. No idea what people felt or thought about me...I hurriedly took it off, and immediately felt so much lighter. It felt heavy to wear, not just in weight but in the way it held my powers down. I carefully laid it back inside the box and tucked it away in the drawer of my bedside table.

I felt compelled to talk to someone, but I was

alone, so I decided to write to my sister. As I wrote, however, I realised that there wasn't a lot I could say. Most of what was looping over and over in my head had officially not happened. I wondered if this was what it was like for the White Elm when they visited family members after a hard day, and, unable to set aside the red tape and political secrets, had to say, 'Yes, work's been fine – I'm great.'

In the end, I wrote a rather short and uneventful letter outlining my scrying practice. I said that I was progressing rather well. I dedicated one sentence to Peter – *We attended a funeral for an ex-White Elm councillor on Thursday morning, which was sad for the people who knew him.* I didn't mention my "dream", or Renatus, or Qasim.

Angela was very perceptive, and would probably read between the lines and realise that there was a lot left unsaid in my letter. But really, what more could I do?

I had just signed my name when the door banged open, and Sterling bounced in, followed closely by Xanthe.

'What happened?' Xanthe asked of me, taking Sterling's key from the still-swinging door and handing it to its owner. 'Qasim didn't say anything about it when he came back to class, but he was *really* angry.'

I hesitated for only a second. Xanthe and Sterling were both watching me, waiting patiently for the juicy gossip they were sure they were about to hear.

'It was stupid,' I began, and the lie tumbled

easily from there. 'I told Qasim I knew a better way to scry, and we had a bit of an argument. He took me to the headmaster.'

I waited for that damning energetic spark to give me away, but it didn't happen. Later, when I really thought about it, I wondered whether how I felt about the lie made a difference.

'Ooh,' Sterling said excitedly, dropping onto my bed. 'Then what?'

'I got detention,' I shrugged. 'I shouldn't have said anything. I guess I was still unsettled from the funeral.'

'Yeah,' Sterling agreed, although I could hear in her voice that my feelings about a funeral were not a concern of hers. 'What's the office like?'

'Uh, big?' I said, as though I hadn't seen it twice and hadn't had a good look around. 'It has a big desk that's covered in paperwork, and some cushy chairs.'

'When's your detention?' Xanthe asked. She put her scrying things away in her cupboard.

'I have three weeks, starting tonight,' I told them. 'It's an hour a night, on weeknights, straight after tea, in the head's office.'

'In Renatus's office!?' Sterling demanded, eyes wide. I nodded, and she pouted. 'But that's so unfair! How come *you* get to spend time with him?'

'If you piss off a teacher, you'll get to join her,' Xanthe suggested.

'You have to tell me *everything*,' Sterling instructed me. Her bright brown eyes were beggars. 'I need to know everything you see or hear. Anything he says.' She sighed, and looked away. 'You are *so lucky*, Aristea.'

'Yeah,' I said in a sarcastic voice, but I meant it, because I knew I was. I had been given a way out of exclusion from the school.

Sterling fell into one of her monologues, as she was prone to do, wondering aloud what level of trouble she needed to get into before she, too, could be sent to the headmaster's office. Xanthe and I went about collecting our things for our next classes, nodding at Sterling periodically.

I shouldn't have worried about how difficult it would be to lie to people about the day's events, because all I'd had to do was tell the lie to Sterling, and she did the rest for me. Over lunch, she enviously retold the story to Kendra and Sophia, and then to Hiroko when she turned up.

'I see,' Hiroko said, once Sterling had finished. Her dark eyes shifted to me, questioningly. I met her gaze, wishing I could use telepathy already. I'd shared the truth with her that morning about my dream – I fully intended to fill her in on the rest, but *only* her. I hadn't known Hiroko long, but I trusted her implicitly, and I felt that leaving her to believe the story she'd just been told would be ten times worse than lying to Sterling or Xanthe.

Luckily, Hiroko didn't bring up the dream all day, even when Sterling continued talking about my detentions to anyone who'd listen right through the afternoon and into the evening. I didn't bother but Hiroko tried valiantly to change the topic, especially when Sterling noticed Renatus enter the dining hall.

'He, like, *never* comes to dinner,' Sterling

reminded us. Her bright eyes followed him from the tall doors over to the table where the White Elm sat eating. As usual, she wasn't the only one – most of the female student population did the same thing. I glanced over the White Elm.

For the first time, I noticed that most of them didn't share the girls' interest. A few councillors glanced at him quickly and then turned back to their conversations; most of them paid very close attention to their meals. It wasn't like they just didn't notice him. I got the distinct impression that the headmaster was being ignored. I had once imagined them all to be close friends, but what I had seen of Qasim and Renatus together told me that there was at least some animosity within the council. Were there others who disliked Renatus, too? Why?

Emmanuelle, however, nodded respectfully to Renatus and glanced once to the empty seat beside her, offering him the spot. He pulled the chair out and sat down, the only councillor without a meal in front of him.

'That must be how he keeps his figure,' Sterling commented, shoving her plate away and dusting off her hands. 'He never eats. He just sits in his office all day. It's about getting a balance between energy input and output.' She frowned slightly and tilted her head to the side. 'But Emmanuelle just eats and eats, and she stays looking amazing, too…' She eyed her plate suspiciously but didn't pull it over again. She suddenly turned to me with bright eyes. 'It's your first detention tonight!'

'Elijah's lesson today was very good,' Hiroko

interrupted – rescuing me – and she kept talking, recounting her whole lesson. The whole group latched onto the conversation desperately.

'I wish I could displace like you can,' Kendra said jealously. 'Teleportation is so, so cool. Are you the best at the school?'

'Probably not,' Xanthe mentioned, not in a nasty tone but I felt a flash of annoyance at her for needing to even say that, and then a second bout of annoyance at Xanthe for ruining my good mood.

'In my Displacement class, I am the only student which can displace unassisted for more than ten metres,' Hiroko told the group. 'Elijah was very pleased.'

'That's great,' I said. 'How far *can* you displace?'

'Probably one hundred metres, because I have never been anywhere with enough to space to practise further distances,' she said. 'I may be able to displace further, but in such a case, the destination must be visible to me, and in Sapporo, there is nowhere with such wide open spaces as here. Soon, Elijah plans to take us out of the school grounds to some hills, and then we can practise long-distance.'

'Our mom has had a go at teaching us to displace,' Sophia said. 'We've both managed some pretty dodgy results.'

'But results, nonetheless,' Kendra asserted. 'It's because we're awesome.'

'I believe that.'

We all looked up at the newcomer who had spoken. The tall, dark-haired stranger was the twins' admirer, and he was standing beside them, his plate in his hand. He was so tall that he cast a shadow over Sophia.

'Hey,' Kendra said, and both she and her sister's faces were lit by identical smiles.

'Do you mind if I sit here?' he asked, indicating the seat beside Sophia with his cutlery. Sophia pretended to dust it off.

'All yours,' she said, as Kendra began introducing us.

'I don't know who knows who,' she said with an air of easy confidence, 'but this is Addison. Addison, that's Sterling and Hiroko from our scrying class, and these two are Xanthe and Aristea.'

'Hi,' he said, grinning around at us all as he took the seat beside Sophia. We echoed his greeting in a girlish unison that embarrassed me – were we twelve?

'So,' Kendra said, before the conversation could lapse uncomfortably. She leaned past her sister to address Addison. 'What brings you all the way from your group of mates to brave our lame, girly conversations?' She nodded once to the other side of the room, and we all glanced over – at the other end of the table, a small group of lads were pretending not to watch our reaction to Addison's presence. They all turned away when they realised that they'd been caught.

Perhaps, after all, we *were* all only twelve.

Addison grinned.

'Don't mind them,' he advised. 'They just wish that they had the balls to talk to cute girls, too.'

Kendra grinned back, and went back to her

meal, unable to stop smiling.

The flirting went on all night, and although Addison was generous with himself – making every effort to engage every member of the group in honest, friendly conversation – it was obvious that his pick was Kendra.

'What's wrong with him?' Sterling asked me quietly just as I finished my beans, shaking my arm and pointing discreetly at the staff table. I shrugged as I turned to look, pretty sure I knew who she was talking about. Renatus was standing, but he looked strange. His head hung and his hands were braced on the table as though for balance. I saw Emmanuelle touch his arm worriedly but he did not react.

'No idea,' I murmured back, slightly disquieted by my own worry. What did I care that the headmaster was experiencing a migraine? It was none of my business and I didn't know him well enough to let his problems concern me.

It was only a few moments later that Qasim strode into the hall, too. My stomach turned anxiously and I tried to look away, not wanting any further contact with my scrying teacher today. It was hard not to watch, though, as he beckoned once to the unresponsive headmaster, face grim, before turning on his heel and leaving again. Renatus couldn't have seen; however, he blinked and murmured something to Emmanuelle, then hurried after the Scrier. The other White Elm stared after the two men in something like shock – perhaps because despite their earlier disagreement they were now presumably off to do something important together –

and I started to feel queasy.

'Wonder what that was about?' Sterling said. She seemed only mildly worried. My stomach was still turning like it had when I'd seen Qasim, but he was gone now.

'Does your lasagne taste strange to you?' I asked, scraping some of the béchamel cheese sauce from the top. It had seemed fine, but could it be causing the ill-feeling in my tummy?

'No, it's good.' Sterling frowned at me. 'Are you alright?'

What else had I eaten? A ham and cheese toasted sandwich for lunch, those beans and a few potato wedges before starting on this lasagne…

'You look a little pale,' Kendra agreed. She reached flirtatiously across Addison and nudged her sister. 'Don't you reckon?'

'Hmm,' Sophia said non-committally. She looked critically at the air around me. 'It's not you.'

I was going to ask what she meant when suddenly it clicked.

It wasn't me, and it wasn't *my* anxious ill-feeling. How many times had this happened before? When someone else nearby was feeling something really strongly, I often found myself unconsciously tapping in and feeling it, too, despite not understanding the cause or the context.

I jumped as I felt a hand on my arm and suddenly I was overcome with mental pictures and strange feelings.

A classy hotel bar with low, flattering lights…A man and a woman sitting in stools sipping drinks…'If you'd told me your name at the outset I probably would have called them on you'...The man laughs...Long black hair hangs over his shoulders...Warmth, honesty, genuineness...His bronze-brown eyes are bright and friendly...'I would have understood'...Smiles, another round of drinks, and the light atmosphere moves to a more serious one...'Is my boy safe?'...Trust, warmth...'I'm not saying they'll hurt your son – not at all. I won't lie about them like they lie about me. They'll treat him right. I'm just saying that their idea of "right" can be different from yours or mine'...Worry...'How different?'...

'Aristea?'

I heard my name, sounding to be in a separate place from what I was seeing and experiencing and was aware that Renatus had a hand on my arm and that less than a second had passed. The images, I knew innately, were from him – he was a channel, and I was tuned in to it, whether he realised or not.

'You know why I left? The story nobody tells? I wanted the power to save one life – just one little life, make it worth living...and they wouldn't grant me that.'

I yanked my arm away from his touch, and the stream of images, sounds and feelings immediately stopped. I was in the dining hall, with a plate of lasagne sitting in front of me and my friends sitting around me, and nobody else had noticed what I had.

'I hope you don't mind but your detentions start *tomorrow* night,' Renatus said, already backing away. I nodded, pretty sure it wouldn't matter if I *did* mind, and he turned and all but ran through the doors.

I was left feeling completely content and warm, just as that classy hotel place had felt.

'*Oh my god he touched you.*' Sterling grabbed my arm as though she could absorb his essence by touching where he'd touched. I didn't tell her he'd also held my hand, just hours ago, because then she might want to amputate the whole arm and keep it forever.

What the hell was that about? It had been both less and more realistic than actually being present at that scene. Able to see and hear everything in the bar while also feeling distinctly distant, like watching a TV programme, made me think I'd scried it all, although feeling what the people felt had been completely surreal. Was that normal in scrying? Who cared? The warm, trusting, friendly atmosphere of the scene had totally relaxed the anxiety and worry I'd been feeling moments earlier. Except last night when I'd accidentally Haunted Renatus's office, I'd never scried anything that clearly before. And I'd never scried anything *through* someone, either.

In my happy and quiet state, I decided it didn't really matter. I was feeling so pleasant that I couldn't even bring myself to feel particularly sad for Sophia, whereas normally I would felt extremely sorry for someone whose sister and Addison actively and unashamedly flirted *over* her for the duration of the whole meal.

I finished off my lasagne, glad for the general simplicity of the existence I led.

chapter eighteen

Qasim was having trouble quietening his mind.

All day he'd felt off, ending lessons early and overhearing the quiet conversation of students as they left, so certain were they that they were out of his earshot.

'He seemed fine to me. Did you hear that he went off at that girl Aristea this morning?'

'I heard she was being a smart-arse.'

Teenagers spread rumours like kindergarteners spread germs, and just like disease, rumour had a tendency to evolve and change as it moved from person to person. Aristea had indeed been too arrogant for his liking, but that wasn't the core of his anger. She was a *scrier*, a powerful one – so powerful and gifted that she could *Haunt*, yet she consistently failed the simple exercises he set her in class. A lot of the time, she seemed to not really understand *how* to do what he asked of her. Given guidance and support, she could be amazing...but Haunting was such a dangerous, serious issue. How many sorcerers had killed others or themselves by projecting themselves from their bodies? She would be charged, of course, for such a gross breach of law and ethics. She would be expelled. She would be out of reach, gone forever.

He'd been too proud, he knew. Renatus had done exactly what he'd really hoped he would – he'd been only too willing to sweep the problem away, make it unseen – but Qasim had been too angry about being overstepped by his least favourite colleague that he hadn't even realised. Aristea was still a student at the Academy. She was not going to be charged. She was not going anywhere. She was still within reach.

True scriers – those sorcerers born with an innate gift for the art – were rare, and often discovered the talent by themselves as children. Qasim had. He was sure Renatus had. Aristea, however, had never learnt to use her gift. Her self-doubting personality had walled it off, and then the trauma of losing her family had further obscured it. Qasim had seen the emotional scars all through her mind. The damage and the talent for scrying reminded him strongly of Renatus, whom he disliked very much more.

This morning, they had both dropped several more rungs down his list of favourite people. Whenever he thought about his confrontation with Renatus, Qasim felt an urge to rage and shout. Who did Renatus think he was? What had Lord Gawain been thinking when he'd picked the boy for

Lisandro's secretive chair? What had *Qasim* been thinking when he'd voted in agreement?

Better him than me, he'd thought. The Dark Keeper could never be the council's Lord, and Qasim was next in line for that. He'd devoted thirty-two years to the White Elm – he'd worked hard and selflessly and he had no interest in ending his career as Dark Keeper, probably dead much too soon as they typically were. Dark Keepers never lasted long. Lord Gawain must have forgotten that when he chose his favourite boy for the job.

Qasim opened his eyes and looked around his classroom. When selecting the best room to convert into their ideal work spaces, most of the councillors had been easy to please. Well-lit, please. Lots of space for practical work, thanks. Qasim had wandered through several rooms and quickly learned to avoid touching things. The Morrissey's had always been scriers, powerful and passionate, and traces of their lives remained all throughout the house on walls and furniture for an attuned scrier to tap right into. Advanced or gifted students in his subject area would be sensitive to these traces and some were confronting, so when he'd stepped into this room and detected nearly nothing, he'd known it would be perfect. Totally traceless. Not long before Renatus's entire immediate family had been wiped out, they'd been betrayed, and this room was probably where it had happened if he'd been upset enough with the room's energy to wipe it.

So there was absolutely nothing here to distract a scrier from working his gift, except himself.

Sitting cross-legged on the floor, Qasim closed his eyes again. It had been just over six months since he'd last seen, heard or felt a current trace of the previous Dark Keeper, and it was easy to lose heart and wonder whether they would ever track him down. Tapping into the energetic echoes of Peter's murder had been a strike of luck – no enchantment could hide something like that for long; had Lisandro slipped up and forgotten that? – but not necessarily *good* luck. They'd been much too late to prevent anything, and still hadn't discovered the actual site of the crime, the only place in the world they *knew* Lisandro had visited all year. There were whispers, sure, that he'd been there, popped up over here, been sighted there…A whisper was only ever a starting point, not real evidence, and each place the White Elm searched based on sightings had turned up nothing at all.

Lisandro.

Visions, images and sounds flowed through Qasim's subconscious, and his meticulous, expert mind sifted through them, easily able to discriminate between the useful and the useless in milliseconds.

A pair of girls strapping on roller skates…'Mom says we're still going skiing this year, even though that Lisandro guy is around'…Useless. *Three teenage boys at the Academy in a disastrously messy dormitory – one is Constantine, a good scrier. He and Jin are mucking around, sparring…'Think Lisandro knows how to get out of this arm bar?'*…Useless.

Qasim could easily wile away hours like this, and did; most scriers became so absorbed by their visions that they lost track of time but Qasim was always aware. Right now, he was mostly just aware that Lisandro was too well-hidden in enchantments.

One more minute, he decided, and opened his mind as far as it would go, the ultimate metaphorical satellite dish. He let go of his focus – Lisandro – so that anything and everything the universe wanted him to see would come.

Peter's grandmother, talking quietly to the ceramic urn above her mantle…

Two hooded figures running in the rain…

Emmanuelle's front door…

A gypsy market…Adult brother and sister admire a handmade necklace while the toothy saleswoman talks about its craftsmanship…'You should get it, or you'll have nothing for her birthday. You always leave things so late'…A shapely gypsy woman with her face shrouded catches the sister's hand. 'They said you'd ruin everything. I can't let you. I'm so sorry'…The brother steps in but the gypsy just turns her attention to him. 'There are two places. Write to them and say you don't want to be considered. Do it or we'll remove you from the pool of applicants. I can't let you stop us'…'Get lost,' the brother snaps, directing his sister away…

Qasim slowly started to come out of his trance, uncomfortably aware that though the gypsy and the brother were unfamiliar, he'd met the sister before…

A classy hotel bar with low, flattering lights…A man and a woman sitting on stools sipping drinks…'If you'd told me your name at the outset I probably would have called them on you'…The man laughs…Long black hair hangs over his shoulders…His bronze-brown eyes are bright and friendly…

This final vision drove all the others from Qasim's mind immediately, and in an instant he was on his feet and running out the door.

'I would have understood'…'You're not what I expected'….Lisandro waves down the bartender and orders another round of drinks…'Well, haven't you heard not to judge a book by its cover?'…The woman laughs…She seems so at ease with him…

This was not an echo of a long-lost past event, like that marketplace or the death of Peter. This was happening right now. But how? How was Qasim able to see this? Lisandro's movements had been totally shrouded from Qasim since he'd left the council. The only means Qasim had of tapping into this was if Lisandro *allowed* it.

If Lisandro wanted him to come, then he would bring the only weapon he had.

He displaced from the top of the staircase to the entrance hall, a tiny jump that he normally wouldn't have bothered with but tonight was different. He only had to take a few steps into the dining hall to know what he'd suspected – Renatus could see it all, too. His eyes were closed as he gave himself over to what he was seeing, but he would still be completely aware of his surroundings, so when Qasim beckoned and turned away, he knew the younger scrier would follow. He had to. This was his job – this was what they'd kept him for.

The woman finishes her drink and puts down the glass with a loud clunk…'You must know I have a son at the White Elm's Academy. That must be why you're talking to me'...Lisandro sips from his glass and smiles over the rim...'You won't believe I just thought you looked much too fabulous to be stood up tonight?'...'Yes, well, obviously I won't be accepting future dates from the loser who forgot me here'...'That's such a great dress. I bet you didn't think you'd be drinking with White Elm's Most Wanted tonight when you picked that out'...They both laugh and order another drink...

Renatus met Qasim in the entrance hall, his usually expressionless face tight.

'He knows we're watching,' was the first thing he said as they started towards the front doors, the confrontation from earlier today completely forgotten for now. 'There's no way this is an accident.'

'Not a chance.'

'We're walking right into his hands.'

'So we'll be careful,' Qasim reminded the Dark Keeper. 'We have to. The woman he's talking to is a parent of one of our students.'

Renatus touched the doors and they started to open, but instead of pushing through them, he paused, and half-ran back into the dining room.

'What are you doing?' Qasim demanded, frustrated. Every second wasted here was another second that woman was in danger of being either harmed or converted by Lisandro. Without even thinking about it, Qasim automatically tuned into the energy of his younger colleague, and, through the wall separating them, was able to scry a glimpse of Renatus briefly exchanging words with a shell-shocked Aristea.

What on *Earth*…? The pair had probably never even spoken before Qasim had brought them together today, so what did Renatus have to tell her that was so important he'd risk this chance?

Unless Renatus didn't *want* to catch Lisandro…

Lisandro smiles kindly, with a small twist of bitterness…'I'm not saying they'll hurt your son – not at all. I won't lie about them like they lie about me. They'll treat him right. I'm just saying that their idea of "right" can be different from yours or mine'…

Renatus was back in seconds and the two scriers ran out the door together.

'Rescheduling,' Renatus said by way of explanation. 'Where exactly?'

Qasim knew already, from the accent of the woman, that he was heading to America somewhere, but it took a great deal of concentration to be able to pinpoint the exact place of the vision.

'Michigan, U.S.,' he said, though Renatus would know almost at the same instant. 'Who's coming?'

The conversation was entirely rhetorical – whatever Qasim asked he would know as soon as Renatus did, just as he knew even as Renatus told him that Lord Gawain and Susannah were preparing to meet them on location. Had those two Seers known or suspected this event? Emmanuelle would stay behind. She possessed the council's other, more reliable, weapon but had had only a day to get used to it. The possibility of her doing more damage with that sort of power than good was too great a risk.

The gate opened obediently for Renatus and they bolted through, trying to get far enough away from the house that its tightly woven spells would not disrupt attempts to warp space and displace. Qasim felt for the Fabric, the stuff from which all space was made, but hesitated when he recognised that it was already misshapen.

Someone was already manipulating this space.

Jadon and Aubrey appeared a few metres away.

'Where is he?' Jadon asked at the same time that Aubrey asked, worriedly, 'What's going on?'

Qasim resisted the frustration that was rising within him. He didn't have the time for this, but already, the Fabric was smoothing, relaxing to its natural state.

'We'll handle it,' he told them, beginning to open the wormhole.

'No, take us with you,' Jadon insisted, and the way he stepped forward demanded Qasim's attention. He was only twenty, the youngest councillor currently on the White Elm, and though right now he seemed older, it was difficult for Qasim to perceive him as the capable adult he probably was. Jadon knew a lot of magic, a great deal more than most modern young sorcerers. Perhaps...?

And Aubrey was a Crafter, an invaluable talent facing Lisandro, and the same age as Renatus...

'I don't know what to think. I can't believe that'...'There are always two sides to every story'...The woman fidgets with the straw of her last drink...Brown eyes and hair, straight nose...Egan Lake's mother...'You should go. They've found us and they're here now'...'The White Elm? Are you sure?'...'Go. They're not here for you; don't get caught in the middle'...

Renatus grasped Qasim's elbow, helping him to make up his mind. He might personally trust the newer two councillors more than he trusted the Dark Keeper, but he couldn't trust that they would hold their own in a conflict.

'Stay and protect our students, in case this is only a diversion,' Qasim told them as he stepped between Ireland and America with Renatus. Jadon's glare stuck in his mind as the wormhole closed behind them.

They were standing in the underground car park of the hotel. Susannah and Lord Gawain stood opposite, looking pale. The last contact with Lisandro had been a disaster and no one was looking forward to this one.

'You shouldn't have come,' Renatus said to the council leader. 'This is your mortal weekend. You should be with your clients or your family.'

'Court has adjourned for the day and this is more pressing than the dishes.'

'Lobby,' Qasim said, leading the way up the nearby fire escape stairs. The others followed closely, and four flights up, he shoved open an alarmed door. A high-pitched bleat started to sound, but Renatus slammed the heel of his palm into a fuse box beside the doorframe before it could finish even one whine. The sound died and the box was left sparking pitifully. Magic and electricity did not mix.

The lobby was exactly as Qasim had seen it, except with slightly more bewildered patrons. They'd all been startled by that brief but loud sound. They were sitting in the same seats, sipping the same drinks, reading the same magazines. The framed vintage posters were the same, the mismatched vases lined along the hall table were the same, and the coasters on the bar were the same.

And sitting in the same seat, waiting for them, was Lisandro. For one horrible second, Qasim knew that all hell was about to break loose here, that dozens of people were about to witness something they couldn't possibly explain and that they could easily come to harm in the cross-fire. There was no way around it and they'd waited for this moment for so long that no one was going to interfere with whatever Renatus needed to do.

But in the next second, when Lisandro spoke, Qasim knew that he was wrong.

'Guys! Join me for a drink?'

No one needed to die. Lisandro wasn't here for a fight. He was happy to sit, totally unworried. He knew exactly what he was doing, as usual. He knew the White Elm couldn't initiate a conflict and would avoid a scene if they could manage it.

A strong sense of calm flooded the lobby, and the patrons went back to their conversations and magazines. Qasim felt himself relaxing, too, and started to release his hold on the energy he'd been drawing to himself in preparation for a fight that would not be.

Lisandro smiled at them all and it was like no time had passed. He looked as he had when they'd all been friends. His bronze-brown eyes were sparkling and friendly. Perhaps things were not as awful as Qasim had assumed. Perhaps this really *was* a misunderstanding.

Renatus elbowed him sharply as he passed, and the resultant second of irritation was enough to snap the contentment. Qasim immediately felt clearer and more alert, and stepped forward as Renatus advanced.

'Ah, Renatus,' Lisandro said cheerfully, 'it'll feel odd buying you alcohol but I do suppose you're old enough now. What'll it be?'

'It would be a whiskey with someone – anyone – else,' Renatus answered coldly. 'Step outside with us.'

'Bring your drink if you like,' Qasim added when Lisandro wrapped his fingers more tightly around his glass.

'Step outside?' Lisandro asked slowly, innocently, putting his glass down. 'Whatever for?'

'Lisandro, we're here to bring you in,' Lord Gawain said, and Lisandro's gaze slowly slid over the four councillors to rest on the leader. 'It would be in your best interests to come quietly.'

The bronze-brown eyes narrowed momentarily, and Qasim knew that look of passive defiance. Coming tonight had been a bad idea, like Renatus had said. He felt along the telepathic circle of minds that made up the White Elm, gauging the ability of each member to get here quickly if this situation got out of hand. Every one of them was totally focussed on these events, trying to interpret images, thoughts and understandings from this exchange from the minds of those present. Qasim tried to keep his mind quiet and organised to help them read his thoughts more clearly.

'In *your* best interests, I think,' Lisandro corrected, still eyeing Lord Gawain. 'And as my very least favourite person in the world, I'm afraid I feel particularly loath to do anything that would serve your best interests.' He left the silence hanging and moved his attention back along the line of former friends. He smiled warmly at Susannah. '*Your* best interests, however, are still near my heart – never once did *you* betray me like our dear Lord did.'

'Save it, please,' Susannah answered without emotion. 'We both know that whatever care we shared for each other is long dead.'

'Alright, perhaps that's true, but your interests still trump Gawain's if it ever comes down to it. Those many takeaway coffees you bought me won't be forgotten.'

'We cremated Peter this morning,' Susannah said. 'So my memories of coffee-drinking with you seem slightly less pleasant tonight. Did you drink takeaway coffees with Peter in the old days, too?'

'Ah, yes, I did drink coffees with dear Peter,' Lisandro agreed. 'Rest his soul. I suppose you think me traitorous and nasty and all that for what's become his fate? Entitled to your own opinion, of course – though you'd hardly think anything of it if only you knew how Gawain had first betrayed *me*, and how Peter exacerbated that betrayal.'

'It's a bit rich of *you* to talk about betrayal, isn't it?' Qasim asked. 'Considering.'

'Yes, considering,' Renatus agreed, harshly. Lisandro looked between the two scriers and sat back on his stool, resting against the bar.

Qasim felt a twitch at the edge of his consciousness. Emmanuelle? Was she here, too? Things could get very messy if she turned up and tried to use that ring before she knew how.

'Considering I walked out on your beloved council, Qasim, and forced you to vote this runt into my old chair?' he asked. Qasim kept his expression firm but felt surprise. 'Yes, I know Renatus is Dark Keeper. Shocking, yes.' He turned to smile at his successor. 'How do you like my old job? Are they keeping you busy? Or does Gawain just like keeping his favourite baby boy close to watch you?' He winked cheekily. 'You know, the naughty way?'

Renatus closed the remaining distance between them in an instant and knocked Lisandro's glass from his grip. It shattered on the bar noisily.

'Watch your words,' he snarled, a warning finger pointed in Lisandro's face. Qasim looked around but nobody seemed to have noticed the broken glass or the altercation between the two men.

Distantly, he felt another twitch. It was Emmanuelle trying to reach him, but she wasn't here. She was at the house. Something was wrong.

'Such loyalty,' Lisandro said smoothly, clearly unafraid and unthreatened by Renatus's show of aggression. 'That's the Morrissey in you. I wonder how far it stretches. Your father had a limit – if only I were able to detail to you the dark depths of Gawain's betrayal of me.'

'What betrayal? ' Lord Gawain demanded, frustrated. 'It was you who turned his back on our friendship and the council, not me.'

Qasim felt no curiosity regarding this supposed betrayal of Lord Gawain's. Lisandro was twisted by years of dabbling in the darkness; anything the frustratingly passive and harmless leader had done to upset the Crafter had doubtless been a true and honest act that Lisandro had taken offence to.

He heard Emmanuelle's voice in his head.

This is a distraction. Someone's at my place. My wards are coming down.

Emmanuelle's wards were among the best in the world and her home was coated in them. They were not infallible but they were challenging to dissect. Furthermore, because of the nature of many of those spells, in order to pull them down, one first had to know they, and the home, were there, and that description only applied to the select few she'd invited inside. The city apartment went unnoticed by thousands of passersby every single day – only someone she knew could see it.

Qasim thought of the Parisian home and directed his mind to view it as it was.

He only saw black. The whole street was invisible to him.

That meant that someone was there, and that person had blocked his energy from Qasim's sight. How many people in the world knew and hated him enough to do that?

Just two...and if one was here, suddenly and conveniently unblocked, that meant that Jackson was at Emmanuelle's home, tearing her wards and possessions apart in search of the Elm Stone Qasim hoped she'd never be stupid enough to leave lying around. He frantically tried to recall whether she'd been home today, whether there was a chance she'd taken it home and left it there...

'We were friends and *you* are the one who chose to end it,' Lord Gawain finished.

'That's your opinion, and you're entitled to it,' Lisandro replied diplomatically, folding his hands in his lap. He ignored Renatus, seething beside him. 'Your opinion is wrong, of course, but I won't fault you for that. I fault you for enough as it is.'

Lord Gawain opened his mouth to respond but Qasim interrupted.

'That's enough,' he said roughly, shouldering past Susannah to reach for Lisandro. This whole situation was by the Crafter's design – he'd drawn them there, he'd orchestrated the conversation and he'd kept the attention of all thirteen White Elm on this place. None of this was within their control unless they took it. 'Let's get him out of here.'

'I think not,' Lisandro disagreed, slipping from the barstool. Qasim's hand closed on air. 'Tonight just isn't your night.'

Susannah and Lord Gawain backed up to give Qasim and Renatus space to make their arrest. Lisandro stayed near the bar, watching his adversaries closely.

'Don't make this difficult,' Qasim warned, flanking Renatus as they closed in. This was it. This was what they'd kept Renatus for – to take down his predecessor. It might be now or never. Lisandro smiled and shook his head.

'Hardly fun if it's too easy, is it?'

Now.

The time to take Lisandro was now. Qasim waited for Renatus's move. It could be anything – light magic or dark, old or new, conventional or unique – so Qasim just needed to be ready to back him up or get out of the way.

Now.

Nothing happened. Renatus stayed where he was, tense but unmoving. He was not taking Lisandro in. The nightmare was real. Renatus was not acting, whether because he was still loyal to Lisandro or out of fear. It didn't matter why. Emmanuelle's voice was still in Qasim's head – *My wards are coming down. Someone's inside* – and something had to be done.

What they're looking for, is it with you? he asked Emmanuelle, and when he got her indignant agreement he added, *Do not leave the estate. Stay exactly where you are.*

Qasim stepped forward, drawing power to his body and preparing a stun spell. He'd only have to grasp Lisandro's arm and the magic would move to attack his nerves. Surprisingly, Lisandro moved to meet him.

Channelling the energy along his arms, Qasim opened his hands to release the magic as a spell. In that millisecond he saw Lisandro's palm open, too, and saw the sparkle of blackness. Lisandro threw it.

Renatus shoved Qasim aside and he felt his fingertips graze the young scrier's wrist. The Dark Keeper stumbled, temporarily paralysed, and caught the bar – for a second Qasim was glad to have hurt him for interfering – but that ball of sparkling black energy in Lisandro's hand now missed Qasim by only inches and blasted a fiery hole in the polished floor.

There was a moment of stunned silence. Lisandro had meant that to strike Qasim. It would have put a hole right through him. The Crafter smirked.

'Are we having fun yet?'

A second ball of crackling black magic began to grow in Lisandro's open hand before Qasim had a chance to build any substantial wards. Nearby and shaking very slightly from the recent attack on his nervous system, Renatus seemed to be recovering. Perhaps now he would want to do something about taking Lisandro in.

'Lisandro, this is stupid,' Susannah snapped, hands out and at the ready.

'I agree,' the Crafter said seriously. 'There's only one person here I really want to see hurt.'

Too quick, he tossed the ball of black lightning at Lord Gawain. Qasim felt his breath catch as he followed the spell with his eyes. *No.*

The ball flew at the old Seer's chest but stopped just short, all motion lost, frozen in space.

Qasim spun on his heel, sure this had to be some surprise power of Renatus's – there were so many of those. The Dark Keeper had a dagger across Lisandro's throat and both stood very still.

'I suppose you think killing me would be like winning, huh?' the Crafter asked softly. 'You think it'll make the past go away?'

'Shut your face,' Renatus hissed, 'and drop it.'

'When you cut your name loose, did you have Gawain adopt you or something?' Lisandro asked, frowning. 'You don't owe him anything – you don't owe him your life. He's not your father. Your father was twice the man-'

'Drop it!'

'Let me go and Papa Gawain goes hole-free, too,' Lisandro bargained. Renatus thrust the blade closer, cutting skin. 'You have my word.'

'Your *word* doesn't mean a whole lot to me these days.'

This was what Qasim had been waiting for. Finally, Renatus's lifelong hatred of Lisandro was coming in handy.

'Well, how about a bet then? I bet I can put a hole through Lord Gawain's heart quicker than you can pull that knife across my neck. You in?'

Keeping the blade tight against the enemy windpipe, Renatus grabbed Lisandro's shirt collar and pulled him over to where Lord Gawain still stood, wide-eyed. Careful not to touch the floating ball of black lightning, he elbowed the old man back. The ball did not follow but waited in place, mirroring Lisandro's own curiosity. Renatus positioned himself in its path and Lisandro, pinned to his successor's side, seemed to shrink. His expression closed off; this was not something he'd expected or wanted. Lord Gawain was still in the spell's path, but to kill the Lord the spell had to first pass through Renatus and Lisandro himself.

'I'm in,' Renatus agreed coldly. 'So do it.'

Qasim watched as Lisandro stared back at Renatus with a calculating look.

'Get out of here,' Renatus said, releasing Lisandro's collar but keeping the dagger against his throat.

'Well played,' Lisandro admitted. Behind his back, the black magic crackled into nothingness. 'Until next time.'

He disappeared, and later, a contented waitress would spot that blackened hole in the floor and wonder whether it had anything to do with the odd crowd that had left through the fire exit.

chapter nineteen

Friday was mostly uneventful. I had two classes, both of which were with Sterling, who, by dinnertime, had well and truly driven me insane with her begging.

'You're so lucky,' she said for the eightieth time as we ate our pasta. 'You have to tell me *everything*.'

'Sterling, I already said I would,' I reminded her, for the seventy-ninth time. 'He probably won't do anything except make a start on that massive pile of paperwork he keeps on his desk. He's the most boring guy around.'

'It's not fair that you've seen his office, and I haven't,' Sterling pouted. On her other side, Kendra rolled her eyes.

'Sterling, it's an office,' she said bluntly. 'There's nothing exciting about a man's office. If Aristea had seen his bedroom, then, maybe, I'd allow you to be jealous. Maybe.'

'I suppose,' Sterling agreed glumly. She glanced

up at the staff table, but very few of the White Elm were present tonight, and Renatus was one of the majority who had chosen not to attend. Aside from those with classes, actually, I'd not seen any White Elm all day. A vague rumour about something big going down outside of the school had circulated among the students, and I suspected that this may be true, from what I'd experienced last night, but I wasn't very worried. After all, it hardly concerned me unless Lord Gawain needed to make some kind of announcement, and he hadn't.

'You're just so lucky,' Sterling murmured again. *Eighty-freaking-one.*

Hiroko met my eyes knowingly over the table. The previous evening, sitting on our bathroom floor, and I'd filled her in on everything that had been said and done on Thursday morning (the real truth, not just the story I was allowing to circulate). As usual, she'd made the perfect audience, listening intently, and cringing and covering her mouth in apprehension at all the right places. She was grateful to be given the truth, I knew, and even though I wasn't meant to share the real truth with anyone, it felt right to do so.

Hiroko was a good friend and I knew I could trust her.

I checked my watch and arranged my cutlery.

'Got to go,' I said, standing and pushing in my chair.

'Aristea – don't forget!' Sterling said brightly. Sophia looked up at me earnestly.

'Yes, don't forget,' she said. 'Enjoy taking notes

on the headmaster's ass, and the way his hair falls into his eyes.'

I poked my tongue at her and Sterling blushed while the other girls laughed.

'Aw, I knew my baby sister had funny in her somewhere,' Kendra said adoringly. Sophia threw a pea at her.

'Yeah, but sadly we're still looking for it in you.'

'What are you on about? I'm the funny twin. You're the quiet, boring one.'

'Bye,' I called, smiling as I walked away. I had made some really fantastic friends here, which I would never have found had I not been brought into this incredible multicultural environment. I had my own dear sister to thank for signing the form and letting me come.

I reached the door of Renatus's office and raised my hand to knock, assuming that if he hadn't attended dinner, he must be inside already. Before my knuckles could connect with the door, though, it opened, and several White Elm walked out.

'Oh,' Lady Miranda said when she saw me. 'Did you need to speak with us?'

'No, I-'

Qasim was right behind her, and cut me off abruptly.

'Then what *are* you doing here?' he asked. His voice was cold and nasty, and made me want to shrivel up into nothingness.

'Aristea has detention with me this evening,' Renatus said, folding his arms and stopping beside me. Two other councillors, Susannah and

Emmanuelle, slipped past him quickly. 'Every weeknight for three weeks, just as you requested, Qasim.'

The Scrier and the headmaster stared at each other coolly for a long, uncomfortable moment. The anger of yesterday's exchange seemed to have been healed by whatever adventure they'd undertaken last night, but they were clearly still not friends. Qasim finally looked away.

'Yes, it was,' he agreed in a tense and reluctant tone. He turned and left. The rest of us stood in awkward silence until Renatus gave the other three councillors a nod, which served as a respectful dismissal. Renatus watched them leave, and then waved me inside.

I hovered uncertainly in the centre of the room, waiting for instructions. I'd never done a detention before. He'd said already that I wasn't expected to scrub tables or write lines. What, then, was I meant to do?

The door closed, apparently of its own volition, and Renatus turned to me.

'Did you have any homework to carry on with?' he asked. I shook my head. 'Do you like reading?'

'Yes, I love to read.'

He went to his bookshelf and withdrew a hardback book. He nodded in the direction of the door, and I looked over and saw that a school desk and chair had been placed against the wall beside the door. 'You can sit there, and do whatever you like, just as long as you're quiet.' He handed me the book, and I hesitantly took it. I remembered reaching out for the books when I was Haunting. It was a beautifully bound book, with nothing written on the cover or spine. 'You should probably read this, though, if you've nothing better to do.'

He went to his desk, and I wandered over to the one he'd assigned me. The book felt nice in my hands. It was old and worn, and the covers were creased along the spine where it'd been held open again and again.

I sat down and opened the book in silence. The inside title page read *A Scrier's Instruction*. Intrigued, I turned the next page and began to read the preface.

A scrier is a sorcerer with the natural ability to perceive past or present events without bearing physical witness. Most scriers discover their abilities in childhood through experimentation, but this book has been designed for those sorcerers who, for many reasons, have not naturally progressed to the level of skill others have achieved.

Scrying is a beautiful and precise art and should NOT be confused with the lesser art of Seeing, which, on its most basic level, relates to the deciphering of the metaphorical and symbolic language of the subconscious. Seeing is an interpretation, while scrying allows the sorcerer to actually witness a situation in its entirety.

Unlike the other five classes, a scrier never takes a capital letter for himself. Telepaths, Seers, Healers, Crafters and Displacers are always referred to, both visibly in print and inferred in speech, as capitalised proper nouns, whereas scriers recognise their class as only one facet of themselves and historically use only lower-case.

The one exception is the White Elm's Scrier, whose honourable title is capitalised out of respect for his position. Some say this habit is derived from the famous scrier pride, and their pride in the White Elm Scrier; others insist this is only another representation of the infamous scrier stubbornness and unwillingness to conform.

There are three forms of scrying, all of which are explained in detail in the first chapter of this book – Conscious, Passive, and Haunting. Each can be highly effective, and each scrier will likely find one form more useful than the others. Conscious Scrying is by far the easiest form to achieve, and many non-scriers are able to develop this skill – however, Passive Scrying and Haunting are skills which require the natural predisposition of a born scrier. The latter has never been achieved by any non-scrier.

I had never realised before now that even in my mind, Qasim was Scrier with a big capital S. How strange that ours was the odd class out, even grammatically.

I skipped the rest of the preface and went straight into chapter one. I had Haunted, though obviously not deliberately. Only true scriers could do it. It was undeniable proof to me, beyond the insistence of Sophia Prescott and beyond Qasim's mentioning of giftedness. I was a scrier.

I flew through the first two thirds of the chapter, deliberately skipping the section on Haunting. The second chapter talked about the dangers of scrying, including perceiving things that the mind or heart was not ready to know. It talked of scriers in history who had scried things they thought they wanted to know – Who murdered my son? Where is my husband tonight? – only to bear witness to the horrific truth, destroying happiness and sanity. *Be careful what you wish for.*

I stared at the wall, my imagination taking over. What kinds of things would I see when I learnt to scry properly? Sophia had alluded to there being good reasons for the mind blocking the ability to scry. Would I scry into the past and witness events that I should never have known? Other than the deaths in my family, my past was relatively happy. And no one could have stopped that storm – what had happened was an accident. Probably the worst I'd see, looking back into my childhood, was Aidan hiding my toys, or Angela blaming me for something she'd done. Right?

'Don't be so sure,' Renatus said without looking up from his paperwork. 'The problem with digging into the past is that we see things as they *are*, rather than as we thought they were.'

Again, he'd picked up exactly what I was thinking and responded to it. How did he do it? A little unsettled, I put the book down with my hand between the pages so I wouldn't lose my place.

'What do you mean?' I asked.

Renatus paused for a very long moment. His eyes were still cast down onto his work. 'Sometimes it just isn't worth taking a second glance at the past.'

I really didn't know what to say to that, and I was spared having to think of something by Renatus opening a drawer and withdrawing an ancient pocket watch.

'We're all finished here,' he said, breaking the quiet. 'You can take the book with you, if you'd like to read it over the weekend.'

I hadn't realised it had been an hour already. I was about halfway through the book, having skipped the sections on Haunting. It was to-the-point and engaging, so I nodded appreciatively.

'Yes, thank you,' I said. I stood.

'I'll see you again, this time on Monday,' Renatus said. He gave me a nod of farewell and waved a hand delicately; the door opened.

'Good night,' I said, turning to leave.

'Speaking of which,' he added, 'how has the pendant worked?'

I stopped and turned back. I had worn his pendant, as he'd suggested. From the second I'd slipped it over my neck and laid down to sleep, I'd known that I never wanted to Haunt again – especially if it meant I'd be issued this *thing* again. The pendant's energy felt like a lead blanket strewn across my body, holding me down, holding back my power. I'd been overwhelmingly relieved to wake up and remove it, knowing I hadn't done any magic (illegal or otherwise) during my sleep.

'It works,' I agreed, wondering if my reaction to it was normal.

'I know it isn't nice to wear,' Renatus said, 'but a few more nights will be necessary before your mind has had a proper chance to close itself back up. Let's give it one week, and then see how you are after that without it.'

'Alright,' I said, pleased with the notion of giving the awful thing back and never seeing it again. 'I'll see you on Monday.'

'Monday,' Renatus agreed, and I left.

I went back to my dorm and took my key from around my neck to unlock the door. I held the book underneath my arm while I turned the key, then stepped inside.

'Tell me everything!'

I slowly pressed the door shut before even looking at Sterling. She was grinning fervently.

'Well?' she pressed. I smiled thinly at her and looked around. Xanthe and Hiroko were sitting at their desks, doing homework. I had no escape.

'Nothing. I read a book for an hour,' I said.

'And what did *he* do?' Sterling asked, jumping backwards to sit on her bed. I shrugged disinterestedly.

'*The headmaster* sat at his desk and got some of his paperwork done,' I said, opening my drawer and placing *A Scrier's Instruction* inside with the pendant. 'Just like I said he would. I told you – he's completely dull.'

Not entirely true, but an entirely forgivable lie in the circumstances. If I could convince Sterling that Renatus was boring and lame, perhaps she'd lay off this stalker routine.

'And,' Sterling encouraged, 'what did he say?'

'Practically nothing,' I said. I collected my pyjamas and headed for mine and Hiroko's bathroom.

'Aristea,' Sterling pleaded. I turned back to her.

'Really, that was pretty much it,' I insisted. 'I went to the office; he told me to sit down and gave me a book to read so I'd be quiet. After the hour, he said I could go. I came back here.'

Sterling nodded, but she looked intensely disappointed. What had she expected me to say? What had she expected me to have seen or heard in a detention? Sophia's parting words replayed in my mind, and I had to turn away so she wouldn't see my smirk.

The weekend passed much too quickly for me. I finished *A Scrier's Instruction* on Saturday morning and spent my alone time flicking back through its suggested exercises to practise. I played cards with the girls, and explored the library with Hiroko. Each night I braved the daunting pendant and awoke from dreamless sleeps, glad to remove the thing but also glad that I hadn't left my body unattended again. I got a letter from my aunt and wrote back. I ate my meals with my friends, trying to ignore the intense flirting that was escalating daily between Kendra and Addison. Afterwards I would laugh as Sophia teased her sister. Then it was Sunday night, and the weekend was over.

On Monday I had a scrying lesson first thing in the morning. It had been slinking around the back of my mind all weekend, inevitable, speeding up time. I apprehensively followed Xanthe to our classroom, wondering what Qasim would say, if he had anything to say to me at all.

Our classmates quickly arrived, sparing me

curious glances. Obviously they could remember the introduction of the last lesson and wanted for me to explain exactly why I'd been dragged so aggressively from the class by the instructor, but by now Sterling's version must have spread far enough that I needn't bother myself.

Qasim opened the door from the inside and ushered us in without sparing me a glance. I sat down with Xanthe, as usual, and he taught his lesson just as usual, except that he treated me as though I were not present. He did not look at me; he did not address me, verbally or telepathically. I tried not to feel offended – it was probably the best treatment I could have hoped for, coming from Qasim.

Walking out of that classroom after two hours was like taking a breath of fresh air. I was delighted to have survived it, really, and to know that I would be allowed back again in future lessons.

So began another week at the White Elm's Academy of Sorcery. Although the content of Qasim's lessons was my favourite, the treatment I got from the other councillors was definitely preferable. Emmanuelle, though she'd become very subdued, was very pleased to see that I was already so adept at her subject – it was the only other field in which I was placed into the top class. We were learning about long-term wards, the kind you cast around yourself and keep there to protect you from mental attack or from being scried. I loved Emmanuelle's classes because I was good at producing wards; at the conclusion of each lesson, I could happily say that I'd achieved something. As well, Emmanuelle was always on speaking terms with me and my peers and she never held back a compliment or encouraging comment.

Lady Miranda was an excellent teacher of healing; Jadon's subject was still in its dull stage but he did what he could to make it worth our while; Anouk taught history so passionately that attending her lessons was almost like listening to a highly entertaining play. Now that we'd covered the theory, Elijah began teaching my class the basics of displacement. He was possibly the most patient man alive, because lesson after lesson, nobody in my class showed any signs of progress whatsoever. Obviously, I'd been placed in the lowest group – I'd suspected I would be, having never tried it before, but it was a little depressing that all of my friends had been placed in the other two classes. Hiroko was in the top class, and the rest of them were together in Level 2.

'Try again,' Elijah encouraged after my thousandth failed attempt. 'You've nearly got it.'

'I just can't do it,' I argued, frustrated. He laughed lightly, and I looked away. Nearby, the British sorceress Willow had her eyes shut tight in concentration, leaning forwards unconsciously. As I watched, she lost her balance and fell over onto the wet grass.

'Of course you can do it,' Elijah said to me as he went to help Willow up. 'Give it another go.'

Displacement always left me feeling rubbishy. It always finished without any success, and the only person who was still optimistic at the end of each lesson was Elijah.

To counter these failures, it seemed, I began to make progress in Glen's class. By Wednesday's afternoon lesson, I found that I was able to alter my perception enough that I could see auras for more than half a second, and as more than simply a small, coloured haze.

'Try again,' Hiroko said, more to herself than to me, after we'd been squinting at each other for about six minutes. She closed her eyes tightly and shook her head, apparently to relax herself and clear away unnecessary thoughts.

I took a deep breath and prepared myself, also, to try once more. I looked directly at Hiroko and willed myself to *see* the energy I could innately sense around her. I could feel it – I knew it was there, because when I reached out to her with my own energetic fingers, I could touch it. I did exactly that even as I thought it, allowing my senses to brush over her aura. I picked up on her mood, her concerns, her frustration at this exercise, her ambition to perform well at everything she attempted, her reds and pinks and greens...

And something switched over in my mind and I could *see* her.

'It's worked!' I told her enthusiastically. The Hiroko I knew was the nucleus of a swirling egg of coloured energy. The colours were intense, and sometimes obscured her. I didn't know much about colour symbolism, but that didn't matter, because *seeing* the aura and feeling it told me everything I needed to know. The reds, I sensed, were symbolic of

Hiroko's ambitious and loyal nature, and also her frustration with this task. The pink and green swirls throughout her energetic field were indicative of her compassion, self-acceptance and her desire to help others. There was white, and there was purple – spiritual, magical colours...

I looked around as I felt my concentration starting to slip, as it so often did. The twins beside us glowed with auras so unalike that I had difficulty believing that I had managed any success at all in the first lesson, in which I'd deduced that their auras were single-coloured and only shades apart.

Had I only picked up on some basic energetic level that day? Perhaps a base colour or something? Kendra was a bright mix of creative orange, dynamic reds, outgoing blues, psychic purples and loved-up pink, while her sister's energy was softer, with various shades of compassionate pink and the greens of a healer. Kendra's aura also seemed to be swirling and changing rapidly. Sophia's and Hiroko's were less lively, more consistent.

Another instant and the colours were gone, but I'd done it, and when I concentrated, I was able to do it again.

'I did it last week,' Hiroko said. She sounded a little glum. 'This week, I am not so clever.'

'It's not your fault,' Kendra assured her. 'I can't see it either. Aristea just doesn't have an aura.'

'Yes, I do,' I insisted, feeling a little defensive. Sophia had suggested the same thing in our first lesson, and after what Glen had said, I had almost completely forgotten about it, because it hadn't really bothered me. Now, however, Kendra and Hiroko were unable to see it, either. What was wrong with me?

Surprisingly, but without a doubt, the most interesting part of each day was the hour-long fraction that was spent sitting in silence in Renatus's office. Every evening, after prying myself from Sterling's annoyingness, I arrived at his door, which would open immediately for me. Each night he had a new book for me to read – how-to books and White Elm history books, mostly, though they were many times more riveting than anything I'd found in his library. So, night after night, I devoured this new knowledge, and if I didn't finish a book within the hour, Renatus allowed me to take it with me, and I would return it the following day. After each detention I would return to my room and be accosted by Sterling, for whom I would have no information except the contents of the latest book.

'It's just not fair,' Sterling complained often.

The detentions continued like this until the second Monday. Today's book (this one about telepathy) was considerably shorter than those I'd read in the previous week, and I finished it before the hour was up. I closed the book and laid it on my little desk, and I began wondering whether I was capable of sitting in absolute silence for however long with nothing to do. Renatus, surrounded by a higher concentration of paperwork than usual, looked up at me.

'Pull up a chair,' Renatus suggested, nodding at one of the cushy seats behind me. I got up and approached, curious. He indicated a growing pile of crisp envelopes. 'Can you seal those, and stamp them with this?' He handed me a rubber stamp with the White Elm's seal and an ink pad.

I nodded and sat, and set about my task. The envelopes turned out to be of the kind that needs to be licked in order to be sealed, so I sat opposite my headmaster in his office, licking envelopes.

I had silently licked about thirty envelopes before either of us spoke again. I glanced at the addressee of one letter and wondered what Renatus was writing to them. What did people write to him in the first place? He responded so casually that I might have wondered aloud.

'It's hate mail, mostly,' Renatus explained. 'People seem to think we're not interested in their wellbeing. Others want us to adopt medieval policies on the non-magical population. It's mostly drivel like this. Have a read.'

So, I did. The letter's author was apparently not a fan of White Elm, or of correct English. A fan of both, I was positioned against him from the start. I had to read the opening line of the second paragraph three times to understand that the author wanted the White Elm to *amalgamate* with "Lisondo" (after all, emellgamit is not a word).

'Why do you even reply to this?' I asked, mildly disgusted with the content and very annoyed with the effort expended on trying to make sense of the letter itself.

'It used to be Glen's job,' Renatus said, 'but I took it on when he started teaching classes. He thinks that sending a personal, handwritten reply will make the sender feel appreciated and will enhance their sense of our "humanity". He thinks they'll be more understanding if they think we care what they have to say.'

I gathered from his tone that he did not.

Apparently I had been deemed trustworthy, because I was allowed to lick envelopes the next day, and the following day I was allowed to write out addresses.

'Is that all he does, all day?' Sterling asked one night as we got ready for bed. 'Write letters, replying to complaints?'

I shrugged and shifted Cedric over so I could get under my sheets.

'There's heaps of other stuff on his desk besides letters,' I recalled. 'He must do that work at a different time of day.' Because Sterling was waiting with an avid expression for any scrap of information I was willing to part with, I added, 'He's really organised – it wouldn't surprise me if he allocates tasks to certain times of day.'

Sterling sighed, and flopped backwards on her bed to smile at the ceiling.

Pathetic was really the only word applicable.

Now, whenever I entered the office, my chair was already in place.

'Is Qasim talking to you yet?' Renatus asked, without looking up from his work. I sat down and began addressing the envelopes piled before me.

'No. He acts like I'm not there.' I tapped the pen against the desk as I scanned the first letter for a return address. 'Is he the same with everyone he hates, or is it just me?'

'He doesn't *hate* you,' Renatus insisted, sparing me a miniscule glance. 'Qasim just doesn't *like* you. He's testing you. Don't worry too much. He doesn't like me, either.'

Qasim, I knew, wasn't the only one.

A question burned at the back of my mind – I longed to know why the White Elm council disliked Renatus so – yet I couldn't exactly just *say* that, could I? Renatus paused in the middle of writing a word, and although I hadn't made a sound, I strongly suspected he knew what I was thinking. I quickly searched my brain for something else to think about.

'How long have you lived here?' I asked before he could say anything.

'My whole life,' Renatus answered. 'This house has belonged to my family for centuries.'

'But now you live here alone?' I asked and immediately wished I hadn't. It was hardly my business, and of all people, *I* should be more sensitive towards people whose families were notably absent.

'Yes, except for Fionnuala and her family.' Renatus looked up and gazed out of his darkened window. I'd hardly said a word but already I'd screwed up this conversation. I really regretted my stupid question, and looked around for topic-changing inspiration. A cracked shard of ceramic floating in a bubble several centimetres above the tabletop – how had I not noticed *that* sooner? – served my purpose perfectly.

'What's that?' I asked. He turned back and regarded the object with me.

'I'm hoping to use the energy traces left on it to track someone. We recovered it from Emmanuelle's place after her house was broken into the other week.'

'What?' I said, shocked that even White Elm councillors fell prey to life's many inconveniences, like burglaries.

'Jackson – another of our former council members, I'm sure you know – was there, looking for something he suspects she has. She wasn't there; she wasn't hurt,' he added, noticing my worried expression and responding to my unspoken, burning question. 'It was a bold move on his part but I know it was Lisandro's plan because Jackson just isn't that bright.'

'What are...' I stopped myself before I could ask another inappropriate question. I rephrased. 'Did he find what he was looking for?'

'No. I don't even know how he knew to target her. But somehow he did, so that's why she's been here almost a hundred percent of her time lately.'

I had noticed that. I hadn't put much thought into it. I reached for a new envelope and, in my usual state of vagueness, bumped a neat pile of papers. The top half fluttered to the floor.

'I'm sorry!' I exclaimed, horrified with myself. I jumped to my feet, wondering how angry Renatus would be – he had so much work to do and everything was so well-organised...had I just ruined his system? 'I'm really sorry. Here, I'll just...'

I stooped to collect the papers, praying I hadn't angered him. We had been getting on reasonably well, and he had the power to expel me if I stepped out of line. But he simply tore his gaze from the ceramic shard and its creepy little bubble and glanced disinterestedly down at the mess I had made of his paperwork.

'Don't bother,' he said, and went back to answering letters. I stood with all the papers in my hands, undoubtedly disordered. I felt really stupid, and opened my mouth to apologise once again. Renatus raised a hand to quiet me. 'Don't apologise to me until you've done something to wrong me. Let's both hope you never have reason to apologise.'

I did hope that, because I really didn't want to get on the wrong side of him, of all people.

Now, I didn't mean to just go reading through Renatus's personal documents and files. I only glanced down at the sheets of paper in my hands to work out where to put them (to dump this messy collection of paper on top of the neat and tidy pile it had come from, or find somewhere else to put it?) and happened to notice the name *Aristea Byrne* in a short, handwritten list.

'This list has my name on it,' I commented, carefully dropping the rest of the paperwork onto my empty chair and beginning to read the list. There were seven other names.

Renatus's reaction was sudden – the energy in the air around and between us immediately became cold and crackly with his emotions...*concern, nervousness, confusion*. He stood abruptly, shoving back his own chair, and leaned across the desk to grab my wrist and jerk it closer so as to see what I was reading. His expression was tense as his eyes scanned the words, but as quickly as the change had come on, his expression cleared and he visibly and energetically relaxed.

'Ah. *That* list,' he said calmly. He released my wrist and leaned back. 'I thought you'd found something else.'

'Where else do you have my name written?' I asked, shaken. His reaction to my simple statement, and the quickness of his return to calm, had really taken me by surprise.

'I don't,' he said. 'I just-'

He stopped suddenly and looked at the door.

'Qasim's coming,' Renatus said. 'You should go. Take an early mark.'

I nodded and headed for the door as he flicked his hand towards it. I was glad for his warning but still a little unnerved by his sudden weirdness. The door opened and I slipped through, almost walking straight into Qasim. Before I could speak, he snatched from my hand the list I hadn't even realised I was still holding.

'What's this?' he asked suspiciously, scanning the sheet quickly. 'Oh. Your scrying class. Off you go.'

He handed the list back to me and entered the office, shutting the door in my face.

chapter twenty

Entering the dining hall on Saturday morning for breakfast, I was immediately taken back to my childhood, and not in a good way. People were upset and confused and I was tapping into their negativity. I worked to armour myself with wards before I could get too agitated and overwhelmed. I'd always been like this. I was always sensitive to the extreme emotions of others, and as a child I had been prone to taking on whatever I felt others feeling. I wasn't so bad for it now thanks to my uncle's tutelage but sometimes it would just wash over me, taking me by surprise, if I wasn't vigilant.

The source of the upset was quickly obvious. Hiroko and I stopped and stood with the twins near the buffet table as a male student argued loudly with Lord Gawain.

'Are you calling my mom a liar?' the student demanded. ''Cause, that's how it sounded.'

'I'm not calling your mother anything, Egan,' the old man said. 'It's Lisandro I'm calling a liar. He's tricked her-'

'Respectfully, Sir, you're talking shit,' Egan responded, earning a buzz of murmured discussion from the gathering crowd of students. 'Who was the girl?'

'I've told you. I don't know what or who Lisandro was talking about.'

'He was talking about the girl whose life you wouldn't save,' Egan said. He folded his arms, standing his ground. 'Who was she? Or have you conveniently forgotten?'

'It's not that convenient,' Lord Gawain answered, clearly losing patience. 'I'm quite sure that she never existed. Neither I, nor the White Elm, as long as I've been on it, has ever refused to save a life when asked. Lisandro is a masterful liar and your mother is not the first to fall for his act.'

The angry student shook his head and turned away. Lord Gawain and the councillors standing around him did nothing to stop him as he stormed out of the dining hall.

Excited conversation broke out immediately, while Emmanuelle and Teresa came to Lord Gawain and led him quietly from the hall. He looked like the argument had taken a bit out of him. The only two councillors left, Jadon and Aubrey took up guard positions either side of the door, keeping an ominous watch over us. We tried to ignore them and went about getting breakfast.

'What was this?' Hiroko asked me as we grabbed some toast for our plates. 'I am not sure I can understand. He said Lord Gawain would save a girl's life?'

'No, he said Lord Gawain chose *not to* save some girl's life,' I corrected.

'Probably just rubbish spouted by Lisandro,' Kendra wrote off, shrugging. 'That guy's such an ass.'

'Yeah, why would the White Elm refuse to save a life? Sounds like a massive misinterpretation to me,' Sophia agreed. 'Psychos misinterpret normality for a living.'

We sat down in our usual spot, where Sterling and Xanthe were already waiting for us. Sterling almost threw herself across the table in excitement.

'Did you see that?' she asked, perhaps rhetorically, because the spectacle had been somewhat obvious. 'What do you reckon that was about?'

'Garbage,' Kendra said flatly.

'Parroted by a mindless loser,' Sophia finished, but paused before eating the spoonful of cereal she'd raised to her lips. 'Not that questioning authority necessarily makes you a mindless loser, but doing so on the advice of a known killer and con artist does.'

'Hey,' Addison said, placing a hand each on the backs of Kendra and Sophia's chairs and leaning between them. Behind him, a friend quietly trailed over. 'How're you enjoying trying to fill in the blanks? Any good theories down this end of the table?'

'I'll have you know that our theories are quite convincing,' Kendra informed him. 'We're an elite group of thinkers, we are.'

'We'll have all of the universe's greatest questions answered by lunchtime if nobody stops us, and there'll be nothing left for experts to wonder,' Sophia said once she'd swallowed her cereal.

Kendra quickly added, 'We've already worked out the meaning of life, what women want and whether there's a god.'

'But now we're stuck.'

'The purpose of men,' Kendra said, shaking her head. 'There's just no logical explanation.'

I burst into a fit of giggles along with everyone else in our group, including Addison and his friend. They pretended to be mildly offended, but couldn't help laughing. We were soon distracted by the re-arrival of the outspoken student from before.

'That's Egan Lake,' Addison told us quietly. 'He's in my dorm. Telepath. Woke up this morning claiming the White Elm is the enemy and his mother's coming to get him.'

'What a loser,' Kendra commented as Egan spoke briefly with a small group of excited students and then left again with them. When he passed the two councillors at the door, he said, in a loud and triumphant voice, 'We'll all see, then, won't we?'

Jadon and Aubrey, standing on opposite sides of the door, shared a patronising glance that told me they weren't concerned by the student's tone. I turned back to the conversation at hand.

'So you knew all along what this was about and didn't mention it until now?' Kendra realised suddenly, frowning up at Addison. 'Pretending to ask about our theories when really you already knew? I feel so cheated.'

'Luckily we'd already worked it all out,' Sophia reminded her sister, 'because we're geniuses like that.'

'It just further proves our other conclusion – no point to men at all.'

'Well, I can't speak for my entire useless species,' Addison said when the fresh laughter had subsided, 'but my current purpose is to take a morning walk around the grounds with six beautiful girls, as there's nowhere for me to sit down this end.'

Addison was, I decided, much too charming to be allowed. With words, he had totally disarmed the lot of us, and had us blushing and grinning like preteens. All six of us stood, left our unfinished breakfasts and followed him and his friend from the hall, and it occurred to me that if Addison wasn't careful, he was going to do more than win over just Kendra.

Addison's friend, Garrett, didn't say much unless spoken to, and even then, averted his eyes when he answered. He had thick russet hair, milky pale skin dotted with several freckles, and a strange accent I couldn't place. Apparently the two boys knew each other from their Displacement class, which, as it happened, was also Hiroko's class.

'So you're a Displacer, are you? Both of you?' Kendra asked of Addison, glancing back at Garrett as well to include him in the conversation. Garrett nodded once and angled his gaze away from her. Addison grinned and, mid step, disappeared. He reappeared several steps ahead of Kendra, and turned to walk backwards.

'That's right. Keeps things interesting.'

Kendra smiled slyly.

'I could do interesting,' she responded, flicking her hair from her shoulder and stepping ahead of Addison to walk through the front doors. Sophia shot me a look of mock-disgust while Hiroko suppressed a laugh by staring at her feet and covering her mouth with her hand.

The group of us had barely stepped outside of the house when Sterling noticed a commotion near the gate. The small group of students who had left the hall earlier were standing in a tight bunch, crowded around the Telepath who had said, 'We'll all see, then, won't we?'

'That's Egan,' Addison commented, squinting in the sharp morning sunlight and rubbing his arms as though suddenly cold. 'And I guess that must be his mum. What the hell do you call this temperature, by the way? I thought it was springtime.'

The elegant wrought iron gates were open, I saw, and an unfamiliar adult stood with the students. The woman pointed up at the house, and the group began moving towards us quickly.

'They left the gate open,' I commented uneasily as we meandered down the path. Very shortly, our two groups would meet. The student leading the other group, the telepath that was Egan Lake, waved once to Addison, flagging us down.

'What did I tell you, man?' he called, waving a small, spherical object in the air. 'Check this out.'

'What now?' Addison asked, though good-naturedly. He covered the remaining distance with a few long strides, and the rest of us hurried to keep up.

'This is what I was telling you about this morning,' Egan said, showing us the glassy sphere. 'Those murderous bastards can't keep the truth hidden.'

'It's atrocious,' the woman said darkly, shaking her head and radiating an unchecked fury. 'I can't believe I entrusted you to these people – what was I thinking? Murderers and liars, the lot of them. The rest of you should just pack your things and contact your parents to come get you. These *councillors* are not fit to be educating and protecting children.' We said nothing in response, so she turned to her son and said, 'Well, show them! Everyone deserves to know.'

I realised with a shock that I recognised this lady. I'd seen her the other night, the night of my confrontation with Qasim, when Renatus had touched my arm and I'd seen that bar and *this woman* sitting in it with some guy...

'Know what?' I heard myself ask in a haughty, grown-up tone I wasn't used to using.

'Don't talk to my mom like that, girl,' Egan snapped, raising a finger to point warningly in my face. I shoved his hand away.

'It's Aristea, and I'll talk how I like,' I answered. I couldn't believe that this was me. I indicated the crystal ball. 'What is that thing, anyway?'

'It's a recording, of everything Lisandro told me. The truth.' The woman smiled at her son.

Kendra scoffed audibly, and her clear disbelief gave me the clout to say, 'You mean lies.'

'Lisandro found me first but he didn't pursue me. I went to him,' Egan's mother told us, ignoring me completely now, 'and he told me everything. He's not at all like he's portrayed – the White Elm betrayed him and painted him as a criminal and a liar, when in fact it's *them* who are the dangerous ones.'

I glanced up at the house behind me, thinking of Renatus. He certainly seemed dangerous, and I was willing to take a stab in the dark and say that he *was* dangerous if crossed, but I felt that he was a good person, like the rest of the council. My eyes sought out the large window of his office, and at that moment I saw him, standing at his window and surveying the scene. Noticing the unfamiliar woman, he turned away abruptly. I imagined that he was not far away.

'It's all in here, everything he told me,' Egan's mother said, gesturing encouragingly at the sphere her son held. At first, I thought it was just a little glass ball, or maybe a ball of clear quartz, but then I noticed the flickers of colour within it. 'How Lord Gawain ignored Lisandro's moment of greatest need and let him suffer for years, and then how he turned him out and poisoned the council and the public against him. It's the greatest cover-up of our time. You won't believe it until you hear the proof.'

'One man's word isn't proof,' I disagreed, 'and Lisandro murdered his friend and follower, Peter, which makes his word rather less trustworthy.'

'I was devoutly faithful to the White Elm only a month ago – I sent my son to them for teaching. What Lisandro told me was convincing enough to turn me around completely.'

There was that. Hiroko gave me an uneasy glance, and I knew she was wondering whether there was truth to Egan's mother's story. I could feel Sterling, Addison and Garrett felt similarly uncomfortable. From Xanthe I felt a growing sense of curiosity, but the twins' emotions remained firm and staunch.

'You only have to touch the crystal to access the information inside,' Egan's mother said. 'I'm here to help you see what's been hidden from you; your parents would want you to be informed, to know the truth. You know it in your hearts, like I realised I did. You've never really trusted these people.'

Her words felt so immediately wrong that I took an unconscious step back in disgust. In the corner of my eye I saw Renatus stride through his front doors, not thirty seconds since I'd seen him standing in his office four storeys above. I felt relief. He'd scared me on occasions but, I realised now, I felt totally and completely comfortable and safe around him. He would fix this situation.

'Even you know it,' Egan told me, meeting my eyes. I shook my head.

'No. I don't.' I exhaled. It felt good to say what I believed.

'Well, whatever. The rest of you must have some sense, then?'

I looked over my friends. I wasn't sure why this

was so important to me – why I was arguing so firmly for a council I'd not really known until so recently – but I wanted their support. Sophia folded her arms.

'I don't know where you've been all month, Egan, but we've been studying under the White Elm, being treated perfectly well and having absolutely no reason to stop trusting them,' she said. 'And perhaps they *have* upset Lisandro, but if I'm to choose between the White Elm and a murderer...'

'What exactly makes you so sure that the White Elm didn't kill Peter?' Egan countered, taking over his mother's role as devil's advocate.

'Lord Gawain said-' Hiroko began.

'Did it occur to you that maybe Lord Gawain *lied*?' Egan asked, rolling his eyes. 'No one can corroborate even one single detail of their story, from how the guy died to who killed him or even where they found him-'

'I can,' I interrupted. 'I'm the one-'

'Aristea!' Renatus cut me off sharply, shouldering between Xanthe and Addison to reach the centre of the circle. 'That's enough.' He gave me a silencing look and turned to Egan. 'What is that?'

'And who, exactly, are you?' Egan's mother asked in the rudest voice she could muster up, but Renatus ignored her except to spare her a small, disdainful glance out of the corner of his eye. The woman visibly deflated, realising that this man was not somebody she could intimidate.

'Egan, what is that?' Renatus asked again. Egan's self-assured air was totally gone in light of the headmaster's arrival. His mother gathered her confidence and answered for him.

'This is Lisandro's way of showing us why he left this sorry council,' she proclaimed, gesturing again to the sphere in her son's hand. 'He's trying to show us that he's a friend and a necessary revolutionist. This is evidence that the White Elm are power-hungry killers, and they're trying to stamp out people like Lisandro who oppose them.'

'You have no idea what you're talking about,' Renatus said coldly. 'You just sound ill-informed and ignorant. Give that to me, Egan.'

My friends, Egan's friends and I stood in silence as the Lakes stared at Renatus and his outstretched hand with identical expressions of mixed fear and resentment.

Egan hesitated for a long moment, and then plastered a self-assured expression across his face.

'I don't think I will,' he said, closing his fingers over the ball.

'Now,' Renatus ordered; Egan's expression slipped. 'I won't have these lies go any further.'

'You're not having it,' Egan said adamantly. He glanced over at one of his friends, who stood behind me, and I figured that they were communicating telepathically, as telepaths were prone to do. Egan turned back to face Renatus, and his voice was cold and firm as he said, 'I hate you – the lot of you – and I'm out of here.'

With that said, he tossed the sphere to his friend. It was a quick throw but I guessed its trajectory and shot out my hand. I caught it with ease, a thousand games of catch with my brother to thank for those reflexes. It was cool and smooth, but that was not my first impression. Voices, pictures and feelings started to overwhelm me.

The man with long black hair, secured in a sleek ponytail...His voice, friendly and charming...A feeling of calm and honesty...'I met Gawain twelve years ago. He wasn't the Lord back then'...

I might have been convinced that there was no real harm in allowing the story to continue – the brain functions so quickly that I could have played the whole recording and known all its contents in only a few seconds – but for the spark of horror I felt at the instant my fingertips touched the crystal. My mind was made up.

I forcibly threw the sphere at the cobbled path and it shattered.

'What are you doing?' Egan yelled at me, angry. I ignored him and looked at Renatus, his hand still held out, waiting. He'd wanted the sphere, to view its contents and assess the situation properly, and I'd interfered in a huge way, well overstepping my boundaries. How furious would he be with me now?

'Aristea?' Sterling whispered, clearly frightened for me. Renatus was still staring at me, though now he dropped his hand. I stood up straighter, trying to think of a reasonable excuse for what I'd just done. I couldn't think of one. I'd really had no right to take matters into my own hands like that, but the flicker of horror I'd felt had been *his* and there had only seemed to be one correct action.

Now there were two things I wanted to say. My

head told me that there was only really one appropriate utterance, but my heart said it was a lie. I took a massive chance, still unable to believe that any of the things I'd said or done in the last five minutes were really said or done by *me*.

'I'm…I'm not sorry,' I said, unable to get much volume. I was really in for it now.

Renatus was still just watching me, and though his expression did not change, I felt acceptance.

'Pack your things, Egan,' he said over his shoulder. 'Turn in your key and you can go. I'm sure it won't bother you that you won't be welcome back. Aristea, Sterling; please close the gate for me. The rest of you, please find somewhere else to be for the time being.'

Like a toddler having a small tantrum, Egan withdrew his key from his pocket and threw it to the ground with much more force than was required. He stalked away, and his mother went to follow but was stopped by Renatus. Egan turned back to watch.

'Not you,' Renatus said to the mother. 'You're not welcome in my house. I will ignore that you have entered my estate without invitation, but you intend to spread your misguided beliefs to our students and for that reason, I won't allow you inside.'

'Misguided beliefs?' Egan's mother repeated, infuriated. She pointed at the shards of glass at my feet. 'That stupid girl destroyed proof-'

'Another word against my council or my students and, I assure you, you will be extremely sorry.'

Sterling and I moved off quickly as the group

dispersed. As soon as we were out of the range of eavesdroppers, Sterling seized my elbow and gave a small, girlish squeal of excitement.

'He knows my *name*!' she stage-whispered. Her brown eyes sparkled and her smile was manic. 'I don't believe it. Can you believe it?'

'Yes,' I said, laughing. 'He knows my name and Egan's name, too.'

'But Egan's trouble, and you're a semi-permanent fixture of his office,' Sterling responded dismissively. She paused. 'Maybe you're trouble, too. Since when do you break stuff and argue with adults?'

'Oh,' I laughed nervously, feeling much less confident now that the situation was behind me. 'I don't know. I just…reacted. I probably shouldn't have broken that ball thing.'

'I've never seen you like that,' Sterling said. 'But that's what got you into trouble in the first place, isn't it? Arguing with Qasim? Can't believe you stood up to that lady like that! And what was with that "I'm not sorry" stuff with Renatus?'

I shrugged uncomfortably. I didn't really want to explain that whole story to Sterling. To sustain our friendship, I had to report daily on my interactions with the headmaster in my detentions. Some conversations I had with him could be mine and mine alone, surely?

Luckily, Sterling had already changed the topic. Back.

'I still can't believe he called me by name. Did you notice he didn't address anyone else by name?'

With an intake of breath so sharp and sudden that I thought she'd been hurt, she stopped and faced me. 'Aristea, what if he's been watching me?'

I started laughing again. 'What?'

'No, really. Do you think it's possible? You've said he hasn't mentioned me to you, but that doesn't mean anything if he's naturally shy...Stop laughing.'

'You're just so hopeless,' I said, trying to contain my laughter and failing.

'He probably thinks that *I* think he's too old, but really, a few years don't make that big of a difference,' Sterling continued, gazing off into nothingness. 'My mom's partner is nine years older than she is, and I don't think Renatus is that much older than us. He's obviously one of the youngest on the council. I don't think he'd even be twenty-five.'

I agreed with her words – people from entirely different generations fell in love all the time and lived happily ever after, and age wasn't really that much of a factor. And she was also right, I strongly suspected, about Renatus's age. He looked to be about the same age as my twenty-three-year-old sister and cousin. However, Sterling's theory had not yet covered the problem of the student-teacher boundary, and I mentioned this.

'That's probably why he hasn't said anything or made any advances,' Sterling explained excitedly, grasping my hands and bouncing on the balls of her feet. 'Of course! He thinks that *I'll think* that it's inappropriate.'

'Isn't it?'

'No. He's not my teacher. He's a politician

acting as a headmaster for a training facility. He's young and he's single.'

'We think.'

'Yes,' Sterling agreed, releasing my hands. 'And he's hot and he's got that *accent* and that *voice*. Did you see how he handled that situation? I love how he just takes control. It's sexy as. I just want him.' Dramatically, she turned away and we started for the gate again.

'So, what's your plan?' I asked when we reached the end of the path. Sterling gave me an inquiring glance as I pulled the heavy, cast iron gate into alignment with its pair. 'Will I be totally embarrassed for you?'

Sterling considered this as she pulled her key out from her bra and locked the gate.

'Well, I don't see how it'll embarrass you,' she said. We began walking back up the path, slowly, because Renatus and Egan's mother were still standing together further along the path. Neither of them seemed to be speaking. 'I might embarrass myself, but that's my business,' she added as an afterthought. She stopped again and turned to me, slightly uphill so that she was looking down at me. She was a little shorter than I was when we stood on even ground, though it was only a few centimetres of difference. 'I'll test him. I'll let him see me with someone else.'

I froze, trying to make sense of this.

'Like…?'

'Like, flirting with someone else,' she supplied, as though this were an obvious implication.

'You're going to flirt with someone. That's it? What will that achieve?' I asked, unable to comprehend Sterling-logic. She sighed again, as if I were a little bit slow.

'I *told* you, it's a test,' she said. 'If he's interested in me, and he sees me with this other guy, or even just hears about it, he'll be jealous, and his behaviour will change and I'll know.'

She beamed, triumphant, and I tried to smile back. I'd seen this attempted in movies, and it never worked. It only ever made things worse.

'You've picked someone out then?' I pressed, waiting. I was really hoping that maybe she'd found a nice guy that she could eventually fall for – someone that was actually possible.

'He's very cute. Nothing on Renatus, obviously, but cute in his own right.'

'Do I know him?' I asked, still hoping.

'Yes,' Sterling said with a nod. 'I'm going to start laying the groundwork as soon as I can, letting people see us together so word will move around the school. I can't assume I'll get them in the same room together, for Renatus to actually see, so a rumour might have to do.'

'So, you're leading some poor boy on,' I verified, 'in the hope that Renatus will see and be jealous.'

'Don't say "boy", you make it sound like I'm hitting on a twelve-year-old. That's so wrong.'

'Who is this unfortunate young man, then?' I asked, choosing not to point out that the age gap between Sterling and a twelve-year-old boy was about the same as the gap between Sterling and

317

Renatus.

'Not telling, you'll spoil it,' Sterling said. 'He's someone cute and someone nice.'

'Oh, no,' I said, a face coming to mind. 'It's *not* Addison, is it?'

'Eww, no!' Sterling wrinkled her nose. 'He's way too weird.'

Like Addison could possibly be considered weird beside anyone as unusual as Renatus.

'This is going to be awesome,' Sterling said with an excited shiver.

'You're so hopeless,' I said again, shaking my head and smiling. We deviated from the path when we noticed our friends sitting on a hill, and headed for them.

'Maybe,' Sterling said with a shrug. 'I don't care. I love him.'

'Love's a big word to use with someone you hardly know,' I cautioned. Sterling shrugged again and gazed sidelong at Renatus.

'Maybe,' she said again.

A cold breeze cut across the estate, and I shoved my hands into the pockets of my jeans. My fingers brushed against crumpled paper, and I pulled the offending page free and slowed to read it. Sterling leaned against my shoulder curiously.

Dylan Wright
Isao Tanaka
Khalida Jasti
Constantine Vogel
Joshua Reyes

Aristea Byrne
Xanthe Giannopoulos
Iseult Taylor

I hadn't meant to take this from Renatus's office, and I'd forgotten until now that after leaving with it the other day I'd shoved it into the pocket of that day's jeans (which I'd not bothered to put in the wash, and which I was wearing once again), intending to return the list shortly. I didn't need to glance back at Renatus to guess that now was probably not an appropriate time.

'What's that?' Sterling asked. I smoothed the crumpled edges with my fingers.

'My scrying class.' Why Renatus would want to keep a list of the students in my scrying class was beyond me, but it wasn't nearly as mystifying as his overreaction to my finding of the list, his ability to read my thoughts, or the visions and feelings I'd channelled from him. Or the way he'd just accepted it without discussion when I'd broken that sphere, interfering with what definitely would have been evidence in a White Elm investigation.

Sterling laughed and pushed away from me.

'You carry around a list of people from your class,' she said, 'and you think *I'm* weird.'

chapter twenty-one

The reach of Lisandro was mightier than the council had ever realised.

On Monday morning, Aubrey stood with Jadon at the door of dormitory one while two of Jadon's students packed their bags for home.

'Got everything?' Jadon asked, apparently at a loss as to what to say. The boys, both sixteen years old, nodded silently. The ever-shrinking world of social networking had made it possible for people to communicate with strangers with more ease and convenience than ever before, and Egan Lake's mother had taken full advantage.

Six families had contacted the White Elm over the weekend to cancel their children's enrolment. Two of these had simply turned up to take their kids home with them, unhappy and sold on Lisandro's story; two more had telepathically contacted their children to tell the White Elm the same story; one had written asking for a councillor to bring her boy home as soon as was convenient. One mother had arrived at the gates in a state of hysterics, insisting she hadn't believed the story but was afraid that the war was looking to be escalating shortly and didn't want her child in the midst after all.

'Let's go, then,' Aubrey said. The boys shared muttered goodbyes with their roommates and left their dorm for the last time. When Jadon extended a hand, both gave in their keys.

'See you, Jadon,' one boy, Michael, said, shaking his supervisor's hand briefly. The other hesitated before doing the same.

'Yeah. See you. Thanks for everything.'

They went down the stairs, one to meet his uncle and the other to meet Elijah to be displaced home. They were gone. Jadon folded his arms and stared down the now-empty stairwell.

'That sucks so much,' he commented.

'Agreed.' Aubrey clapped his friend's shoulder. They'd only had the students for a month or so and it seemed unfair to lose them so early over something so ridiculously small. Hearsay? An overreacting mother's fanciful tale? It was hard not to be impressed with Lisandro's storytelling if he could incite such passion and trust with only words.

And just a little hint of magic...

'I'm down to two students, just like that.'

'You can have one of mine if that makes you feel better,' Aubrey offered, steering Jadon up the stairs with him on his way to his classroom. 'I still have four.'

'At this rate we could all be down to none by

next weekend,' Jadon said negatively. Aubrey didn't bother to counter that. There was no reason to think every student would go, but also few reasons to expect that any would be able to stay. He also knew that in his current mood, words would do little to bolster Jadon's spirits.

Aubrey had only known Jadon, and everyone else on the White Elm, for about half a year. Initiated at the same time and similar in age, Aubrey had immediately connected with the sociable and impulsive American, as well as the sweet and sensitive Romanian Teresa. He'd not expected those initial friendly exchanges to transform into friendships as deep as family bonds, nor had he intended them to. This was meant to be just a job – a means to an end; a way to secure his future with his beautiful girlfriend Shell – but it had become a life. Distanced from the rest of the council by mistrust and uncertainty of competence, the three new initiates had banded together, intent on proving themselves and demonstrating their worth to the senior councillors. Aubrey had never known two other people so supportive and emotionally invested in his successes as Jadon and Teresa were – even his three blood brothers showed less care than these two new friends.

If only the rest of the White Elm would take Aubrey as seriously as Jadon and Teresa did.

Aubrey sifted through the mountains of crap on his desk, looking for his lesson plan for this morning's class. The students were still at breakfast but would soon be here, expecting to be taught something.

'*Merde*,' Aubrey muttered, pausing to look at a stack of papers bound with elastic bands. 'These will need to be all adjusted now.'

'What is it?' Jadon asked, taking them to look. 'Enrolment forms?'

'Just copies for the records, but some of those students have left now so I'll need to add that before I can enter them as current.'

The White Elm was hundreds of years old, with tens of thousands of various paper records, from minor stuff like minutes of meetings, public statements, publications and surveys to major things like private journals of long-dead councillors, confiscated dark spells, documentation of investigations and records of criminal trials and verdicts. It was necessary, of course, that this all be kept safe, and so a secure archive had been established. As Historian, Anouk was the only White Elm with access to this treasure trove of information. Aubrey didn't even know where it was, but as the White Elm's Scribe, most records added to it this year were written in his hand.

A bell rang to signal students to head to class.

'Man, do me a favour,' Aubrey said, still searching for that lesson plan. 'Take those to my place? I'll work on them tonight and have them back tomorrow for Anouk.'

'Yeah, no worries,' Jadon agreed. He tucked the stack of forms under his arm and held out a hand while Aubrey dug through his pockets for his house key. 'Will Shell be home?'

'Doubt it.' Aubrey handed over the key. 'She had an appointment this morning so she's probably taken that as an excuse to have breakfast with a girlfriend or go shopping. You know, since she's out of the house already. Or because it's overcast, or because a new café opened, or any other excuse she can think of.'

'How is she?' Jadon asked quietly as the first few students entered the classroom. Aubrey went back to looking for that stupid lesson plan. He'd left it here somewhere, hadn't he?

'She's good,' Aubrey answered, but he knew that Jadon was asking about more than just in general. Unlike the rest of the White Elm, Jadon and Teresa knew that Shell was due to have Aubrey's baby in about three months. It had been unexpected and ill-timed, considering that Aubrey was twenty-two and his partner only nineteen and neither had been planning to start a family for many more years, but her family, and especially her foster-father, had been so delighted and supportive that Aubrey had quickly gotten past his fear and embraced this for the blessing it was. He hadn't intended on telling anybody White Elm – after all, the council had done so little to prove its trust in him, so why should he share his joy with any of them? – but Jadon, a Telepath, had stolen the news straight out of Aubrey's head the very day he'd learned it.

How had he managed to lose a page of dot points he'd written only two days before? Jadon gave him a resigned look and pulled a sheet of paper out from under a folder. Aubrey grabbed it from him, knowing he'd overheard his thoughts. The trade trick of Telepaths. No matter how well-guarded your thoughts are, thinking in questions immediately voids any wards you thought you had protecting your inner monologue. By their very nature, questions are intended to be answered, which was perhaps why they were always broadcasted for the listening pleasure of nearby Telepaths, and which was why Jadon knew exactly what Aubrey was looking for without needing to ask or be told.

'She's got some appointment in Glasgow this morning,' Aubrey added, reading over his dot points quickly. 'A scan thing. We couldn't see last time what it was; she wants to know whether to buy pink or blue.'

Jadon grinned and pulled a Euro coin from his pocket.

'It had better be a boy or I owe this to Teresa,' he told Aubrey as he left.

The students arranged themselves in their seats and a few wrote the day's date in the margin of a fresh page. Some of the Academy's younger girls entered and took seats near the back. Aubrey recognised one as Aristea Byrne and resumed going over his notes to avoid looking at her.

Aristea Byrne. Seventeen years old and local. Renatus's pet. She was pretty enough, though did nothing to accentuate it. She dressed as though she were somebody else; she was not yet comfortable with who she really was. Of thirty-whatever students in the Academy, she was the only scrier. He knew that Qasim had been watching her progress very closely. Word was that she and Qasim didn't actually get along – she'd apparently crossed him somehow and landed herself almost a month of detentions with Renatus, which seemed to suit Renatus just fine. Renatus, most unusually, had also taken an interest in her, asking other councillors about her abilities in their specific fields. Aubrey had told him the truth as he knew it: Aristea was a powerful sorceress, certainly, but with no particular gift for spell-crafting or spell-writing. Her talents obviously lay in other areas.

Like disobedience.

On Saturday, after a confrontation with Egan Lake's neurotic mother, Aristea had destroyed a precious memory sphere that might have contained Lisandro's every motive, idea and plan. The information was irretrievable. Yet Renatus was perfectly unfazed; indeed, he'd seemed almost proud when he'd reported this to the council. Aubrey had wondered several times what it was about her that so intrigued and impressed the Dark Keeper.

Maybe he just liked to look at her, or maybe he just liked the idea of someone with the potential to be even more trouble than he was.

The students were all gathered, so Aubrey began his lesson. They were a good bunch. They just sat silently, writing anything he told them to write, putting their hands up to respond whenever he asked a question and always, always watching attentively.

Again, teaching magic to teenagers wasn't something he'd intended to do with his life, even when he'd applied for the White Elm, but it was something Aubrey had come to really enjoy. The students were interested and interesting, and Aubrey was surprised each day by how much *he* learned by working with them.

He set them copying a spell from the blackboard and wandered between the desks. One student, Jacinta, put her hand up to ask for help. Aubrey stood beside her and leaned over to check her careful handwriting.

'It doesn't look right,' she said quietly, frowning at her words with searching blue eyes. Aubrey could see what she meant. She'd been careful to copy his spell letter by letter, even going so far as to replicate his slanted font, but it still appeared incorrect. He ran his fingertip along each line as he read it under his breath, looking for the error. He soon felt the problem, and his eyes – always slower than the magical senses – confirmed it.

'For this to work, you'd need to close your o properly,' he explained softly, pointing to a few examples of the second-last vowel that were not closed circles. He took her pen and rewrote the beginning words a few lines lower, deliberately etching each letter as they were intended to appear. 'Try it slower.'

'Thanks.' Jacinta smiled up at him, taking back her pen. They were good kids, if kids was still the right term for sixteen to nineteen-year-olds. They were only a few years younger than Aubrey was – the eldest was born the year after Jadon. Despite that fact, they were very definitely kids in Aubrey's mind.

The girls were pretty and the boys were funny and friendly, but Aubrey was careful to keep a cool, detached distance from them all. Professionals did not make friends with their students.

Renatus should be told.

The lesson eventually ended and the students filed out. Aristea was among the first out the door, but was stopped just outside by a friend. Aubrey found himself wishing she would go away, and immediately felt bad. She was one of his students and he should regard her the same way he did all the others, but it was becoming difficult not to associate her with the Dark Keeper, who Aubrey very much resented.

Renatus was an idiot. He'd had a rough trot, admittedly, but he'd spent years under the wing of one of magical history's greatest men and squandered away the incredible opportunity this presented with every breath he took. Every step was in the wrong direction. Every scathing word burnt another bridge. His tenuous loyalties were unclear even to those close to him and Aubrey knew he'd never succeed in his own role if he allowed himself to rely on Renatus.

Aubrey quickly turned his thoughts away from this dangerous path before anyone could overhear and lecture him on how Renatus had never actually *done* anything wrong and that the council had never had any *real* reason to question his loyalties…

Right.

Aristea's friend waited until most of the other students were gone before coming inside, and

Aubrey, now shuffling through the crap on his desk once again, attempting to put everything into some semblance of an order, recognised her as Sterling Adams. Nice girl; bubbly; talkative. She'd not seemed all that interested in his class previously, though, so he wasn't sure what she wanted.

'Hi, Sterling,' he said. 'What is it that you need?' He made an effort to paste an approachable expression across his face, even as Aristea trailed uncertainly behind her.

'Nothing much,' Sterling said. 'I just wanted to, you know, talk.'

Aubrey looked up, immediately wary. Talk? About what? He glanced at Aristea (*Why can't you just talk to her?*) but she appeared just as confused as he was.

'What would you like to talk about?' Aubrey asked, speaking slowly but his mind working at the speed of sound. Shit, this was the *counsellor* part of his job. *Please, goddess, please don't let her cry in front of me, and please, please don't make me listen to any talk about boys.*

'Uh, like, school stuff,' Sterling said with a small shrug and a coy smile. *Thank you, goddess.* 'I was just thinking, you know, how all the subjects are so linked together, and how spell-writing is really at the core of it all.' She smiled wider. 'Your subject is kind of the most important of all, and I'm no good at it.' She glanced back at Aristea. 'I've got this. You can go if you want.'

The young scrier nodded and began to slowly walk away. She shot an uncertain glance back, and

Aubrey knew why. Sterling's entire demeanour, her tone, her body language, had all changed abruptly. She'd shifted her weight onto one leg, one hip jutting out, calling attention to her curvy female shape, and her cute face was tilted to one side. What on Earth was she doing?

'I wouldn't say it's the most important one,' Aubrey disagreed, wondering whether he was meant to be flattered by that notion, 'and you're working on it, which is all anyone can ask of you.'

Aristea had paused just inside the doorway to retie her shoelace. Aubrey was kind of glad for her remaining presence.

'Well, *I* think that creating magic with your words is the most impressive magical art, and I want to be better at it. I've been practising. See?' Sterling withdrew a folded sheet of lined paper from the pocket of her denim miniskirt and moved closer to hand it to him. Aubrey accepted it, and weirdly, she held onto the page for a beat too long. He met her eyes, and she was looking straight at him, smiling. She let go. Starting to feel uncomfortable, Aubrey turned his attention back to her handwriting as she continued speaking. 'I know my calligraphy isn't great, but yours is so perfect. Could you rewrite this for me?'

'Sure.' That request seemed harmless enough. Stepping back over to his desk to put some much-needed space between Aubrey and his overeager student, Aubrey grabbed a pen and began to rewrite her amateur spell underneath the first. Sterling moved close again.

'I love watching calligraphers,' she commented. 'I just love how the pen just glides across the paper, like a caress on skin.' She giggled girlishly. 'And when you use the proper pens, and dip it into the ink, it's like the pen kisses the ink-'

'Sterling,' Aristea interrupted, straightening suddenly with a knowing look of dread on her face.

'Aristea, just go. I'll see you soon,' Sterling insisted, smiling brightly. Aristea looked unconvinced and did not move. Sterling turned her attention back to Aubrey. 'You hold that pen really well,' she admired, and Aubrey knew he was in trouble. 'Does the grip make a difference?'

'A little bit.' Aubrey remained focussed on writing. She didn't let up. She rested a hand on his forearm.

'Like, is it better to keep your grip loose...or really *tight* and *firm*?'

She tightened her grip to accentuate her words, and Aubrey was saved the humiliating horror of having to ask a seventeen-year-old sweetheart to back off by Aristea.

'Sterling,' she said, her tone pleading, and Sterling pulled her hand away. 'We have to go to-'

'I'll meet you there,' Sterling said meaningfully. Aubrey recognised his cue.

'I actually have to go, too,' he decided, handing the page back, unfinished. In his haste to avoid her contact, he let go before Sterling had a grip, and the paper fluttered to their feet.

'I'll get it,' she said, bobbing down at Aubrey's feet and reaching around his legs to collect the sheet as it fluttered further away.

'No, don't bother,' Aubrey protested, still trying to maintain a casual air. His desk prevented him from backing away. 'Really, just leave it.'

'No, it's okay, I've got it,' Sterling said brightly as she got back to her feet, way too close. 'I-'

'What is going on?'

Qasim's powerful voice scared all three of them. Sterling sprang back, Aubrey turned quickly and Aristea was immediately encased in an invisible bubble of magic. None had expected that Qasim was near. He stood now in the doorway, looking angry.

Everyone stood in stunned silence for a very long moment. Sterling's face went steadily redder with every passing second.

'Nothing's going on,' Aristea eventually managed, moving over to her friend and grabbing her hand. 'We were just leaving.'

Sterling practically ran behind the young scrier as they left the classroom. Aubrey collapsed into his chair, suddenly exhausted with relief.

'What on Earth?' was all Qasim could ask, and Aubrey could only shake his head helplessly. Qasim folded his arms, and Aubrey knew that his response wasn't going to be enough.

'I have no idea what that was,' he admitted, sitting up straighter. The Scrier commanded a sort of respect that few men could ask for, and Aubrey couldn't help but give it. Qasim was a man he admired, with his firm morals, unshakable standards and no-nonsense attitude. The other senior councillors had welcomed their new three with warm smiles and endless patronising kindness, but Qasim had remained distant, determined that Jadon, Teresa and Aubrey would *earn* his trust and respect.

Qasim would be the next Lord of the White Elm, and he would be great, probably better than placid, eccentric Lord Gawain. Despite finding him terrifying, Aubrey had made the effort to familiarise himself with the Scrier. He felt compelled to earn Qasim's respect, to be properly accepted. He was sick of being "one of the new kids", almost grouped in with the students, left to baby-sit the students while the older councillors went about important business without him.

'Sterling has never acted like that before,' Aubrey elaborated, still surprised and confused by her odd behaviour. It had seemed extremely flirtatious, yet, in his classes, all she talked about was Renatus. 'I've never said or done anything to encourage anything more than a professional relationship. I can't think of what might have brought that on.'

Qasim's sharp gaze clung to Aubrey as the senior councillor considered his words. Aubrey waited, nervous but patient. He hadn't lied – he'd never done anything to incite Sterling's behaviour, and he'd *never* have touched her even if he had – so all he needed was for Qasim to realise this, however long that took. Eventually Qasim unfolded his arms and moved his hands to his hips with a sigh.

'They're a pool of potential, but they'll not be in control of their magic until they're in control of their hormones,' he conceded finally. 'It was probably fortunate that Aristea was still present. It would serve you well to avoid being alone with students. You are young and friendly, and some of these children have blurred boundaries.'

Aubrey nodded immediately. Qasim was still regarding him shrewdly, and for a too-long moment, neither man spoke. Aubrey was determined not to crack, and so he waited.

Qasim took a small cloth bag from the inside pocket of his jacket and held it up.

'Can you write me a trace? Two of them?' he asked shortly. Aubrey blinked, wondering before he could stop himself what sort of test this was.

'Uh…Yes,' he answered warily. 'What sort?'

'Jackson broke a vase at Emmanuelle's when he was tearing around looking for…the treasure. Some traces of his magic or his essence should remain on this piece. Also, there's a possibility that some trace of Lisandro may remain in the orb Aristea shattered, but after all the hands that thing moved through, it would be a very slight one. Jackson is clumsier and more likely to have left energy lying around. I want you to write a trace spell to track him. Can you do that?'

Aubrey didn't know what to say. *Of course* he knew how to write a trace – he was a Crafter; he wrote magic as naturally as he breathed. But this was the first time in half a year anyone on the council had actually *asked* him to write anything more interesting than a document. This was what they should have been using him for all along – the council's only Crafter – but nobody had trusted him enough up to this point to give him such tasks.

'I...Yes, I can do that,' Aubrey agreed finally, still surprised. He'd been waiting for this day for so long, and now it was here. He really hadn't expected Qasim to be the one to finally branch out from the old White Elm family and ask for "outside" help.

The aging Scrier strode closer and dropped the bag into Aubrey's hand. When the Crafter opened the top and looked inside, he saw that the shard of ceramic was encased in a bubble of magic. A few slivers of glassy crystal lay inert at the bottom of the bag, almost certainly useless.

'No one else has touched it?' Aubrey checked, referring to the ceramic. Qasim shook his head.

'Not to my knowledge. Emmanuelle locked it into that orb and nobody would be getting through that to interfere with it. It's been sitting in Renatus's office.'

Aubrey nodded slowly, feeling a strong sense of satisfaction growing within him that he didn't bother to hold back. Renatus had had these for days, and had experienced no success tracing Lisandro or Jackson. The council had exhausted all their usual options, leaving them with only Aubrey – who should have been their first port of call. The idea that Renatus was in any way superior to Aubrey (except in his freakish capacity for power) was stupid anyway. His lineage was corrupt and embarrassing. And his extra year of service to the White Elm definitely did not warrant the extra respect he got for free from Lord Gawain, like he was some kind of honorary senior councillor. There were mere months between the ages of Aubrey and Renatus.

'Do not screw this up,' Qasim advised, quite lightly, and left. Aubrey shook his head again.

No, he wouldn't screw this up. This was what he'd been waiting for. Finally, a chance to do what he was here for. Finally, a chance to do his job.

chapter twenty-two

There was no nice way of describing how I felt about Sterling right then.

'Well, I *told you* to leave,' she defended, trailing behind me as I dragged her by the hand as far from Aubrey's classroom as I could. 'There would have been no problem if you'd just gone when I said.'

'Oh, no problem, you reckon?' I asked, mildly hysterical. How was I ever meant to show my face in that room again? How would Sterling? 'Tell me, how did you picture that escapade ending? A handshake?'

'No, I-'

'Only,' I interrupted, pulling her behind me as I took the stairs, 'I could only see that ending with your suspension from his class, or the two of you having sex on his desk.' *Ew.* I shook myself in disgust. Sterling started laughing. What was funny about this? 'Your grand plan to Renatus's heart was to get yourself suspended for sexually harassing one of his colleagues? Or is this all just to get into detention like me?'

'Aristea, your imagination is so crazy!' Sterling told me, still laughing. I couldn't disagree with that, but I was quite sure that her moral compass was crazier. I recalled the horrifying moment when I'd worked out what she was doing in Aubrey's classroom.

Don't say boy, you make it sound like I'm hitting on a twelve-year-old...

She'd picked out another councillor, another *teacher*, to play with until Renatus noticed her. No boy at all. Oh, no, *Sterling*.

'You said you wouldn't embarrass me!' I reminded her.

'I wasn't trying to!' Sterling said defensively. Her flush was clearing, and I could see that she wasn't remotely abashed by how she'd behaved.

'You were flirting with a *teacher*!' I covered my eyes with my free hand, remembering. 'Couldn't you have at least picked someone our age? How old do you think he is?'

'I don't know. Twenty-two or twenty-three?' Sterling followed me into the dining room, where we stopped just inside the door, off to the side to keep out of the way of others coming in.

'You didn't notice that he was feeling uncomfortable?'

'Aristea,' Sterling sighed, '*he's* not the point. The point is that if I hit on another student, Renatus will never hear about it, and the guy will probably assume I'm serious.' She rolled her eyes here, as if anyone making such an assumption would have to be a complete idiot. 'Aubrey actually *is* my teacher so he probably won't try to pursue anything, but he's on the council with Renatus, so he might pass it on.'

'I don't think they sit around and talk about which teenage students they think are cute,' I commented.

'That doesn't matter,' Sterling insisted, taking my hand imploringly. 'All Aubrey has to do is say, "Sterling was acting weird with me today, like, really friendly", and if Renatus has an eye on me he'll become suspicious, and next time he sees me...'

I shook my head and smiled in spite of myself. Sterling trailed off, apparently glad to see my expression.

'Sterling,' I said clearly, still smiling, 'I don't think I'll ever understand you. You are utterly incomprehensible.'

'Like you're so normal!' Sterling laughed, still holding my hand affectionately. Her laugh ended, and she added, 'Like any of us here are normal.'

She was right. The whole point of the school, I'd reflected several times that day, was that the students were as far from normal as the White Elm could find. I mean, instead of going to English and Chemistry this afternoon, I'd be going to Swordplay and Scrying, and that was actually the most appropriate sort of learning a person like me could be doing.

'Cool tat,' Xanthe commented to me, very quietly, as we sat in our Scrying class. I followed her gaze to Qasim, who had raised his left hand to accept Isao's candlestick. His sleeve had slipped back, and on his wrist was an obscure black marking, about five centimetres long. I'd never noticed it before. It was distinctly Middle Eastern in appearance, yet also not at all. I couldn't decide whether it was a symbol, like a letter or hieroglyph of sorts, or just a design he'd liked. I wanted to ask what it meant, but thought it best not to push my luck after what he'd seen me associated with this morning.

'I'm getting a tattoo when I turn eighteen,' Xanthe informed me. 'A dove, right here.' She reached across her chest to grasp her opposite shoulder, and tapped a spot on her shoulder blade. 'What about you?'

Xanthe rarely spoke so casually with me, so I wasn't prepared with an answer.

'Uh…I never really thought about it,' I said, honestly. 'If I found a design I really liked, I'd probably get one. My sister would kill me, though.'

Angela was slightly adverse to tattoos, along with other non-traditional customs such as excess body piercing and internet dating, so such an act would probably not go down so well with her. There, she might finally draw a line and say no.

'My mother doesn't know yet,' Xanthe said, shrugging. I could sense her getting bored already; she had withdrawn, emotionally, from our conversation, and if I'd bothered to respond, she would not have been interested, no matter what I'd had to say. So I didn't bother.

The lesson ended, and Qasim requested we try a new homework exercise.

'For some of you, this may not be new at all,' he

said. 'Some of you will have accidentally divined visions or images from objects or people by touching.'

I recalled the images and feelings I'd received when Renatus had touched me, the night before my detentions started. Was that the sort of thing Qasim was talking about?

'Physics tells us that whenever there is contact, there is a probability of transference. When somebody touches something, or manipulates something with magic, they leave something of themselves behind – a trace of their energy. Sometimes, very sensitive sorcerers are able to identify that trace and tune into the energy left behind, resulting in a scried image or short vision, depicting the event leading to the contact between the person and the object. Used consciously, this skill can be a valuable tool. With your roommates' permissions, please find something in your rooms that is *not* yours. Hold that item and allow yourself to see whatever comes to you. It may take a while before you note any real progress, because traces do fade over time and some traces are only very light. It is not easy. We will begin work on some techniques in our next lesson tomorrow, but in the meantime I would like for you all to attempt this on your own. Tomorrow we'll talk about what you come up with.'

This time, I was determined to have something to show for my efforts by the following day. I refused to be the disappointment again. Qasim seemed to have forgiven me, and I wanted it to stay that way. At lunch, when I told my friends about the exercise, they willingly handed me small items of theirs – Kendra pulled a pencil out of her hair, Sterling lent me her favourite hairclip and Hiroko unfastened her bracelet – but though I concentrated, no images or visions came to me.

'It probably takes much practice,' Hiroko assured me. She clipped her bracelet back around her wrist. 'Once you work out the trick, you will be very good at it, I am certain.'

'Well, you don't really know that much about scrying though, do you?' Xanthe asked, with a slightly sympathetic smile. Hiroko's expression faltered and I felt immediately irritated by Xanthe's blatant rudeness.

'Not very much,' Hiroko admitted. She forced a small smile at me and waited until Xanthe turned her attention away, and whispered, 'You will learn the trick and be very good at it anyway.'

Her confidence made me smile.

'Do you ever wonder what boys talk about when there're no girls around?' Kendra asked, gazing across the dining hall. We all glanced over to where Addison was sitting with his group of male friends at the other end of the table, their usual spot. One of them must have said something funny, because all five of them laughed loudly. Addison was careful to share his time between his guy friends and us, so we never knew if he would be sitting with us or not. Kendra apparently did not like the arrangement at the moment.

'No,' Sophia answered pointedly, picking the lid of her meat pie off with her fingernails.

'They talk about sex,' Sterling informed us earnestly, 'and cars and bikes. And they try to impress each other by telling big, exaggerated stories. I asked my stepbrother once.'

The rest of us didn't have big brothers (anymore, in my case) so we had to take her word for it.

Kendra had finished her lunch, so she helped herself to Sophia's. I briefly wondered whether Sophia ever had the chance to eat her own meal, undisturbed by her twin, and why both twins were the same size if Kendra usually ate both her own meal and half of her sister's.

'Marcy went home last night,' Sophia mentioned, stealing back a chip that was halfway to her sister's mouth. 'Her parents sent for her and she left last night after dinner with Elijah.'

'So that's, how many?' Kendra wondered aloud. She silently counted on her fingers. 'That's seven students gone so far.'

'The White Elm's gone on damage control,' Sophia told us. 'Anouk told Kenny and me that the council spent most of yesterday and last night visiting the families of those of us still here to rectify the situation. They don't want to lose any more students.'

Had they been to my house? Had someone visited Angela and neglected to invite me along?

'I'm going to see if he wants to go for a walk,' Kendra said suddenly, standing and walking away and leaving nobody wondering who she was talking about. Well, I didn't *think* anybody was wondering.

'To see if who wants to walk?' Sterling asked, looking up from the magazine she'd been engrossed in.

'Her *boyfriend*,' Sophia clarified simply. Xanthe, sitting right beside her, whipped around suddenly, and I felt her energy shift.

'He's her boyfriend?' she asked sharply. I was surprised by the barely contained waves of envy and dislike that suddenly radiated from her. 'Why didn't she tell us?'

'It's not official, I guess,' Sophia answered, shrugging dismissively. She acted as though she hadn't noticed Xanthe's change of mood, but I suspected that, sensitive as she was, she must have been pretending. Her next words made me less sure, because I'd figured her for a more tactful type. 'Maybe he's not her boyfriend yet, but I don't think either of them is looking at anyone else. Do you?'

We all looked over just as Addison playfully pinched Kendra's waist and she swatted away his hand, beaming. Nobody bothered to answer Sophia's rhetorical question – the evidence was quite plain.

Xanthe said nothing else for the rest of the meal, although I seemed to be the only one to notice that she was silently fuming. I assumed she'd had her eye on Addison, too, and somehow had missed the weeks of intense flirting that had led to this point. Either that, or she'd thought her friendship with Kendra was close enough that she should have been informed earlier. Whichever way, she was hurt and annoyed.

I had only four detentions left by this point, and

that realisation was actually more depressing than exciting as I made my way to Renatus's office that night.

Usually, the door just opened for me, but tonight it did not. I knocked, and still I was not answered. I waited for more than a minute, wondering whether I should sit at the door and see if he was running late, or just return to my dorm.

I shoved my hands into the pockets of my jeans and felt the scrunch of paper. I had thought to bring the list containing the names of my scrying class, because I hadn't meant to take it in the first place and I didn't know whether he needed it back.

I heard footsteps behind me, and turned my gaze down the hall. Renatus was heading towards me.

'Thank you for waiting,' he said, striding past me and pushing the door open easily. I followed him inside, and the door closed behind me. 'We have things to talk about.'

'What do you mean?' I asked. The chair I'd used for the previous few nights had been returned to its usual position amongst the other chairs, so Renatus dragged it closer to his desk before indicating that I should occupy it. He sat down opposite me in his own chair and presented an envelope, showing me only the back.

'Do you recognise this hand?' he asked as I read the return address. I felt my face light up as I saw my own address under the name *A. Byrne*.

'That's from my sister.'

'I thought so. We, also, received a letter today

from an Angela Byrne, regarding you.'

'That's her name,' I agreed, uncertain. His voice and her name didn't sound right together, from totally different corners of my life as they were. I watched as Renatus unfolded an A4 typed letter.

'We can't match the handwriting because it's typed, but both envelopes had the same handwriting. Can you open yours and confirm for us that she sent both of these?'

I wasn't listening. I took the typed letter from his hand and started to read. It was short and tense.

To whom it may concern,

My sister Aristea is a student at your Academy. Through social networking sites I have been contacted by the parents and guardians of other students, presenting me with unsavoury information about the council and encouraging me to cancel my sister's enrolment. Though I cannot vouch for the validity of these claims, discussion of cover-ups and murders is rife among the online community of Academy parents. I am evidently eager to resolve these issues immediately in order to preserve Aristea's position in the school if that is what she sincerely prefers; however, if she feels any uncertainty at all, I would like to be notified so I can collect her at the earliest possible convenience. I have sent a letter to Aristea as well and expect that she will be able to make this decision independently and without interference.

Regards,
Angela Byrne

I frowned at the paper. Angela could not seriously be buying into this crap Egan Lake's mother was selling about Lisandro and the White Elm. I knew that other families had been contacted as well, and had pulled their children out of the Academy over the past few days, but surely *my* sister had more sense than those silly people. Renatus was watching me closely.

'Do you think your sister wrote this?' he asked.

'Definitely.'

I reached for the letter addressed to me and Renatus let me have it. I ripped it open, knowing with certainty that this was the accompanying letter to the first. Angela was worried for me. Whether she believed that garbage or not, a seed of doubt had been planted in her mind, and until it was weeded out she'd be trapped with her protective guardian mentality.

Aristea,

I don't know how they tracked me down but some mums from your school have contacted me on Facebook. I logged in today and found a bunch of messages about the White Elm being responsible for the death of some girl that Lisandro was trying to save, some examples of supposed cover-ups and information on how to have "my child" removed from the White Elm's school.

I haven't heard from you in a little bit and I haven't heard any complaints in any of our correspondence but if there is even a grain of truth to this stuff or if you don't feel comfortable there anymore, please, just write to me and let me know and I will be there so quick for you.

*You don't have to do anything you don't want to do.
Ever.*

I love you so much. Write back straightaway!

-Angela xoxoxo

I read the letter a few times fast. Angela wanted
me out. She hadn't said it to me but I could read
between the lines. And it was my fault. I should be
writing to her more, keeping her updated. Of course
she would worry. She felt responsible for me, and
despite what she always said, she *was* my mother in
many ways.

'What's a Face Book?' Renatus asked, reading
the letter upside down as I laid it onto the tabletop.
He had no business reading my personal mail but I
felt no resentment at all. Hadn't I read dozens of
letters addressed to or written by him?

'Oh, it's just a website, where you can have a
profile and your friends look at your photos and
status updates, and you tag people, and...' I watched
for a signal of understanding on my headmaster's
face but saw none, and remembered what sort of life
he'd led. Social crazes that took over the rest of world
didn't even catch his notice. 'Never mind, it doesn't
matter. I need to write back to my sister.'

Renatus produced a leaf of paper but held it
back from me.

'Saying what?' he asked. I reached for it and
waited; he waited, too.

'I need to tell her that Egan's mum is an idiot,' I

348

said, 'and that I'm staying here.'

I'd known it would be my answer even before I'd opened her letter. I had crazy friends and daily misadventures of varying degrees of awkwardness, but I had no intention of going anywhere.

'You seem certain,' Renatus noted, giving me the paper. I grabbed one of his beautiful fountain pens from its perfectly aligned position at the top of the desk.

'I am.' I began to write. *Dear Angela.* 'I'm only just scratching the surface of what I can do. I can't leave now. And she won't make me. She'd never make me do anything I didn't want to do.'

I wrote for twenty minutes in total silence while Renatus sat opposite me, reading an old hand-written book, possibly a massive journal. I told Angela how Egan and his mother had bought into Lisandro's stupid stories, how I'd seen some of this through Renatus when he'd touched me (I made it clear that he'd touched me to get my attention, not wanting any confusion, especially after this morning) and how happy I was here to be learning so many new and exciting things. I finished by asking how work was going and promising that I would try to write more.

I signed off and slid the completed text across the desk. Renatus looked up from his book and glanced at it. He didn't seem to be looking close enough to be actually reading, more just skimming, but then he must have noticed something that caught his attention. Frowning, he turned the letter around to read it properly. Again, I felt no invasion of privacy.

'What you said here,' he said, pointing as he read. 'Is that true?' He showed me. 'You scried *through* me?' Renatus paraphrased, frowning slightly. 'When? And how?'

'I don't know how,' I admitted. 'And I only assume that's what I did. The night you went with Qasim, and you touched my arm...' He was staring at me, and I felt suddenly uncomfortable. Scrying had gotten me into deep trouble in the recent past. 'I don't know...'

'What did you see?' Renatus was insistent.

'I had this sudden rush of feelings and blurry images. It felt like they were channelled from you.'

'What did you see?' he repeated.

'I saw a man and woman having drinks at a bar, talking about a life Lisandro wanted to save,' I said quickly, 'and everyone felt really content and curious. That's it. I didn't mean to scry anything, I promise.'

I'd been in enough trouble last time. I didn't need that whole adventure again. Why did this keep happening?

Renatus sat back, regarding me with interest.

'You aren't in trouble,' he assured me. 'I just...didn't expect this. Do you usually feel things when you scry?'

I considered this for a moment. When I'd scried what turned out to be Peter, I'd felt the desperate hunger of the birds; when I'd wandered around this office as a disconnected spirit, I'd felt Emmanuelle's outpouring of grief.

'I always do.'

'Has anyone ever suggested that you may be empathic?'

I'd heard the term thrown around by my uncle and father since I was young. They said it was when someone felt things more intensely than others, and that it explained why I was like I was.

As a child, I was sensitive. My mother had often complained to me later on that I had been a tearful baby and a moody toddler – much higher maintenance than either of my older siblings. In primary school I was the weird girl. I didn't have many friends. Several times, other kids tried to single me out and pick on me, but they usually ended up in tears themselves. I had a knack for knowing what to say – what would hurt the most – and before I was old enough to know better, I was happy to use this knowledge to protect myself. These days I was usually more tactful.

As primary school neared its end and secondary loomed, my sensitivity suddenly increased (psychic changes often coincide with biological changes, and early adolescence is usually a pretty hectic time, regardless of whether you're a witch). It began as waves; I would be sitting in class, writing an essay, when I would suddenly be swamped by the unchecked feelings of my non-witch peers. The overwhelming jealousy felt by Siobhan of Aisling would suddenly make my vision blur. Shamus's fear of ridicule would threaten to choke me. The mixes of stress, confusion, anger, worry and nervousness would wash over me again and again until my body responded by running to the bathrooms and throwing up.

Understandably, my parents decided against sending me to high school until this was under control. My family and their nearest friends taught me how to protect myself from all of this by barricading my mind. My father and uncle had home-schooled me to the end of compulsory schooling. I was much more controlled now than I'd been before the training, but I still felt a lot of what was being emotionally processed around me.

It had become an unspoken issue among members of my family. It was just Aristea's little problem – not a big deal, but ever-present. Not something we talked about outside the home.

'I've heard the term,' I agreed. 'I feel stuff all the time. Other people's stuff. I feel it most around non-witches.'

Renatus nodded. I was about to keep speaking, but then remembered who I was talking to. This was my headmaster, not my friend or parent – why was it so easy to forget that? I realised, with something of a shock, that I trusted him almost as much as I trusted Hiroko, even though I knew nothing about him.

That didn't seem to really be true anymore, though. More and more, I felt like I *knew* Renatus. Somehow, I felt as though we shared something, like an interest or an experience, but when I actually thought about it, I couldn't really identify anything that we had in common. He was mysterious, intense and intelligent and I was, well, me. I considered myself the epitome of boring – or at least, as boring as it is possible to be when you are an orphaned witch. What could I possibly have in common with an adult man who was influential, all-powerful and so incredibly organised?

In the ensuing quiet, Renatus folded up my letter and sealed it inside an envelope. He left it for me to write the addresses.

'I haven't yet thanked you for the way you stood up for the White Elm when Egan Lake and his mother came slandering our name with Lisandro's lies,' he said. I finished writing his estate's name as my return address and put the pen back where I'd found it initially.

'I haven't yet apologised for breaking that orb thing that probably could have answered a lot of your questions,' I countered.

'I'm not concerned that you destroyed it. There could have been much worse outcomes to Saturday's events.' He paused, and when I gave him a questioning look, he elaborated unhelpfully by adding, 'You could have accessed the information left inside the orb instead.'

I recalled the jolt of horror I'd felt *him* feel when that had almost happened. What was he scared of me seeing? And why did he care what I saw?

'The less people Lisandro's stories reach, the better off we'll all be.' Renatus nodded at the door. 'Your time's up. You can go.'

'Will you send that letter to my sister?' I asked as I stood up.

'Consider it halfway there,' he answered, and I noticed that the envelope was nowhere to be seen. I remembered something else that had once been on this desk and no longer was, and dug into my pocket for the scrunched list I'd taken last week.

'I took this by accident,' I said, careful not to even sound apologetic. He accepted it back from me with interest.

'I don't think it was really an accident,' he mused, and I felt slightly offended.

'I assure you it was,' I said firmly. I left him with it and walked out. 'See you tomorrow.'

'Aristea,' he called after me. I stopped and looked back. He looked strange. 'You are going to hear things in the coming weeks, about the council and about myself, which will be incorrect. You won't believe a word without careful consideration first. Can you promise that?'

'I promise that,' I agreed, ignoring the weirdness of yet another odd exchange with Renatus and just going with it. 'Night.'

chapter twenty-three

Anouk was a brilliant teacher, like all of the others. Her classes had no active or hands-on component, however, so there was a lot of opportunity for complete boredom, but she taught her council's history with such fervour and zeal that I didn't really mind sitting, just listening and writing for two hours at a time. Plus her accent was amazing. She rolled her r almost into a d and pronounced each syllable so fully. Kendra and I liked to try to imitate it after classes.

Today we wrote as Anouk dictated. She was explaining the current structure of the White Elm. We'd been building to this for weeks, learning about the how the White Elm was first formed from a band of warrior spell-casters in the Dark Ages to protect local villages from dark sorcery, how its purpose had evolved and how various nations had eventually pledged allegiance to the council. Starting as just a little group, the council had later been called abroad to solve international problems, slowly amassing a global following. Today, the White Elm council was generally accepted as the supreme authority of the magical world. It helped that less than a century after forming, Fate itself was invoked to bless the White Elm as a part of the Natural Order, basically meaning that it would be awarded its own powers to do Fate's work. That part seemed a bit wishy-washy for me, but it was still an engaging story.

'Each White Elm councillor takes on one of thirteen traditional roles when initiated,' Anouk said, waiting for us to write that before continuing. Those r's sounded like a cat purring. 'We use Lord Philip's 1512 model, but we are flexible on the ranking of most roles. Today, only three are formally recognised and given authority – the others are allocated to those best suited to the role, rather than the next in line – and there is only one that allocates authority irrespective of seniority.'

I paused with my pen in the air and it took a moment for me to process that, because the phrase "allocates authority irrespective of seniority" was too full of big words. I put my hand up.

'So...usually, authority in the council is dictated by age?' I asked when Anouk gestured to me, and she nodded, although by now I'd guessed this.

'That's correct.' It sounded like cord-eckt. 'The eldest male is the High Priest, entitled Lord; the eldest female is the Lady, or High Priestess. Those roles are the ultimate goal of every councillor. Fate awards the possessors of those chairs extra powers, and no position is more respected in our society.'

Anouk paused again while we wrote madly. 'Statistically, most White Elm councillors pass away while still in service, but many others have chosen to retire when they feel that they can no longer serve effectively. In both of these cases, their role becomes available and others on the council, or a new initiate, may take that role. If the departing councillor is a Lord or Lady, the next in line will automatically take that position. If the new position is another...' Anouk trailed off to let us catch up, and gestured to the blackboard behind her, where she'd written thirteen titles and a short description of each. I'd started writing that list when I'd come in, before she'd started talking. I glanced up at it as I scrawled about statistics.

Lord Philip's Council Structure, as at 1512:
Lord Philip – *leader, priest and judge*
Lady Catherine – *leader and priestess*
Keeper Nathaniel – *researcher and warrior*
Scrier Christopher – *researcher and strategist*
Seer Edward – *philosopher and strategist*
Healer Anne – *doctor and counsellor*
Displacer James – *tracker and transporter*
Listener Daniel – *chief telepath and researcher*
Illusionist Isaac – *defender and trick-maker*
Wandcrafter Hannah – *creator of council wands and minder of weapons*
Swordcrafter Walter – *creator and minder of council weapons*
Historian Rowland – *keeper of council histories and researcher*

Scribe Allen – *scribe of council documents and writer of council magics*

It was pretty easy to guess who a couple of these long-dead former councillors had most recently been replaced by. Lord Gawain and Lady Miranda were givens, obviously, but Anouk was evidently the Historian of this modern incarnation of the White Elm, Elijah the Displacer, Qasim the Scrier and Susannah the Seer. I recalled a conversation with the twins and Marcy that indicated that Emmanuelle must be the Healer. It still seemed strange to me that this should be Emmanuelle's job – she didn't *seem* like the kind of gentle, compassionate soul I'd envisioned the Healer would have to be – but later, when I knew her better, it would seem obvious.

It was Renatus that I kept wondering about, because lots of those descriptions seemed to suit him. He was so strange. Monday night's detention had been so tense, then last night's had been totally boring, back to licking envelopes. I had two left and no idea what to expect from either one.

Anouk moved on to discussing the roles in depth, and I wrote half-heartedly until she reached the third and fourth.

'The Keeper is the White Elm's researcher and warrior in apparent peace-times,' she began, and then moved onto the Scrier without any elaboration, whereas for the previous two she'd spoken for several minutes about the expectations and a number of famous councillors former to that role. I looked around but seemed to be the only one to have noticed; I quickly forgot, however, as Anouk began to describe the position of the White Elm Scrier.

'The Scrier is the gatherer of information both past and present, and due to the secretiveness of the job, has often been used as something of a spy,' she said while I listened attentively. 'A great deal of the White Elm's wartime research is carried out by the Scrier, and much of our successes over the years can be attributed to the work of Scriers. This role can only be held by a natural scrier because of the demands of the job.'

She went on to list various famous Scriers through the council's history, and I promptly forgot the names and neglected to write them down. It didn't matter anyway. It was irrelevant who'd been in the role before. What mattered was that I'd be the next one.

'Anouk.' I grabbed my pen and notebook as everyone else filed out at the end. Kendra stopped at the door and waited for me while I spoke with our teacher. 'Anouk, is there anywhere I can read more about this stuff?'

The rake-thin Russian sorceress waved a hand across the chalkboard and the whole thing cleared itself. Chalk dust fell to the floor as she turned to me.

'About the White Elm?' she clarified. I nodded.

'About anything,' I agreed. 'About the council, about the positions, about the traditions...'

Anything about the Scrier, and about how to get that job?

'Oh.' Anouk smiled thinly, going to a small shelf behind her desk. 'You should be so specific in speech, Aristea.' Ard-iss-tay-ya. I loved it. 'This book should tell you everything you want to know about the various positions on the council, including the Scrier, and about the traditions and processes involved in entering the White Elm.'

She pressed an old book with a tatty dust jacket into my hands. I stared at her. *Now, I know I didn't say anything about-*

'I know, you didn't say anything about the Scrier,' she guessed, keeping her voice down. 'I'll let Glen cover that one in his classes.'

I couldn't believe how un-private a place my mind had become since arriving at the Academy.

'I love her lessons,' Kendra told me as we left a little while later. 'She makes history so inspiring and makes the council seem so incredibly complex and interesting.'

'She makes me want to sign up for the White Elm's waiting list right now,' I admitted. We went to the dining hall even though dinner was ages away. It was kind of the central meeting point for students. I was sure that the ballroom had been intended as a social common room of sorts, but staging a funeral there just a few weeks into term had really turned most of my classmates off that particular part of the mansion.

'Which would you be?' she asked, taking a seat in our usual section of the table. 'I would want to be the Seer. I think that's Susannah at the moment.'

'I think it is,' I agreed. 'I want to be the Scrier.'

'No "would" for you,' Kendra noted playfully. 'Just plain old "want".'

I grinned back at her.

'No harm in wanting something.'

'Too true,' Addison said, announcing his arrival at Kendra's shoulder. He playfully tipped her chair to the side, partly unseating her, but he was quick to catch her, steal her seat and set her down on his lap. 'What's happening? Forming a boy band?'

'Close. We're joining the White Elm,' Kendra informed him. 'We're just discussing the various spots and taking the best ones for ourselves.'

'Well, as long as you leave the "hot, bad-boy guitarist" spot open for me,' Addison warned.

The rest of our friends filtered in over the course of the afternoon and evening and I enjoyed the conversations, but I was still thinking about scrying for the White Elm the whole time, even as I walked into Renatus's office, still holding the book.

'For that to happen,' he greeted me as I walked in, 'Qasim would need to rise to High Priest.'

'And I'd have to hope that you wouldn't want that spot,' I added, because I'd guessed by now that he was a scrier, too. Why else would he have countless books on scrying lying about his office, and how else would he have been receiving those images I'd channelled through him?

'That wouldn't be an issue,' he told me. I sat down and put the book down on the desk in front of me. 'I have a position I can't step down from.'

'What's that?' I asked. 'Like Lord Gawain?'

'Similar. I'm actually not allowed to discuss it.'

He looked up and met my gaze. The challenging

look in his violet eyes was unmissable. I wasn't sure what he wanted me to say to that.

'I see. Perhaps I should stop discussing it, too.'

'You can discuss whatever you like.'

I paused, trying to understand what he was *really* saying. I decided I had no idea, and that I'd just cycle back to this conversation later if I worked it out. I noticed the list I'd accidentally stolen last week sitting in front of him. It was different now.

'I'd like to discuss why some names have been crossed off that list,' I decided, not sure why. Renatus turned the paper around so I could read it easier.

'I suspected you would.'

'Why are you crossing our names off?' I asked, noting that Dylan, Isao and Joshua were all scratched off. Khalida Jasti was at the top now, followed by Constantine, then me, Xanthe and Iseult.

'This is your scrying class, with Qasim,' Renatus said, which I knew already. 'How well do you know these people?'

'Um, Xanthe and I are friends, sort of,' I said, pointing to her name. I made no attempt to pronounce her surname. 'The others I know only superficially. Why?'

'To overcome Lisandro in a conflict, I will need access to magic and power that I don't currently have,' Renatus explained. 'I will need to become a master.'

I stared at him. He wanted Lord Gawain's job? He shook his head, as always, answering my thoughts before I could ask them.

'I knew when I was initiated to the council that

I'd never be the council's Lord,' he said. 'That became certain when I took my current role last year. It is not possible to go from...what I am, to High Priest. That isn't what I mean. I need an apprentice.'

'Oh,' I stated, understanding. I looked back at the list. 'And these are your first choices?'

I couldn't believe that *I* was in that top eight. Admittedly, I was sixth, but I was before Xanthe. That had to count for something. But seriously. Were Khalida and Constantine really that much better than me?

'It's listed by age,' Renatus informed me, with a slight tone of amusement. He laced his long fingers together. 'Qasim tells me that these eight are his best students. Realistically, as scriers, it makes sense for him and me to choose apprentices who show early promise in scrying. So we're both considering this same group.'

'And...you've already removed some from the running.'

Renatus seemed to sigh as he took the list back. I wasn't sure what I expected but it wasn't what followed.

'I overheard Isao Tanaka talking with friends this morning in the dining hall, and I realised that I have no time to untrain stupidity,' he admitted bluntly. 'I observed Dylan Wright briefly and realised I require someone...slightly less...' Renatus struggled to think of an appropriate word.

'Soft?' I suggested, thinking of the nice blonde boy.

'That'll do. I need someone less soft. What I

do…it isn't for the light hearted.'

I sat back, forgetting totally that this was my teacher.

'Are you the White Elm's Keeper?' I asked, thinking of Anouk's lecture. 'The "researcher and warrior"?'

'I'm not allowed to discuss it with you,' Renatus said automatically. He paused. 'But yes. The true title is Dark Keeper. It's my job to defend the White Elm in times of crisis.'

'Why aren't you allowed to discuss this, if other councillors use their positions as public titles and Anouk teaches it in class?'

'Nobody but the council, and now our students, knows that my position exists,' he explained. He nodded at the publication in front of me. 'It isn't even properly described in the book you've found – and I'm glad you found it, by the way. I couldn't find my copy to share with you. The creation of the Dark Keeper was a precautionary measure. A council of well-meaning, decent sorcerers all practising only white magic is beautiful in theory, but in reality, as soon as somebody comes along with knowledge of darker arts, they stand no chance of holding their power.'

'But good should overpower evil,' I argued. Everyone knew that. It was a common theme of modern storytelling, and one that I liked to believe in. Our conversations were so deep and academic that, as usual, I forgot to feel embarrassed for my outburst.

'Maybe in *Cinderella*,' Renatus answered, 'but

Lord Philip felt – and I happen to agree – the world is very rarely as simple as good and bad, right and wrong, black and white. There are shades of grey, and many of them. His council structure resembles what we now think of as the yin-yang concept. Nothing is inherently good or bad. There is flaw in everything light; there is beauty in everything dark. A White Elm council that was only light could not be balanced and could have no understanding of the dark. We cannot hope to compete against that which we do not understand.' He sketched a faint yin-yang in the corner of the list as he spoke. 'So, Lord Philip chose his cousin, Nathaniel Tynan, another councillor, to be the first Keeper of the Dark Arts. His job was to study dark magic and remain up-to-date with dangerous spells as they became popular, so that the council was able to effectively combat uprisings of dark sorcerers. The secrecy of the position has also allowed the White Elm to be continually underestimated during conflicts.'

I allowed this new information to sink in and assimilate itself with what I'd read and learned earlier in the day.

'And now that's *your* job,' I said. He nodded, and things started clicking into place. 'That's why, on that Thursday night, Qasim came and got you, instead of just going ahead by himself?'

'That's right,' Renatus agreed. 'I am much better suited to a confrontation with Lisandro than he is, and he knows that. It didn't help us much, though. Lisandro knew to expect us.'

'If you study dark magic, are you evil?' I asked

before I could think about how awful that sounded. I shook my head quickly and added, 'I mean, people. Not *you*.'

'No one answers that question with "yes",' Renatus said immediately, 'regardless of the true answer. No one thinks himself evil. Academically: yes, if you use dark magic, if you do bad things, you will do damage to your soul and the more you use it, the further and faster you'll fall. There's no coming all the way back, either. Some scars can't be erased. Reading about it or talking to people about it, though, that doesn't hurt you.'

I started to think on what I'd just learned (the White Elm had a secret weapon, a *person*, someone they trained to use dark magic, and that person was *Renatus*, and he was my headmaster, and he was *well-suited* to a confrontation with Lisandro, and that meant he could easily kill people, and he was sitting right in front of me, perfectly capable of blowing my head off with a click of his fingers if he so wanted...) and decided to ward off my imagination's wanderings by quickly changing the topic. I took the list back.

'All of the people you've left on here are pretty good scriers,' I reported. *Including me, obviously.*

'You're friends with some,' Renatus noted. 'Like Xanthe Giannopoulos.'

'We're *sort of* friends,' I corrected. 'Some days she's chatty, other days she won't look at me.'

A bit like Qasim's behaviour towards me, really, except that I always knew *why* he was angry. Xanthe would just switch off me for no apparent reason.

'I think perhaps I just don't understand her,' I finished diplomatically.

'And Iseult Taylor?' Renatus asked, indicating the last name on his list. I considered the tiny, self-powerful blonde who hardly ever spoke. She was in my wards class with Emmanuelle, and my illusion class with Teresa.

'I've never spoken to her,' I said truthfully, fiddling with the strap on my watch, 'but if I were you, looking for an apprentice, I would choose her.'

Renatus sat back, seemingly surprised.

'What makes you say that?' he asked.

'Because she's so powerful,' I said, shrugging. 'Doesn't it make sense to find a student with a power level close to yours? And besides that, she's good at everything.'

There was a knock at the door, and Renatus sighed, closing his eyes briefly.

'Who is it?' I asked him softly, but he shook his head. He sat up straighter and flicked his hand irritably in the direction of the door. I turned to look.

Three older girls stepped inside the office, smiling and emanating nervousness and delight. One was Khalida Jasti from my scrying class, and the other two were her roommates. The Asian girl was clutching a pink diamante-covered notebook. All three had gone all-out on their hair and make-up this evening. Hair curled, straightened, pinned up – you name it. How they'd managed those styles without access to power points was beyond me. They all wore tight, dressy jeans and trendy black tops. They looked grown-up and glamorous.

'Good evening, girls,' Renatus said, professional as always. 'What can I do for you?'

'I'm not sure whether you really know who we are,' Khalida gushed, ignoring me completely, 'but I'm Khalida, and this is Suki, and Bella. We were hoping to talk to-'

She was interrupted by the girl I assumed was Bella, a pretty European with shiny brown hair and eyes so heavily lined with black kohl that I couldn't guess the colour. She had just dragged her sultry gaze from Renatus to take a quick look around the office, and spotted me.

'What's *she* doing here?' she demanded haughtily. Khalida and Suki turned to stare at me with the same demanding, expectant air. I felt a spark of indignation – what, they had a right to be here and I didn't?

'I'm in detention,' I said, deeply annoyed. 'Why?'

The three beautiful teen queens blinked almost in unison, looking uniformly stupid, and then relaxed, sharing snide, smug looks.

'Oh, that's right,' Khalida said airily. 'Sterling told us about that. Anyway,' she turned her attention back to Renatus, 'the three of us are interested in starting a student events committee, with your permission, Sir. Our tasks would involve organising social events for the students here, as presently there's not a whole lot to do here outside of classes.'

'I see,' Renatus said, nodding once.

'It would require *some* collaboration with you, Sir,' Suki said, looking positively enthralled by the notion, 'but mostly we'd organise everything ourselves. We've come up with a few ideas already.' She showed him the book she held.

'We thought you might like to have the worry of arranging these kinds of events off your shoulders,' Bella added.

I quickly turned away so the girls wouldn't see me struggling not to smile. Like Renatus had *nothing* better to do than arrange movie nights for a bunch of bored teenage drama queens.

'Yes, that would definitely be a weight off my mind,' Renatus said, absolutely seriously, and I tried my hardest not to roll my eyes and smirk. I bit my tongue and flipped open Anouk's book to a random page. *...councillors continued the then-common tradition of taking an apprentice to ensure succession of talent and skill within...* I could tell without looking that the girls were beaming with pride. 'Who would this committee consist of?'

'Us,' Khalida, Bella and Suki answered all at once, as though the answer was obvious.

'Of course.'

'These are some of our ideas,' Khalida said sweetly, positively wrenching the pink and sparkly notebook from Suki's jealous grasp. She stalked forward, earrings jingling, until she was standing right beside me, pretending I didn't exist, and leaned past me to hand Renatus the book. 'We'll give you some time to have a read over what we've got, and perhaps we'll come back in a couple of days to talk about what you think?'

'That will be fine.'

Khalida smiled widely, an expression echoed by her friends. I was vividly reminded of a documentary I'd seen on lionesses, and envisioned a pack of hunters, trying to close in on their prey.

Except these girls had no idea what they were hunting.

'Thanks so much,' she said graciously, slowly backing away to rejoin the other two. 'Goodnight, Sir.'

'Goodnight, Sir,' Bella and Suki said together. As one, they turned and left, each taking a moment to cast triumphant looks my way. I watched them leave. I supposed they thought they had won a round. I supposed they thought I *cared* if they'd just made complete fools of themselves. The door closed behind them.

Renatus didn't say anything for a long moment – he just stared at the back of his office door. Then, abruptly, he snatched the list from me and slapped it down before him. I watched as he found a pen and crossed out the third name: Khalida.

I couldn't have said what made me do it – what made me think I had any right to do it – but I reached across the desk and took both the pen and the list from him. He didn't try to hold onto either one. I scanned the list quickly, and drew a line through Xanthe's name.

Actually, I knew exactly what made me do it. Xanthe had been nasty to Hiroko and I couldn't bear the thought of her getting a privilege so undeserved. As to where I got off thinking it was my right to influence Renatus's decision as a result, well, I'm not so sure. He didn't seem offended.

'I thought she was your friend?' Renatus asked, his tone hinting at amusement.

'She's not.' I still had Anouk's book open, and flicked the cover to close it. Renatus's hand snapped out and caught it, maintaining my page.

'Don't,' he said. 'No page is random for people like us.'

'What are you talking about?' I asked. He pushed the cover back so the book fell open again.

'You opened the book without thinking. There is information on this page for you. Maybe not for today, but for one day. You should memorise the page number and come back to it.'

'How do you know I didn't?' I teased, knowing it was a stupid question – of course he knew I hadn't committed the page number to memory! I looked around for a bookmark, or something to use as one, and Renatus unlocked and opened his drawer.

'Use this,' he suggested, offering me a strip of red ribbon. My eyes lingered on it as I took it.

A beautiful teenage girl with very long black hair sitting in the library...She uses the red ribbon to secure her plait...Loneliness, resentment, hurt...She has tears on her face...

I whipped my hand back instantly. Renatus blinked, surprised by my reaction.

'What is it?' he asked.

'Whose is this?' I demanded, startled. I could still feel the girl's pain. 'She's upset.'

He stared at me, apparently lost for words. His face didn't say much, but his eyes told me that my words and my distress had brought up a hurt deep inside him. His whole energy shifted, and something seemed to break. I could suddenly feel everything he was feeling, whereas usually he was in complete control of his emotions. His fingers closed over the ribbon, tighter and tighter, mirroring the feeling of tightness in my chest.

'She's...' he began, but couldn't continue for a very long moment. He looked to his window, as he often seemed to do when he was lost in thought. This time, though, I wasn't going to leave him to his thoughts. I was worried for this girl, distressed by what I'd felt, and I wanted to know what was going on.

'She's what?' I asked, not caring if I sounded pushy. 'Who is she? *Where* is she?'

'She's been dead for seven years,' Renatus said finally, clearly struggling. I had never seen him so distraught. He wouldn't look at me. 'Her name was Ana. She's...' He wiped his brow with his hand, upset. He paused for another long moment, and this time I allowed it. I was trying hard not to cry. He finally dragged his gaze back to me, and to my surprise, there was an apologetic look in his eyes. 'She's why you're here.'

I closed Anouk's book, losing my place, but I was finding it hard to care. My head was swimming – all I could feel was grief, powerful grief, and it was clouding my thoughts. I stared at Renatus, trying to make sense of his words. The parts of my brain still functioning began producing outlandish and improbable possible meanings. Was this Ana a prophet who had foreseen my coming to this school and my eventual ascension into the White Elm as the Scrier? That would be too nice and convenient. Perhaps she'd died as a part of some psychotic ritual, and I had been selected as the next sacrifice? Did Renatus have contact with the other side? Was that the sort of dark magic the council let him use? Had I been tricked into coming here?

Could I possibly think up a crazier prospect?

'I don't understand,' I said, making an effort to keep my voice even. My heart was hurting. His pain was too intense, too real to block out. Renatus held my gaze.

'She was my sister,' he explained softly, 'and you remind me of her.'

I stood suddenly, not really knowing what I was doing. My heart felt broken. All I knew was what he was feeling, and I was connecting so deeply that I was completely unable to block it. It was overwhelming. I realised how much it must have hurt him to get to know me, having grieved for his lost sister for seven years and suddenly meeting a living reminder. I wondered briefly why he had bothered with me if that was the case. This was *my* fault. I'd brought this up. For the first time in my life, I couldn't stand myself, and I knew this wasn't my own, personal feeling. I could feel tears welling in my eyes, blurring my vision.

'I'm sorry,' I blurted, backing away. Distance usually helped whenever this happened to me. *I'm sorry that you lost the person you loved most in the world. I'm sorry that I remind you of what you lost. I'm sorry that I'm here and she's not.*

'Aristea,' Renatus said, standing also, 'that isn't what I meant.'

His voice was calmer, and he was making a conscious effort to rein in his emotions, but I had already felt it all, and I was still drowning in it. I didn't know any way of calming down other than simply running away from the problem. It was the only way that always worked – I didn't seem to have the self-control to wait it out.

The last thing I wanted was to burst into tears in front of Renatus and completely lose control to a bundle of powerful emotions that weren't even mine. I'd backed almost all the way to the door by this point, and Renatus, his expression one of concern, raised a hand and the door opened. I turned to leave, but managed to make myself pause in the doorway and look back quickly.

'I really am sorry,' I said, then left.

chapter twenty-four

Renatus watched her leave. So much potential, all wrapped up in the form of an overly-trusting, uncertain teenage girl. She could so easily go astray, with demons like hers, and she could be so easily led down the wrong path, so willing was she to follow anybody who was nice to her.

Who is she? She's upset.

Renatus had once been like Aristea – young and ignorant of his true potential. He had, thankfully, known himself better, known his gifts, but he'd been short-sighted and unable to imagine himself as he now was. He'd been much, much further away from the light than she was, though, when Lord Gawain had brought him back.

Most of the way back, anyway. Apparently some of his own demons still haunted him.

'Apparently,' he muttered bitterly, locking the ribbon back into the drawer. There was no apparently about it. He *knew*. He *knew* how ridiculously messed-up he was and he *knew* that this deep unresolved pain lay at his inner core. What he hadn't known until now was that there was a person – other than Lisandro – who could open him up and shine painful, nasty light on that core.

Renatus had found that stupid ribbon years ago, a few days after he'd officially inherited the mansion. He'd picked it up accidentally, tapped into the impressions left on it by his sister's touch and reacted similarly to Aristea. He'd thrown it back into the drawer. Years later, on a whim, he'd found it again and grabbed it…and received nothing from it. Some faint impressions dissolved over time, or after they'd been accessed. Renatus had assumed the ribbon had shared all it would.

He'd dropped her straight into that. He should have at least suspected Aristea would read more into it than he had. She was an incredible scrier, and so shockingly like Ana. He should have been more careful with her.

Aristea had no idea who or what she could be in five years' time. Less, even. Properly instructed, she could become an incredible force.

And who said you'd properly instruct her?

She wouldn't necessarily become like him. She was stronger than she knew, and with his knowledge, she could perhaps be better. Perhaps she wouldn't break, like he had.

Renatus shook his head firmly and got up, restless, ashamed and anxious. He'd expected his search to take a long time – he'd imagined compiling list after list, observing quietly, taking notes, eliminating names until there was only one option left. That name, he'd decided, would belong to the *one*.

He'd written a list. He'd listened to Qasim's comments on the Academy's top scriers. He'd even made a point of talking to a few of them, although only Aristea had really stood out, odd and unusual as she was.

Then she'd crossed Qasim and landed herself right in front of Renatus's eyes.

Fate.

Then she'd turned out to be the only scrier in the whole cohort. The best scrier of her age anywhere.

Fate.

Then she'd been both reserved and outspoken, both self-doubting and quietly confident, both obedient and stubborn, a medley of paradoxes and contradictions that reminded him so, so much of the person he most needed to replace.

Fate.

It seemed – *seemed* – as though he'd already found what he was looking for.

As it turned out, he hadn't really known what he was looking for, because Aristea was nothing like the cold, fierce, self-powerful male he'd imagined he'd need to win his war. Instead, she was emotive (an Empath!), trusting, and of course, she was a girl.

She was perfect.

And he'd hurt her. That was reason enough to feel ashamed, but even more, he'd hurt her by the act of hurting *himself*. Remembering his sister brought up old feelings of guilt, inadequacy and loneliness, which had for years simmered and festered in his dark, tortured soul and reformed themselves into a single emotion. Now when he reflected on his old life he generally only felt self-hatred, because, really, all the other feelings were only going to lead there anyway. Might as well skip to the good bit.

Speaking of skipping to the good bit…

Renatus let his head fall against the window, staring out across the dark estate. Eventually he'd have to talk to Aristea about this, and it would be awful. She'd be upset, like she was tonight, and she could be angry and distant. If he left it until tomorrow night's detention she'd have a whole day to ponder which nasty emotions to bring with her. He'd seen into that imagination. Best not to let it go too long.

The right thing to do would be to go and find her right this instant and tell her everything.

Yes.

It would be the right thing to do.

Right now.

A minute passed and Renatus didn't move, his forehead still against the window glass. He was a coward, a pathetic coward, and he deserved all of this agony, every little twinge of it.

But Aristea wasn't, and didn't. He straightened and walked to the door. He froze at the doorway, procrastination striking again. What exactly was he going to do? Walk into her dormitory and ask her to step outside for a talk?

He wasn't good at this.

Why did Aristea have to feel so much like the

past when she looked so much like the future?

'Fate,' he reminded himself. There would be no future until he buried the past, or otherwise dealt with it appropriately. He couldn't bring himself to walk the path into the graveyard, and as a result he was drowning in the darkness of his own past, but Fate was throwing him a lifeline.

He raised a hand and the door opened. He had barely taken a step when a familiar presence registered with his senses.

Aubrey?

His fellow councillor exited the stairwell and approached down the hallway.

'Renatus, can I have a word?' he asked brusquely. He was no Empath; he couldn't guess what an emotional mess the Dark Keeper was at that moment, how inappropriate this time was for any sort of "word".

'Uh,' he responded, torn. His colleague didn't seem to find his sudden lack of articulation concerning or surprising.

'Lord Gawain wanted your opinion on something,' Aubrey began, tensely. He was already wondering, thinking about Teresa's task, worrying, and Renatus grabbed those thoughts right from his mind before he could verbalise them.

'You can tell him I know already,' Renatus said. He glanced down the empty hallway. 'She already told me.'

'Did she, or was it your idea?' Aubrey demanded, his expression stony. Renatus turned his attention to him, and their icy gazes locked.

'If it's a good idea, does it really matter?'

'You're putting her in unnecessary danger,' Aubrey said, his voice barely controlled. 'Emmanuelle is handling the situation fine.'

'Emmanuelle handles everything fine. It isn't the point. I'll talk to you later.' Renatus went to step around him, his thoughts with his distraught student, but Aubrey took a step forwards, blocking his way.

'No,' he said, angry. 'There's no need for what you're doing. You've chosen to risk Teresa in order to protect Emmanuelle, and you've somehow convinced Lord Gawain that it's a great idea. Teresa isn't prepared for this risk. Now, I don't know what your game plan is, but ever since you started involving Emmanuelle in it she's changed. We can all see it. Jadon is going to flip out when he hears about this. We can't trust you, and we can't even trust Emmanuelle anymore. Do you really think we're going to leave you and Emmanuelle alone with Teresa and that ring?'

For fuck's sake...

Renatus would have done it himself, weeks ago, if he'd thought it was possible. The fact remained that Teresa was a better illusionist than he was. It was why she'd been chosen to replace him on the White Elm for that exact position when he'd been stepped up into Lisandro's empty seat.

'Still unable to perceive the difference between what is best for the one and what is best for the whole?' Renatus asked coldly, taking care to glare *down* at Aubrey, who was only slightly shorter than he was. Sometimes people needed to be reminded of the status quo. 'I asked if she thought she could do it; she says she can. She knows the stakes. If you and Jadon are so worried, make yourselves present when Emmanuelle goes to make the exchange. I won't be there.' He deliberately dragged his gaze from Aubrey to check the hallway again, and when he spoke again, his voice was dripping with sarcasm and resentment. 'Make sure I don't send a pack of wolves with her, won't you?'

With a furious scowl, Aubrey turned and stalked away. Renatus watched him leave, disappointed in himself because defeating Aubrey had made him feel better, stronger. Confrontation would have weakened a good man like Lord Gawain.

Just another snippet of evidence to suggest that Renatus would never be what the Master had hoped he'd be.

Aubrey entered the stairwell and paused, looking down a few steps.

'Isn't it a bit late for you to be up here?' he asked somebody. Renatus extended his senses and was deeply surprised by who he detected.

'I left my book in detention,' Aristea explained as she moved past her spell-writing teacher. 'Good night, Sir.'

Aubrey echoed her farewell and descended the stairs. Aristea stepped out of the stairwell and stood still, facing Renatus from the opposite end of the hall.

'So, you've proved you're the better of us,' Renatus commented, unsurprised by this conclusion.

Of course she was. She was the child, and yet she was the first one to go back and face the problem. While Renatus had deliberated, she must have walked to her room, stopped at her door and walked straight back.

'Sir, I'm sorry about before,' she said, deciding it was best to be straight up. Renatus could read most of her thoughts as she thought them.

Is he mad at me? Why did I have to overreact like that? Why did he?

'Aristea,' he said, using a very clear and precise voice, 'if you ever apologise to me again without good cause, you will be excluded from this academy. I've spoken to you about this before. As much as I want you to stay here and fulfil your potential, I am tired of your self-worth issues.'

'Oh, you're a fine one to talk,' she snapped, forgetting for a moment who she was talking to. She quickly remembered, eyes widening, and opened her mouth. 'I'm–'

'Ah!' Renatus raised a hand, forbidding her from continuing. How could she apologise for such brutal and necessary honesty? 'No apologising. You owe me nothing. If you voice an opinion, I want to hear it. I do not expect an apology. I don't want one. You should never apologise for having independent thoughts. Nor for curiosity. If you have a question, ask it. I don't want to talk to you about this again. Are we clear on this?'

'We're very clear, Sir,' she said, voice small again. Like Ana, after blowing up at their father.

'And I don't want to hear "Sir" anymore, either,'

he added. 'Do I look like a knight to you?'

'No.'

'Good, so we're on the same page,' Renatus said. He regarded the teenager momentarily. She didn't really look much like Ana, except for the long hair and the similar height. It was really just the demeanour, then, and that aura. 'I am the one who is sorry. I forgot about your sensitivity. I lost control. I promise I will be more careful in future. I'm sorry for what I caused you to feel.'

Aristea looked away, struggling with his words for a moment. She didn't like being apologised to any more than he did.

'Perhaps it's better if you don't say sorry to me, either,' she suggested. 'That way it's fair.'

He nodded obligingly.

'That's fine.'

'And since I can ask you anything,' she continued, thinking of ways to make things equal, 'you can ask me anything.'

Perhaps it was strange that a powerful White Elm sorcerer in his twenties should be so pleased to see his friendship with a seventeen-year-old girl developing so well, but Renatus didn't care.

'Alright,' Renatus agreed, determined not to let this opportunity go to waste. 'Would you like to stay a while and talk? I think we have a few questions for each other.'

Aristea nodded, and walked over. Renatus waited for her to pass him before following her back into the office.

'Absolutely anything, right?' she asked warily as

the door closed behind them. Renatus nodded, steeling himself.

'Absolutely anything,' he agreed, detecting her question long before she asked it. Why did she have to be so fixated on that awful place? 'Ana is just one of the people buried in the graveyard in the orchard. She and my parents died together seven, nearly eight years ago. And before you ask that,' he added, overhearing her next wild thought train, 'yes, they died in the orchard.'

They were just facts. He didn't have to feel them. Perhaps this wouldn't be as painful as he'd feared.

'Which is why it feels so...' Aristea searched for the right word, and Renatus tried to hide his reaction to what he heard in her head. *Alluring? Magnetic?* '...dark?'

Now it was Renatus's turn to hesitate and think of an appropriate response.

'Partly,' he admitted, but refrained from going into detail, because it would mean admitting to the very worst he'd ever been, and he didn't want to be that, ever again. 'It definitely could be.'

But probably wasn't.

'My family died during a freak storm,' she stated, unexpectedly. She hadn't planned on saying this; it had just come out. She crossed her arms across her chest and leaned back against the closed door. 'My mum, dad and brother were all killed. I was fourteen and my sister was nineteen.'

Her voice was detached and distant. She was recounting facts, too, choosing not to feel them. She was an observant learner. When Renatus answered a few moments later, his voice had the exact same tone.

'By "freak storm", you're referring to the kind of wild storm that wasn't predicted or even typical of the season,' he said. He wasn't expecting an answer, and she didn't yet give one. 'You're talking about a massive storm that rolled in so quickly and unexpectedly that nobody had any time to think about what to do. The winds were so strong and fierce that whole branches were ripped from trees. Trees uprooted. The rain was sharp and heavy, and the wind flung the raindrops around like nails. And everywhere people ran, or went, or thought they might be safe, danger followed. Suddenly you felt their deaths, successively, like three rips through your soul. Suddenly, you were alone. And just as quickly as it hit and destroyed your whole life, the storm just drifted away.'

There: the whole dark tale, as horribly poetic as it deserved to be told.

Aristea blinked, her mouth hanging open. She wouldn't, couldn't have described the event as he did, but his words painted a picture in her mind that he read and recognised.

It was the same story. He'd suspected it – no, deep down, he'd known it must be…Fate had orchestrated this whole thing – but her face confirmed it. This was the first time she'd thought of her past in his presence, and he saw that in this one aspect, it was a mirror to his. Was this why Fate had brought them together?

Her thoughts were a wild mess even he could

barely follow. He caught wisps here and there but he had no chance of keeping up.

How did he know? Did he read through my memories the same way he reads my mind? Had he guessed? No...description was too real...too detailed...Was he actually there, out of sight? Why didn't he help? He couldn't have stopped the weather, of course, nobody can...could have at least pulled Angela and I free of the wreckage of our home, instead of leaving us to dig our way out...

'How do you know all this?' she eventually asked. Her hands were shaking with the effort of trying to rein in her insane imagination. Good to know she did actually try. Somehow, despite it, she hadn't actually realised the truth of the situation. Of all her wild theories, she hadn't connected the dots.

'Aristea,' Renatus said, calmly, firmly, gently. 'I was not there. I promise.' He waited a few seconds as she calmed down. *Relax...Relax...*'What I described was not your experience. It was mine.'

He tentatively reached out and touched her forearm, hoping to soothe her. She met his eyes but Renatus barely noticed, because his attention was drawn to another vision.

Nobody had any time to think...

Whole branches were ripped from trees...Trees uprooted...

Rain was sharp and heavy...like nails...

Everywhere people ran, or went, or thought they might be safe, danger followed...

Their deaths, successively...like three rips through your soul...

Suddenly, you were alone.

He was *scrying*. Was this what Aristea had meant when she said she could scry *through* him? How fascinating that she'd discovered this possibility before he had. Was she seeing this, too?

She shoved away from him and stalked away. When she stopped in the centre of the study she turned back and glared at him.

'It happened to me, not you,' she said, angry and upset. 'I can't believe you would try and steal credit for *my* traumatic experience! Why would you even want it?'

What an imagination.

'It happened to us both,' Renatus said, remaining calm and keeping his voice even. 'You and I have suffered the same trauma. My parents and sister were killed in a storm here seven years ago. I got away with a scratch across my shoulder.'

She shook her head slowly as this filtered through her thoughts and beliefs, accommodated and rejected over and over. Renatus could understand her difficulty. How was it possible that two people could suffer the exact same insanely unlikely, random ordeal four years apart, miles apart, and then meet and learn of the other's ordeal? How often did freak storms strong enough to rip trees from the earth hit Northern Ireland and kill three people from the one witch family? Maybe it happened from time to time – who knew? But how often did two people with nothing else in common realise that their memories of totally different events *matched*?

387

The odds must be pretty incredible.

'Well,' Aristea said eventually, 'what does this mean?'

Renatus stared at her. She stared back.

'What does it mean?' she repeated. 'It has to mean something, doesn't it?'

'I don't know,' Renatus admitted now. She frowned.

'Why would you tell me something like this if you don't even know what it means?' she asked, annoyed. She stopped herself and took a moment to regain her composure. 'I mean, don't you have any ideas?'

'I have theories, each as unlikely as the next. All I know for certain is that Fate is a sentient thing and it has plans we aren't always meant to understand.'

Aristea sighed and began slowly pacing. Renatus let her alone, allowing the silence to expand into minutes as she explored the office. He'd seen in her thoughts that she'd wanted to do this for weeks, ever since she'd accidentally stumbled into the study in the midst of a dream. She looked for a while at the books in the bookcase, not touching a thing, and after some time moved over to the desk where they'd sat, night after night, slowly getting used to each other's company. This was a private working space, but not one Renatus felt particularly sentimental towards. This was where his father had spent his days, avoiding the family, and it was where he'd summoned his children, most usually Ana, when they'd been naughty. This was where he'd yelled at them and told Renatus he needed to shape up and told Ana she was nothing. This was where the Morrissey children's problems had begun.

Perhaps one day he'd walk in here and only be able to remember addressing envelopes with Aristea.

The chairs were where they'd been before, and Aristea sat back down in her usual seat. She opened the cover of the book she'd brought in with her and began to turn the pages, one by one, scanning each.

'You said there were no random pages for people like us,' she noted. 'You said there's information on that page for me. You were talking about Fate then, weren't you?'

'I've seen a lot to convince me that Fate is very real and very much entwined with everything we do,' Renatus said. He remained by the door.

'And you think my mum and dad and Aidan dying is just Fate nudging me in the right direction?'

Aidan? The brother, apparently. Aidan Byrne.

Aidan Byrne. Angela Byrne. Aristea Byrne. They were all on Lisandro's list, the one Emmanuelle had found with the ring. He had been watching this family, too.

'Fate only makes sense in hindsight,' Renatus admitted. 'One day, not this day, but one day, it could make sense.'

'Does *your* past make sense in hindsight?' she asked pointedly. She scanned each page and turned it, looking for the one she'd lost earlier.

Renatus took a moment to answer. It shouldn't have been a tough question.

'It...Some,' he decided, unsure how much he wanted to say. 'They're dead. It hurt, and confused me, for a long time. It still does. But if they'd lived I'd be different now. I wouldn't be on the White Elm. Lord Gawain wouldn't have found me.'

Aristea pretended to read for almost a minute, but Renatus could hear her thoughts and knew that none were with the book. She struggled with her feelings about what she was thinking.

'When…When Qasim came to my house,' she began, haltingly, 'he…my sister said, my mum, if she were alive, wouldn't have let me come. She would have said no.' She looked over. 'Maybe if she'd lived I wouldn't have minded. But…*this* me would mind.' She folded the corner of a page down and snapped the cover shut. 'What an awful thing of me to say.'

'Wanting what your parents *didn't* want doesn't make you a bad person,' Renatus insisted, recognising the internal debate. He walked over and rested his hands on the desk in front of her. 'I can promise that.'

The best things I've ever done have been the opposite of what my parents wanted for me…

'Well, since you promised,' Aristea replied, obviously humouring him. Renatus sat down across from her.

'I do promise that. What about what the rest of your family wants? What about what *you* want?'

'My sister was the only one who wanted me to come here,' she admitted. 'Except me, of course.' She fiddled with the edge of the book's dust cover. 'Have you ever read a book called *Magic and Destiny* by Cassán Ó Grádaigh?'

Renatus sat back in honest surprise.

'Yes.' But he had not for a second expected that *she* would have. 'Did you find it in the library?'

'No.' It was her turn to look surprised. 'I didn't know you had a copy. I didn't think it was widely published.'

'It wasn't,' Renatus confirmed, feeling slightly wary. That was why it seemed so odd that someone like Aristea – with such a limited experience with the traditional magical world that both Renatus and Cassán Ó Grádaigh's books inhabited – would know about that text.

'I have one of the first editions,' she told him. 'My sister gave it to me when I got here. Cassán Ó Grádaigh was our grandfather.'

Now Fate had to be messing with him.

'He's been missing for over forty years,' Renatus said slowly, thinking over everything he knew about the infamous author. 'I didn't think he had any children…'

'He had a wife and a daughter, my mum.'

Aristea Byrne was Cassán Ó Grádaigh's granddaughter. How had that escaped *anybody*'s attention? Let alone his? Ó Grádaigh had written a number of prominent, influential but very underground texts during his younger years about his investigations into the relationship between Fate, Magic, the Fabric (of space and time) and the nature of human relationships. In a time when such complex dissection of magic was being heavily discouraged by a paranoid White Elm, Ó Grádaigh's work was sought out and quashed by the council but also widely regarded as ground-breaking science to magical academics and a deep inspiration to the magical "freedom fighters" of the sixties – those hippie sorcerers bent on keeping access to magic "free".

And Aristea was that man's granddaughter.

'Well, I haven't really read it,' Aristea admitted now. 'I've just opened it and, you know, glanced through. I was just wondering if you had, because what you said before reminded me of a passage I read in it.'

'Your grandfather and mine belonged to the same circles,' Renatus told her. 'I don't know if they were friends but they knew each other. They shared a lot of the same views about the nature of magic. Your grandfather was quite famous in our world. Did you know that?'

Aristea shook her head.

'Maybe I should read his book,' she suggested with a small smile.

'Maybe you should. The rest of his publications are in the library.' Renatus paused, thinking. 'I remember getting one down from a top shelf. They're up high.'

'Thanks. I might have a look tomorrow.'

They'd been in this office for a very long time. Renatus opened his desk drawer and checked the time on his father's old pocket watch.

'You should go. It's getting quite late.'

Aristea checked her own wristwatch and nodded in agreement.

'Yeah, okay.' She got to her feet. 'I'll see you tomorrow?'

'No, don't worry about your last detention,' Renatus dismissed. 'You've more than made it up tonight.'

'Oh. I suppose so.' Aristea looked at her watch again. 'Are you sure? It'll feel weird not coming here after dinner.'

It *would* be strange to not have her company for that hour each evening.

'I'm sure, but you can decide for yourself.'

'We'll see what Fate organises for us,' Aristea said with a smile as she turned to leave. Renatus had the door open for her, but she stopped before she reached it. 'Oh, oops.' She came back and grabbed the book from the desktop. 'I really did leave my book behind before.'

She was almost out the door again when Renatus called after her, 'I'm glad you came back for it.'

'Me, too,' she called back. The door shut behind her and Renatus's eyes darted to the list in the centre of his desk. There was never much point to that stupid list, he realised now. This had never been *his* choice, anyway. Fate had plans and he was just a chess piece on a massive chequered board.

chapter twenty-five

My scrying lesson was great. *Nobody* had experienced any success with their homework, so when Qasim looked mildly disappointed, it wasn't directed at me. I neglected to mention that I'd accidentally managed the task last night with an old ribbon, regretfully forgoing the praise I would have received but happy to avoid the topic of Renatus with Qasim.

In the familiar scrying environment of our usual classroom, I found that the exercise was much easier than when I was sitting, half-hearted, at the dining table or in my room. Qasim had us stand in a circle around a table, with enough space between us that we weren't touching. We each placed one personal item – a hairclip, earring, watch, whatever – onto the tabletop.

'Your minds must be clear,' the Scrier said. I closed my eyes in an attempt to lock new thoughts out of my mind. *Clear my thoughts; clear my thoughts...* 'It is important that you are *receptive* and *open*. Expect nothing. If there is something to be seen, let it come to you. Do not seek it out, or you will lose it. Take something from the table that is not yours.'

I heard light scraping sounds as some of my peers picked up some of the things. I took a few slow, deep breaths, focussing on nothing. It was difficult, so when my mind seemed empty enough, I reached a hand out to the table. My fingers closed on something cylindrical and plastic.

Khalida, carefully applying pink lip gloss in front of her mirror...Two other girls giggling behind her...'Maybe he prefers older women?'...'We'll give him a few days to get used to the committee idea...' Suki washes her hands in the sink...'Did you see my jerk brother checking you out, Bella?'

It was much the same sensation as yesterday, except without the grief and the intense reaction. The brief and erratic flow of disjointed images, sounds and feelings abruptly ceased, and I opened my eyes. Xanthe, Isao and Joshua had their eyes very tightly closed, concentrating much too hard. Dylan's eyes were open but out of focus. Khalida placed a boy's watch back on the table, looking annoyed. Constantine seemed to have given up – he was examining the charm bracelet in his hand with mild interest. Iseult was waiting patiently, looking around. She met my gaze. We'd never spoken before, so I didn't know whether or not she was nice. I offered a smile, hoping. Her return expression reminded me of Renatus; a kind of almost-smile where her mouth didn't move at all, but her sharp eyes softened significantly.

Despite what he'd said about power not being a deciding factor, I felt even more now than before that Iseult was the perfect apprentice for Renatus. Who on that list was more like him, better suited to him?

'Any traces of energy will now be either lost or too mixed up for you to find,' Qasim said, breaking the concentration of those still trying. 'Go around the circle now and let the group know what you saw, if anything. Isao?'

'Nothing,' the Japanese boy said, returning a gold chain to the tabletop.

'Nothing,' Constantine agreed, swapping the delicate charm bracelet for his gold chain and securing it back around his neck.

'I saw nothing,' Xanthe said moodily, dropping a stud earring onto the bracelet. It caught one of the charms as it landed, so it didn't bounce. Joshua took his earring back and put down an abstract silver ring, which Isao fitted onto his middle finger.

'I thought I saw Xanthe fitting this in her hair in a blue-tiled bathroom, but it was such a fleeting image, so I can't be sure,' Dylan said, always so modest, handing her back a black bobby pin. She took it without comment, sliding it into her short, sleek hair. Quietly, Dylan took the watch from the table and strapped it back onto his wrist.

'I saw nothing,' Khalida told us. I put her lip gloss down.

'I saw Khalida in a bathroom with two other girls,' I said. The Indian girl gave me a sharp look, but I continued. 'She applied the lip gloss and they were all chatting.'

'Did you hear anything?' Isao asked, grinning. 'What were they gossiping about?'

'When I was putting this on this morning,' Khalida informed him harshly, snatching up her makeup, 'your sister and I were talking about how *you* are always checking out Bella.'

I startled, amazed that what I'd seen was exactly as Khalida remembered it. I'd gotten it right! Isao sighed loudly, looking more amused than embarrassed.

'Come *on*,' he said, but anything else he was about to say was cut off by Qasim.

'Joshua?' Qasim asked loudly, turning the class's attention to the next person in the circle.

'I didn't see anything,' Josh stated. We looked to Iseult, the only one left. She put my watch down and took back her delicate little bracelet.

'Aristea was in an office with the headmaster,' she said, most of her attention on the clasp of her bracelet as she put it back on. 'They were sitting on opposite sides of a large desk, talking. There was a lot of paperwork – piles of paperwork. Aristea was playing with her watch strap.'

'Very good,' Qasim said, while I tried to work out what moment in the recent past Iseult had witnessed through energy traces left on my watch. I took it from the otherwise empty tabletop and refastened it on my wrist.

I did quite well at all of Qasim's exercises for the remainder of the lesson. When a bell sounded, and he released us to lunch, he called Iseult and I back.

'Iseult and Aristea,' he said, and we paused. My

hand was on the door handle, and Xanthe had just stepped through the doorway. Qasim spared us a respectful nod as he said, 'Well done today. I'll see you next lesson.'

I smiled my thanks for the acknowledgement. With a tiny glance at one another, Iseult and I left. Xanthe had not waited for me, which I decided didn't bother me. Iseult walked in silence at my side all the way to the staircase.

'Aristea,' she said suddenly, before I could descend the stairs. I turned to her. She was so short, barely up to my shoulder, making me feel painfully tall. I thought she'd look positively miniscule beside Addison. 'Thank you for what you said to the headmaster.'

'When?' I asked, bewildered. I hadn't spoken to him all day.

'When you fidgeted with your watch,' she reminded me. 'You were in his office, talking. He asked about me.'

I suddenly recalled the moment she must have seen when she held my watch. Last night, when he'd told me he wanted an apprentice. When we started talking about Iseult, I must have been playing with the loose strap on my wristwatch.

Was that conversation meant to be secret? Was I allowed to pass this stuff on? Did it matter if Iseult had overheard some of it without my knowing?

'I'm grateful that you recommended me, even though you don't know me,' she said in an accent exactly like mine. I wondered which town she was from. 'You could have tried to promote yourself.'

I laughed, surprised.

'There's no way he's going to pick *me*,' I said. 'I'm the delinquent who ended up in detention for a month. I'm the least reliable scrier in our class.'

'Well, let's keep it between us. The less the others know, the less opportunity they'll have to muscle in. Whatever he decides, thanks.' Iseult offered me her little hand to shake. I did, smiling.

'You're welcome.'

With a grateful nod, Iseult squeezed past me and hurried down the stairs before me. I inhaled deeply, glad that I'd already given up on being chosen. Iseult seemed very competitive, and I didn't want someone like her to think I was a threat to her success.

At lunch, I piled my plate with hash browns, sausage rolls and a slice of pizza before I was stopped by one of the house staff giving me a letter from my sister. I rested my plate on the edge of the buffet table to tear open the envelope. The letter was short – grateful in tone, to have heard from me and to know everything was alright, but firm, too. I had to keep in regular contact with her. She worried about me constantly. I considered Angela's expression if she could see what I was eating. I reluctantly added a small, healthy-looking salad sandwich to the edge of my plate. I'd have at least one bite of it.

Kendra was delighted by Addison's decision to sit with us this meal, but looked markedly put out when he decided to leave early with Hiroko.

'I heard from Garrett that Elijah's going to be

taking us out of the grounds for today's lesson,' he told Hiroko excitedly, quickly finishing his juice. Hiroko's eyes brightened. Addison turned to Kendra and showed her his almost-empty plate. 'Do you want another spring roll? I want to get to class early to practise.'

Kendra shook her head, trying not to look moody or upset. Sophia raised her hand slightly.

'I'll have it, if she doesn't want it,' she said. Addison turned his body towards her and offered her the plate so she could take the spring roll, but he kept his eyes on Kendra. She forced a smile that fooled nobody. I took that one bite of my salad sandwich, wondering how this would turn out.

'Have fun,' Kendra said, trying desperately to avoid sounding bitter. Hiroko stood and tied her hair up, not looking at Kendra. The short side of Hiroko's asymmetrical cut always fell straight out of any ponytail. Addison put his plate down and pulled his jacket off the back of his chair.

'I will,' he said, shrugging his jacket on. He rested a hand on Kendra's shoulder and leaned down to kiss her forehead. 'I'll see you at dinner.'

He waved farewell to the rest of us and headed for the door. Hiroko followed on the other side of the table, shooting Kendra a subtle encouraging grin.

We waited for Addison to leave the dining hall before breaking into massive smiles. Kendra scooted over into Addison's vacant seat so she was sitting beside her sister.

'That's the first time he's kissed me,' she admitted. She took Sophia's knife and fork and began to slice the spring roll in half. Her twin snorted in disbelief. 'I'm serious. He's just so *sweet*.'

'So sweet,' Sterling agreed whole-heartedly. Kendra ate her half of the spring roll in two quick bites and glanced subtly at Sophia's half. Sophia picked it up and took one bite, then obligingly handed over the remainder.

'How come you get the sweetheart?' Sophia complained. Kendra swallowed the last of Addison's spring roll.

'I get the sweet boy because you love me and you don't mind missing out from time to time if it makes me happy,' she explained.

'Oh. That's right.'

'And besides, you'll get a sweetheart one day, too,' Kendra promised. 'I won't let anything short of a perfect male near you.'

'I'm going to die unmarried and childless,' Sophia announced. 'No such male exists, and if he does, you've already got him. And even *if* there's another one out there, somewhere, he's never going to bother with me if he has to get past Mom, Dad *and* you just to talk to me.' Sophia glanced at me. 'Kendra thinks that because she's twenty minutes older, she's in charge of me and who I see.'

The conversation progressed steadily from there. A younger student had been called out of Sophia's last Healing class to pack his things up and return home to his parents, the eighth person to leave. Kendra mentioned that a roommate of Addison's had received a letter that morning from their former friend Egan, encouraging the remaining three boys in the dorm to leave the school.

'They ignored it, of course,' Kendra assured us. 'It turns out he's a lunatic. But that's still a lot of people gone already just because of him and his mom.'

The staff entered the dining hall and began packing up the buffet table. I watched as one woman pushed a trolley through the door and noticed Renatus and Emmanuelle walk in behind her, talking in low voices. Despite that he did nothing to call attention to himself, several of the girls in the hall glanced over.

Emmanuelle looked mildly annoyed as she grabbed a plate and scooped whatever was left onto it. Renatus continued talking to her, staying close enough that he didn't have to raise his voice. He collected no lunch, but followed her to the table. She sat down at one end and began to eat while he stood beside her, resting his hands on the table, leaning close to talk quietly.

I looked around the hall. Of the fourteen girls still enrolled, six were openly glaring at Emmanuelle. Sterling had lowered her head so that her fringe swept into her eyes, supposedly for the dual purpose of making her look more alluring and hiding the jealous expression shining in her eyes. I saw Khalida with her two roommates sitting further up the table, whispering darkly and shooting nasty looks at the French councillor. Even my non-obsessive girlfriends would occasionally glance up to take part in passively admiring Renatus.

At times like this I had to wonder if there was

something wrong with me. Why was I the only person around who didn't find the headmaster sexually attractive? Other sensible girls, like Hiroko and the twins, were able to observe and regard an attractive person in an entirely objective manner without becoming ridiculous like Sterling or totally disinterested like me.

Well, it'd be wrong to say I was disinterested. But it was a different kind of interest to theirs. I enjoyed his company and I found our conversations intensely compelling.

Last night had been a perfect example, both intense and compelling. The visions held by the ribbon had only startled me; it was the heart-wrenching grief and sorrow that followed that had ripped at me. Renatus was carrying around a great deal of repressed guilt, loneliness and self-loathing. He hated himself. He hated being him. How did he deal with that kind of self-disgust all day every day?

And how could he be dumb enough to believe he was worth so little?

When I returned to the office it was to tell him that he was stupid for hating himself, but thankfully I'd realised on my way that it would be rude and unfair. Feelings could not be controlled. I could not help disliking Xanthe. Renatus could not help disliking Renatus.

I was so, so glad to have gone back. He'd said it made me "the better of us", whatever that meant, but I was just glad because of how much had become clear and how much I now understood. Renatus had had a sister, who had died. I reminded him of her, although I couldn't see how. Ana, like her brother, had possessed film-star good looks, and I was certain that I looked nothing like her. The picture of Ana's tear-streaked face had stayed with me all night, clear in my mind, even as I fell asleep.

I didn't dream. I never dreamed anymore.

'You're so weird, Aristea,' Sterling commented mildly.

'What do you mean?' I asked, startled out of my reflections. Sterling blinked.

'I don't know,' she said, apparently surprised that she was expected to provide a reason for her statement. 'You're just weird. You were just plucking at your buttons and it made me realise that you're weird.'

I looked down at my front. In my unfocussed state I had indeed been playing absently with the buttons of my blouse. Sterling decided to elaborate.

'You run a brush through your hair twice like you couldn't care less, and I don't think you could, and you don't bother with makeup, and you don't wear jewellery…And that's you. You're minimalist and it's usually like you don't give a shit what anyone else thinks.' She shrugged and smiled. 'But then, in the morning, you spend fifteen minutes trying to decide what you'll wear, and you always end up in an outfit that looks like you're heading to a job interview, and then you spend all day fidgeting and looking uncomfortable. It's just weird.'

Her words echoed in my head. She was right. These weren't *my* outfits. This wasn't *my* style. It wasn't in my nature to worry about how I looked.

From the moment I'd realised I was coming here I'd had this idea that I needed to prove myself, and that *I* wasn't good enough as I was. I'd been trying to be perfect. I'd been trying to be Angela.

But Qasim hadn't picked Angela. He'd picked me. The White Elm had accepted me into the Academy as I was, weird and untidy me. They didn't care how I dressed.

'I'm going to be right back,' I told the girls, getting to my feet and hurrying from the hall.

Here I was, so insecure about my own self-worth that I'd spent six weeks trying to emulate my big sister, and I'd had the nerve to attack Renatus last night about self-esteem issues when I was so obviously a walking bundle of them.

I let myself into my dorm and pulled my clothes off, feeling freer with each neatly pressed item that came away.

'Bear with me, Ange,' I murmured vaguely, stuffing the blouse into a drawer. I dug through the clothes stored there until I came across a tight black t-shirt with rows of silver stars across the front. I'd found it on sale when shopping with Angela two years ago, and she'd allowed me to bring it here for weekend wear.

And I'd been *dying* to get back into my favourite purple tartan skirt, which had "accidentally" found its way into my bags…

I slowly redressed, feeling a little disloyal to Angela as I chose clothes she didn't like. The feeling quickly passed though. She wanted me to have the best chance of being chosen as an apprentice, and she'd sent me here with what she thought would help. Presentation is key, she'd said, and I'd agreed at the time. If this was a normal university application process, then dressing like Angela would be the ideal starting point. However, no councillor on the White Elm was going to choose a girl without an identity.

I admired my handiwork in the bathroom mirror. The cropped jacket and stockings were a decent compromise, I assured my conscience, which had Angela's voice. The look worked. It was cute and unique. This was the real Aristea.

I was going to return to my friends but noticed with a distinct sense of embarrassment the state of my part of the room. I was such a mess. If I wasn't going to wear what my sister picked out for me, I might as well do what she'd be nagging me to do right now.

It took nearly an hour before my bed was made and my junk was back where it belonged. Granted, I didn't hurry. I glanced through Anouk's book; reread that random page about apprenticeships within the White Elm, but nothing stood out to me. When I was done I wandered quietly down the hallways and took note of the expensive-looking paintings and tapestries hanging everywhere. I'd noticed before how recent everything seemed to be for such an old estate, but today I allowed myself to wonder what this place had looked like prior to 1999 and 2000, which seemed to be the top contenders for Year of Most Morrissey House Artwork Award. Were the walls just bare before then?

I might have just told myself, *yes, the walls were bare before then*, except that right then I noticed a discolouration to the wallpaper. Was it a trick of the light, or was there a distinctly brighter panel of paper directly below the frame of one of the paintings? I stood back to better observe. Yes, definitely, it was there. I moved on to the next picture and noticed the same thing, except this time it was either side of the frame. When I shifted a tapestry aside, I found a discoloured square beneath it.

For every painting and tapestry hanging in this hallway at least, and maybe in the whole mansion, there had once been another. Someone (and I could guess who) had replaced every single one. I pressed my fingertips against the wall, wishing I could tap into its secrets like I had Khalida's stupid lip gloss. What had hung here in the nineties and before, and why had Renatus felt the need to replace it all?

I was nearing the staircase now and heard the vestiges of an adult conversation I was, no doubt, not meant to hear.

'My first choice would be to keep it *here*.'

Emmanuelle's voice and classical accent were impossible to mistaken.

'*Here* isn't really ideal. He let Lisandro go free – what does that tell you?' Susannah was harder to place, but I got it after a second. I backed up to a distance that seemed far enough away that I wouldn't be able to hear, but I couldn't un-attune myself from the exchange.

'Do you think 'e can't 'ear you, in 'is own 'ome?' Emmanuelle asked scornfully. 'For your information,

I offered it to 'im already. 'e doesn't want it. He suggested I pass it to someone else to throw Lisandro off the trail. Teresa 'as a fantastic idea. Tell 'er, Teresa.'

I strained to hear as Teresa spoke for the first time. Her voice was softer and weaker than the other two councillors.

'It mightn't work,' she protested. 'I'm not sure I have the skills…'

'That is rubbish,' Emmanuelle cut her off. 'You 'ave exactly the skills.'

I imagined that she had shoved past her colleagues to ascend the remaining stairs and exit the stairwell, because suddenly I could see her, and she could see me. I smiled what I hoped was an innocent smile and pretended to go back to admiring the tapestry in front of me. Naturally, it was the most boring piece of art in the whole mansion, so I was thankful when all three sorceresses continued up the stairs without approaching me and noticing that I was staring at a huge red blanket.

chapter twenty-six

The girls were sitting at the table where I'd left them, but they hadn't been there the whole time, apparently. Both Sterling and Xanthe were sporting new hairstyles.

'Nice look. Suits you way better. What have you got tomorrow?' Sterling asked me as I sat down. Both twins had just refused her offer of a free haircut. 'I've got the first lesson free.'

'No you don't, we've got two hours of shame with your favourite toy boy,' I answered, not looking forward to Aubrey's lesson, but glad because now Sterling couldn't chop my hair off. Admittedly, Xanthe's bob looked really good, but I was still nervous about the prospect of an eccentric teenage witch going to town on my hair.

'What about Hiroko? What does she have on tomorrow?'

'Uh.' I frantically thought of a good excuse to save Hiroko's beautiful, satiny hair. 'She's trying to grow her hair out.'

Sterling looked put-out, and made sure to make a comment about trims being healthy for growth when Hiroko did turn up. I caught my friend's eye deliberately and ensured she saw me shake my head the tiniest bit.

'It was, um, just cut the day before when I came here,' she said diplomatically as she sat down.

'Nice save,' I whispered as she settled into her seat beside me. In a more reasonable volume, I asked, 'How was Elijah's lesson of hell?'

'It went well. You are not enjoying Displacement?'

'It's not enjoying me, either,' I responded, but she didn't really understand, so I clarified. 'No. I hate it. I'm really bad at it.'

'Perhaps we can help each other,' she suggested, sounding very hesitant.

'What do you mean?'

'On weekends and in our spare times, perhaps I can help you with Displacement, and other times, you can help me with making wards?' Hiroko asked, blushing lightly. 'I cannot make any wards yet.'

I was surprised, because Hiroko seemed like such a studious, clever person. In our classes together, we were rather evenly matched. There were a few fields in which my friends excelled and I found challenging, but I'd not really considered that some people found difficult the things that came naturally to me.

'That would be great,' I said, pleased with her idea.

'Once you have done it some times, it becomes much easier,' Hiroko assured me while she fiddled with a piece of clumsily folded paper. 'When you can...When...' She clicked her fingers a few times, trying to remember the right word. She gave up. 'When you know what you must look for, it becomes easy.'

'I'll help you with your wards, but you should know that I am incapable of displacement,' I informed her.

'That's silly,' she disagreed. 'Everyone can learn. I will help to teach you.' She paused, looking around. 'Do you...Shall we practise now?' she asked, pushing her chair back slightly. I nodded, suddenly eager.

'Yeah, let's find somewhere,' I agreed, standing.

'But you only just got back!' Sterling complained when she noticed us leaving already. 'I have a lesson soon but I could probably do something with your ends before then.'

I protectively tugged on the ends of my long hair.

'Lots of study to do,' I apologised, following Hiroko from the hall. We headed for the stairs automatically, and I nodded in the direction of her hand and the scrunched paper she held. 'What's that?'

'It is from Garrett,' she said, and her eyes brightened with amusement as she twirled it between her fingers.

'Garrett? As in, Addison's friend, Garrett?' I asked, interested, examining the paper shape in her hand. 'The very shy one?'

Hiroko nodded and started up the stairs, and her step suddenly lightened.

'I think it should be a crane,' she said, holding the gift up so we could both admire it.

I squinted at the object, and could see that it had once been a lined page from an exercise book. The shape had been constructed from a series of folds, many of which I could see had been attempted several times, leaving extra creases.

I guessed that this was Garrett's first attempt at origami.

'We went outside the gates to practise today,' she told me, her eyes sparkling. 'Elijah talked about the intuition of displacement. We came back inside for a theoretical lesson. Garrett did not sit with me, but when the lesson was concluded, he walked past my desk and dropped this. He did not say anything.' She smiled affectionately at the crane, or whatever it was. 'I think perhaps he assumes I must enjoy origami because I am Japanese. I do not mind. It is very funny.'

'It's very cute,' I agreed. 'Have you spoken to him?'

Hiroko shook her head.

'He never speaks to me. I wish he would, because I do not know what he means by giving me this crane. Perhaps he wishes we could be friends?'

'Or?' I said, and we both smirked.

'We will see,' she said. Her tone was carefree, but I could tell that she was flattered by Garrett's attention and was hoping that it would continue.

We found an empty classroom and shut

ourselves in. It was unlikely that we would be disturbed, as everyone else should be enjoying their break between midday and afternoon classes. The room's furniture had been pushed against the walls, as if someone had known we would come here and need the space, and the wooden floor was covered in a number of ornate old rugs, as if someone had known that I would be falling over a lot.

'So, what do I do?' I asked, looking around. Hiroko looked stumped.

'I am not sure how to explain,' she admitted. She pointed to a ruby-red carpet overlapping the edge of the brown-and-beige one we stood on. 'You must know where you want to be, and you must cease to be here,' she pointed at the floor beneath her feet, 'and just *be* there.'

She turned as though to walk over to the other rug, two metres away, but she arrived there within one step, having completely avoided the space between.

'That's amazing!' I said, realising that I'd never seen this done before by anyone but Elijah and once by Addison. To see such a trick performed by a friend made it so much more real. She smiled, pleased.

'You see, it is not so difficult,' she said. 'It is only difficult to explain. You must identify the *space* you are in, and identify the space you wish to be in, and then...' She paused as she considered how to phrase the next part. 'You must then bring the two spaces together so you may step between them.'

I blinked, confused. How could I possibly move

space? Hiroko walked over so that she was standing opposite me, and placed a hand on the side of my face, which seemed weird until she said, 'I will show you how it feels to displace.'

I let my guard down mentally so that she could bring me into her mind, like we'd been starting to learn in Glen's class. It was entirely non-obtrusive. I was soon aware of both my thoughts and hers, although I couldn't understand much more than vague impressions from hers.

'Watch,' Hiroko instructed. I waited, and presently I noticed a thought of hers that I could mostly understand passing into *my* head.

It was a memory. Paying attention to it was exactly the same as reviewing one of my own memories. I could see what Hiroko had seen, feel what she'd felt, all very vaguely and blurrily.

I, or Hiroko, was standing in an elegant, modern apartment that I personally didn't recognise but that Hiroko felt safe in. A tall, smiling Asian man with thinning hair closed a door to a neighbouring room and stepped back to watch. I as Hiroko used some sense I'd never before used and grasped something immaterial with her magic. Space? Next, she'd visualised the neighbouring room, her father's bedroom, and grasped that same immaterial substance there, and stepped forward. As she did so, she pulled that second space towards her so that it was in her path. The well-lit sitting room disappeared, and then I (she) was standing in a darker room. The door opened, letting some light in, and Hiroko's father stood there, beaming with pride.

Hiroko took her hand away from my skin and waited for my response.

'That's amazing,' I said, again. 'You didn't even need to see where you were going.'

'It was the first time I did not see my destination,' Hiroko said. 'Did you understand how it was done?'

I remembered how she'd utilised a part of her brain and mind I'd never known existed, and manipulated magic in a way I'd never considered. Like when I'd first learnt to scry, I suspected that displacing was going to be just like straining a wasted, unused muscle.

'I think so,' I said. She turned me around so I was facing the ruby-red rug.

'You must identify the *Fabric* of this place,' she explained, waving her hands through the space around me. 'You must feel it and hold it. You must do the same for this space.' She went to the red carpet and waved her hands again in demonstration. 'Then you bring them together.'

I tried, I really did. I felt better armed with her knowledge and advice and than I did with Elijah's mere encouragement and pages of theory, but a further twenty minutes of hard concentration yielded no results. I officially gave up for that day, and we went on to wards.

'I think it's easiest to cast wards without a wand,' I said, not sure where else to begin. I wasn't a teacher. 'Wards are just protective barriers, so you need to consider what you want to be protected from and channel your magic into a barrier against that threat. You might want to be safe from mental attack, or from magic, or you might even want a physical barrier.'

'Can you make a physical barrier?' Hiroko asked, intrigued. 'It can stop anything from getting past?'

I outstretched one hand, facing away from my friend, and summoned the magic required. It seemed natural to channel it through my body, giving it purpose, and to send it along my arm and out of me. A tiny bead of white light shot from my palm, mushrooming outwards at an incredible rate. I cut the power, so to speak, and the whitish, membranous shield ceased to grow and hung in midair, a metre before me, waiting. It was dished, hemispherical in shape, and quivered very lightly as air particles bounced off either side. *Nothing* was allowed through.

'Wow!' Hiroko said, hurrying over. 'It is a wall of magic! Nothing can get through this?'

'Nothing physical,' I agreed, keeping my right hand outstretched to maintain the ward. I was thinly connected to my creation. When I broke the connection by willing it to end or by forgetting about it, it would dissolve. It needed me. It had been a long time since *I* had properly needed *it*, and hopefully it would be a long time yet before I needed a ward that badly again. 'See if you can find something small.'

Hiroko returned to the door, beside which there was an armchair and a small reading table. She came back with a ballpoint.

'Throw it,' I suggested. She looked hesitant. 'It

should just bounce off.'

As requested, she tossed the pen at my patiently waiting ward. It sailed through the air and struck my ward. With a faint hiss, it bounced off and landed on the ground, as if we'd thrown it at a wall or window. The ward wobbled slightly, like a taut canvas, and quickly returned to its still state. I dropped my hand, ending the channel, and the ward died. Without my magic to sustain it, the energy dispersed.

'That is very cool,' Hiroko informed me. 'Soon, I will be able to do the same.'

She was a much more confident, optimistic student than I was. Within twenty minutes she was channelling magic through her body and through her hands and casting small, very brief wards. Most of the magic required seemed to be getting lost somewhere between its source and her spell, though, and her wards appeared as puffs of blurry white just a few centimetres from her palm, gone almost before they were created.

Hiroko had still made ten times the progress I had.

'You are a very good teacher,' she praised me, as we left the classroom. 'I am sorry that I am not able to teach you as effectively.'

'It's not your fault,' I disagreed. 'I'm just not any good at Displacement. You can't help that.'

We met our friends in the entrance hall, just heading out for a walk. Through the doors of the dining hall, I saw Garrett sitting with Addison and the other boys. I saw his milky white cheeks redden when he noticed Hiroko, and he looked away quickly.

Too cute.

'Aristea, is Renatus seeing Emmanuelle?' Sterling demanded as we headed out the front doors. I froze.

'What? No! I mean,' I amended, realising how odd that had sounded, 'I don't think so.'

'Oh, good.' She relaxed, beginning to smile, and I thought I was going to be okay, but then her face fell. 'It didn't work.'

'What didn't work?' Kendra asked, pulling her sweater tighter around herself as she stepped out into the quickly cooling breeze. Sterling looked pointedly at me.

'*It* didn't work. Renatus hasn't changed his behaviour or said anything. I'm running out of patience.'

'Oh, well,' Sophia murmured, unsympathetically. 'Maybe it's not meant to be.'

'It is. I know it is.' Sterling beamed at me. 'You'll have to just ask him for me.'

'Ask him what? What he thinks of you hitting on inappropriate people?'

'No!' Sterling laughed while the other girls made various queries and exclamations. 'What he thinks of *me*.'

'Oh. Right.' I didn't really know what else to say. I sensed that she would only beg and argue the point if I refused. I looked over at Hiroko for support.

'It will be okay,' she assured me. 'You may be saving the rest of us from listening any longer to hour-long discussions about the headmaster's eye colour. You will stop talking about him after Aristea talks to him, won't you?' she asked Sterling sternly. Sterling grinned.

'If he tells her that he likes me, you won't hear another word about the colour of his eyes, which I would definitely say are violet,' she promised. We all groaned, knowing that this promise meant nothing, because Sterling wasn't going to get what she wanted to hear.

'You'll be saving us all,' Xanthe agreed. 'A few minutes of total embarrassment in exchange for our sanity is a worthy sacrifice.'

'You poor little lamb,' Sophia commented, linking her arm through mine for warmth and patting my hand apologetically. 'You're such a team player.'

'Apparently.'

'You have your last detention tonight, don't you?' Kendra asked conversationally. I paused, unsure.

'Uh, well, technically,' I agreed. Renatus had told me not come if I didn't want to, and I kind of *did* want to go, but how to say that to my friends without sounding weird? Fate, I'd suggested, would tell me whether to go or not. So far I'd received no particular sign.

'Well, that's perfect,' Sterling assured me. 'If you think it'll be embarrassing, at least you never have to go back. At least until you next pick an argument with another adult.'

'I'm sure Aristea never meant to get in trouble in

the first place,' Kendra defended.

'Maybe she did?' Xanthe wondered. 'Maybe she was just beating Sterling to it.'

Sterling and the twins laughed, and I smiled, but I chanced a quick look at Xanthe. Her tone was difficult to determine – it had sounded both playful and meaningful at once. Was she suggesting something? Her face told me nothing.

'I'm planning to keep my confrontations to a minimum in the near future,' I informed them all.

The sign I was waiting for hit me like a pile of bricks dropped from a skyscraper. We followed our usual route, circling beyond the rolling hills down the back and passing near to the orchard, which was very dark and creepy and becoming more so with each step closer we came to it. It was windy and the uppermost branches, fresh baby leaves sprinkling the ends, swished about but very little light seemed to be getting through to the ground level. I alternated between gazing absently at the tree line, looking out for rabbit holes and nodding agreeably with whatever Sterling was rambling about. She'd fallen into one of her famous monologues, and everyone was responding appropriately by nodding and taking turns to murmur "yeah" or "that's right" during the pauses. Sometimes it was really just easier to let her go for it, and in the past six weeks I'd learned that she was quite easy to ignore. She liked the sound of her own voice, and really didn't require responses or feedback to sustain her one-sided discussions.

'Yeah, exactly,' I said, because it was my turn

and Sterling had stopped for breath. There was a ninety-five percent chance that my response would work, but I listened in briefly just in case I'd agreed with the wrong thing.

'And Suki, she's like an artist, so she's drawn all these really incredible pictures of him...'

I phased her voice back out, safe for now. A biting-cold breeze cut past us and I felt Sophia's grip on my arm tighten as she pulled closer and shivered. I was glad now for my change of outfit into the little jacket but somewhat regretted the skirt. I turned my face away from the wind as the ends of my hair got caught up in it, and in the corner of my obscured vision I noticed movement to my right.

Something red, black and white.

In that second of inattention I felt my footing slip. My shoe slid into a rabbit hole, taking my foot with it and rolling my ankle. I stumbled, only managing to stay upright because of Sophia's tight grip on me.

'Whoa!' she exclaimed, almost coming down with me. I steadied myself quickly and looked up, my heart thudding with the fright of falling unexpectedly.

The orchard was quiet and dark, and there was nothing to be seen. There was nothing red, nothing black and nothing white. I was staring right down that pathway again, which remained still and dark even while the treetops rustled about in the wind and even though the sun was hours from setting.

Was that pathway haunted? For half an instant I'd imagined that colourful flash in my peripheral vision to be almost *person-shaped*.

Was that why I wanted to follow that path, *so badly*? Because I did – even now, I could feel an almost physical pull that made no sense whatsoever.

'Are you alright?' Hiroko asked, moving closer to check on me. I stared past her.

I was imagining things.

'Uh, yeah,' I managed eventually, stepping away from the hole and testing my ankle out. It was only a little bit sore, definitely not damaged. I looked up again. Still, there was nothing there to see. None of the other girls had noticed anything, either. 'Bastard rabbits.'

'You sure?' Sophia asked, critically eyeing the air around me. 'You've gone all pale and you're all messy.' She waved indistinctly at what I supposed was my aura. Hiroko still watched me with concern while the other three stood a few metres away, waiting patiently for the walk to continue. 'Coincidence? I think not.'

No page is random for people like us. That's what Renatus had said. Did that mean the same as when people say that there are no coincidences? I was waiting for a sign. A freaky unexplained vision might count.

Stranger things had happened to me.

'I'm okay,' I said. 'I just thought…' I didn't want to say what I'd thought. I didn't want to talk about the ribbon misadventure last night, or Renatus's reaction or our ensuing conversation. I didn't want to start rambling about storms and dead people and a ridiculous desire to walk into the creepiest part of the orchard. I didn't want to talk to any of the girls about this – not even Hiroko, not right now. There was only one person I wanted to talk to. 'I just remembered that I have to go to detention.'

'What, now?' Sophia asked, surprised. I disentangled myself from her arm. 'You don't normally go until seven.' She checked her watch. 'Oops, we're going to be late for dinner. I hope our seats haven't been taken.'

My assertion that I was going to detention was ignored and I was led to the dining hall to eat with my friends. I picked a couple of odd things for my plate and scoffed them quickly, barely registering the tastes. I'd been waiting for a sign and I knew I'd received it, whatever it was, and now I just wanted to follow it.

'Alright, see you all later,' I said, getting up and pushing my chair in. Xanthe frowned.

'You're strangely eager tonight,' she mentioned coolly. I chose to ignore the tone; I didn't have time to decode it.

'I want to check something in a book before I head up,' I said, waving as I turned away.

'No, wait! Aristea!' Sterling called me back. I walked backwards as she said, 'Don't forget! You *have* to ask!'

I wondered whether this was the payment for whatever new information I would learn tonight.

Because, though yes, I'd probably imagined it...I was *sure* that the apparition had been a young woman with white skin and black hair. And blood. A lot of it. And Renatus was the person to ask about these things.

I shook my head. That was stupid. There was no such thing as ghosts, and if there was, they'd have better things to do than stand around on cold, windy days in orchards – the whole point of ghosts was that they had unfinished business, none of which would get done if they wasted time popping up and scaring unrelated people like me.

I went first to my room and dug out Anouk's White Elm book from my bedside drawer. I sat on the edge of my bed and stood its spine on my lap, and let the covers go experimentally. The covers fell onto my knees and pages fell to either side...by this point, the fact that the book opened to last night's page did not surprise me at all.

'It became expected practice that councillors continued the then-common tradition of taking an apprentice to ensure succession of talent and skill within the White Elm,' I read aloud, tracing my finger along the line that had caught my eye last night.

'Magic and Fate were drawn on to officiate and formalise partnerships once both the councillor and his preferred student had consented to the ritual. Apprentices of councillors were guaranteed a position on the council at some point following their coming-of-age, usually succeeding their own master following his passing or retirement. This was especially common as apprentices of White Elm councillors were trained for their master's specific role and...' I trailed off and skimmed the rest of the page, bored. It was the most long-winded page I'd yet found in this otherwise engaging text. Apprentices *had to* succeed their masters. If your master was the Seer you had to eventually become the next Seer. You could be something else for a while, as you waited for them to die or retire, but then you had to take their place. It took a whole page to spell that out. I pushed the covers back up to kiss in the middle, closing the dull page inside. 'Least. Useful. Random. Page. Ever.' I threw the book back into the drawer, annoyed that I'd wasted my time on that. I saw my grandfather's book in there, too; today I lacked the patience to try the same no-random-pages theory on that early edition.

Despite his unhelpful page-related advice, I still wanted to speak with Renatus, so I marched up the stairwell to the top floor and down the hall to his office. I slowed as I got closer, noting a piece of paper tacked to the door. I knew straightaway what it was. I recognised the scrunched paper that had lived for days in the pocket of my jeans, and I recognised the eight names written in the spidery print of Renatus's handwriting. I battled a smirk; he *knew* I'd come. I pulled the list free of the door without giving it a proper look.

If I had, I would have noticed new lines crossing out all remaining names, bar one: mine.

chapter twenty-seven

Teresa nervously checked the oven again. Her rich vegetarian lasagne was coming along perfectly, cheese bubbling cheerfully on the top. Would the homemade fries be ready in time to be served with the lasagne? What about the steamed vegetables?

'Relax, Teresa,' her boyfriend, Samuel, soothed, speaking English. He was Italian, and when she'd first moved in with him they'd only spoken Italian at home and in their community. When she'd been initiated onto the White Elm, the need to speak fluent English had become prevalent, and Samuel had had the idea to speak only English at home so that her fluency could improve.

'I'm trying,' Teresa said, tucking strands of curly brown hair behind her ears. 'I just want everything to go perfectly tonight. I don't want any hitches…'

'Everything will be fine,' Jadon assured her. He, Aubrey and Samuel were sitting around the small table, playing a game of cards. 'We're here in case there are any complications. And stop staring at the oven,' he added. 'You haven't managed to burn or ruin a meal in all the times we've bludged here. There's no way you can possibly screw it up.'

Samuel very subtly glanced up from his hand of cards to eye Jadon. Neither of her colleagues noticed, but Teresa did.

Teresa had never been a very social person, but upon her initiation onto the council she had formed very strong and close bonds with both Aubrey and Jadon. Just like her, they were young and new, and just like her, they were mostly treated like outsiders by the rest of the White Elm. It became routine to spend time with them outside of work, hanging out like normal friends did.

Samuel had at first been distant with her new friends. She knew he had felt suspicious, not of her but of them. Why else would two guys want to spend time with his girlfriend? Slowly, though, he had come to accept that both Aubrey and Jadon were nice young men, worthy of his trust and friendship. He had warmed to Aubrey much more quickly, upon learning that Aubrey had a girlfriend of his own, Shell. Apparently, despite appearances, Samuel was still cautious of Jadon.

Teresa knew it would help matters if she spent less time with Aubrey and Jadon, but she cared about them and felt responsible for them. Neither of them had a clue how to take care of themselves. Shell was always travelling somewhere, leaving her domestic disaster of a boyfriend to fend for himself, and Jadon lived alone in a granny flat under his mother's house.

Neither of them knew how to cook a meal from scratch. Jadon thought that "real food" meant drive-through burgers and fries because it wasn't from the freezer. They *needed* Teresa. She was surprised they'd lasted twenty years without her.

'So who is it that's coming tonight?' Samuel asked, laying out his cards for the others to see.

'Emmanuelle,' Teresa answered, adjusting the heat setting for the vegetables.

'I don't remember her,' Samuel said, watching as Aubrey also laid down his cards.

'You will when you see her,' Jadon assured him. He dropped his cards triumphantly. 'She's nice to look at.'

At the trio's initiation, Samuel, Shell and other family members had been present as witnesses. It was the only time Samuel had met anyone on the council except for Aubrey and Jadon.

'So long as you're not looking at her forehead, which has "traitorous bitch" written across it in bold print,' Aubrey muttered. Jadon and Samuel tried not to laugh, while Teresa struggled to pretend the insult didn't offend her on Emmanuelle's behalf.

'Aubrey,' she said, firmly.

'What? She's family. I'm entitled to think of her like that.' He sipped his beer and reshuffled the deck. 'I certainly can't think of her like Jadon does.'

'I said she's nice to look at,' Jadon said again. 'I think she's hot, and she is. I wouldn't dare think anything else. Can you imagine what would happen to me if anyone happened to be browsing my thoughts at that moment? She'd tear me to shreds.

Not worth it. I'll stick to looking – no thinking.'

Aubrey and Samuel laughed. Teresa pretended to preoccupy herself with cooking. Aubrey's attitude towards Emmanuelle had gone a long way downhill in recent weeks. Teresa didn't like hearing it. She quietly admired the French Healer, who embodied many qualities that Teresa wished that she herself possessed. Emmanuelle was strong-willed, defiant, determined and confident. When she wanted something, she went forth and got it. She was an intelligent, independent and empowered woman. She showed her feelings, which Teresa really respected. When she was hurting, she let it show. She was open and stronger for it.

Teresa found it difficult to consider herself equal to the other White Elm councillors. They seemed so imposing and superhuman. It was rare for any of the male councillors to ask her for an opinion, although Lady Miranda, Susannah, Anouk and Emmanuelle easily held their own during council circles, so it wasn't because she was female. It was because she hadn't proven herself yet.

The lasagne was ready, so Teresa donned her oven mitts and pulled it free of the oven. There was a soft knock at the door.

'Can someone get that?' Teresa called over her shoulder, feeling nervous. It was like being ten and having a friend over for the first time. What would she think of your family home? That terror of being judged was still very real.

'Yeah, I will,' Jadon said, carefully setting down his cards. 'Keep an eye on these two for me, will you?'

'Don't you trust us?' Aubrey asked, grinning.

'With my life, yeah,' Jadon said. He approached the front door. 'Just not with my cards.' He opened the door and smiled easily at the person on the other side, stepping aside for her. 'Hey, Emmanuelle.'

Emmanuelle smiled in return, a golden smile, and swept inside. In her scarlet dress and black corset, and with her wavy blonde hair, she looked every bit a medieval princess. Teresa had difficulty ignoring the soft voices of her insecurities – jealousy and inadequacy were the loudest.

That was what a White Elm councillor should look like. Self-assured and confident: *that* was how the ring's guardian should be.

Why had Teresa ever agreed to this?

'Hi,' she said, trying to smile normally.

'Hi, Teresa,' Emmanuelle answered, smiling warmly. 'Thank you again for inviting me to stay for dinner.'

'You're very welcome,' Teresa said, feeling nervous as she began to dish up the food. She had thought that by having dinner first there would be time for her nerves to settle before she had to work, but now she wasn't sure. Maybe prolonging the inevitable would only make it worse.

'Let me 'elp,' Emmanuelle said, her tone too firm to argue with, as she moved into the kitchen and took the vegetables off the boil.

'Thanks,' Teresa mumbled, meekly handing over a ladle. She hurriedly collected five plates and spread them across the limited bench space.

'So, you're alone tonight, Emmanuelle?' Aubrey asked from the table.

'If by that you're asking whether Renatus is joining me 'ere, no, 'e isn't,' Emmanuelle replied. 'He made it sound as though you were afraid of 'im being 'ere tonight. I *hope* that isn't true.'

'It isn't,' Aubrey assured her, lightly punching Jadon's arm to get his attention. The American councillor had not yet taken his seat and resumed the game; instead, he was hovering beside the table, watching the women prepare the meal, apparently wanting to offer to help but unable to see any way of being able to do so now. 'What else did your boyfriend say?'

'Renatus isn't my boyfriend,' Emmanuelle answered easily, spooning the last of the vegetables onto the fifth plate. Teresa admired the calm and grace with which Emmanuelle dismissed Aubrey's jibe. ''owever, 'e asked me to ask you to do something, but I won't repeat it. It wouldn't be polite.'

'*Pourquoi, qu'est-ce qu'il a dit?*' Aubrey asked, his voice challenging. Why, what did he say? But Emmanuelle refused to say.

'*Demandez-lui vous-même,*' she suggested. Ask him yourself. She went to the oven to collect the fries while Teresa served out the lasagne.

'English, remember,' Samuel reminded Aubrey. Jadon, the only non-European present, nodded.

'Yes, please. Keep in mind that your ignorant mono-linguistic pal is still here.'

'Please finish the game,' Teresa asked of the

boys. 'We need the table. Samuel, can you please find the spare chair so we can all sit together?'

It would be a squeeze, five people eating around a small table designed for four people. But Aubrey and Jadon had been insistent – they wanted to be here tonight, just in case.

Dinner was slightly awkward to begin with but improved as stomachs became fuller. Emmanuelle made every effort to be friendly and talkative, despite being an outsider to a tight small group, and though Aubrey didn't respond much, Teresa tried her best to keep conversation flowing, and soon Samuel and Jadon were chatting away, too.

Time just keeps on moving forwards, and those future things you dread eventually become the present. All too soon, Jadon and Samuel were kicking Teresa out of her kitchen, taking over the washing-up, reminding her that she had important work to do.

It was a brilliant idea, really, although Renatus had brilliant ideas all of the time. Teresa could understand why Lord Gawain had kept him around for so long, even if no one else could. He was terrifying but he was clever.

He'd caught up with her in the library at Morrissey House while she searched for material for her lessons. At first, when he'd entered the library behind her, she'd expected him to ignore her completely, so she'd been more than a little surprised when he'd actually called her name. He'd quietly described the all-important ring that Emmanuelle was guarding – everyone knew she had it, but only a few councillors had actually handled it and she always wore so many rings that anyone who hadn't seen it before wouldn't know which one it was.

'She wears it on her thumb,' Renatus had explained, while Teresa had wondered why he suddenly felt like sharing information with her. 'It's a thick, solid thing made from silver, with a crest and a black stone set into it. The Elm Stone. You must have seen it.'

Teresa had, and had considered it probably the plainest of Emmanuelle's lovely collection of "everyday" jewellery. She'd assumed it to have some kind of sentimental value, and apparently she had guessed correctly. It was the ring left to her by her old friend, Peter.

'I know you can cast illusions as convincing as life,' Renatus had said next. 'Can you recreate that ring?'

Teresa had deliberated, uncertain. Yes, she could very easily create a visual and tactile illusion so true-to-life that no one could tell the difference between the two rings, but she did not know how effectively she could fake the illusion's energy. A typical illusion had *no* energy. The real ring had an aura all its own – it was visible on Emmanuelle's right hand, emanating from her bejewelled fingers. Could recreate that? Maybe. Possibly. Probably, if she exercised a great deal of skill, effort and care.

'Yes,' she'd replied at length. 'I think I can.'

'How long can you make it last?'

'The visual and physical illusion could probably last up to two days outside my auric field,' Teresa had said then, feeling oddly professional. It seemed strange to be talking to Renatus like this (talking to him at all was unusual – talking to him like an equal was just strange). 'I don't think the energetic illusion, if I can cast it, would even last an hour. Maybe only half.'

'You would be its guardian – the illusion's guardian.' Renatus had glanced over his shoulder at the closed door, perhaps sensing someone passing it in the entrance hall. 'If it was taken from you, half an hour should be enough time for you to get away before Lisandro realised he'd been tricked. What do you think?'

Teresa had not told him what she thought, because she had only been thinking of how terrifying the idea of meeting Lisandro really was.

'Sounds great,' she'd said finally, because it did, in theory. Renatus had nodded then, and turned as if to leave, but something had suddenly occurred to him, because he had paused.

'Lord Gawain arrives in an hour. I know he'll love to hear your idea about the ring.'

Her idea?

'Are you alright?'

Teresa blinked, suddenly brought back to the present by Emmanuelle's voice. The idea was insane but it was a good one and the decision had been made. She had work to do.

'I'm fine,' Teresa agreed, brushing her hair from her eyes and taking a deep breath to steady herself. There was important, very important, work to be done. She was standing beside the now-clear table;

Aubrey had moved all of the chairs to the edge of the room, and he and Emmanuelle now stood either side of her. Jadon and Samuel were making every effort to keep their dish-washing very quiet, to avoid disturbing Teresa's concentration.

'Are you sure?' Aubrey asked, crossing his arms. 'You know you don't have to do this if you don't feel up to it.'

He shot a subtle, dark look at Emmanuelle. Teresa hesitated. He was right, this could end badly – what sort of trouble could she get into if the other side thought she was carrying around the ring they wanted? But Emmanuelle rolled her eyes.

'She's fine,' she insisted. 'Teresa is strong and capable. I know that; Lord Gawain and the rest of the council knows that. She's up to it. Aren't you?'

Emmanuelle met Teresa's gaze and waited. This was the chance to show she was made of the same stuff as the rest of the council – bravery, talent, selflessness…

'Of course I am,' Teresa said firmly. She could be scared; it didn't have to stop her from doing what needed to be done. 'I'm ready.'

Emmanuelle removed the chunky silver ring from her thumb and placed it in the centre of the table. Teresa observed it for a few moments, committing its appearance to memory, before she took it and began to turn it over in her hands, learning its dimensions, its every curve and scratch. Its energy, too, had to be fully understood and appreciated if it was to be recreated. For a simpler illusion this much preparation would be unnecessary, but this one had to be perfect. There could be no mistake.

Minutes passed in silence. She thought of nothing but the ring, *this* ring, which could cause so much trouble. Its surface was warm with touch, but would cool if left alone. The stone set into it was dented with several scratches, and the shape engraved into it was worn, but still distinguishable. The metal of the band had a slightly swollen feel to it, undoubtedly the result of the incredible power pumped through it, and which it still held. This ring had served the White Elm for centuries, and Teresa could feel the memories, pains and joys of each long decade etched eternally into every millimetre of silver.

Eventually, the ring ceased to feel unusual in Teresa's hand. She understood it now, and it was familiar. She closed her eyes, keeping her understanding of the ring at the forefront of her mind. Her fists closed, too, and power surged through her, willed and directed. She loosened the fingers of her left hand as she felt something cold growing against her palm. Her creation was taking shape, and it needed room.

Teresa opened her eyes and her hands. In each palm, a chunky, plain silver ring lay, shining dully in the light, projecting identical auras of potency and dark power.

'It's done,' she said, unnecessarily. The proof was evident, sitting in her outstretched hands.

'I knew you could do it,' Emmanuelle said, smiling as she admired the two rings. Teresa tipped them both onto the tabletop, where they rolled and clinked together, eventually coming to stillness. Aubrey picked one up and held it to the light, narrowing his eyes and trying to find fault. He couldn't.

'How do we know which one is real?' he asked.

'It doesn't matter,' Emmanuelle said, holding the other out to Jadon and Samuel to see – they had given up on the dishes and they were leaning over the bench top, curious. Samuel took it. 'We will keep them both as safe as if they were both genuine.'

Samuel squeezed the ring he held between his fingers, and tapped it gently against the bench top.

'I can't believe this isn't real,' he admitted, throwing it lightly into the air and catching it. 'All of my senses are telling me this is real, but it isn't.'

Teresa smiled, but didn't bother to tell him that the one he held *was* real. The two pieces were perfectly identical, with no way of knowing which was which, but she, the creator, would always be able to tell. The real thing was familiar, but the illusion was connected to her being by the constant, fine stream of magic it required to exist.

The rings were compared and then swapped hands. Emmanuelle turned to Jadon and Samuel, and the three of them began to search their ring for the distinguishing markings Emmanuelle recalled. Teresa folded her arms, pleased with her work, and sidled closer to Aubrey to view the illusion she had created. Nobody would ever guess that it wasn't real, at least not until she lost it and it began to fade away, as all wishes, ideas and fabrications do when there's no one around to believe in them.

'Which one *is* real?' Aubrey asked, rolling the illusion between his fingers. His senses believed that it took up space – so it did. Teresa smiled.

'I'll let you guess,' she said, teasing, feeling light and carefree. The stresses of the past few days seemed to have lifted from her shoulders in light of her latest achievement.

'It really is incredible work,' Aubrey confirmed, as though he'd known what she was thinking.

'I wasn't sure I could do it,' Teresa admitted, though Aubrey must have known this already. 'I kept thinking what a crazy idea it was. I couldn't understand what I'd been thinking, to tell Renatus that I was capable of that kind of magic. But apparently I am.'

She felt herself smiling, but Aubrey's face took on a dark look at the mention of the Dark Keeper.

'Do you trust him?' he asked, keeping his voice soft so that Emmanuelle wouldn't hear. Teresa shrugged, her eyes on her creation. How to answer a question like that? Yes; but no.

Yes, because it seemed clear that Renatus loved Lord Gawain as much as the old Seer loved the Dark Keeper. He showed it very differently but the feeling was there. He served the council. He'd never yet stepped out of line or done anything wrong.

No, because, in short, he scared her. He had a life story that could be adapted into a horror film. He didn't seem particularly nice and nobody else liked him.

'I have to,' she said finally, in response to

Aubrey's challenging question. 'We all have to.'

Aubrey went back to looking at the illusion he held and said nothing for a few moments. Teresa blinked, feeling a strange energetic twitch somewhere in her vicinity. She looked around, bemused, but couldn't pick anything amiss.

'I honestly believe that this is real,' Aubrey said, handing the illusion ring back to Teresa, obviously not distracted by what Teresa thought she'd felt. He looked over at the others. 'I would swear that it is, but they think theirs is just as real. You've done a great job.'

'Thanks,' Teresa said softly, turning her creation over in her hands as she felt another tiny flicker of misplaced energy. Was her illusion fading already? She cast her senses over it, searching it for flaw. There was none, and when she felt a third flick, right at the edge of her consciousness, she knew it was unconnected to her illusion.

The twitches became more frequent, so faint that she mightn't have noticed, except that she was sensitive to her own spells. Something was happening to something of hers, though what, she had no clue. She had never felt this before – it reminded her of that irritating sensation when a fly creeps across a bare shoulder, but disappears before it can be swatted away, only to return.

'Can you feel that?' she asked of the others. Aubrey's gaze was blank when she met it, and Jadon and Samuel only glanced at each other, confused, wondering what they were meant to be able to feel. The twitches became twangs – what was breaking?

'What do you feel, Teresa?' Emmanuelle asked, a tiny frown forming. Teresa could only shrug, unable to communicate the weird energetic itch she sensed.

'I don't know...like a twitch, somewhere near. It's something connected to me,' she added, feeling stupid. She couldn't explain, and it was probably something really simple. She looked down at her hands, sliding the illusion ring onto her fingers. It was loose on every one – she had thinner fingers than Emmanuelle did.

'Do you have wards up here?' Emmanuelle glanced between Teresa and Samuel.

'Of course; I cast them around the house when I was initiated,' said Teresa. 'Lord Gawain said-'

'Are they still up?' Emmanuelle interrupted. Teresa blinked – she'd put several nets up last year and not thought of them since – and took a moment to spread her magical senses through the rooms of her small home, across her vegetable garden outside, out onto the street...

The net was gone, cut to pieces. One strand remained, holding up one flimsy cloaking ward like a tent, guarding her entire property. The other layers had been carefully cut away – one by one, twitching like severed elastic.

Teresa didn't know what to say. She stared at Emmanuelle, frozen in confusion and indecision.

'But...where have they gone?' she asked after a long, tense moment. Nobody said or did anything for a second.

Then everything happened at once.

The last strand of magic protecting Teresa and Samuel's little cottage snapped and was gone. Emmanuelle had her wand in her hand and cast some kind of ward on the ring in Jadon's palm, and it was suddenly energetically invisible, just as if it had become like any other ring. Teresa became aware of something wrong outside the door – masses of nothingness, impenetrable by air, dust particles and miniature insects – and realised what it must be just as she saw Emmanuelle's spell.

They were people, energetically cloaked, conspicuous only by their apparent lack of substance. There were people outside who had pulled the house's wards down. This was, and could only be, an attack.

Emmanuelle and Teresa acted at the same time in the instant before the door smashed open. Teresa flung her hand out towards the kitchenette, willing her magic to shield the people in it. Her wards were not the flashiest, so an illusion was born – a picture of an empty kitchen, dishes for two strewn across the bench, silent, the energy dull and unmoving, the auras of the three occupants impossible to detect. Emmanuelle cast her powerful wards through Teresa's magic, building two opalescent walls between Teresa and the door.

The door was opened with such force that chips of wood were splintered away from the lock. The door itself swung inward and hit the wall with a bang, bouncing back into the sides of the men who streamed through the door, armed with wands and knives.

There were nine of them, Teresa became aware vaguely through her panic; too many for her to take on. Aubrey drew his wand and stepped in front of her, his mouth set in a determined line. Teresa's heart clenched – she had not acted fast enough or effectively enough. Her illusion had not stretched far enough to envelop him, too.

The men hit the first ward with force, like running into a glass door. Two fell, stunned. The third, a tall, black man with a wide, white grin, slashed with his wand, and the wall was gone.

Aubrey pointed his wand at the intruders and a small globe of bluish light shot from its tip. It cut straight through the second ward (Emmanuelle had thought to use proper defensive combat wards, which worked much like two-way mirrors) and struck the temple of one of the men struggling to his feet. The man's eyes rolled back, and he slipped back to the floor, unconscious. His fellows behind him hesitated when they saw Aubrey turn his wand on the next man in line, but the heavy-set, black man stepped forward, his grin still in place.

'You can't win, boy,' he said, as though amused. His accent was American, although Teresa couldn't guess the locality.

'Stand down,' Aubrey commanded. 'This is private property, and we are councillors for the White Elm-'

'I know who you are,' the man said, looking around while Teresa silently assessed him from his aura. He was a Crafter; powerful, but not complete, somehow. 'Frankly, I think you're a poor replacement for someone like me. I just want to know where you've hidden Emmanuelle.'

Teresa resisted the urge to glance into the kitchenette.

'She's not here,' Aubrey said coldly, and the intruder scoffed. Without warning, he shot a stream of flame from his wand. Teresa's instincts had her hand up straight away and casting a ward, but to her dismay her quick reflex meant nothing – no sooner had her thin sheet of magic blocked the flame than it shattered like eggshell. It was Emmanuelle's ward that repelled the dangerous magic, ricocheting the flame into the kitchen and blasting a cupboard door clean off.

Teresa turned to look, glad for the excuse to check on the three she had hidden. Clearly, the intruders could not sense through her illusion. At first, neither could she, but a change in focus and her eyes were able to pick out three people ducking to avoid the cupboard door as it fell. Emmanuelle was standing very still, recognising the need to stay hidden until the right moment. Jadon had a hand clamped across Samuel's mouth; upon meeting his girlfriend's eyes, Samuel made a sudden movement as though to go to her, but Jadon pulled him back. There was nothing Samuel could do, after all. It was better he stayed safe. In that same instant, Jadon sought Teresa's gaze. She felt their minds click together just as she turned back to face the trespassers.

It's okay, Jadon's reassuring voice sounded in her head. *Em and I have him; just worry about yourself and*

Aubrey. We'll jump in soon, we'll take them all on together.

'See that ward?' the American asked, nodding at the silvery wall protecting Teresa and Aubrey. The kitchen light glinted dully off his bald head. 'Did you think I wouldn't recognise her work? It's Emmanuelle's – where is she?'

'She's not here,' Aubrey said again. 'She's gone.'

'I don't think so,' the impostor disagreed, looking around but not moving, still grinning as though this was all very funny. He raised his voice. 'I know you're in here somewhere, darling. I've been looking forward to seeing you again.' He paused, waiting, and his grin widened snidely. 'I promised Peter I'd find you.'

'Who are you and what do you want?' Aubrey demanded, apparently losing patience.

'I'm your predecessor, and I'm here to collect something for a good friend.'

Predecessor? Teresa had the word confused with ancestor, and couldn't make sense of the American's claim, but she had a good idea as to what he wanted to collect.

Teresa, Jadon said, forcibly calm, *baby girl, you're on your own. Lord Gawain has ordered Em and I to stand down.*

Her heart skipped a beat.

He won't let us step in until backup arrives. You and Aubrey have this, though. You're okay. Just stay calm. You're doing great.

'You need to leave,' Teresa said, stepping forward to stand at Aubrey's shoulder. 'You are

444

trespassing.'

'That's her, Jackson,' another intruder, another American, this one bearing a hunting knife, exclaimed suddenly, pointing at Teresa. 'She's the one I seen. He said she'd be the one with the Elm Stone tonight.'

Teresa's stomach flipped over. He'd *seen* her? *How*? No one knew what she looked like. The world knew only her name, as well as Aubrey's and Jadon's – Lord Gawain had refrained from introducing the new three publicly, enjoying the fact that three of his councillors were unknown to the enemy.

And *Jackson*?

How does he know you? Jadon demanded, less reassuring now. Teresa could only wonder, her thoughts disordered and flustered. *It doesn't matter. Renatus is coming, and the rest of the council.*

Teresa's mind froze on that thought.

Renatus.

Teresa's illusion was Renatus's idea.

The ring's presence here tonight was Renatus's idea.

Was it possible, at all, that this raid was yet another of his ideas?

'She's got the ring,' one of the trespassers at the rear of the group pointed out, and they all looked to Teresa's hand.

'I think you ought to hand that over,' the leader (could it be *the* Jackson, who had left the White Elm with Lisandro?) said, stretching out a hand. Aubrey shifted forward again to put himself between the intruders and Teresa.

'This is the last time we're going to ask,' he said, his voice hard. 'Leave.'

Jackson only smiled wider and began to walk forwards. Aubrey cast another stun, and the bluish light shot towards Jackson's chest, but the bigger man raised his empty hand to catch the magic. The light dissipated in his hand, ineffective, and he shook his head. Aubrey raised his chin slightly, defiant and determined not to show his fear.

The intruders were all advancing now, slowly, taking care to keep behind Jackson. Teresa took a big step backwards, pulling Aubrey back with her to give them some space. He cast another spell, and the bright globe of light was bigger and brighter this time, but Jackson just caught it again.

Try something else, Teresa found herself begging silently, knowing only Jadon could hear. Other White Elm councillors were brushing past her consciousness, confused and scared, but only Jadon was listening.

One of those presences, one of her brothers or sisters, had instigated this. It was the only explanation. Nobody else knew this was happening tonight, nobody but the White Elm. Even Samuel, her own boyfriend, had only found out a few hours ago when she'd started preparing for dinner. For Jackson to know, somebody on the council had to have told him.

Her instincts told her who.

Aubrey thankfully decided to change his tact, and his next spell was something different of his own make. Jackson closed his hand on the bolt of sparkly green and flinched as his skin seared and the muscles in his hand experienced a sudden spasm. It was better but it didn't slow him.

Another ward, Jadon commanded suddenly, and Teresa did as he said, just as Jackson tore down Emmanuelle's and another intruder blasted dark magic at her. Her ward was instantly in shreds, barely existent, but it had served its purpose.

Aubrey tried something else, missing Jackson when the target ducked aside, but striking his nearest fellow in the neck. The man who was struck fell back, clawing at his own neck, shouting incoherently as imaginary pain took hold. Buoyed by success, Aubrey turned back to Jackson and tried the spell on him.

In an instant, Aubrey had lost. Jackson cast a hasty reflective ward, good enough to send most of Aubrey's spell right back. He had no chance to deflect. The spell caught him in the stomach, and he fell to his knees, gasping as though he'd been stabbed.

'Aubrey!' Teresa clutched at his shoulders, trying to pull him back to his feet. He couldn't be down; she couldn't fight these people, not without him. Jadon's voice still streamed through the back of her mind: *You're doing fine, he's going to be okay, you're going to be fine, too, I swear*...But even that was becoming less and less comforting as the situation worsened rapidly.

'Just give me the ring, pretty thing,' Jackson said, reasonably. 'We'll go.'

Teresa nodded, recognising her chance. She kept

one hand on Aubrey, channelling healing energy through him, giving him strength. It was slow work because there was no actual wound or damage. She began to twist the Elm Stone free of her finger but Aubrey grabbed her wrist.

'No, Teresa-'

'No, what?' she hissed back, trying to get him to understand. They could have it. This was the whole point of tonight, making a convincing fake for Jackson to steal. It wasn't worth dying for. But he wasn't the Telepath, and he was in too much pain to be thinking clearly.

'Just don't-'

Two of the intruders hit him with stuns, and he crumpled.

And Teresa was alone, or as good as. In the corner of her eye, she saw Jadon release Samuel and step forward, but Emmanuelle had the sense and the strength to fling her arm into his path and catch him across the chest, stopping him from throwing himself into danger. They'd been forbidden to step in. Lord Gawain had to have his reasons for that. Teresa understood that. Emmanuelle understood that. Jadon did not.

I want to help you, Jadon said, almost pleading. Teresa stepped over Aubrey, her every instinct craving to check his vitals, to tend to him, but she could not. He was alive; that was enough.

You cannot, was her answer to Jadon as Jackson raised his wand. Lord Gawain must know that the situation was hopeless. It was better to lose only two councillors than four.

'Stop,' she ordered, when she saw that Jackson's wand was still aimed at the motionless Aubrey. 'He's not a threat.'

'I know.' Jackson laughed loudly. 'That was disappointingly easy. I was promised a decent fight.'

By whom? Did Renatus tell Jackson who would be here tonight, and suggest that the boys would pose a formidable threat?

Where are they? Teresa demanded of her best friend. *You said Renatus was coming to help!*

He is coming, Jadon promised, disengaging from her slightly to check in on another conversation. He returned momentarily, sounding more stressed and angry. *He's still at the estate, arguing with Qasim.*

It felt like the final nail in a coffin. Lord Gawain could be at the end of the street right now, but wouldn't go into battle without his secret weapon...who was still at home, picking arguments with their other best chance of survival.

He was doing this on purpose. Renatus was deliberately holding up the council to give Jackson a head start.

Jadon, it's Renatus. This was all him. He's a traitor.

She waited for Jadon to disagree, to rationalise, but he didn't try.

Teresa lifted her hand, disappointed to see that it was trembling slightly. The ring glinted there.

'Leave,' she warned. Jackson smirked.

'Looks good on you. Maybe I should let you keep it.'

'Maybe I will.'

Jackson's smile slipped away.

'You know, you are full of good ideas,' he said, and showed her the burnt skin of his palm, the result of Aubrey's spell. 'You'll use it to fix the mess your boy made of my hand. You're coming with us.'

Teresa didn't have a chance to argue. A spell struck her shoulder and the energy was absorbed into her whole body, intoxicating her. She could feel it taking effect, dragging her into the drain of unconsciousness, that dank, dark place...

Teresa!

Jadon's voice, scared and worried. Because she was on her hands and knees now? Because her vision had already blacked out? Because he could see strange men moving towards her, lifting her roughly, and could do nothing? Why didn't he specify?

Jadon, you have to know, Teresa said, just as she slipped away from reality, *Renatus did this.*

She lost her connection with Jadon and was alone in the dark, left to regret ever trusting the Dark Keeper.

Acknowledgements

While talent, hard work and tenacity will get you a long way in life, having wonderful people alongside you will get you a fair amount further, and though I have only this one section on which to thank them all, I should first remind them that every single page of this book is dedicated to them all. *Chosen* would never have gotten from my jumbled mind, to my computer screen and out into the world as paper and ink without the following people:

Sabrina Raven, fairy godmother – editor, agent and explainer of things – without you, this book would still be a Word document on my computer, trapped behind the monitor screen, banging with angry fists and unable to find a way out and onto bound paper. Thank you for your patience, support, understanding, industry knowledge and willingness to believe in me and in *Chosen*.

Through all phases of the writing process there are the betas – the ever-patient, ever-willing friends and family members upon who falls the task of reading, rereading and painstakingly recounting the manuscript – and they are to be hugged and thanked profusely. Deep gratitude goes to LJ, Ellen, Matt, Danielle, Mia, Mel, Tiffany, Katherine, Mum and Dad for the part you each played in moulding *Chosen* into the story it has become. Accepting criticism is no one's strong suit but I'm glad I listened to all of yours.

We always say not to judge a book by its cover, and yet we all know that we still do, and for this simple fact I knew I needed the artistic talents of you, Laura-Jane MacNamara. We've come a long way from our days as eccentric outcast schoolgirls sitting in the back of a classroom writing fanfiction and drawing anime but the fact remains that no other artist on the planet could put up with my frustrating perfectionist nit-picking or understand my crazy mind. No book of mine could have been complete without a cover of your creation. As always you have created something more amazing than I could have ever envisioned, and I continue to be awed by your talent and honoured to count you as my friend.

On the topic of friends, thank you to each and every one of mine who have loved and believed in me, or even just not patted me on the head and told me my dreams are very sweet. Thank you for letting me believe, thank you for understanding when I chose to stay home and write over coming shopping, thank you for dragging me out anyway sometimes when I needed the break from my own mind. Thank you to the wonderful and inspiring people I work with, both past and present, who keep me afloat in my professional life; thank you to the encouraging and generous people I have connected with online in the writing communities, who shower me with praise and glowing feedback that keeps me believing in myself. Thank you to Kirsten Lund for your generous assistance with the French translating and your willingness to help me achieve my dreams without ever having met me.

Thank you to my teachers, who made me love learning, who made me literate, who made sure I knew I could do whatever I wanted with my life. Thank you for taking notice of a little girl with a messy desk, a pile of novels too old for her and a notebook full of stories, and nurturing the skill you found there.

The biggest and most heartfelt thanks, of course, must go to my loving family, from my beloved grandparents who have loved me and supported my ambitions without a moment of doubt, through to the extended family who have always let me talk about my future as an author like a given. Thanks to Graham for acknowledging your own curse, whereby fantasy authors seem to immediately die once you start reading their unfinished series, and for refusing to read anything of mine until I get the Elm Stone Saga done. And for love and support and stuff, too. Reegan, I'll never have another brother and I'm so grateful to have you around to keep me grounded. Thanks for being reasonable about sharing the computer, and thanks for the countless times I've stayed up too late writing and you've been the only person awake to help when I've found spiders in my room. Mum and Dad, I don't have enough pages to thank you for everything you've done, everything you've sacrificed, everything you've put up with from me, so I can be here today writing an acknowledgements page to my first novel, so please just know that I am grateful for it all and that I know I wouldn't have any of it without you, and that I love you both so very much. Lastly I need to thank

Matthew, the deuteragonist of my life's story, for all these years of unconditional love, for putting up with my craziness, for reading your then-eighteen-year-old girlfriend's 'book' even though you were convinced it'd be terrible, for getting hooked on the story, for endless days and nights of detailed discussion about the story, for your patience as I bounce ideas, for inspiring me...I love you, and thanks, always.